CARINA ALYCE EMKAY CONNOR
KARIGAN HALE LOLO PAIGE
LC TAYLOR SAMANTHA THOMAS

A 9/11 CHARITY ANTHOLOGY

About the Anthology

Heal your heart with stories of love and heroism!

In honor of the 20th anniversary of 9/11, some of your favorite romance authors joined forces to create a charity anthology to raise funds to honor the memories of the heroes we lost that day. For the first three months, starting in September, every single dollar without exception goes to the 9/11 Memorial & Museum.

So grab a fan for some heat and tissues for some tears, and fall in love with the men and women first responders in this collection of heroic romances.

Enjoy all-new first responder romances from:
Carina Alyce
EmKay Connor
Karigan Hale
Lolo Paige
LC Taylor
Samantha Thomas

To keep up to date on the progress of our donations, join our newsletter at https://carinaalyce.com/911-charity-newsletter/

As a wildland firefighter, I remember each time I heard about the death of a fellow firefighter. The grief, the pain of losing a single teammate breaks your heart. But twenty years ago, the world blew open. Those brave, unflinching 412 first responders went up the stairs and never returned. Everyone else was fleeing, and they ran toward the danger to save the lives of thousands of innocents

We can never replace what we lost, but we can dedicate ourselves to preserving their memories. So thank you for buying this book and helping us keep watch over their sacrifice. Feel free to laugh, cry, and fall in love with the heroes in these stories who we hope carry the legacy of the ones that we will never forget.

Lolo Paige
Alaska, September 2021

"Through blurred eyes we find the strength and courage to soar beyond the moment. We look to the future knowing we can never forget the past. God Bless America."

-Unknown / Quote from 9/11 Memorial Plaques

TEMPTED

Carina Alyce

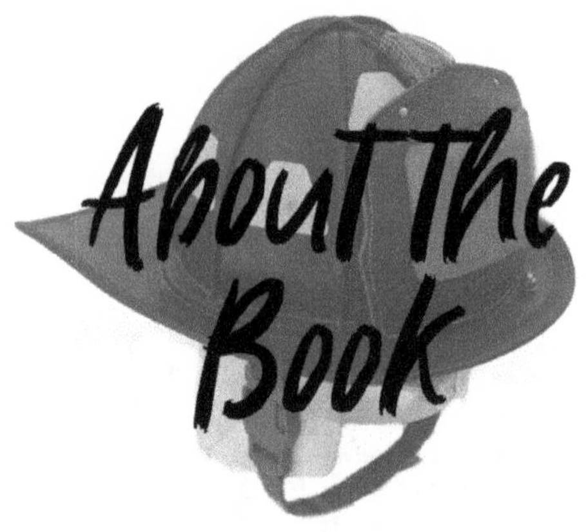

It takes a certain type of person to work nights in the ER, and Cassie Odon has always been that person. She was hoping for a slow night, but all bets are off when Firefighter Fabian Santos stops by after a scene. They've known each other for a while, and he was mostly naked the last time she saw him . . .

Fabian Santos has seen cute and fun Cassie on occasion when their paths had crossed over the past few years. He wasn't ready for the scorching kiss they shared on his way out of the ER. They have a date planned, but will fate keep him from seeing her?

Find out in Tempted, your first taste of the MetroGen Universe where the women are strong, the guys are brave, and the scenes are steamy – all written by an actual doctor.

TEMPTED

Tempted: Verb (past tense) 1. To have been enticed by something desirable, though unlikely to be in the best interest of those involved

The New Catholic Dictionary

"You are a professional," Cassie reminded herself, wheeling her computer through the MetroGen ER. The wee morning hours of Thursday night shifts in the minor care pod were supposed to be slow.

The bars didn't have extended hours. No major concerts. The light drizzle should have kept people in on a late July night.

Unless it was a full moon.

In which case—definitely the best time to google hangnails, calluses, splinters, and toothaches.

Lest anyone think she was joking, the minor care census included a hangnail, cut lip, and stubbed toe.

For the two ladies waiting for urine pregnancy tests, Cassie totally recommended the one-dollar pregnancy tests at Dollar Tree. Skip the three-hundred-dollar ER co-pay. It would take Cassie far longer to process their insurance in her job as the ER clerk than waiting for the store to reopen in five hours.

The triage nurse at the front door was having a ball because her triage reasons became more outlandish as the night wore on.

Seriously, why were Fabio and Glen sharing a room? And

what did "get checked out" mean? They couldn't be too sick if they were in the minor care pod and not one of the two standard care pods. At nineteen and twenty-eight years old, they shouldn't have been taking a ton of meds.

Group STD testing, perhaps?

No, the triage nurse'd have written 'personal concern w/ testing' on that.

Object in the butt? While everyone said 'they fell on it,' it usually appeared as 'OITB.'

Sex accident? Ideally, they weren't drunk. Drunk guys, gay, straight, or in between, were obnoxious when she had to file their insurance.

It made her long for the trauma pod. There, she worked with the charge nurse, fielding phone calls, test results, locating consults, specialists, and directing human traffic. Her main company here was an attending, a PA, and two custodians cleaning the floor for the fifth time after another visit from the Vomit Comet of Minor Care.

She opened the door to Room 78 and understood triage's note.

There sat two shirtless firefighters 'getting checked out.' Even better, she recognized one of them, who had been similarly naked during their last conversation.

Chapter Two

Rookies were the most dangerous and unpredictable part of firefighting. Not fires, not bombs, not axes, but rookies. Despite six months of fire academy, one whiff of smoke and they went rogue, forgetting everything they'd learned.

Which was how Fabian had ended up here.

Glen had gotten confused in the smoke and failed to find the evac when the ceiling started to come down. Fabian had found him and dragged him out just in time to get hit by some of the rafters.

Sure, they'd walked out on their own power, but their captain had insisted an actual physician check them and decide if they required chest x-rays. Had they not gotten buried, the other firefighter-EMTs would have done their health checks. However, according to the captain, until someone invented x-ray vision, they would go to the ER.

"I'm sorry," Glen said for the twentieth time.

"I know," Fabian answered. "These things happen."

"Really, lieutenant, I'm sorry."

"Yes, you told me several times. It's fine." Fabian tried to wring out the wet mass that had been their uniform T-shirts. The other guys had doused the rookie with water for his screw-up but caught Fabian in its wake. Hospital gowns were possible replacements, though it wasn't worth it if they were getting checked for bruises and breaks.

The door opened, and the desk clerk entered with her computer to start their registration. Her eyes widened as she recognized Fabian.

Some time back, he'd been in Vegas for a firefighter conference. Fabian's former captain had had a crush on a woman from his neighborhood who had been at a bachelorette party. ER clerk Cassie Odon had more than supported bringing the lovebirds together.

She glanced down at her forms and then back at his face. "This can't be right."

"It's right," Fabian assured her. This wasn't the first time a problem with his name had come up.

"Not possible. Prove it. Insurance card and ID." She held out her hand, but her eyes were on his shoulders.

At least that part of him impressed her today. "I promise, it's legit."

Glen asked, "What are you talking about?"

Fabian rolled his eyes, "My name."

"Yeah, Lieutenant Fabian Santos."

Cassie, the troublemaker he remembered in Vegas, stifled a giggle. "I'm sure there's a very exciting story behind it."

"I don't understand what's going on. Is this another rookie hazing thing? Fake names after getting drenched?" Glen guessed.

"Tell him." Cassie tapped his information into the computer

and gave his cards back.

“In the nineties, my mom loved romance novels and models… I’m not clear exactly on what it was he did…” Fabian hoped to stave off the explanation.

“His mom named him Fabio,” Cassie said. “After the shirtless model on many romance novel covers. Best story ever. ID please.”

Glen went from crestfallen to stunned to cackling. “No way. Lieutenant. New Old Spice guy versus old Old Spice guy? I remember that commercial from elementary school.”

Cassie took his driver's license, “And not yet old enough to drink, Glen Lindsay Smith.”

“It's a family name,” Glen said.

“I’m sure.” Cassie kept her face straight, which was difficult for her if Fabian’s memory served. She had been at the height of the Vegas antics with his friend Jared, another trickster.

“I've never had the ER clerk do this to me before.” Glen was confused.

“Because your mom brought you last time?” Cassie winked when she leaned forward to return Glen’s cards.

Poor Glen’s jaw dropped.

Fabian got it. Cassie had that effect on anyone around her. She was a bright ball of energy with her smooth skin several shades darker than Fabian’s tawny tone. He tried not to stare at the generous curve of her chest and focused instead on the long red extensions braided through her hair. Still, the MetroGen ER logo on her left breast mocked his attempts to keep his thoughts PG.

Now she caught him looking, and her deep brown eyes were laughing at him. Cassie Odon was damn fine, and she didn’t look the least bit sorry about it.

Her eyes flicked back to Fabian's bare skin. He was suddenly glad they'd been too busy with the fire to eat dinner. Never hurt to be shirtless without the after-meal pouch. She was checking out his mat of coal-black chest hair. Unlike Glen who hadn't even grown any yet.

"Is this normal?" Glen asked Fabian.

"Only when you've met before and gotten acquainted." Fabian didn't bother to avert his eyes.

"Yeah, me and Fabio are really close friends. In fact, he wore this the last time I saw him." Cassie said.

"You wore a tube-top made of scraps when we danced at Coyote Ugly," Fabian reminisced about one of the tamer events during that notorious weekend.

"All for a good cause."

"Mine too." Fabian felt the room's temperature rising. Glen was forgotten because the forecast called for a dead heat with a heavy shower of flirtation.

"You did fulfill every woman's fantasy. It's universal."

Fabian was drawn to the way the words rolled off her lips. This woman radiated loud, friendly temptation, just as she had in Vegas. Being near her reminded him he was alive and getting more tempted by the moment.

Glen cleared his throat. "Universal fantasy?"

"Yep." Cassie crept closer to Glen, fake leering. Fabian was amused and annoyed. "You know what every girl wants with the strong arm muscles of our neighborhood firefighters?"

"To be rescued," Glen stammered.

Cassie's hair fell over Glen's pale arm, but Fabian awareness climbed as her leg brushed his knee. Other parts of his body took notice. Her voice purred, "No, that's not what he did. That's not what he gave all of us."

"All of you?"

"Me and my five best girlfriends. All six of us. Just the way we wanted it."

Fabian resolved to have Cassie stop by the firehouse and mess with his rookie regularly. Then again, Fabian didn't need her around his firehouse if it made him think with his other head.

His poor rookie wasn't coping well. "All six of you, and the lieutenant? My lieutenant got gang banged? By chicks? Did you pay for him?"

"Oh no." Cassie kept applying the pressure to Glen and, incidentally, Fabian's knee. "Pay? He came over so well, and he did it for free. We would have paid if that's what it took to get his clothes off. You interested in my next friendly get-together? I already have your phone number."

"…you do?"

"Of course, I do. You gave me your ID." She pulled back. "Now that you're registered, a provider will see you soon."

She grabbed her computer and rolled out the door.

Glen immediately turned to Fabian. "Is the universal fantasy firefighter prostitutes?"

Fabian cracked up. "That is not the universal fantasy."

"Firefighter orgy? Threesome? Reverse harm? Menage?"

"What are you reading in your bunkroom?" Fabian sighed, "Hate to break it to you, kid. I've never kissed her, let alone slept with her. The closest thing I came to a date with her was a few dances at a Vegas club."

"Then what was… that?"

"That what, rookie?" Fabian didn't want to put him out of his misery yet.

"The sexy talk. And the breathing. And the leaning. And the staring at your chest? She said she'd seen it before."

"She was referring to stripping."

"Is there a troupe of strippers? Does our firehouse strip? Are we really getting checked out by a doctor, or is this part of the city's stripper training and recruitment?"

"We're here because you're a lunkhead who got us hit by burning rafters. This is a real hospital with a real exam by a real doctor. There is no stripper troupe thus far that I am aware of. Even Lieutenant Jared Pickford hasn't started one."

It took another minute for Glen to grasp the important points of the conversation. "You stripped for free?"

"It was for charity. Sort of."

Cassie popped her head back in and threw them a set of scrub tops. "Put these on. Can't have my doctors fainting because of the hotness."

Fabian chuckled and sincerely wished he had Cassie's number and not the other way around. Hopefully, any minute, a doctor would come by to clear them, and he'd ask for her digits on the way out.

Or not because less than five minutes later, they heard an overhead announcement. "Code Orange, minor care pod."

Fabian was out the door before Glen even sat up. Code Orange was the standard hospital code for a chemical spill… or Haz-Mat situation.

The second he exited, he got the scent of the danger, literally.

The air smelled of peppers and pineapple, which meant one thing. Someone had mixed ammonia with bleach, leading to the release of chlorine gas.

The most likely cause was the janitorial staff who carried those products in their cart. At 2:00 a.m. in a busy ER, mistakes could happen. Or poor labeling perhaps left them unaware of the potent and dangerous combination until it was too late.

Chlorine gas was no joke. It corroded the skin by forming hydrochloric acid with moisture and could destroy the lungs if breathed long enough. Gas masks were unnecessary when a damp cotton cloth could be pretty damn protective. People on the ground near the source were in the greatest danger.

Cassie was in the thick of it with her eyes streaming red. She was trying to drag one of the two janitors away from the sickly yellow cloud emanating from the floor. Fabian shoved on an isolation gown and gloves before dousing two hospital masks in water. He flipped one over his mouth and the other over Cassie's before grabbing the arms of both janitors and pulling them down the hallway.

The staff arrived with gurneys on a run. Fabian waved them onward. "Chlorine gas exposure. Get them decon showers and respiratory support. We need to evacuate this entire pod."

With the efficiency he'd expected from MetroGen, the nurses and residents whisked away the janitors. Rapid-fire orders from the charge nurse were issued for an orderly evacuation. Other staff members moved the patients to the regular care pods and cordoned off the area.

Fabian had to strip off his clothes and take a quick decon shower in the staff emergency shower by the back ER lounge. The scrub top and his uniform pants bit the dust. He ended up in a new set of scrub pants after rescuing his trauma shears, boots, and wallet. That's when he noticed no one had seen to Cassie.

He found her at the edge of the standard care pod behind a desk. She was still wearing the same clothes.

"What are you doing?"

She stated the obvious. "Working."

"No, you're not."

"Yes, I am. Why are you out here? You're a patient. Why is your shirt off again?"

"Yours is still on," he said. "And it shouldn't be."

A younger White doctor, Attending Ryan Yates by his badge, walked by Fabian without comment to speak to Cassie. "Didn't we call Haz-Mat? Or call a Code Green?"

Code Green stood for a belligerent or dangerous patient. Though shirtless guys weren't exactly rare in the ER, they typically did not hang out near the staff desks.

"Haz-Mat is on its way," Fabian said, "but Cassie needs a decon shower."

Dr. Yates gave Fabian a once-over, noting the lack of patient bracelet and overall general good health. "Not a patient and not one of my residents?"

"Cleveland Fire. Lieutenant Fabian Santos. I lost my clothes getting the custodians away from the chlorine gas." Fabian showed the doctor his ID.

"He knows Kyra," Cassie put in. "And he's supposed to get his lungs listened to before he puts on a stupid shirt."

Yates whipped out his stethoscope and did a focused exam on Fabian's breathing. "Sounds good, and you were able to move two human beings without pain. What happened?"

"Got hit by the edge of burning rafters with my rookie and then helped out here. No medical problems, and I used a wet mask over my mouth to move those guys." Fabian glanced at Dr. Yates. "Do you know Kyra?"

"You could say that," Yates agreed and put a portable pulse ox on Fabian's finger.

"I met her in Vegas," Fabian said. Kyra Washington had been part of the bachelorette party. She used to be a nurse at MetroGen but had joined the FD paramedic training program. The local paramedic shortage had led to their paths occasionally crossing.

"In that case, Cassie, take a decontamination shower in the staff shower," Yates suggested and glanced at Fabian. "Bachelorette firefighter Vegas?"

"Amy's Vegas Before Vows," Fabian confirmed.

Yates broke into a smile. "That was a busy night. I'm Ryan. And, Cassie, decon shower, please."

"I barely touched anyone." Cassie clicked a couple more keys on her computer. "I can shower when I get home."

"Or now. That's in four hours." Ryan nodded at Fabian. "All

yours."

"On it." Fabian stepped up to Cassie and rolled her chair backward.

"On what? What are you—"

Fabian scooped her up into his arms and carried her tossed over his shoulder. "I know my way."

"Ryan Yates!" Fabian got the sense that Cassie was pointing her finger at the doctor. "I'm telling on you. Kyra will have your head. I'm sorry I helped you two get together."

"Kyra will have my head if her bestie gets chlorine toxicity," he called back.

How humiliating. First, she flirted with the sexy firefighter, then she got exposed to toxic chemicals, and now the sexy firefighter actually carried her away from work.

Her fantasies about shirtless sexy firefighter showers did not involve decontamination.

This was not the universal fantasy.

Fabian indicated the open shower. "Step in and give me your clothes."

"Turn around." Cassie kicked off her flats and closed the curtain. She tried to remember what underwear she'd worn today. Sexy or functional? "You can go somewhere else."

"I would, but your clothes are contaminated, and I don't want a second shower if I get whacked in the head with them."

She tossed the scrub pants and her t-shirt over the top of the shower. Luckily, laundry day had gifted her with a white lace bra and panty set, which followed her clothes. "Can you go now?"

The bra and panties landed back on her side. "Put them back

on, please."

"You told me to strip."

"I did not," he protested from the other side of the curtain.

"Yes, you did."

"No, I didn't. I said 'clothes.'"

"You said my clothes were contaminated. Why am I putting these back on?"

"Those don't seem touched, so you can keep them. We have to deal with your hair, and I doubt you want to be naked during it. I have trauma shears."

Her brain filtered out the naked comment. Then his intent dawned on her. "You want to cut my hair?"

"You have to wash your hair," he said wearily. "Since when are synthetic braid extensions washable?"

"No, but…"

"'But' what?" Now it sounded like he was standing right next to her.

"Then people will see my hair. Without product or styling."

"I'm sure they've seen messy Black hair before."

"I don't care what they've seen. I love my hair, but I don't want to be at my job with awful, dry hair because I couldn't get it oiled." Cassie didn't regret cultivating her appearance one bit.

"It'll be okay," he said. "I'll just go down to the cafeteria and steal olive oil."

"Are you being a jerk?"

"Absolutamente no. Solo quiero que te sientas bien." He responded in Spanish. "Eu adoraria beijar seu pescoço por trás e provar sua linda boca gloriosa."

"That last part wasn't Spanish," she said, re-snapping her bra.

"Spanish and Portuguese, paixão, the languages of love." His voice suddenly dropped deeper.

"I thought that was French."

"They're missing out. Once your good parts are covered, I'll wrap you in a towel while we deal with your hair."

A towel flopped over her side, and she slid out with it on. Flirting with the hot shirtless firefighter was one thing. Sitting next to him half-naked in a towel with him half-naked and letting him cut her hair…

That was far too intimate.

"Can't you put a shirt on, Fabio?"

He gave her a sly grin. "Do you want my shirt on?"

Cassie hedged, because as far as she was concerned, he was always shirtless. "Maybe if you weren't so arrogant about it."

"You're just mad because we're cutting off your poisoned hair."

She poked him in the chest, tingles spreading up her fingers when they touched his tan skin. "Don't think I won't use those trauma shears on your balls."

He glanced down at her hand, still on his chest, daring her to do more. Cassie didn't move, so he walked his fingers down her hand to her wrist, guiding her hand away while he glided closer.

"The first cut—me or you?" He picked up the tie at the end of an extension.

"I'll do the first one." She borrowed the shears to snip off the tie and the end of the red braid.

"That wasn't so bad," he said.

"Speak for yourself." She threw the end of the braid into the nearby trash can.

"I will." He plucked the trauma shears out of her hand, grabbed his own bangs, and cut them off.

For once, she was speechless.

"Do you feel better?" he asked.

"A little. A tiny amount," she said when she recovered from her shock. She touched the uneven edge of the remains of his bangs. "You look goofy. I do feel better."

"How high do you want me to cut?" he played with one of her braids.

She felt about six inches down. "My real hair is about here. Don't give me a haircut like yours."

"I won't. This isn't my first rodeo."

She teased the shortened edge of his silky black hair, "We don't have the same."

"My dad's Brazilian. Total luck of the draw with what kind of hair you get. My older sister has the same as yours. Do you know what tortures a little brother? Helping her take these out when she was going through a phase of trying a different color every other day."

"Poor baby."

"It got worse because then my little sister wanted the same, every single time. Fabby, eu preciso de você. Me ajude, Fabby. Bonito por favor," he imitated in a high voice as he cut off the indicated sections.

He was trying to distract her, which was working. He'd cut, she'd unbraid. After he ran out of braids to cut, he did the sections she hadn't reached. Soon, the trashcan was full of red strands, and Cassie's hair stuck out every which way, confused on why it had been treated this way.

It was going to be even more unhappy soon.

"I take it you forgot your emergency hair kit?"

"I didn't think this would happen. My clothes or my hair. Can I have my T-shirt back? It's one of my favorites."

"Hell no. I'm taking your shoes and socks too," he said. "Take your shower. I'll be back with scrubs and stuff."

He bagged up her clothes and extensions. She jumped in the shower and used the terrible liquid shampoo.

Stupid ammonia plus bleach. Stupid killer chlorine gas. Stupid unnecessarily shirtless firefighter.

It was a shared fault of everyone. The janitors had been tired and made a mistake. She shouldn't have run toward the poison gas cloud. Others had been coming to help, but it wasn't brain surgery to know people passed out in a reeking yellow cloud were in danger.

Thank goodness she'd gotten to keep her underwear at least. The hospital kept a frightening supply of postpartum mesh undies, but bras were generally not in the supply closet.

Fabian returned, wearing a shirt this time. He had a pile of scrubs, a pair of firefighter boots, an unopened bottle of coconut oil, and a fork.

"Is this The Little Mermaid, Fabby?"

"Someone in the lounge must have gone keto. These should get you through the shift." He unraveled a length of green fabric from a few rubber bands.

"You made me a hair scarf?"

"Yep, from scrubs. You can do almost anything with trauma shears. It's the duct tape of firefighting."

She checked out his feet, which were still in his boots. "Did you take Glen's boots?"

"He won't miss them. The nurses are holding his hand for the torture of wearing the paper hospital slippers. It might be his fantasy." He produced a pair of double-sided bright orange socks, aka, the socks of shame. "And here are these sweet socks."

A cell phone beeped. It wasn't hers because it was in her desk. Fabian checked the message. "That's my ride on its way."

"Thank you," she said, unable to come up with anything better because she didn't want him to go.

His hand was on the door. "Be careful when you wear the scarf, no singing that the hills are alive with the sound of music."

"Sound of music?"

"Yeah, how Julie Andrews makes clothing out of curtains?"

"Interesting childhood you had. Extensions, Fabio, and the Sound of Music. So cute and nice and sweet."

Somehow, he was across the room, holding her face in his hands. "I'm not that nice."

And then he closed the distance.

The first brush of his lips was tentative like he wasn't sure if she would be onboard.

An excellent time to disabuse him of that notion. She pressed herself upward, opening her eager mouth to his.

Tentative was abandoned, and their kiss sprinted straight to steamy hot. Cassie plastered her body against his, those muscles that needed another close examination. She ran her hands back up over his poor chopped-up hair.

The towel fell on the floor, and his strong callused hands shaped her back and then her ass. The way he toyed with the back of her bra told her where his mind had gone.

A tiny whimper escaped her throat. She was at work. There were plenty of rumors about who had done the dirty in the hospital, but she liked having a job, and he probably did too. This was not the time or the place.

Before things got more frantic, and she ended up naked again, she drew back. Her body was not happy, but she forced the words out. "I'm at work. You're at work… sort of. This is not a work activity."

Hair thoroughly mussed, his eyes were roaming over her chest. "Not a work activity?"

"Definitely not." She suppressed the temptation to restart. Instead, she threw the scrubs on, aware of his gaze. Covered up again, she sternly said. "You go back to your firehouse. You might be cute, but no one is going to watch me brush my hair with a fork."

"Lucky you. When we get back to the house, the rookie gets to shave my head. I need a real haircut now anyway, but I let him think he's getting something in exchange for his boots." He backed up to the door. "If you were wondering, my shift ends at 9:00. I live alone. By myself."

"My shift ends at 7:00." She answered. "I live alone too. I usually catch a post-shift nap . . .unless I have company."

"Do you want company?"

"We'll see," she said, hoping she could play it mysterious or slightly cool as he left.

Best not to share her fantasy of stripping him naked and letting him do any good, bad, or naughty thing he wanted to her body. She'd finally answer the eternal question if the real universal fantasy was screwing a firefighter.

No, she couldn't wonder how big his hose was or how wet it would get her. She had a shift to finish. She was not doing the hot firefighter.

Or at least not until after his shift ended.

Cassie was definitely regretting the last several hours.

She'd been on her way out to the door when the charge nurse begged her to stay. Cassie pointed out that she had been exposed to chlorine gas and was wearing firefighter boots and a hair scarf made out of scrubs. Charge upped the deal with the promise of triple overtime and a switched shift to get an extra day off.

Hopefully flirty firefighter rendezvous weren't limited time offers. The ER was the hospital version of Grand Central Station, and some of the firefighters got around. Not as much as the hook-ups going on between the doctors and nurses, but still, firefighters were a universal fantasy for a reason.

Her universal fantasy could take a nap and meet her for dinner, or so her text with her address instructed.

As the day shift rolled in, Cassie understood the charge nurse's desperation. It wasn't the minor care pod being closed from the Haz-Mat incident. It wasn't Darren, the new desk clerk, being on the job for three weeks. It wasn't the new medical students and residents wandering through the ER like the lost puppies they were in July. It was that the ER Chief, Dr. Mankia Gupta-Carver, was working on the same day as her husband.

A few years ago, this wasn't a big deal, because they used to work in the ER together. However, unfortunately, Dr. Jacob Carver had quit the ER in dramatic fashion and somehow made his way into the fire academy. His assignment to the nearby Firehouse 15 supposedly had her grudging support.

There was only one solution to this problem—which was to make the day run as smoothly as possible. She helped Darren stay ahead of the labs and consults. He'd been unprepared for the number of pages he'd be doing from the desk by the trauma pod.

Cassie was printing lab requisition forms when Darren frantically waved her over. "I have a transfer from Cincinnati. They say they'll be here any second."

"What?" Cassie clomped over in her giant boots and took over. One glance showed the 513 area code of Cinci and not the 216 of Cleveland. "This is Clerk Odon, MetroGen ER."

"Medic 15. Two minutes out. We have a burn patient with facial injuries and two firefighters exposed to gasoline." The voice on the other end of the line said.

"Copy Medic 15. ETA in two minutes. We'll have the team meet you at the ambulance bay." Cassie snapped her fingers at Darren and said, "Get Doyle and the resident team. Tell charge nurse."

Darren looked around wildly while Cassie scribbled down 'Trauma 2, Burns, Medic 15' on a big piece of paper. "Just follow me."

She hopped over to the glass fishbowl and tapped on it, holding up the sign. Two attendings and their residents headed immediately out the side door toward the ambulance bay.

Cassie made a beeline for the red-headed Marcus Doyle. “Medic 15 is arriving with the burn victim and two firefighters who need exams. Doesn’t sound like Carver’s one of the firefighters.”

Doyle sighed happily, “Small favors. Can you page the burn team?”

“No problem, boss.” Cassie got a quick glimpse of firefighters rolling in a gurney. None of them were Dr. Carver, but even at this distance, she could smell the gasoline.

One of the firefighters, a Black woman, pushed another firefighter away from Trauma 2. “Can we get him a decon shower? He reeks, and he could combust when they turn on the oxygen.”

“All me!” Darren volunteered and led the firefighter off. Judging by the firefighter’s unhappy expression, Darren wouldn’t be getting kissed in the decon shower.

Cassie quickly forgot about them as the nurses descended on the patient like a flock of locusts. She was back at the desk entering information on the unnamed burn patient when Darren returned.

“I got him in the shower they used last night. These are Cleveland firefighters. Why did they call us from Cincinnati?"

"They called us on their cell phone. If they can't get through to Dispatch, they call the desk directly."

Darren said. "Is that common?"

“More common than we'd like. The city’s emergency dispatch splits to police or EMS-Fire. The police dispatch is fine, but EMS-Fire was designed to work for about a tenth of what it's handling now."

"A tenth?"

"There used to be six hospital systems—Lake Hospitals,

University, Cleveland Clinic, MetroHealth, Fairview, Merdian, and now there's only one. Then the fire department doubled in size three years ago without upgrading anything.

"No upgrades?" Darren glanced at the doctors and nurses in Trauma 2 and sat down in his chair behind her.

"Not yet. Dispatch does the best it can, but if there's a full scene going on, sometimes the medics get missed. Too much traffic or rotten luck or, in this guy's case, bad juju."

"Bad juju?"

"Juju. Karma. Black magic. Same way that you can't use the 'Q-word' in the ER."

"The 'Q-word?'"

"The second a shift seems easy, the Q-word gets said and it goes to hell in a handbasket."

"Like last night?"

"That wasn't awful," she hedged. Seeing Fabian didn't count as bad juju.

Darren sat up in his chair, "Oh, hello, what do we have here?" A medical student was standing in front of their desk. May I help you?"

"Student-Doctor Michael Harper. I got paged from nephrology," the man said.

"Trauma 2," Cassie said neutrally as the medical student trotted off. She added a nephrology consult into the chart, guessing that the nurses had paged him from inside Trauma 2.

"There's no way that's a medical student. Not a chance. They're usually nervous, slippery mofos. That one is a MAN! Just like that firefighter."

"That one is a unicorn," Cassie observed. Student-doctor Harper was a Black man in his mid-thirties, which made him a decade older than most of the other medical students.

"Do you think he's single? Could he be my type? The firefighter didn't look twice at me," Darren said.

Cassie kept typing. "I don't know, but you're not supposed to hit on the medical students during traumas. If you run into them in the lounge, you can hang out with them. Offer them a graham cracker."

"Man, Orientation did not cover this stuff," Darren said. "Note to self, wait until things are quiet to hit on medical students."

She closed her eyes. "Did you have to say that?"

"Say what?"

"The Q-word. You just freaking brought bad juju down on this entire shift." She circled her hand to encompass the ER. "You yelled 'fire' in a theater or 'Nick Jonas' in a crowd of preteens."

"Come on. It's only a word."

Charge nurse Marianna sprinted out of Trauma 2 with an EKG printout in her hand, "He's having a STEMI. His troponins are climbing, and he's in kidney failure. Lock and load him to cath."

"On it." Cassie rolled Darren further away from the computer.

"Did I do that?" Darren asked.

"Absolutely, you gave the unnamed suicidal patient a heart attack. Great job. For that—you get to call cath lab. I hope the mean cardiologist is on, not the nice one." She handed him the phone.

"How will I know which one I get?" Darren checked the flip

sheet of 'IMPORTANT NUMBERS' and started dialing.

"Bradley Leyman's a dude with attitude. Angela Perkins is a cute blonde lady, and she won't bite your head off."

"I'm sure it will grow back," Darren said with his ear to the phone.

"Lots of things grow in the ER. Usually the line in the waiting room."

The phone rang the second Darren put it down. Whatever triage had said gave him an expression of panic. "Are you serious?"

Cassie took the phone and started typing into the triage sections, "Yes, two more chest pains walked through the door… fifteen kids incoming… food poising at summer camp. Excellent."

Darren nudged her back in front of the computer again. "You should get going, this is my mess. I take back everything I said about the Q-word. You were right. I was wrong. I solemnly swear that I was up to no good and will never say it again."

"They're paying me triple time. With only two hours left in the shift, I'll see this out. I bet I can get Marianna to open up the minor care pod for the kids." Her phone beeped, and she checked it. It was NOT a message from Fabian. It was Kyra, reminding Cassie about the barbecue at their friend Caroline's house. "Drat."

"Did you say 'drat?'"

"Yes, I'm channeling my inner Church Lady, and because this isn't a swearing level of mess yet. I thought I was going on a date tonight, but I forgot I have to go to a barbecue."

"Bring your date to the party."

That was an interesting thought. The bachelorette crew had organized a party for Caroline's firefighter husband. Fabian should be familiar with all players involved.

Hope he was ready for her girls again.

“That’s not something you see every day," Fabian said, climbing out of Engine 10 and regretting getting lassoed into overtime. Cassie's address was in a text he hadn't had time to answer yet.

The event in question was a fire engine crashed through a garage door. The main issue was that the engine was nine feet tall and the garage door was seven feet tall. The roof listed inward onto the engine since it had probably destroyed all the rafters in the garage.

“Forgot which one was the brake?” Fabian asked one Lieutenant Luna Rodriguez who apparently was in charge of Firehouse 15 today.

“People were trapped inside,” she said briskly. “As acting captain, I made a decision to save my people.”

“The victim set himself on fire, and two of us are already at MetroGen getting checked out for gasoline exposure,” the redhead beside her added. “Soto would have done the same.

Fabian examined her with a slightly jaundiced eye. That redhead was Vanessa Knight, former beauty queen, and rumored to be stacked like a brickhouse. She didn't seem like the hottest thing on two legs, unless you counted all of them sweating like pigs as the sun reached midday in July heat.

"Que diria tu tio?" Rodriguez's uncle, Captain Mateo Soto, was a legend for his position of captain of Firehouse 15. His retirement had caused quite a stir in both the firefighting and Puerto Rican community. Even Fabian's own mother had wanted Fabian to apply for Soto's position.

He heard they'd appointed Clarke from inside 15, but perhaps things were not as they seemed.

"Deja a mi tio fuera de esto," Rodriquez told him to keep her uncle out of it. "My firefighter was in danger and the rest of my ladder team couldn't get to him.

"Where is the rest of 15?" he asked. There was supposed to be a third woman on their shift, but the only other person with the two women was an older White guy. "He's not Clarke."

"He's our rookie, Carver," Knight said flatly.

"This is all of 15. The other four are at the hospital," Rodriguez admitted.

Fabian nodded. Poor recruitment had left everyone scrambling to fill holes. Firehouse 15 must have been operating their Medic, Ladder, and Engine with seven people instead of the usual ten.

This was exactly why Fabian was still working. This shift'd had two guys call off because they had covered a different firehouse the night before. His captain was arranging relief, but it would be a long time coming.

This wasn't putting him in any better position to reach that amorphous meeting with Cassie.

"You're lucky that Bat Chief McClunis isn't on call because

she'd skin you alive. You're getting Chief Haskell."

"We are? Did he just start?" Knight asked.

"Today," Fabian said, and he felt like something else went along with that piece of info. He clicked on his radio to the rest of 10. "Hook up the water. Engine 15 isn't going to be much help."

"We've established a collapse zone. I called the power and gas companies while we waited for help to show up late," Rodriguez said archly.

"We came when we got the call," Fabian said, sharing a look with her. They both knew that Dispatch had been unreliable at best lately. "Here's the bat chief."

A white Cleveland FD SUV, called the Chief Car, pulled up and two men got out. One wore the standard navy-blue uniform of chief's aide and the other wore the black blazer and white shirt of battalion chief.

Fabian grinned, despite the situation, because he was familiar with both of them. Jared Pickford had been with him back at Firehouse 5. Jared was a big clown, but he and Fabian shared an intense loyalty to their former captain James Haskell. James had saved Fabian's life a few years back at the near cost of his own.

The new battalion chief listened carefully to the explanation from the crew from 15. He allowed them to walk him around the building while Fabian helped Jared set up the safety board and sent his team to mark off the collapse zone.

As soon as the chief was out of earshot, Jared said, "Santos, what the fuck happened to your hair?"

"That? Well, there was a chlorine exposure, and this new girl…"

"Another one? You and your ladies. Did she give you a bad

haircut?"

"You and your guys," Fabian retorted since he and Jared didn't play on the same team. "And no, I cut my own bangs. It made sense at the time."

"Probably the same way driving an engine into a garage did," Jared said. "This is a great first day. If I were still in a firehouse, I'd never have done this."

"Would have broken a nail?" Fabian tried to rejudge the roof's lean onto the engine. "Could we back it out? It's worth a million dollars, right?"

"Not worth your life or explaining to Fire Chief Baker how we got someone killed on James's first day. Would definitely put a damper on his party."

"The party… oh no." That's what Fabian had forgotten. James's former officers, in tradition of ambushing their reticent superior, were throwing a surprise 'congrats on bat chief' party tonight.

Which he had forgotten about. Which meant there was no date with Cassie.

"You forgot?"

"Not exactly. Do you remember Cassie from our trip to Vegas?"

"Cassie the ER clerk from Vows Before Vegas?"

"She's the reason I cut my hair ... we were going to see each other tonight."

"And you will again since she helped organize the party. The ladies from that bachelorette party are very motivated to throw more parties."

They didn't have more time to speak because Haskell came

back around, trailed by the firefighters from 15. "Get your shift off Cleveland Fire property and cool your heels in the sin bin. File your paperwork immediately and expect a meeting at HQ tomorrow."

Rodriguez opened her mouth like she would protest, but Knight grabbed her shoulder. "We understand, and thank you, sir."

They fled toward their ladder truck and pulled out faster than Fabian thought possible.

Haskell sighed and rubbed his eyes. "Why on my first day? Pickford, call Urban Search and Rescue. Maybe they can shore up the garage."

"On it." Jared walked behind the Chief Car to make calls, and Haskell handed Fabian a water bottle.

"It's only going to get hotter," Haskell said. "Make sure your team takes rehab breaks… and what did you do to your hair, Santos?"

"I was going to fix it if I hadn't gotten my arm twisted into staying over." Fabian said and put his helmet back on, even though he was far out of the collapse zone. "If they stabilize the roof, we can back it out?"

"It'd be nice, but I think it'll take a wrecker."

There was a sudden whooshing sound, almost like the air was being sucked into the garage.

"Down!" Fabian tackled the battalion chief and covered him with his body as the gasoline in the garage and its vapors ignited, washing the scene with a brief blast of fire.

Vapor ignitions in open air dissipate quickly, so he rolled off Haskell, who sat up, shaking his head. "Thank god the Engine's a diesel. Let's get this fire out before that explodes too."

The garage had fully collapsed on the engine, which was now

gaining a char pattern. Fabian stood back up and issued commands to his team. Those texts to Cassie would have to wait.

It wasn't fair, but Cassie was feeling a bit prickly as her clock chimed five in the evening.

Maybe prickly wasn't the word. Bitchy might have been better.

She'd finished the ER shift, saving Darren's butt several times. And, despite multiple checks, she'd gotten zero messages from Fabian.

Yes, she'd sent her address and several updates about being late. Then she mentioned she was going to the party for his former fire captain. Then she flat out invited him to meet her at the party.

With every text, she felt she was bordering on desperation. Was she pathetic to keep sending messages to someone with whom she'd never been alone with for more than twenty minutes? There had been the flirting, the chlorine exposure, the kiss, and then her theft of his number from his insurance forms.

No date for sure, even though she'd gone to the trouble of taking a relaxing bath in her cucumber melon body wash and shaved her legs. Just in case, she'd left her hair out rather than risk another hair extension bad luck disaster. Bad juju invited more bad juju.

Just for one stupid firefighter who was obviously not

interested.

Too bad for him. She wore her favorite curve-hugging, but not slutty, pink halter dress, and she was due at Caroline's to help watch her toddler. Caroline was making an insane number of cookies while Cassie was much more of the 'I'll bring the chips and beer' team player. Never in charge, but always happy to help.

Back in the bathroom, she reapplied a final layer of bubblegum pink lipstick. She liked to think she glowed when she wore it. Hot shirtless firefighters beware of the sexy goddess incarnate.

Her phone rang, and she answered it. An unfamiliar voice said, "Sinto muito, flor da paixão. I'm outside."

Rather than hang up on his inconsiderate self, Cassie said, "I'll be there in a minute."

She took her time to finish that last swipe of makeup and went to find her pink sandals.

He was sorry? He'd better be.

Cassie took a deep breath. It was the zilch-ola sleep talking. If she didn't get a nice nap after a night shift, she tended to dance between bitch and heinous bitch. He probably had a good reason.

Then again, she'd worked a double and still found time to text him.

She walked over to the door and opened it.

An ash-covered half-asleep firefighter stumbled into her entryway.

Cassie was surprised at the change since yesterday. He was practically grey with exhaustion and still wearing the scrub top he'd borrowed from the ER. "What happened to you?"

"I got stuck working extra. There was a garage and a fire

engine and—"

"And a patient who set himself on fire?" Cassie suggested. "If you read my messages, you'd know I covered an extra shift."

"My relief just arrived. I haven't even showered. This isn't how I thought I'd be doing this." His eyes focused on her dress. "You're looking really cute."

She crossed her arms under her breasts, lifting them slightly. "All this work and you came up with 'cute?' No naughty words in some other language, especially after how great my boobs look?"

His brown eyes blinked. "Well, paixão, I thought more would be coming on too strong before our first date. Usually, I'd get flowers. And for breakfast, donuts before the nap that we didn't take.

"It's a little late for donuts, though a nice cup of coffee and a cream stick would be appreciated after a double shift," Cassie checked her sparkly golden watch. "As fun as it is to chat, I don't really have time for this. I've got to head over to the party."

"Caroline's and James's?"

"That's the one. It's not your fault I'm a little cranky and annoyed that no one returned my messages."

"I wanted to. I was dying to check my phone. I could feel it buzzing, but it was under my turnouts. And it's July, so I was getting sweaty and—"

Cassie inhaled, "Wow, you do smell manly. Not the good kind."

"I'm disgusting, and I'm screwing this up."

"Let's call it's a mutual screw-up. Why don't you hop in my shower? I'll put your clothes in the wash instead of Haz-Mat and give you a dress out of my collection to wear."

"I have my street clothes. And I think my chest hair won't go with your dresses." He gave her a tired smile. "What about these?" He flicked his mangled bangs.

"Slick'em back with water." She reached out a hand to touch his coal-colored locks and then thought better of it. "You're almost Haz-Mat level of grimy, and I can't do grimy right now."

"Cassie, please. I can do better than this." He sounded so pathetic she blew him a kiss.

She smiled. "I hope so, Fabio. Strip, and I'll wash them." Cassie led him to her bathroom, and he seemed more than grateful she wasn't tossing him out on his cute butt.

Honestly, she really could have. They'd flirted and kissed one time last night. They both clearly had busy lives of their own… but she did want to see what that nap with him felt like.

Ten minutes later he was dressed, with a great deal more color. His polo shirt stretched over his broad shoulders and a hint of chest hair peeked out. "Thanks, I feel almost human."

"Good. Hope you feel mostly human," she traced the edge of his bangs.

The man grasped her hand and kissed the inside of her wrist. Her insides did that panty-twisting squeeze which they had no right to do. "Você é linda demais e quero te beijar de novo, paixão."

"You are unfairly sexy when you do that. I think the universal fantasy needs to add Latin lover to firefighter stripper." She followed his tug into his arms, almost close enough to kiss again.

And her phone made a warning beep. "That's a text from Kyra. I'm supposed to get the Haskells. Do you want to come with me?"

He frowned. "I thought the party doesn't start for over an

hour."

"I'm babysitting while Caroline makes cookies. I'm off tomorrow, and I don't cook, so that's my job."

"I'm in. I love kids," Fabian said, proving he was probably a good guy. "I'll drive."

The universe had decided it did not want Fabian to kiss Cassie. In fact, the universe wanted to make things as difficult as possible and drive him absolutely crazy horny.

First, Caroline Haskell had welcomed them home and put them in charge of playing with the toddler. The kiddo had taken to Fabian and insisted on climbing on him to pull his hair. This game was great for the kid, not so great for Fabian's hair. He swore Cassie was laughing at him the whole time.

Meanwhile, Cassie and Caroline stacked and passed out cookies to a steady stream of neighbors that passed by. James Haskell hated attention and parties, which made the entire clandestine operation even funnier. He'd be polite while it happened, but a grumpy bear if he caught wind of it.

After another clump of his hair got pulled out, Caroline let Fabian in on the secret. They'd skipped the nap today so the toddler would sleep through the party. The name of the game was to get the kid so tired it guaranteed sleep through what would likely be a rambunctious get-together.

Sleep finally won out right after six, and upstairs went the tired toddler. They were relaxing with Caroline in the living room when someone opened the front door.

"Nyet. He's early," Caroline shoved Fabian and Cassie into a corner by the kitchen and opened the door to block them from sight.

Fabian was very aware of Cassie pressed up against him. He placed his finger over her lips, rather than kiss her like he wanted to. The dim light made him notice the slight sheen of sweat over her arms and into the valley of her breasts.

They waited as quietly as possible, but it was so cramped, Fabian was having difficulty thinking straight. Her dress was thin, and he tried not imagine cupping her ass and breasts.

She wasn't making it easy, either. She laid a hand on his shoulder and rubbed the sinew in his neck, right next to his pulse.

Footsteps approached their door and Fabian wondered wildly if James could hear the throb in his pulse or the answering throb in his cock through the door.

The door creaked. Cassie and Fabian tensed.

Then Caroline saved them from discovery. Whatever she said in Russian made James release the door and not spoil his own surprise party.

They exhaled quietly and waited.

While Fabian had no idea what Caroline had said, it was more than effective because the talking stopped to be replaced by the unmistakable moans and groans of his battalion chief making love to his wife.

While it was great to know that the Haskells were in love and very happy together, it was inappropriately erotic to witness the breathy sounds of pleasure.

He wasn't alone in being affected. Cassie bucked slightly

against him, her pupils wide with arousal.

Fabian carefully placed his hand on her face, running his thumb over her lips. She opened her mouth and bit down with blunted teeth. He controlled his exhalation while he plucked at the front of her dress with the other hand.

Her nipple instantly pebbled through her dress, and he did it again, reveling in the way she thrust forward against him and bit his thumb with more force. He squeezed her nipple, feeling her muffle her whimper into his thumb. If she was wearing a bra, it had to be quite thin.

On the other side of the door, the amorous encounter was reaching its crescendo. Fabian was trying not to imagine what James was doing to Caroline, but the smell of sex was equally unmistakable.

Technically, it smelled of fresh baked cookies and arousal.

How would Cassie smell when he went down on her? Would he have her scent layered on his skin, marked with the evidence of a woman fulfilled? Fabian leaned forward just enough to lick the side of her neck as he tugged her crest again.

There was a masculine shout and a feminine moan. It wasn't over though, because they could hear James say something in Russian to Caroline and carry her into the kitchen, closing the door behind them.

Fabian didn't care what was going on the kitchen because he needed and wanted Cassie. She willingly spun to get her back to the wall, lifting one leg to wrap around his hip. His hard-on was a big fan of that and pushed forward, wishing they were naked.

Someone coughed loudly. They froze.

Jared came out from the entryway. "Not the couple I expected in the living room."

"Hey, Jared," Cassie smoothed down her dress, completely nonplussed.

"What are you doing here?" Fabian tried not to sound too annoyed.

"I'm James's aide, and I planned the party. I dropped James off, drove around the block a few times, and came back." He shrugged. "He had to think I left. Caroline was supposed to distract him."

"She did," Cassie said.

"Going at it like rabbits again?" Jared eyed them carefully. "Though I guess they aren't the only ones."

Before Fabian could say anything, paramedic Kyra Yates, resplendent in a Cleveland Browns themed dress, arrived with her husband, Ryan and then an entire gaggle of firefighters and women crept in.

After hushed greetings were passed around, Jared tapped on the door and Caroline—fully dressed—let them into the kitchen, and the surprise party was on.

The sex must have put James in a good mood, because he greeted his unexpected guests with smiles instead of scowls. Or maybe it was the fact that Caroline wasn't drinking for the best of reasons.

However, since it was a team-up between the firefighters and the survivors of Amy's Vegas Before Vows bachelorette party, there was a lot of drinking. It was many vodka shots before anyone made it outside to the barbecue.

As nice as it was to see the firefighters that had served under James, Fabian couldn't stop sneaking glances at Cassie. She was smiling and giggling with Kyra, who was fake yelling at her over the chlorine incident.

Fabian itched to steal some alone time, but the little old ladies kept trying to feed him more cookies and introduce him to single women in the neighborhood.

Usually, Fabian would have been on board with that. In the past, he'd have kept his options open, but Cassie was right there in front of him. Tempting, delicious… was she wearing a bra or not?

Six shots and three hours later, he found himself roped into carrying several trays of cookies into the house from the outdoor tables with Dr. Ryan Yates.

"Are you and Cassie official now?" Ryan asked.

Fabian looked around to make sure no one else was nearby. Most guys wouldn't have been so upfront, but this bespeckled doctor in a Brown's Jersey seemed relatively harmless. "We're working our way there."

"I see," Yates said. "I assume you're single, STD-free, and intensely believe in mandatory use of protection."

Fabian noted the abrupt shift in Ryan's voice as he was significantly less friendly now. "As if it's your business, perrera."

Having clearly understood the term for 'Dawg Pound,' Yates straightened his jersey. "Kyra and Cassie are best friends. Cass has always been knee-deep in navigating other people's drama at work, but she's kept her stuff outside the hospital. She's made an exception for you. Don't make me sorry I gave you an opening yesterday."

"Or what?" Fabian let annoyance into his tone. This guy didn't even know him. He only assumed. "You're going to threaten me?"

"Of course not. If you come to MetroGen, I'll provide the best medical care possible. You'll receive a head-to-toe exam by my medical students, then my residents. They'll even check your prostate because, remember, their education is paramount."

Fabian winced. "Point taken."

The doctor, totally calm again, patted Fabian on the shoulder. "Anytime. With that out of the way, you can make you move, and I can tell Kyra I appropriately threatened you."

Now Fabian laughed. "I thought you were serious for second."

"I was. I'll let the medical students probe you like an alien abduction with zero regrets. Fortunately, I have pretty good instincts, and I have a good feeling about you." He paused before he threw a parting shot on his way out the door. "In case I didn't threaten you hard enough, Kyra wants you to know she's not above talking to Fire Chief Baker."

And that was far more ominous than anything else Yates could have said.

Never cross Fire Chief Baker, the unyielding boss of all Cleveland Fire.

There was a bottle of vodka on the counter, so Fabian took two shots and asked himself what he was doing. Flirting with Cassie in the ER had seemed simple, as had planning the nap.

But it didn't sound simple anymore. They'd been in each other's periphery for almost three years, and nothing ever happened. Their friends had weighed in already before their first date and assumed this would be some type of real relationship.

Exhaustion and alcohol were not helping this make sense. Regrouping and figuring stuff out was the best course here. Fabian hadn't planned much beyond the nap and seeing if they clicked enough to date. Flirtation may or may not have led to something physical.

Had he treated her like a badge bunny—a woman who went from firefighter to firefighter for sex? What did she expect now? Was Yates serious about the Fire Chief?

"Hey!" Cassie carried in more cookies. "I had no idea you could party after eleven into your eighties, but there they are. Unless these cookies are laced with more than sugar."

"Cassie, can we talk for a second? Someplace with less traffic," Fabian started uncertainly.

She considered his words before giving him a giant grin and leading him past the living room to a dimly lit room that appeared to be an office based on the desk and plaques.

Fabian closed the door and turned to Cassie. He took a slow breath and gave his brain a mini pep talk about not stripping that halter dress down her arms. "So, about us."

"My thoughts exactly." She kissed him open-mouthed and stopped whatever stupid idea he'd been about to suggest.

She tasted amazing, like powdered sugar from the cookies they'd been eating. Fabian swooped in to trace the outline of her lips, savoring the confectionery goodness.

"Fabian. Fabio," she cooed while pulling on his abused hair. "No more talking. It's over-rated."

"But Yates… the Chief." Fabian tried to force his brain to remain on topic. It was more difficult than he thought possible with a warm, wanting woman in his arms.

Said woman was also not interested in his words. "For the love of God." She untied her halter top and let it fall, answering the

$10,000 question about the presence or absence of a bra.

Fabian's mouth watered at the sight of plump breasts with erect nipples straining against thin pink lace. Talking was completely over-rated because he already had one nipple in his mouth. With each pull of his mouth, she moaned and twisted his ravaged hair.

He boosted her onto the desk for better access. “Precisa de mais, paixão? Eu vou dar para você.”

“No idea what you said but get back to it. Please.” She caught the collar of his polo as if she could guide him and strip him at the same time.

Since no answer was necessary in any language, he resumed the feast of his new favorite meal.

Though maybe it wouldn't be his favorite meal. When he moved to her other side, he began to roll up her skirt.

“Just like that,” she urged him on, opening her legs till his fingers encountered wet lace.

“Não se preocupe. Vou provar seu doce néctar.” Fabian hiked her skirt up and moved his head down.

There was a sudden explosion of bright light. They scrambled apart and readjusted their clothing.

Jared said, “Again? Get a room, you two. Or find a door with a lock. I’m constantly amazed by the loose women from Vegas Before Vows.”

Fabian bristled because no matter what they had been doing, no one was allowed to say that about women in front of him. “I suggest you reconsider your words, babaca.”

“I love it when he uses whatever he uses,” Jared said. “Take a joke."

"I'm not offended," Cassie said, straightening her chest, though there was a hint of wetness from her bra soaking through her dress. "We hadn't gotten far enough to count as loose."

"See, she's fine with me being an asshole." Jared walked toward the desk.

"What are you doing?" Fabian asked in confusion.

Amusement beamed from Jared's face, and he picked up a messenger bag with the insignia of Cleveland Fire. "The guy from the garage fire died. We're going to MetroGen."

That was sobering. The battalion chief wouldn't have been sent to the hospital for just any victim. "There's more, isn't there?"

Jared nodded. "He attacked the firefighter who tried to stop him from burning the building down. The firefighter defended himself with force… the Fire Chief will want a full update."

Even Fabian got that. James was tasked with determining if that firefighter from 15 had mistakenly killed the victim. Fabian had no idea how Chief Baker would respond to the outcome of this scene. "Wow. Chief Baker. Wow and wow."

"He won't mess around," Jared agreed.

"Why is everyone so scared of the Fire Chief?" Cassie chirped.

"Because he's the Chief. Have you met him?" Jared said.

"Of course. Blonde guy with beautiful blue eyes. Cute."

Fabian's blood pressure rose unexpectedly, and he sputtered, "Cute?"

"Actually, hot. Handsome. We see him sometimes since the ER is Grand Central Station. And when he gets interviewed for the news, he seems nice… and hot," Cassie declared as Fabian fumed internally. Had she flirted with the Fire Chief the same way she had him? Did she swipe his phone number off his insurance card too?

"He is not a nice guy," Jared said. "He is the Chief. That guy who you think is friendly sees into your soul. His beautiful blue eyes penetrate skin, flesh, bone, and cement blocks."

She waved a hand. "Commanding is hot. No straight woman would complain if he ordered her into his bed. Intense and focused is dynamite in bed."

"No. The Fire Chief is an asexual being issued from the Cleveland Fire Department factory. So you can't think about whether or not he's attractive. He's the Fire Chief. El jefe." Fabian couldn't control the anger creeping into his voice.

"I bet his penetrating gaze is less of an x-ray and more of a smolder. Definitely a smolder. I can use that word, right? We are talking about firefighting," Cassie continued relentlessly.

"No, the Chief does not smolder. You don't look at the Fire Chief that way. If Jared says you can't look at him that way, it's legit," Fabian said.

"You can't tell me what I can say and can't say. I was being funny." Cassie stiffened and stepped away from him.

"I don't think it's funny," Fabian hissed.

"I can leave now," Jared said. "I'd rather go to the morgue at MetroGen than be here for the first fight between you and lover-boy with your dating and everything."

"You can't have a fight if you're not dating," Fabian grumbled.

Cassie responded by snapping her head up. "Oh. So I guess your whole date plan with the coffee and donuts was bullshit?"

"We haven't even been on a date! Sounds like you'd rather

fuck the Fire Chief anyway!" Fabian shouted.

"Go to hell, Fabio!" Cassie made a beeline for the office door, and Fabian didn't stop her.

"You escalated that quickly." Jared gestured to the door. "What are you doing? Go after her!"

"Why? Didn't you hear her? She talked about how hot the fire chief was! She said he'd be great in bed!" Fabian felt the fury burning hard and fast.

"No kidding. He is hot, and untouchable. I'm gay, but even I can tell she was teasing you. Hell, she was testing you to see if you would get a little bit jealous."

"She definitely got the jealous part. I've dated enough badge bunnies to know I'm not interested in another one," Fabian raged, pissed that she'd had the nerve to share way too much lust about a guy who was NOT Fabian.

Jared poked him in the center of the forehead. "Why the fuck do you think she's a badge bunny? If she was a badge bunny, she had plenty of opportunities to fuck you in Vegas and after our group strip show. How many badge bunnies wait almost three years when a woman like that could stop by her nearest firehouse and ride as many firefighters as she wanted?"

Jared was starting to make too much sense. "Crap."

"Is there more to this than what I assumed was Flirty Desk Clerk with Flirty Firefighter?"

"Not really. I ran into her last night in the ER. We flirted and messed with my rookie while we waited to get checked out. That was when I remembered how fun she was. Then we got exposed to chlorine gas, I helped her take a shower, and I cut off my hair for her."

Jared raised his hand. "Wait, you cut your hair for her? And you helped her shower? Was she naked during her shower? Were you?"

It took a couple of seconds for Fabian to catch up with the number of questions. "She had extensions and looked sad about taking them out. I wanted to make her feel better, so I cut my bangs with trauma shears. Then I found her clothes while she showered—naked—without me."

"Did you get hit in the head since this morning? How much have you had to drink?" Jared accused him.

"What does that have to do with anything?"

"Listen to yourself. You've always been a flirt. Not a man-whore, but you never turned a lady down. All night, you ignored the ten women the neighborhood welcome wagon threw at you. I caught you all over Cassie twice, and then you blew your stack—not in the sexy way—when she made a few jokes about the hotness of the Fire Chief."

"What are you saying?" Fabian didn't follow, as he could barely think past how it felt to hear Cassie talking about the Chief.

"Tell me why you're so pissed off at her… and then why you aren't chasing her right now!"

Fabian swallowed hard, trying to make sense of his own behavior. The alcohol wasn't helping, but eventually, he admitted the truth. "I'm mad because I really like her. And I'm not chasing her because I'm incrivelmente estúpido."

"I hope you called yourself a dumbass. Try to catch her." Jared pointed to the door.

Fabian ran through the house and then outside. He arrived just in time to see Cassie climb into a car with Kyra Yates at the wheel and her husband glowering at him through the window.

He stared dumbly at the departing tail lights, the bottom dropping out of his stomach and settling somewhere around his feet. "I need to go after her."

"Not tonight. Give me your keys." Jared confiscated his key ring. "You pulled a double, drank too much, and have blue balls. No driving till tomorrow."

"You're driving."

"Yeah, because I, like James, only had one shot three hours ago. You were so busy staring at Cassie and drinking that you didn't notice. James has a guest room. Sleep it off there."

"But…"

"She's not in any mood to talk to you, and I'm not dropping your inebriated ass on her doorstep. This isn't How to Lose a Guy in 10 Days."

"Fine. I will fix this." Fabian took out his cell phone. "But I'm texting her I'm sorry, and I'll see her tomorrow."

James joined them, dressed in a clean uniform, looking every inch the battalion chief. "Ready to go?"

"Yep, Fabian's crashing in your guest room. He screwed things up with Cassie."

"That was fast." He patted Fabian on the shoulder. "Whatever you do, go big. It's easier for them to forgive you that way."

"But it can't be stripping. We already did that," Jared advised as they loaded into the Chief Car. "Strip after you make up."

Fabian woke in the guest room only slightly hungover and in full command of his facilities.

A good night's sleep had restored his brain to working order and at 5 am, and he knew exactly what he had to do. The nearest Dunkin Donuts was already open, and he threw on an extra Firehouse 10 shirt to be there bright and early.

Unfortunately, he was not the only insane person with that plan. It was the morning rush with two cashiers ringing people up while another took his order for four dozen donuts.

Other than her request for cream sticks, Fabian had no clue what Cassie's donut demands would be. It wouldn't hurt to be prepared, and he'd be a hero at the firehouse if he came in with a bunch of donuts anyway.

His arms were loaded down with boxes. To his annoyance, a blonde guy in front of him was taking an eternity to pick out a single cup of coffee.

"It's coffee, perezoso. Pick up the pace," Fabian grumbled. "It's not a life-changing decision."

The man turned around with his ice-blue eyes and said,

"Donde esta el fuego, Santos?"

"Holy fuck… Chief Baker, I am so sorry," Fabian choked.

"You'd better not be scheduled to work today after pulling a double yesterday." The Chief nodded at the pile of donuts.

"I'm not working… I was…" Fabian was not telling the Chief about his romantic challenges. "I was hungry. I'll share the leftovers at my firehouse later."

"If that's the case, these are on me." The Chief signaled the cashier to ring up Fabian and paid with his credit card. "Need a hand?"

"Sure, sir." The Chief grabbed his coffee and held the door for Fabian to exit. Then he helped Fabian unlock his truck and maneuver the boxes inside. "Thank you, sir."

"My pleasure," the Chief sipped his coffee.

Fabian reexamined the Chief and exclaimed without thinking. "Those are workout clothes… I've never seen you without your uniform on."

The Chief raised his eyebrows, waiting to see if Fabian rethought that comment.

"I meant… hell… fuck. I'm not hitting on you. It's that you're always in the white shirt and black blazer." The Chief was wearing a tight blue performance shirt which brought out his legendary eyes.

"Neither are very conducive to yoga or meditation."

Fabian couldn't believe his ears. "Yoga? You do yoga?"

"Only on occasion. I prefer punching things, but that often doesn't fix the problem."

Without thinking, Fabian said, "It doesn't put the garage back together for sure. Or the fire engine."

"Yes, I know," the Chief said. "There will be repercussions for that—not for you. Your report was excellent."

"Don't be too hard on them, patron." Fabian decided he might as well go in for the whole enchilada, the hamburger, and the supersized fries. "Yes, they broke protocol, but it was to save the life of a teammate. Five years ago, you broke protocol and led the rescue of James yourself as battalion chief. I was there at your side when you did his CPR."

It was more than bold to call the Chief out on anything, let alone breaking protocol. But yesterday, Jared had called Fabian out for his behavior and been willing to help him. It was only fair he remind the Chief of his own actions and help the team at 15 who had suffered for being understaffed.

The Chief stared him directly in the eye, almost penetrating his flesh and bone, just as Jared had said.

"And much to contemplate I have," the Chief smiled mysteriously, "Don't let me keep you from your girl."

"How did you…"

The Chief pointed at Fabian's hair. "No one gets a haircut that bad unless it's for a girl. Don't forget to give her coffee if you're visiting her this early."

Cassie had said she wanted coffee during their discussion of their imaginary date. "Holy crap. Thank you, Chief."

The Chief walked away and Fabian doubled back, passing an African American woman in purple yoga tights at the donut display. He made it to the front of the line and ordered two coffees.

The clerk handed him two cups and said, "That's the last of it.

We're going to have to brew another pot.

The woman groaned, “What do you mean ‘another pot’? I'm going to be late for yoga. I will not stay awake in yoga without coffee.”

Fabian turned around. “Sorry.”

“I don’t suppose you could let me have one of your coffees?” she asked in a light tone.

Two days ago, Fabian would have been interested. This woman was tall and cute—if he were on the market. Her hair was similarly textured to Cassie’s, pulled back in a poof, and she had long lean lines that could have been appealing.

To some other guy…and Fabian’s heart was loyal.

Wow, his heart . . .

“Nope,” Fabian said. “I promised my girl coffee.”

“Of course,” the woman said, “Firehouse 10, huh?”

“I work there,” he answered in a tone that ideally would dissuade her interest. Still, she didn’t give off the badge bunny vibe because she seemed to be measuring him.

“I heard you guys showed up late to our scene yesterday. If I act sad, would it change your mind? I have a debrief today at HQ.” She batted her eyes with exaggerated speed.

“We were late because the call never came through. Dispatch issues again.”

“You’d think they’d have fixed that.” She introduced herself, “Erin Hudgens, Firehouse 15.”

So this was the third woman at Firehouse 15. “Fabian Santos, lieutenant at 10, and I’m taken.”

“Please. Firehouse dating only leads to destruction, rain of body parts, and a plague of frogs without cool Yul Brenner. If you're going to try it, it should be not in your firehouse or battalion and reserved for drunk dials only."

"No clue. There have never been enough women in Cleveland firehouses to know." Fabian paid for his drinks.

"I'm from Seattle till I transferred here last year. Way more women. Also way fewer crashed fire trucks."

"Yeah, I heard. Incident debrief today?" Fabian's phone beeped and he opened it.

Cass: You're sorry.

Fabio: The sorriest. I am coming over.

Cass: Today?

Fabio: Now. I promised you a nap date.

Cass: You're serious.

Fabio: So serious. And so SORRY.

There wasn't a smart remark following so that was positive.

"Sorry," he said to Erin, having forgotten she existed for a few seconds. "I'm… well… my girlfriend."

"I see. You got it bad."

Fabian grinned. "But it feels so good. Even the groveling."

"Good luck with that. I guess I'll be going without coffee."

"Good luck to you. That debrief is going to be rough," he warned her. "Watch out for the Fire Chief."

"That old stick? I'm way more concerned about our battalion chief."

Erin was out the door and gone before Fabian could ask her

exactly who she thought the Fire Chief was.

She'd find out soon enough.

But Fabian had a nap date with Cassie.

Or so he hoped.

Cassie woke up this morning kicking herself. Last night had ended in a disaster. Her phone was full of 'sorry' messages from Fabian and one that said he was coming over now.

She rolled out of bed, untied her hair scarf, and tried to recreate some mystique of 'attractive woman,' not 'woman who dragged herself out of bed.'

Her doorbell rang as she finished brushing her teeth. Barefoot and in her favorite comfy pink bathrobe, she checked out the peephole. Fabian, jealous firefighter/Latin Lover fantasy, had four boxes of Dunkin Donuts and coffee.

Cassie pulled back the chain and opened the door a few inches. "It's 6 am."

"I said I was coming over now. I promised you donuts, OJ, coffee, and a nap. This seemed like a great way to make it work."

"Or a great way to get a restraining order." Cassie shook her head. "I'll let you in, but only because you brought donuts."

"Thank you." He followed her into the kitchen and set everything down on the counter.

She flipped open the first box to oohh and aaahh at the wide variety. “You certainly got enough—”

Fabian snaked out an arm past the boxes and spun her into his arms. His mouth came down, hot and hungry on hers.

She met his kiss with an intensity of her own—frustration, anger, confusion, and this undeniable attraction. Even though she wanted to be pissed, her body was softening against his muscled one. Unbidden, her hands helped him throw her robe on the floor, making the hot pink lace beneath available for his taking.

When they came up for air, he kissed one side of her neck. “Eu sinto muito. Lo siento. I'm so sorry. You're beautiful and gorgeous and wonderful, and I'm an idiot. Give me another chance. If you don't want to date me, we can just hang out and watch TV or nap. Whatever you want.”

He was melting her token resistance. She panted with her head pressed against his chest. “I should tell you to go. Last night, you were out of line. So far out of line.”

“I don’t deserve anything from you, but please let me grovel. I really like you. And what I said last night was inexcusable. Lo siento,” he apologized, dropping a kiss on her shoulder.

She leaned into him, wanting to give more, but not wanting to get hurt. “You need to sweeten the deal. A lot.”

“I’ll strip. I’ll do the full monty. I won’t even lay a hand on you unless you ask.” He whispered into her neck. “If you ask, I’ll make you come over and over again. Please, paixão.”

Cassie wanted to take him up on his offer. She took the middle road by putting a little distance between them and stepping away.

"Fine. You'll get naked. I'm going to cut your hair."

"Deal."

"And I get to keep the donuts and the coffees."

"All yours." Fabian did a double-take when he noticed his clothes from yesterday, including the scrub top, were folded on her counter. "You washed my clothes?"

"I thought about dousing them with gasoline and burning them in my garage, but it was someone else's horrible idea."

"Can I mention again how sorry I am?" He trailed her to the bathroom.

"It won't hurt." She pulled towels out and opened the drawer, getting out of pair of barber scissors.

"Do you know how to do this?" He eyed the scissors.

"You were going to let your rookie do it. You'll be fine. I know ER doctors. They'll sew your ear back on if I miss."

"Probably without lidocaine," Fabian said. "Yates said—"

"I did not ask Ryan to threaten you. That was one hundred percent Kyra Yates. God, I don't know what they're going to do when the baby comes." Kyra had been the designated driver for a reason.

"Maybe that's why he came on so strong. You want my shirt off?"

"You did offer the full monty. I'll settle for the shirt first." Cassie waved the scissors at him.

He shrugged and said, "This was not how I imagined our first date going."

"Strip. This is exactly how I imagined our sixth date going."

"Sixth date?" He rolled his shirt and undershirt over his head and Cassie had to remember to talk. He was half a foot taller than her but definitely cut with glorious, copper skin. "Cassie?"

"Just staring. Take off your pants." His ripped chest and easy-going attitude was making it easier to forgive him and admit how much she wanted him. "Since it's my rules, I've decided it's our sixth date."

"When did we go on these other five dates?" He stripped down to his underwear. The man wore briefs today, unlike the boxers she'd washed yesterday. Interesting.

"In Vegas, our first two dates were when we had lunch together and then we danced at Coyote Ugly. Date three was your group strip show at Larissa's. And then our kiss in the shower and our fight yesterday counted as four and five." She set a chair in front of the mirror. "Get naked."

"I haven't even bought you dinner yet." Fabian wrapped a towel around his waist and played reluctant to give up the goods.

"You guys chipped in for lunch in Vegas, so that should count. I think I can handle naked by the sixth date."

He held the towel tightly around his waist. "I screwed up badly enough that I don't want you to think I disrespect you or that I expect…"

"Are you saying you don't want to get naked with me?" The way his towel was tenting made her think he wasn't exactly unaffected. She put her hands on the sculpted muscles of his shoulders and traced her fingers across his nipples and his six-pack. She rested her hands lightly on the edge of his towel. "When you imagined napping with me, what did you want to happen? I'm going to get that towel one way or another."

He was breathing heavily, almost close enough to kiss her

again. “I don’t want you to think I’m easy. Turn around.”

“Suit yourself.” Cassie went back to the counter to take out the hair clippers. The bathroom mirror wasn’t low enough to give her the full show. “Between what you did to your bangs and then Baby Haskell’s hair pulling game, it’s tough to salvage your hair. Want to go full cue ball and get rid of that goatee you’re sporting?”

“It has to go. I skipped shaving it when I started my shift, which is three days ago. If it goes any longer, my SCBA—my air—won’t fit. Take it all.”

“So I’m shaving your chest?”

“I don't think I know you well enough.”

“I shaved my legs for you yesterday.” She took out the scissors and begin trimming off his hair. She could have used the clippers immediately but getting rid of the bulk of it made it easier. He had nice thick, luxurious, black hair.

His chocolate-colored eyes were watching her closely. She couldn’t help giving him a tiny hip wiggle. “You’re torturing me, woman.”

“Possibly a little. Tell me what you want to do on this date.”

His hands grabbed her hips, making her almost drop the clippers. He was definitely staring at her eyes, and she felt every part of her swell. “Because this is the sixth date, I want to cover you with sugar and eat you up like the donuts.

She laid her hand across the edges of his goatee where it had become unruly. Her body thrummed with want, nipples peaking. “You won’t ask me to suck the cream out of your stick?”

He shifted uncomfortably. “Definitely too forward for the sixth date. Date eight?”

She glanced down at the bulge under the towel. “Am I too

forward if I take that towel?"

"You get to do whatever you want to me. It's your house and your rules, paixão." Fabian's voice rumbled way too pleasantly through her.

She needed to cool things down a notch, or she'd jump him and end up covered in hair. "Hands off, Fabio… for now, or we'll never finish."

"At your command." He let her go and sat quietly while she worked. He didn't even move when she buzzed his head and took out shaving cream for his face. "I presume you're completely single or you wouldn't be here. Though I don't see why you're single—other than the jealousy thing."

He blushed slightly. "The jealousy thing is new. I'm single because of the job. My last girlfriend was three or four months ago now. As usual, dating a firefighter is fun until the math sets in."

"The math?" Before she covered his face with the shaving cream, she decided to get permission. "Mind smelling like cucumber melon?"

"Not an issue. My sisters used to do my hair, so I ended up braided and smelling like lavender through all my teenage years."

She laughed at the way his face scrunched up. "Extensions and cornrows?"

He nodded. "I looked weird, wrong hair, wrong face. But you were amazing with those extensions in the ER."

"I do okay with it, but I like it better like this, free." She began to rub cream into his cheeks and chin, briefly closing her eyes at the rough texture. "What is firefighter math?"

"I work twenty-four hours on and forty-eight off with an occasional seventy-two off. There's times like this week where I work more, and it feels like I'm in the firehouse more than I'm out of it."

"Still, you're a hot single firefighter. You should be in high demand. There's a guy from Firehouse 15 who flirts with anyone who has an X-chromosome and at least one leg when he stops by the ER."

"Random tail gets boring. There has to be more to life than that. Look at James and Caroline. The man used to be a storm-cloud and now he's blissfully happy with one woman." Fabian gestured with his hand and almost got an eyebrow of shaving cream.

"Regular infusions of hot sex with the right person can do that… you said the jealousy thing was new. What do you mean?" She wished for a second she hadn't asked and turned away from him to trade the cream for a fresh razor.

His face, buried in the shaving cream, was unreadable. "I don't know. Last night… it sounds stupid. I had too much to drink, and then you mentioned the Chief. I had this beautiful woman in my arms, and I realized I was never going to be able to give her what the Chief could. I'm never going to be a blonde White guy with a penetrating stare. I'm never going to be Fire Chief."

Cassie decided it was time to admit her part in it. "You weren't the only one with a jealousy problem. The little old ladies kept introducing you to new women, and, after a few drinks, I decided to stake my claim. Then I took it too far."

"I was still an ass."

"I didn't help you much. What kind of woman talks about another guy right after a guy was engaged in heavy petting?"

"I was about to do more than heavy petting."

She cleared her throat and managed not to climb on his lap.

“The point is. I egged you on. And for the record, I don’t actually care about the Fire Chief or that you aren’t going to be a future fire chief. You’re at least an officer. I’m the shiftless lazybones.”

“What are you talking about?”

“I'm over thirty and an ER desk clerk. Or, as past boyfriends have said, ‘a glorified secretary.’ I don't have a college degree, and I don't plan on getting one. I own this house. I don't have any loans. I work the shifts I want when I want to work them.”

“Nothing's wrong with that. Who complains about their woman having a job?” Fabian protested on her behalf.

“That's what I thought. However, my sister is a lawyer in Chicago, and my brother got an MBA from Cleveland State so I'm under achieving. I didn't want to become a doctor or a nurse. I'm a valuable part of the ER team.”

“You tried to pull that guy out from chlorine gas poisoning. You're brave; you're tough. Those aren't things that you buy with education.” His burning gaze was penetrating her. She felt hot, wobbly, and extremely wet, with her bra uncomfortably tight. She wanted to steal his towel and suck off his cream stick.

He caught her wrist. “Stop looking at me like that.”

“Like what?” She licked her lips.

“Like I should forget my manners and get you naked again in the shower.” He took the razor out of her hand. “Let’s make a deal. I’ll finish my face while you clean up. Then I’ll shower by myself, and you can decide what we do next.”

Cassie fled and spent the next ten minutes wandering her house and not bursting back into her bathroom. She got rid of the bra so he would know exactly what her nipples thought about him.

A bald and clean-shaven firefighter exited her bathroom with a new towel around his waist. He stopped a few feet from her, eyes black with hunger. "Cassie, before we get going. We need to talk. Make sure we both want the same thing."

She stepped forward and ran her hand across the towel, enjoying his moan. "We want you to take that towel off and get busy."

Fabian used one hand to capture her wrist and the other one to pull her second hand behind her back. His mouth teased her nipples through the robe. "You're so much trouble - temptingly delicious. I want you, but it won't be just once. And if we're banging, it'll be just the two of us. No side pieces, no Fire Chiefs. Can you live with that?"

"Hmm, should I say yes to the almost naked firefighter giving me exclusive use of his body and seeing if it works between us?" She pulled the tie on her robe and let it fall to the floor. He gasped when he took in the full effect of her brown skin with her dark nipples and pink lace panties.

“Madre de dios,” he panted.

“Hell yes,” Cassie beckoned him to her bedroom. “I’ve done everything I can to ward off bad juju. The door is locked. My phone is off. My smoke detector and carbon monoxide detectors have new batteries. The weather report is slightly cloudy with no risk of thunderstorms, tornadoes, floods, or blizzards.”

“We’ve had enough bad luck.” He almost stalked into her bedroom and saw the string of condoms on her nightstand. “We’re both on board for exclusive relations with mandatory protection?”

“So moved. Now get naked before I eat you.”

“Not if I eat you first,” he said and dropped the towel.

Burning lust washed over her. In addition to the chest hair, the six-pack, the happy trail, Mama Santos must have been a traditionalist because his sizable erection lacked a turtleneck. “I'm going to live the universal fantasy of riding hot firefighter cock.”

He smiled and shook his hips, completely unashamed of the impressive erection jetting out of his dark hair. “Então você gosta do que vê sim?”

“I have no idea what you said, but I think I need a closer look.” She placed one hand on the base of his cock and tapped the tattoo of an angel with a cross on his left thigh. “I see you're a good Catholic boy. What’s this?”

“St. Michael the archangel, protector of firefighters. Got it when James Haskell saved my life. Then the Chief saved him…” He grunted through gritted teeth because she jerked her hand up and down the length of his shaft. “Girl, if you plan on riding my cock, you'd better be careful."

"Or the firecracker will go off in my hand, Fabio?" She released him, though his cock stayed pretty much where it had been, stuck straight with its one eye fixed on her. "Bed, now."

"There's something I've been dying to do first." Two seconds later she was on her back with her panties off and a bald firefighter between her legs, murmuring in three different languages. "You're so wet. I've kept you waiting too long. I need to taste seu néctar. Seu açúcar."

Cassie couldn't respond because every swipe of his tongue on her clit brought forth more of that nectar. He held her hips in place with one hand on her thigh and used the other to slip two fingers in her channel.

"Do that again," she shrieked, and he obliged. Between the thrust of his fingers and the motion of his mouth, he brought her to the brink.

She couldn't help herself as she scrambled to grab his non-existent hair. Finally, she found his ears and tugged him upward, near mindless with lust. "Fabian. Stop."

It didn't work the way she intended. He sat back on his heels, pulling away from her. "Okay. I can… okay."

Inches from orgasm, Cassie sat up in bed in total confusion. He was almost comically starved looking with her juices smeared on his face. "What are you doing?"

His voice was strained, as was his monster erection, with every line of his body tense. "You said 'stop.'"

"Yes, 'stop eating me out so I can come when your cock's inside of me.'" She found a condom on the nightstand and welcomed him onto the bed by rolling it on.

They tumbled together, kissing, touching, until he was on his back, suckling her breasts. He was quite the talker in his three languages, and Cassie decided she was on board with his language of love. He'd worried her nipples to the point of unbearable desire when she decided she didn't want to play anymore.

She wanted him, all of him.

Fabian's eyes bulged after she climbed over top of him and positioned herself. He watched her with rapt attention as she slowly slid down, impaling herself on his length. He let out another string of words she couldn't understand, his ability to stick to English failing with every heated second.

She stayed on her knees, riding him, and he let her control the pace. Fabian's cock was amazing, stretching her with the right amount of give. The heady sense of pleasure mixed with need was exactly what she'd craved from the moment they'd laid eyes on each other again.

Speaking of pleasure, he moved one hand to her clit right above where they joined and started stroking her. "Fuck!" the word exploded out of her mouth.

His face was feral as his hand rubbed her straining bud. "Foda-me, paixão. Pegue tudo. Você quer isso. Pegue."

"English," she cried, the tightness in her body ratcheting up.

"Claro, paixão. I love how you feel. I love the noises you make when you get wet. So, take it, lovely." Each sentence was punctuated with a deeper thrust.

That was enough to push her screaming over. His hands clamped down on her hips, and he surged upward to completion.

Finally satiated, she laid down on top of his chest and rested her head on his strong shoulder. "Okay, you lived up to the universal fantasy. I can die fulfilled after Caroline and I compare notes about the wonders of sexing firefighters."

He chuckled and fluffed her hair, which was newly sweat-streaked. "You're the one who's the fantasy."

"Jaded ER clerks are the fantasy?"

"The fantasy is the passionate real-life girl you meet in Vegas—full of trouble and temptation. That's what paixão means—passion."

She rewarded him with her best drugging, passionate kiss. "Passion, huh? It took us close to three years and—" she checked the clock "—twenty-seven hours.

"It was a busy twenty-seven hours." He rubbed her back, "I was interested three years ago, but I'd just been promoted, and life got in the way. I wish I'd called you after we did that strip show."

"I wish I'd asked you to."

"We can make up for that now. Because after our nap, I'm going to enjoy you with decadência—decadence. And I'm going to kiss that borboleta right here." He playfully flipped her away from him and bit the butterfly tattoo on the upper slope of her buttocks. "Any special meaning?"

"Yes, I like butterflies. Sorry, no deep dark secrets, no death, no rebirth. Just like butterflies."

He nipped her butterfly again and then twisted back around to her lips to kiss her with each word. "I like my woman as she is. Cynic. Sarcasm. Sexy."

"Your woman? I like that."

"Sim, minha mulher. My woman for as long as you're willing

to keep me."

"Then that depends on how good the donuts are." She got out of bed and came back with a box of donuts… and her best wicked smile.

Fifteen minutes later, she'd sucked the cream out of his cream stick. Then he'd covered her with sugar and licked it all off, and they'd collapsed in bed, due for another shower.

But first—they were napping.

At last.

Not everyone was napping because some people were trapped at yoga.

Erin Hudgens was definitely reconsidering her plan to attend yoga without coffee. The second they closed their eyes in lotus pose mediation, she dozed off.

Basketball might have been a better choice. Get the blood pumping and clear her mind in preparation for Firehouse 15's big meeting at FD headquarters today.

It was a relief when the teacher asked if anybody would volunteer to get water for the class. Erin's hand shot up.

She wasn't the only one, because a blonde guy in a tight performance shirt and workout shorts jumped up too. It took more control than Erin typically displayed not to do a double take. The man was gorgeous, with blue eyes and gold hair that had a hint of gray.

Erin hoped he wasn't gay because she was unabashedly checking him out. Based on the planes of his muscles, this man knew his way around a weight room and the cardio machines.

Their eyes held for half a second, and Erin suppressed a

shiver.

No, no. Not gay.

The instructor directed them to a storage room in the hall opposite the studio. Erin and the man padded across the hallway in bare feet to the propped open door and didn't notice it swing closed behind them when they entered. It shut with a loud thunk.

All of Erin's senses went on high alert. Firefighters do not rooms without exits. She set down her load of water and tried the handle. "It's stuck."

"Stuck?" The man set down his twenty-four-pack of water.

"Yes, stuck." She tried it again with more force.

"Maybe together?" He came up behind her and pushed while she struggled with the handle.

"I guess that's why they leave the door propped." Erin contemplated her options for opening the door. She could kick it in at the lock or shoulder it. However, her yoga tank and pants were not suited for either of those activities. It was possible, provided she didn't mind a lot of bruising.

Would it be a tragedy if she needed to find a different yoga studio because she broke down the door?

She checked the room for other options. No tools to work into the frame. Neither of them had their cell phones because yoga clothes didn't exactly have pockets. "Pound on the door?"

"Or in ten seconds someone will let us out." The man was still sizing up the door.

"True. Hopefully, your wife won't be mad at you for being stuck in here with me." Erin leaned back against the wall next to the door and laughed slightly at her blatant attempt to gauge his status.

"No wife. Divorced. You?" He faced her, and she was near

breathless from the full force of his bright blue eyes.

"No wife or girlfriend," she said and quickly amended her statement when those azure eyes dropped in disappointment. She couldn't have that. "Or boyfriend. In high school, this is where you play Seven Minutes in Heaven. Don't you think?"

"I was five-foot-three and scared of girls," he replied wryly.

Considering that he was now six-foot-two and ridiculously hot, she doubted that was the case anymore. "That's the problem with high school boys. I was taller than almost all of them, and not one tried anything. If anybody made a move, I'd have been game."

"Not one?" he asked. "Beautiful woman like you, and no one made a move?"

"See, if one of them had your confidence and had said that—he could have gotten lucky." Erin had no qualms about getting closer to Blue-Eyes.

"Confidence?" The man watched her with avid interest now, taking three steps toward her.

"A confident guy would try to cop a feel and ask for my phone number."

"That guy might also be creepy," he said.

"Only when it's not encouraged." She had no qualms about hitting on a hot stranger. "A confident-not-creepy-one would steal a kiss."

His face transformed briefly to a large grin as he comprehended her statement. "Then it's not stealing, is it?"

Erin sidled closer to him, pursing her lips. The idea of even thirty seconds in heaven with a cute guy had accomplished what one hour of yoga class had not. Why not start this long day with something good?

The man drew near, his mouth inches above hers. She could see the details of his red lips, the tiny stubble on his cheeks as if he hadn't shaved this morning. He started to lean, closing those inches that separated their mouths.

A knock interrupted them. "Anybody in here?"

Two minutes later, they were out and Erin skipped the rest of yoga class. Today was a big day and they'd already missed their moment so she'd simply move on.

There was no point in looking back. No one should ever obsess over what could have been when the next thing was coming shortly.

Besides, a little flirting did a body and mind good.

Fire Chief Noah Baker reflected that the highlight of his day was violating the etiquette rules of yoga class: Straight guys were not supposed to ogle the women in class.

Even if they were super-hot and half-naked in skin-tight yoga gear.

Even if said super-hot and half-naked cute woman might have fallen asleep in class and then hit on him when they were stuck in a storage closet.

It was unfair to call her cute; truthfully, she was stunning. Bronze skin, sable, frizzy, poufy hair tied back on her head, wearing form-fitting purple yoga tights and top, he'd failed to keep from salivating as they moved from sun salutations into the vinyasa meditation pose.

She did very little to help with his actual reasons for attending yoga. He preferred boxing, but today was going to be something of a trial with a long morning incident debrief over the Firehouse 15 disaster and then more department business till late at night.

Too bad someone had interrupted them before he took the kiss she'd been offering. Her smile had been full of promise.

Maybe he'd get lucky and see her again some day...

If you think the Fire Chief has just met his match at yoga class, stop by the About the Authors section at the end of the book to learn about Carina Alyce's MetroGen Books.

BRAVE ENOUGH TO LOVE

EmKay Connor

S.W.A.T. team member Lou Quinn makes a living taking risks and rushing into danger. Courage is one of the requirements for the job, and he has it in buckets. He's an everyday hero in every way…except to the one person who matters most.

With his marriage in peril, Lou needs to face his fears and entrust Katie with his vulnerabilities. He's a man of action who refuses to walk away, even when the odds aren't promising, so he'll do whatever it takes to make things right with his wife.

When Lou finds himself in the middle of a robbery gone bad, he realizes he may have missed his chance to tell Katie what's really in his heart. Can he protect the other hostages and make it out alive for a second chance with the love of his life?

Brave Enough to Love is a Heart of the Hero short romance. Look for more stories about these everyday heroes and heroines as the series continues.

"Appointment with the therapist at three today." My wife's voice—the husky, intimate tone she reserved for me—sounded flat and cold on the voice mail she'd left. "Please be there."

I deleted the message, letting anger override my guilt at what she left unsaid yet I heard clear as day. *Please be there instead of canceling at the last minute like you've already done twice.*

She made it sound like I called off to have beer and wings with the guys from my S.W.A.T. team when she knew my schedule could change on a dime if our unit was deployed. It wasn't like I could turn in my sniper rifle and body armor in the middle of a hostage situation. My lieutenant didn't give a rat's ass I was paying Dr. Harding $150 an hour to figure out why my marriage was falling apart.

The job came first.

I warned Katie about marrying a first responder. Shifts are long, and hours are unpredictable. I'm as much married to my teammates as to my wife. Danger and risk are a fact of life. There are parts of my job that I can't—and won't—share with her.

Four years ago, so deep in love with Katie that anything

seemed possible, I allowed her to convince me that none of those things mattered, that together, we could overcome the obstacles and create a family together. She sacrificed so much, and all for me. For my career.

Holidays spent alone or celebrations delayed because the team was out on a call. Making friends with the other police spouses and embracing her blue family. Developing restraint and not blowing up my phone every time the local news media announced a standoff with some desperate guy hellbent on ending his problems by committing suicide by cop.

Katie only wanted one thing from me…and I couldn't give it to her.

I fought with the padlock on my locker, swearing under my breath when I twisted the dial too far. My stomach roiled like I'd eaten bad sushi and my hands shook. Not good for a guy who needed rock-steady nerves to avoid making fatal mistakes in life-and-death situations. I leaned my forehead against the cool metal and sucked air between my teeth.

We'd been trying for a baby for eighteen months. The first six, it was no big deal. "Patience," her OBGYN advised. "Fertility begins to decline at thirty." So each month, Katie tracked her ovulation and alerted me with an eggplant emoji when the time was right. After three months, making love to my wife began to feel more like duty than pleasure.

Katie was thirty-six to my thirty-eight. All of our tests came back negative. There wasn't any medical explanation for our inability to conceive a child. The monthly roller coaster was taking a toll on both of us, me more than her. Katie wanted to try IVF. If that didn't work, we could always adopt, she said. She remained hopeful, convinced this was just another obstacle our love would see us through.

I wasn't sure love was enough.

When you're a first responder, courage is one of the job requirements. I had it in spades. First through the door on a drug raid. First to volunteer when there was an active school shooter. Biggest, strongest, bravest guy on the team, but a first-class coward when it came to facing the disappointment in his wife's eyes when the little plastic stick only showed one line—for the eighteenth time.

I'd pulled away from Katie, unable—more like unwilling—to admit our baby-making problems were my fault. They had to be. The doctor said the only lab result that could potentially indicate a problem was my sperm count. It wasn't *quite* lower than normal…but it was close.

What's that famous quote?

Close only counts in horseshoes and hand grenades.

Bullshit.

Close counted when you were trying to make a baby with your wife.

I yanked open my locker and shoved keys, wallet, and phone on the top shelf. I stripped off my uniform and pulled on shorts and a t-shirt. A workout was exactly what I needed right now to work off the resentment and frustration pouring acid into my veins.

How the fuck was I supposed to give Katie a baby when I was going off half-cocked? Normal sperm count is between fifteen and two hundred million; my count came in at a measly seventeen mil. That was the equivalent of loading my firearm with half the number of bullets it took. An unreliable weapon didn't the job done when lives were on the line. Clearly, the same logic applied to impregnating a woman.

"Lou!" Bobby Briggs, the newest member of our unit, sauntered around the row of lockers and dropped onto the wooden bench a few feet away. Clad in gray shorts, socks, and four-hundred-dollar Nikes, sweat runneled over his heaving chest and plastered his hair to his scalp. "Hope there's enough tread left on the tire for ya. I killed it in there today." He jerked his thumb toward the gym.

Blond, brawny, and cocky as hell, he landed a spot on the team when a bullet to the shoulder forced Antonio Perez into early retirement. Briggs came in already at a disadvantage. It was hard to warm up to a guy who benefited from a tragedy. Tonio was a third-generation cop. His dad was a cop. His dad's dad was a cop. It was the only thing he ever wanted to do, and now his choices were desk duty or disability. Tonio's loss was Briggs's gain, reason enough to dislike him. Top that off with an ego the size of Texas, plus the fact Briggs was several years younger than the rest of us, and you can see how integrating him into our well-oiled machine might require more than a few tweaks with a monkey wrench.

Briggs swiped at his forehead with the back of his hand, flicking droplets in my direction.

Asshole.

I clenched my teeth and then gave him a feral grin. "Don't forget. You're on ARV duty. Hale's nosebleed left a huge mess. Make sure you get it all."

As the FNG—Fucking New Guy—Briggs caught hell. His credentials and skills might have satisfied HR that he was qualified, but everyone, even Big Balls Briggs, had to earn his place on the team. Cleaning out the armored rescue vehicle was a rite of passage…and a legit excuse to give him shit.

His dimples shallowed, but then his arrogant smile was back in place. A slow shake of his head conveyed regret. "Guys get old, and their reflexes slow. Next time let me handle the entry. Hale breached the door okay but couldn't move out of the way fast enough to avoid the suspect's fist."

I didn't have the bandwidth to deal with Briggs's attitude. The guy got off on triggering reactions. The best strategy for dealing with an egomaniac like that was to not respond at all.

What I wouldn't give for Briggs to be the worst part of my day instead of fifty-five minutes on the hot seat in front of my wife and our marriage counselor.

Forty minutes of jacking steel and bare-knuckling the punching bag was better therapy than sharing my feelings using "I" statements.

I feel like a failure.

I feel powerless.

I feel like less than a man.

I feel petrified I'm losing my wife.

My hands curled into fists, and I battered the bag with no thought for style or form until my triceps and deltoids screamed. Thank God the gym was empty because I didn't know if the wetness on my face was sweat or tears. I bent, palms on bent knees, lungs heaving like bellows, ribs expanding and contracting until I regained control.

Good timing because Briggs stuck his head through the door and shouted that the commander wanted to see me.

I stood and used the bottom of my shirt to wipe my face. Time to pull it together.

Mid-day on a Tuesday, the station was quiet. Most of the

officers were out on patrol, so there were a few civilian employees, the police chief and other admins, and the desk sergeant. My athletic shoes squeaked on the linoleum as I strode from the locker room and down a short corridor that led to a huge room reserved for the S.W.A.T. unit. The LT had a closet-sized office in one corner of our space which looked like a cross between a gun store, a garage, and a warehouse.

I lifted a hand to acknowledge Hale Gibson and Ladd Dupree who were examining a map detailing every block and street in Jacksonville Beach pinned to one wall.

Briggs was nowhere in sight, probably out in the yard restoring order to the ARV. I snickered; August in Florida was miserable. Hot and humid, and this close to the beach, the ocean air made your skin sticky. Let's see how cocky Briggs was with sweaty, salty balls.

I hooked my fingers around the door jamb and leaned in. "You wanted to see me?"

Lieutenant Niad looked up and nodded, chin jutting toward the door. "Shut it."

Several inches over six feet, Jack Niad had the weathered look of a career military officer. He wore khakis and a golf shirt with the department logo that revealed corded muscle in his forearms and a still-flat abdomen. His face was angles and slashes—narrowed eyes that made him seem eternally suspicious, thin lips, and a narrow-ridged nose. He was tough but fair. Because of his role as team commander, he needed to maintain a few degrees of separation, but Katie and I were well-acquainted with him and his wife, Denice.

"I hear we might have a problem," he growled. A kick to his throat at a bar fight in Nice, France, on his first deployment with the

Navy had permanently damaged his trachea, resulting in a voice that sounded like sandpaper being dragged over cinder block.

"Wha—" The word hung in the air as he continued.

"I already know too much about what's going on with you and Katie." He bent his elbows and folded his arms on the edge of the desk, reminding me of a praying mantis. "She and Denice had lunch yesterday."

I pursed my lips, wondering about the conversation between the two women but not sure I really wanted to know. It was out of character for Katie to overshare, even though the guys and their wives were like family to us.

"I can't afford to have one of my team members distracted, Lou." His tone softened, but his ice-blue eyes hit me like twin lasers. "Should I be worried?"

Should he?

I was worried.

The problems in our marriage were my fault. Somehow, despite the month-after-month disappointment, Katie remained patient and loving. She endured my broody silence without judgment and tried to entice me back into her arms when I avoided her. She should have been angry. She should have shouted accusations. She should have called me out for being a coward.

Her *request* that we attend couples counseling had been her line in the sand. She would not continue to tolerate my behavior. Something had to change, and that something was me.

I wanted to change. I hated knowing she was unhappy, and the cause of that misery was me. Not just my failure to make a baby with her, but my inability to open up and reveal my vulnerabilities.

"We lost two babies before Cherry came along." Niad looked

out the window as if examining the brilliant Florida sunshine and row of shaggy palm trees between the police station and the parking lot. "After that, Denice couldn't get pregnant again, so we stopped trying."

I grunted, not sure what to say.

"On our wedding night, she said she'd go wherever the Navy sent us, as long as that didn't interfere with having a large family. She wanted six kids. I got her down to four." He swung his gaze back to me, the line of his mouth tilting at the corners for just a second. "It was tough. Denice handled it better than I did. I was one of the Navy's best fighter pilots, but I couldn't perform a basic biological function."

"Huh." I did not want to have this conversation with my lieutenant, but he got it.

"Failure is not an outcome men like us are well-acquainted with." Commander Niad's eyes blazed. "We're heroes. We walk into situations others run from. We protect and serve. We sacrifice our time, our families, and sometimes our lives. We dare, and we do. But sometimes we're just men, and nothing we do can save the day. You need to accept that."

His words hit me like bullets, piercing my skin and channeling through my flesh.

This was what I couldn't convey to Katie.

I wanted to be her hero. I wanted to pick her up in my arms and leap into the sky like Superman. I wanted to slay her dragons.

But I was only a man, and that wasn't enough.

"Stopping at the cleaners and credit union before heading to Dr. Harding's office."

As I stood in front of my locker, a damp towel draped around my neck and my skin still prickling from a cold shower, I listened to another voice mail from Katie.

It wasn't an FYI about her schedule and the errands. She was underscoring the fact that I'd better show up.

I didn't want to consider the "or else".

Lieutenant Niad's words whirled through my head like waterspouts forming over the Atlantic.

We're heroes.

We sacrifice…

We dare…

But sometimes we're just men…

Failure…

My inability to give Katie a baby wasn't the first time I failed at something that shook me to my core.

One of my sniper shots had missed its target and struck a

hostage. The kid was twelve.

A fugitive, wanted by the FBI for mailing pipe bombs to politicians, blew up his home, taking his wife and twin daughters with him because we didn't move in fast enough.

Lionel Massey, my S.W.A.T. brother, who took a bullet to the face while serving a high-risk warrant. He died on my watch, literally—we'd traded shifts so I could attend a Jaguars football game with my brothers who were in town for the weekend.

Any one of those episodes was enough to drive me to my knees. In order to keep doing the job, I compartmentalized. I nailed a lid on my emotions. I didn't talk about it.

None of those techniques would work with Katie. Not if I wanted to hold on to my wife and save my marriage.

Fuck.

I didn't know how to fix things, but I knew I had to try.

It was one thing to fail when you'd done your best, and another thing entirely when you just plain quit and walked away.

I checked my phone—2:03 p.m.

Niad had concluded our private chat with a directive to clock out and take the weekend off.

"Spend it with Katie," he rasped. "Surprise her with some flowers or a box of Peterbrooke chocolates. Go up to Savannah and stay at a bed-and-breakfast. Quit making everything about having a baby. Can't tell you the number of stories I've heard about couples who couldn't get pregnant and the minute they stop trying…"

What if we never got pregnant? What if we tried IVF and it failed? What if we weren't approved for adoption?

For the first time, I considered life without a family. Just me and Katie.

That wouldn't be so bad.

Sure, we still had to find our way through this rough patch but failing to bring a child into our lives was nowhere on par with shooting a twelve-year-old kid or burying a fellow officer.

Something clicked in my brain, and I pounded my fist into the locker next to mine.

Goddammit.

How had I missed it? While I was beating myself up about incompetent swimmers, Katie never lost sight of what mattered most. Me. Her. *Us*. She wasn't punishing me for failing her. I was doing that to myself. So far, that self-castigation had done nothing but cause my wife more heartache and suffering.

I tossed the towel into a nearby hamper, an urgent need to see Katie tightening my muscles. I pulled on cargo shorts and a white t-shirt, jammed my Ray-Ban Aviators on top of my head, dropped my cell in a side pocket on the shorts, and flew out of the station.

Heat rose up from the concrete sidewalk as I headed to the parking lot. I waved at Briggs who tried to shoot me with a blast of water from the green rubber hose he held, but he missed by several feet.

"Hale's going to check your work with a UV wand," I yelled. "Make sure you get it all."

I ignored his comeback, intent on facing Katie. I trusted that when we sat down together and I took her hands in mine, the right words would come to me.

The Jacksonville Beach Police Station, a single-story brick building constructed in the eighties, was an eight-minute drive from Ocean Tower. One of those trendy work/live/play buildings, the six-story structure housed shops and restaurants on the first level, office space on the second and third floors, and luxury condos at the top. It took up a full block, and we could see the behemoth from the rooftop deck of our house, a mile away.

The clock on the dash of my Mustang read 2:21. I was early. It was too hot to wait in the—

I remembered there was a florist inside the complex. I'd start with flowers and an invitation to dinner at Salt Life Food Shack, Katie's favorite restaurant at the beach. She could decide how we spent the rest of the weekend.

Feeling more hopeful than I had in weeks, I thumbed the door lock on my key fob and strode off toward the main entrance.

Beach Blooms occupied a glass-fronted space across the hall from A1A Jewelers. Brightly colored bouquets in tin buckets where artfully arranged amid stacks of driftwood. A huge, fabricated sandcastle was draped with seashell ornaments, chimes, and rustic textiles products. I vaguely remembered Katie buying her mom a handcrafted table runner and placemats from the shop for Christmas a few years ago.

"Hello." A tanned young woman with a long blond ponytail greeted me from behind the counter. "Can I help you with something or are you just browsing?"

"I'd like a bouquet." I scanned the displays but didn't see what I wanted. "Can you put something together? Nothing too fussy."

"Sure." She pointed to a large, refrigerated display where blooms were grouped on shelves in black buckets. "Who is it for?"

"My wife." I hoped the flowers would express to Katie what I couldn't put into words. "Maybe a dozen roses? The yellow ones are pretty."

She smiled. "Is it a special occasion?"

"Every day is special when you're married to an amazing woman." I shifted on my feet, hoping I didn't sound like an idiot.

"Aw, that's so sweet." The young woman plucked a small square of cardstock and a pen from beside the cash register and pushed them across the counter. "That is exactly what you should write on the card."

If my team heard me utter something sappy like that, they'd blow air kisses at me all day or mime sticking their finger down their throat.

Good thing they weren't around to overhear.

The shopgirl might approve of my sentiment, but there was something more important Katie needed to know. I scrawled out "Sorry I've been a jerk - I love you" and added my initial.

It only took a few minutes for the young woman to assemble the roses and some greenery in the center of a large sheet of tissue paper which she folded into a cone. She rang up my purchase and then handed me the bouquet with the notecard tucked into the front.

"I hope she likes them." She watched me leave the store and then turned to straighten a display of ceramic vases.

I checked my phone. 2:36 p.m. I considered waiting for Katie in Dr. Harding's reception area, but I was too antsy. If I hung out near the entrance, maybe I could catch her for a few minutes alone before our session.

The glitter of gold and gemstones caught my attention. I strolled over to the jewelry store. Necklaces, bracelets, and earrings sparkled against gray felt. Most of the pieces were gaudy, but a series of chains, each with a simple, engraved medallion, made me look closer.

A single, inspirational word was etched onto the flat, metal disk—*Believe, Friend, Love, Dance*. The next one stole my breath. It was perfect. What Katie meant to me in four letters.

I had just enough time to buy the necklace and get to our appointment.

When I entered the shop, I headed to the back where an Asian man with gray hair and round wireless glasses was examining the internal mechanism of a wristwatch. At my approach, he looked up and set the watch aside.

"I'd like to make a purchase." I glanced over my shoulder and indicated the item.

In short order, the necklace was given a quick polish, boxed, and wrapped. I handed over my credit card, trying to decide if I should present the necklace with the roses or wait until we were at dinner. I pictured it against Katie's creamy skin just above the swell of her breasts, the medallion warmed by her body heat. Then the image shifted to Katie wearing only the necklace, a red thong, and my favorite pair of black stilettos.

Fuck yeah. I wanted hot sex with my hot wife instead of—

The store's glass-paned door crashed open, banging against the wall with a heavy thud. Two men in jeans, dark, long-sleeved shirts, and ski masks they were still tugging into place wheeled around and pointed guns at me and the shop owner.

"Hands up, old man," one guy shouted as the other closed and locked the door. "If you press that panic button, you're dead."

He swung the gun toward me, eyes darting around the store, hands shaking, pitted teeth grinding. His clothes hung off skinny arms and legs, and my stomach dropped.

Meth head.

When his accomplice turned, I realized they were both hopped up on speed.

Tweakers posed an increased risk in that long-term meth abuse leads to paranoia, confusion, anxiety, violent behavior, and even psychotic symptoms. They were unpredictable, irrational, and often delusional.

Robbing a jewelry store in a busy complex like Ocean Tower was stupid. Their chances of making a clean getaway were close to zero. We just needed one person to look in the shop, see what was going down, and call the police.

Unfortunately, the florist and jewelry store were at the end of a long hallway. The foot traffic here was light.

Muscle memory took over. I relaxed my stance and regulated my breathing. I kept my face blank and cleared my mind except for one stray thought.

If I was late for our three o'clock appointment, Katie was going to be pissed.

A door I hadn't noticed earlier, probably connecting the showroom to an office and storeroom, popped open, a chiding, high-pitched feminine voice preceding an older Asian woman, presumably the shopkeeper's wife. She stopped mid-rant, hands flying to her cheeks.

"Shut her up," the first man screamed, his outstretched arms quaking.

Her husband said something in a language I didn't recognize.

"English. I wanna know what you're saying," the man warned. "Don't make me shoot you. We just want the money and the gold, and we're outta here."

His partner jerked his head over his shoulder every few seconds, watching for people in the hallway outside the store. He held his gun in one hand, the nose dipping and lifting.

I had to defuse the situation or risk a gun going off when one of the robbers panicked.

Lifting my hands in a gesture of surrender, I kept my eyes on the thieves but directed my words to the man and his wife.

"Raise your hands so they can see them, move slow, and speak clearly," I said.

"Good advice," the lead man sneered, "but don't try to be a hero. That way everyone makes it out of here alive."

Don't be a hero.

What did that mean? Let these two tweakers intimidate people weaker than them, take advantage of their apprehension, and ruin their honest business? Let them bully us with their guns and threats? Go along with their demands so I could go home to Katie?

My wife was a hero. My hero. She knew when to push and when to back off, but she never gave in. Things might look bleak, but she never gave up, biding her time for an opportunity to set things right.

"You're scaring them," I told the two men, my voice steady and respectful. "Calm down, tell us what you want, and we'll comply."

"Come on, Mikey." The second man inched toward the door. "You're wasting time. If that old bitch pressed the alarm—"

The store owner lunged over the counter, but his wife pulled him back, jabbering in fear. I stepped between them and the robbers, arms spread.

"Don't do anything you'll regret," I cautioned, then turned my head to the side. "Sir, what's your name?"

"Mr. Park," the woman said in heavily accented English. "Gong and Lolly Park."

"I'm Lou Quinn." I lifted the small gift bag, still dangling from my left hand. "Just picking up a gift for my wife. You're

Mikey, right? Who's your friend?"

"Don't give 'em my name, Mikey," the second man whined. "They'll turn us in."

"Asshole." Mikey rolled his eyes and spat on the floor. "Donald Huggins ain't never been able to keep his piehole shut. You three, park it on the floor, up against the wall over there."

"Fuck you, Mikey Dombrowski!" Huggins turned his gun on his partner in crime.

As the two squabbled, I motioned for the Parks to follow instructions and sit. I joined them, quickly sliding my hand into the side pocket of my shorts. Blocking my actions so Mikey and Donald couldn't see what I was doing, I pulled out my cell, speed dialed Niad's office, hit the mute button, and tucked it back in my pocket.

After a few seconds, hoping the lieutenant had picked up, I addressed the two thieves, upping the volume of my voice slightly.

"Why did you two guys decide to rob this place? You could have picked any jewelry store in Jacksonville Beach, and you target the store in Ocean Tower. Do you have a beef with Mr. and Mrs. Park here? I must have the worst luck of anyone, doing my shopping in the middle of an armed heist."

If Niad was listening, I'd given him critical information. Two perpetrators, two civilians and an off-duty S.W.A.T. officer, the location of the crime in progress, and the fact that the men were armed.

"Shut up," Donald screeched.

"You don't look so good." I feigned concern. "Do you need some water? Maybe a fix?"

Hopefully, Niad would figure out we were dealing with addicts. That increased the danger in a situation like this because of their unpredictability and paranoia.

If Niad was listening in, he'd already be deploying the team. As soon as they were on the scene, they would secure the perimeter and start evacuating the complex. It had to be close enough to 3 p.m. that Katie was in the building.

The hair on my nape lifted, and my breath stuck in my throat as the image of Katie caught in crossfire flashed in my head. I blinked it away and forced myself to focus on the here and now. Niad was right—being distracted put everyone at increased risk. The Parks. My team. Civilians. Even the perps.

Movies and TV glorified S.W.A.T. teams bursting into dangerous situations, guns blazing, knocking bad guys to the ground, shouting commands in the midst of choking smoke from tear gas grenades.

It wasn't like that in real life. The majority of operations concluded with fast and efficient containment of a potentially high-risk situation. That required stealth, accurate information, well-rehearsed procedures and protocols, and intelligent decision-making from leadership. Even though I wasn't in uniform and riding to the scene in the back of the ARV with the rest of the team, I was as much a part of the operation as Gibson, Dupree, Briggs, and the other guys. My job was to stall, give them time to secure the scene.

I didn't know how long Mikey and Donald would last. They were both breathing heavily and sweat darkened the back of Donad's shirt. They might grab what they could and scram. The downside to that was the loss for the Parks and the risk of two gun-toting junkies on the loose. Getting away with a crime once created repeat offenders. The crime spree continued until the wrongdoers were apprehended and jailed…or killed.

"Dude. Chill." Mikey shook himself, a measure of control seeming to return. "Let's get this done."

With one last look out the door, Donald slunk behind the counter and began yanking at the display cases. "They're locked. We need a fucking key."

Mikey stalked over to us, lowered his gun, and pressed the muzzle between Mr. Park's eyes. Mrs. Park squealed, a piercing exhalation of fear, but she did not move.

I slid a sideways glance at the older man, and our eyes met. I gave a tiny nod, and he slowly raised trembling hands to show his empty palms.

"He has to get it out of his pocket," I told Mikey. "I noticed him put it in his pants pocket when he opened the display to pull out the necklace I bought. Is it okay if he reaches in for it?"

"Who made you master of ceremonies?" Mikey squinted, eyeing me with distrust. "You're pretty calm, cool, and collected for someone in the middle of a robbery."

"Maybe he's a cop," Donald squeaked, his voice cracking. He lost hold of his gun, dropping it onto the glass display case with a noisy clatter. It skittered across the surface, circling like a criminal version of spin the bottle.

"God *damn* it." Mikey twisted toward his accomplice, momentarily distracted, the gun no longer aimed at Mr. Park.

I lunged, intent on grabbing Mikey's wrist to wrest the weapon out of his hand. Mrs. Park must have had the same idea because she launched herself upward, the blur of movement jerking Mikey's attention back around.

Time froze and then unfurled in slow motion. Each second

ticked distinctly, like individual frames on a movie reel, the fearless old woman and the matte black metal gun moving into alignment. Noise filled my ears, Mr. Park's terrified shouts and Mikey's enraged commands seeming to come at me as if I was underwater.

Adrenaline flooded my system, acting like a boost of rocket fuel. I thrust myself between Mrs. Park and Mikey as time slowed. I saw the revolver's hammer fall in the nanosecond before the deafening *crack* of a gunshot exploded. Suddenly, my upwards trajectory changed, and my body snapped back like an overstretched rubber band.

I hit the wall and slumped over, fiery pain searing my side. I looked down and saw blood.

Complete and total silence settled over the jewelry store. Donald peered from behind the counter. Mr. and Mrs. Park huddled together, wide-eyed with terror. Mikey stared down his arm, past his gun, to the damp red stain spreading over one side of my shirt. I struggled to breathe, paralyzed by disbelief and shock.

Thirteen years on the job without more than a black eye, dislocated shoulder, and concussion. Now, I was shot.

Katie.

My thoughts flew to my wife, waiting for me in Dr. Harding's office, assuming the worst about my absence. If the building was being evacuated and she saw the S.W.A.T. ARV, would she try to check on me? Find out what was going on?

The thought of my wife learning I was one of the hostages and waiting to see if I'd make it out alive made me want to vomit.

That was IF my call to Niad had gone through. For all I knew, Hale and Ladd were harassing Briggs for a shitty clean-up job on the ARV while Niad ran numbers for the month-end finance report.

The melodic chirp from a cell phone shattered the tableau. It continued to ring as the Parks and I remained silent, Donald moaning dramatically as Mikey scanned the store, searching for the phone.

Darting past the door, Mikey scurried behind the counter and picked up an iPhone near the cash register. He scowled at the store owner. “Is this yours?”

Mr. Park nodded.

The phone stopped ringing for a second and then began chirping again.

“Answer it. In English.” Mikey glared a warning before tossing the phone to Mr. Park. “Put it on speaker.”

It took the old man three tries to press the right buttons. Before he could say anything, Niad’s raspy voice sounded.

“This is Lieutenant Jack Niad of the Jacksonville Beach S.W.A.T. Unit. I’d like to speak with whoever is in charge.”

Mikey’s face darkened with rage, his eyes skipping between me and the Parks.

“Hang up,” he whispered furiously.

Mr. Park disconnected the call.

The phone immediately began to chirp.

Mikey vaulted over the counter and crossed the shop in angry strides, leaning over the Parks threateningly. “Which one of you pressed the silent alarm?”

“Neither of them.” I winced and pressed my hand harder against my side, feeling the warm trickle of…blood? Sweat? Probably both. “I called it in when you weren’t looking, idiot. I’m a police officer. Robbery with a firearm is a first-degree felony. If I die, you’re both facing charges for first-degree felony murder of a law enforcement officer. Do you know what the penalty for that is? Donald, want to take a guess?"

The tension in the store skyrocketed. Between the incessant ringing of the phone and my incendiary statement, Mikey's tenuous control of the situation unraveled.

"I'm not taking a needle for anyone," Donald shouted from where he cowered behind the display case. "Get us outta here, Mikey. You promised no trouble. 'We'll grab the goods from the old man and be out before anyone knows what happened,' you said."

Mr. Park's cell abruptly stopped ringing. If Niad was still monitoring the situation via my phone, he'd realize it was time to back off, let things calm down, give the perps a chance to realize what their options were.

"Why do the cops always have to play hero?" Mikey crouched in front of me. "If you'd just followed directions, you wouldn't be bleeding out. Me and Donald would be buying enough meth to keep us high for a month, and the Parks would be filing an insurance claim. No one any the worse off."

"It's not about being a hero," I ground out between clenched teeth, my own fury sparked. "It's about protecting innocent, hard-working people from assholes like you. You think just because you have a gun, you can take what you want, do what you want. You think robbing these folks and getting away clean doesn't have consequences? What if Mrs. Park has a heart attack right now? What if Mr. Park has to close his shop because of PTSD? What if you OD and die next to a dumpster behind Home Goods? You got a mom or wife or kids somewhere? What do you think that news is doing to do to them?"

Mikey's face crumpled like a wadded-up sheet of newspaper,

then hardened again.

"No one gives a fuck about me," he scoffed. "Why would they?"

"Give them…a reason." My words caught as a lightning bolt of pain shot through me. My vision grayed at the edges. That hot liquid was definitely blood. Mine. Shit. "You're in trouble, no doubt about that, Mikey, but you can stop it from going from bad to worse. Call Lt. Niad and surrender."

"Don't do it, Mikey," Donald blathered. "We shot one of their guys. They'll take us out or mess us up on the way to the station."

"You watch too many Jean-Claude Van Damme movies," I snarled at Donald. I focused on Mikey's face, inches from mine, and locked eyes. "That's my team out there. Do the right thing, and they'll be fair with you."

Indecision wavered on his face.

"Come on, man." I sighed, suddenly exhausted. My arms and legs were lead. My hand was losing its pressure on the entrance wound. I could see blood pooling on the store's gray-flecked carpeting from the corner of my eye. I weakly lifted my other hand, the ribbon ties of the small gift bag tangled in my fingers which—unbelievably—still held the bouquet of roses. "I got in a fight with my wife. She deserves an apology."

"You should be in bed." Katie hovered around me, fingers plucking at the blanket she'd draped over my legs where I was stretched out in the living room recliner.

"I'm fine." My grimace gave me away when I tried to shift position.

"Bed." She braced her hands on her hips.

"Only if you join me. Completely naked." I grinned, my smile widening when she blushed.

God, she was beautiful. I inhaled slowly, my chest expanding to accommodate the swell of emotion. I admired the sheen of her dark, silky hair and how it framed high, elegant cheekbones and thick-lashed brown eyes shining with concern and desire. My gaze dropped to her shoulders, toned, tanned arms and ample breasts showcased in a tight, pink crop top. Her nipples jutted out, assuring me she shared my hunger for a physical connection. My appreciative examination continued down long, satiny-smooth legs, and then back up to her flat midriff, a band of skin revealed between her top and leggings.

"Babe." I choked on the single word and reached out for her

She linked her fingers between mine, and I pulled her onto my lap. The reassuring weight of her against my groin and thighs overrode the discomfort of the gun wound.

"Why didn't you tell me?" My heart jerked against my ribs, trying to escape the pain of coming so close to death without knowing my wife carried our child in her belly.

"I did tell you." She wound her arms around me, burying her face against my neck.

"You shouted it at me when the EMTs were loading me into the ambulance." I stroked her back, over the bumps of her spine and smooth bands of muscle, soothing us both. "I thought I was dreaming."

"I wanted to tell you." Her voice was thick with emotion. "But you'd become so distant. You wouldn't talk to me. We rarely made love. I was afraid you wanted to stop trying. That you didn't want a baby if it took so much effort."

"I couldn't stand disappointing you month after month." I kissed her temple, inhaling the heady scent of feminine perspiration, coconut shampoo, and peach body wash. "The one thing you wanted—"

"You gave me." She leaned back to look at me, lips curved in a blissful smile as tears coursed over her cheeks.

"The doctor said ten weeks?" Now that I was no longer hospitalized, surrounded by Niad and my team, answering questions for IA and the DA, being poked and prodded by doctors and nurses, I wanted time to savor this miraculous news. I wanted Katie to repeat each precious detail so I could etch it into my memory.

"When I first suspected I might be pregnant, I took a home test. It was negative. I talked to Dr. Gillespie, and she said it isn't uncommon for stress to affect menstrual cycles." She brushed the back of her hand over her face. "When another month passed, I wanted to believe it had finally happened, but I was too afraid to hope. That's why I kept it to myself. I was going to tell you at the appointment with Dr. Harding. I wanted her there in case you didn't take it well."

I fingered the gold medallion around her neck. It flashed as a beam of sunny afternoon sunshine caught it. I read the inscription.

HERO.

Katie was a real hero. My hero. When I lost hope, when I didn't have the courage to open up to her with my fears, she had the courage to fight—for our marriage and for our dream of making a baby.

The local newspaper ran a story about the robbery, hailing me as a hero for convincing Mikey and Donald to give themselves up. I made sure Mr. and Mrs. Park shared the spotlight and insisted the article include a side piece about the S.W.A.T. team. People called us heroes, but the truth was that we're all just regular guys doing our best.

Sometimes it's enough. Sometimes…

"I love you so much, Katie."

Her mouth found mine, and my eyes drifted shut. I tilted my head, automatically finding the perfect angle to deepen the kiss. Her lips parted, and I plunged my tongue into the warm wetness. She did the same, teasing and taunting and tasting. For the first time in months, there as no urgency or ulterior motive overshadowing our intimacy. Blood raced to my cock, arousal sensitizing the nerve endings, lust fueling my physical need as love spurred an emotional need to bond and fuse with my wife. My hero. The mother of my child.

"Bed," I muttered. "I should be in bed."

Katie moaned in agreement, carefully extricating herself from my lap. She eased the arm on the side of the recliner, so the footrest slowly dropped and helped me up.

"If it gets too painful—" She curved an arm around my waist as I leaned against her.

"It's already painful," I jested.

It took far too long to make it down the hallway, strip off our clothes, and climb into bed. Katie urged me onto my back, her knees straddling my hips. She nestled atop me, coating my rigid length with creamy juices as I wedged myself in the heat of her slit.

With all of our energy and attention focused on getting pregnant, sex had become mechanical. I forgot how playful the pursuit of pleasure could be. Should be. I lost sight of what made fucking the woman you love so fulfilling and satisfying.

It all came rushing back.

I was the only man with the privilege of spreading her legs. Tonguing her nipples. Lapping her clit until she writhed and begged for more. Piercing and filling her core in a sacred union.

Likewise, she was the only woman who would take my cock in her mouth and drive me to the edge of insanity. The woman who knew and satisfied my deepest longings and desires.

The only woman entrusted with my heart and my fears and my insecurities.

"Let me in," I urged, rocking my hips in search of her

opening.

"I'm so—" Katie panted, her face creased with pleasure. "It's so easy with you, Lou. So fast. So instantaneous."

She lifted up, sliding onto my length with a contented sigh.

Bracketing my hands around her hips, I ignored the pull of the stitches in my side. She eased into a slow, rocking rhythm that nudged her clit against my pelvic bone.

"I missed this." She opened her eyes and looked down at me.

"I promise it will never happen again." Tears leaked down into my ears as I vowed to never pull away again.

No matter what happened—if we lost this baby or had six more—Katie would always know I loved her.

Want to meet the rest of Lou's team? Learn more about EmKay Connor's new series Heart of a Hero in the About the Authors section at the end of the book.

INCENDIARY

Karigan Hale

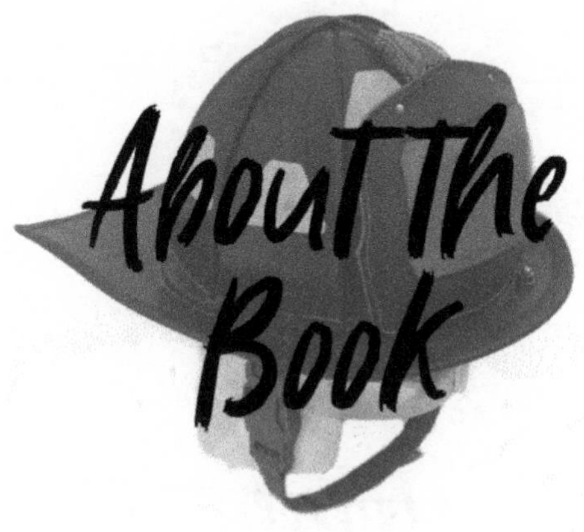

Fire Captain Nicole Flint has two problems. First, there's a serial arsonist intent on burning the town down. Second, she's depending on the help of a nosy reporter who happens to be her ex boyfriend. He never let their relationship get in the way of a story.

Reporter Marcus Dunlevy knows he betrayed Nicole in the past, but it was the biggest regret of his life. Now she's pulled back into his orbit as the arsonist escalates, bringing them closer to each other, and danger.

And fire isn't the only thing that is *Incendiary*.

Chapter One

Nicole

My cell phone buzzed seconds before the deafening scream of the firehouse siren. With one last, longing look at the cheesecake in front of me, I answered the call on the run.

"Tell me this isn't what I think it is," I said.

"Looks like it," dispatch responded.

I groaned. We needed to catch this asshole soon. I'd wasted two desserts in as many days.

"Two-alarm this time. I'm sending in a hazmat unit," dispatch informed, rattling off the address.

"Ten-four. On the way." I disconnected and jumped into my turnout gear. The rest of my team was a crackle of activity beside me. We were on the road in less than five minutes.

We'd had a shit ton of fires set with the same MO around our small city, nearly doubling the yearly average in three weeks. It could only mean one thing: serial arsonist. And he was escalating.

Or she, for that matter. If I could be a female fire captain, then so could our pyro.

My unit pulled up to the scene, a small shed at the back of our ghost-town of a mall, where several bystanders were already watching the blaze.

"Let's set a record, boys," I called to my team, who sprung expertly into action. In no time, the only reminders of the once hungry flames were the seared carcass of the storage shed and the thick, gray smoke billowing into the air.

I pulled off my helmet, rubbed the ache in my neck, and walked over to the bystanders, hoping to find the first on scene. A hand on my arm stopped my momentum before I could reach them. I followed the arm up to the man it belonged to: Marcus Dunlevy. My brain and body warred with their reactions to his touch.

As a nosey reporter, general pain-in-my-ass, and ex-big mistake, Marcus caused my brain to want to recoil from his touch and douse him with the fire hose. As a Hollywood handsome hunk with a panty-melting smile and very skilled hands, Marcus made my body want to climb him like a ladder truck and hang on for the ride.

"Nicole. What can you give me? Is this the same guy?" he asked, stepping into my space with a glint in his ice-blue eyes and a smirk playing on his lips. I was having trouble finding my breath. Which obviously had everything to do with the billowing smoke and nothing to do with Marcus.

Nothing at all.

"That's Captain Flint to you," I said, pulling my arm from his touch and taking a step back.

"Come on, Nicki. Work with me here. We both want the same thing—to catch this bastard."

"What you want is a headline."

"That's not all I want," Marcus said under his breath, his deep tenor voice hinting at our past.

He took a step toward me, that smirk morphing into a playful smile. Before I could react, he cupped my jaw in his large hand and ran a thumb across my cheekbone. I ignored the shock of heat it sent through my system.

"Soot," he said, holding up his thumb.

"Hazard of the job." My voice sounded husky and thick. Damn him.

"Meet me tonight," he said. "Please. We don't have to talk about the fire."

"Been there. Done that. Didn't bother to get the t-shirt," I said flatly. "I'll be holding a press conference in an hour. You'll hear the details with everyone else."

He placed a hand on his heart in mock hurt. "You're killing me here. One drink. I've changed, Nicki."

"Captain. Flint," I repeated. Then turned on my heel to do my actual job—investigating a fire not babysitting a grown man's feelings.

Later that evening, instead of gobbling down a sweet treat, I sat at my desk chewing on a pencil. A cupcake seemed like tempting fate. Anytime anything resembling sugar came near me, the siren sounded. Great for my waistline. Not so much for my current mood.

Adding to my grumpiness was the sinking feeling that Marcus may be right. We were working toward a common goal. I would never admit it to his face, but his stories had matured from sophomoric sensationalism to border-line investigative reporting.

Okay, that wasn't exactly fair. He'd become one of the premier journalists in our area. Too bad he ran over anyone in his path to get there. Including me.

Now I found myself in the precarious position of possibly needing his help. People were more willing to open up to a civilian, especially one who could provide their five-seconds of fame, than to a uniform. If someone knew something, Marcus was the better bet to charm them out of the information. Much like he charmed a much less world-savvy me out of my pants, and heart, years ago.

"Flint!" Chief Finnegan's booming voice announced his presence in the hallway. I dropped the pencil and sat up straighter.

"In my office!" I shouted back.

He came barreling in, face red and hands fluttering, as he harrumphed about our lack of progress finding the arsonist.

"We're doing everything we can," I assured him when he took a breath. "We can link the series through the combustible. That'll help prosecution."

He continued to pace around my small office. "Candle and gasoline, right?"

"That's right. We can't figure out how he's releasing it yet. No trail. And no trace of the arsonist at the scene, so it has to be a delay technique."

"Figure it out faster. We look like fools." He spotted the newspaper on my desk. Marcus's report on the rash of fires was top story. "What about that reporter, Dunlevy?"

"What about him?" I asked uneasily.

"Could we use him? Feed him bits of information? Maybe lure

this arsonist out?" he suggested, echoing my earlier thoughts.

I sighed. "He's willing. He said as much at the scene today."

"Good. Meet with him. Come up with a strategy."

"Sir," I called, stopping his momentum out the door. "I'd appreciate if someone else handled the press connection. Just this time."

"Press conferences are part of your job. You've never been shy before."

"Marcus and I"—I struggled for a polite way to say I'd rather eat nails—"have a complicated past. A complicated, personal past."

Realization dawned on Chief Finnegan. Then his face clouded. "I hired you to do a job. Put your personal beef on ice and do it."

"Yes, sir." I sighed.

He lingered a minute in the doorway. "You know, if you were a man, we wouldn't even be having this conversation."

I showed his back my favorite finger as he disappeared down the hallway. Then pulled up my big-girl pants and called Marcus.

The headline ran the next morning: "Amateur Arsonist Annoys Again." I smiled at the alliteration then read through the article. Marcus and I decided on the details over the phone last night. Part of me hoped he messed it up so I could go back on our deal. This article came with a high price—dinner with Marcus. I must have been in some serious sugar withdrawal when I agreed to that.

To my personal dismay, but professional delight, the article was damn near perfect. We leaked the candle, calling it juvenile and ridiculous, hoping that would entice the arsonist to respond. Marcus made some not-so-subtle comparisons to the minuscule size of the fires and the arsonist's genitalia. I posted the link all over the fire station's social media.

And now, we waited. Hopefully for a call or letter from the arsonist and not another fire. I sat on the edge of my office chair all day and didn't even look at a dessert in hopes of swinging our luck away from more fires.

"Hey, Cap?" Charlie Ortega, my second in command, called

from the doorway. I glanced up and motioned him to come in.

"What's up?"

"A bunch of us are heading to Champs after shift. Wanna come?"

I sighed. Usually that would be a hell yeah, no questions asked. But I had my sights set on a large pizza from Rinaldis and anything with sugar for dessert. Maybe the curse didn't extend beyond the walls of the station.

"Not tonight. But thanks for asking," I answered.

"Got a hot date?" he asked, waggling his eyebrows. "Maybe with that reporter we saw you talking to?"

I scowled at him. "Definitely not with the reporter. I'd rather stab fish hooks through my eyes. Or his eyes." I smiled. "Yeah, that'd be much better."

"Damn." Charlie laughed. "Remind me not to get on your bad side."

"Don't talk about me too much while I'm not there," I said.

"No promises," he called on his way down the hallway.

My superstitious "no sugary desserts" ban may have worked too well because the end of my shift came with no retaliation from the article. Oh well, worth a try.

Marcus called as I walked to my truck. Guess my suggestion to delete my number from his recent calls fell on deaf ears.

"Did you see the article?" he asked smugly.

"I did. Nicely done. I assume since I didn't hear from you, our guy didn't contact you today?" I asked.

"Not yet. But it's only been a day. Gotta give the bastard time to stew. I'll keep playing our angle in the coming issues too." His voice dropped and smoothed. "We still on for dinner?"

I sighed and made one last ditch effort to get out of it. "The deal was to get a response from the article."

"Oh no. No, it wasn't. The deal was to run the article to your exact specifications and *hope* for a response. I held up my end of the bargain," Marcus clarified. Damn his journalistic mind for remembering exact conversations.

"Fine. But not tonight. I already have a date." Not a complete lie. The pizza delivery guy and I were practically in a relationship. I saw him more than my own mother.

"A date? With whom?" Marcus asked.

"Why do you sound so surprised? Did you assume I would be waiting around for you to get your head out of your ass?"

"I'm an investigative reporter, Nicki," he said as if that explained everything.

"And now you sound like a stalker," I pointed out. "I'll text you when I'm free, okay?"

"Don't wait too long," he said.

Ninety minutes later, I was settled into my comfy sweats, worn-in Smokey the Bear t-shirt, and a glass of wine. I'd pulled my shoulder-length blond hair, wet from a shower, into a messy bun on top of my head and shoved my tired feet into fuzzy socks.

My cell phone rang as I was scrolling through Netflix. I checked the screen and smiled.

"Kennedy!" I practically screeched into the phone. "Did you get in? How was the move?" My good friend had just moved to the mountains of Maryland for her job. And to get away from her crazy parents.

"Finally unpacked. From the car at least. There are still boxes everywhere," she said.

"I miss you already," I admitted. "Sorry again I couldn't help you move."

"Yeah, I can't believe you let a serial arsonist get in the way of helping me move across the state. Some friend you are," she teased. "How's that going anyway?"

I snorted. "You'll never guess in a billion lifetimes who Chief Finnegan is making me work with."

"Don't tell me it's He Who Shalt Not Be Named."

"The one and only." I ran down the events of the last few days. "And so, in a moment I can only describe as hallucinatory, I agreed to have dinner with him in exchange for the article."

"You didn't. You really are a glutton for punishment," she said.

"What am I going to do?"

"I'll tell you what you can do. Hop in the car right now and come visit. There are a lot of hot cowboys here just waiting for some city girls to chafe their chaps."

I laughed. "Is that even a thing?"

"I don't know. But it's on my to-do list for sure. God bless the bio-diversity of our small state where we can have big city bad boys and sexy small town cowboys."

"Don't forget tanned beach lifeguards by the ocean."

"How could I forget? That was a great summer."

"Ollie Gulden," we both sighed, remembering a childhood summer fling at Ocean City. Then laughed.

"It's quite the buffet." I paused, then sighed dramatically. "I guess there are worse things that having Marcus buy me dinner. You know, like water torture. Or Guantanamo Bay. Or doing taxes."

"You'll be fine. Eat fast, excuse yourself to go to the bathroom, and sneak out the back door. Done and done."

I perked up. "Actually, that's brilliant. I knew you were my friend for a reason."

The doorbell sounded just then.

"That's the doorbell. I have a date with comfy clothes, fuzzy socks, and a large cheese and bacon from Rinaldi's."

"Mmmmm. Perfection."

"I know, right? I'll call you soon. Miss you, love you." She made a kissy noise and then disconnected.

"One minute, Giancarlo," I called, grabbing my purse on my way to the door. Rummaging in the deep pockets, I opened the door with a "Right on time as…" but my voice trailed off when I looked up.

My ex-biggest mistake stood next to Giancarlo on the stoop, an amused smile playing on his deceitful lips.

"I didn't order that," I told Giancarlo, hooking at thumb at Marcus. "Take it back."

Giancarlo laughed. "Here's your pie, Nicolina Mia. The gentleman has already paid," he said in his thick Italian accent. Then waggled his eyebrows at me.

I scowled at them both, snatched the box from Giancarlo, and slammed the door. Only it didn't shut. Mr. Show-Up-Unexpected had shoved one shiny Oxford in the way.

"Excuse me," I said impatiently, slamming the door against his foot again. Still there. I opened it wider to get a good throw, and hopefully cause some bone damage, except Marcus used the momentum to push it open with his arm, surprising me into stepping backwards and giving him room to cross the threshold.

He closed the door behind me as I tried to process what the hell just happened.

"Hi," he said.

"What are you doing here?" I asked, my astonishment turning quickly into annoyance.

"I was in the neighborhood and noticed the Rinaldi's car parked by your house. Figured we could share while we hashed out our next steps." He took the pizza box from my hands and carried it to the kitchen.

I did not approve of how comfortable he was making himself in my home. A home that, until today, had been gloriously free of Marcus cooties.

"In the neighborhood?" I asked, crossing my arms and popping a hip. Yeah, right. And my mom was the Queen of England.

He shrugged, a mischievous glint in his eyes, and avoided answering by taking a big bite of pizza. My pizza.

Marcus settled into one of the bar stools and flipped the box to face me. "Grab a slice. I almost forgot how good Rinaldi's pizza is."

As I reached for the box, he captured my hand, rubbing a thumb across my wrist. I snapped my eyes to his as a wave of electricity coursed through my traitorous body at his touch. He held my gaze. "You know why I stopped going there."

His implication was clear. Rinaldis was our spot when we were dating. It was where we met. And I refused to give it up in our break-up. If he thought he could guilt-trip me into going out with him again, he had another think coming.

“Your loss,” I said, pulling my hand out of his grasp.

“In more ways than one,” he mumbled around another bite.

Smokey the Bear. She was wearing the goddamn Smokey the Bear t-shirt. Did she know I was coming over? Or was this karma kicking me in the ass again? Either way, I was screwed.

I'd given her that stupid shirt when she applied for the academy. Seeing her open the door in that shirt, now faded from age and use, was a punch to the gut. And a fast trip down bittersweet memory lane.

I couldn't take my eyes off her as she reached into a cabinet for a plate. The side of that t-shirt rose at her waist, revealing the smooth, muscled skin beneath. Touching her a moment ago was a tease. A drop of water for a dying man. I wanted more. I needed more.

I clenched my fist on my thigh so I didn't run my fingers over the expanse of exposed skin. I wanted her, but I didn't have a death wish. Touching her now, in that spot, unexpectedly, would undoubtedly land me with a black eye.

Instead, I enjoyed the view and tried to settle on my next move in the Win Nicole Back game plan. The fact that I actually made it through the door with my groin still intact was more than I expected.

Thank you baby Jesus for pizza and impeccable timing. Now I needed to capitalize on being here.

If only my senses weren't clouded by her familiar smell or the smattering of freckles across her nose or the way her nipples pressed against the thin fabric of her shirt.

And now my jeans were tight. Great. Having a very obvious hard-on would absolutely engender her to me. I concentrated on baseball stats and waited for her to retrieve her wineglass from the living room.

When she didn't return, I grabbed another slice of pizza and peeked around the corner. She sat on the couch with her feet curled up under her, her wine in one hand and the television remote in the other. Completely ignoring me. I couldn't really blame her since I caused our initial break-up. I'd hoped time would heal some of the bad feelings, but from her icy welcome, I guessed not.

I grabbed the wine bottle from the fridge, knowing it was Pinot Grigio without even checking the label, and refilled her glass.

She turned her wide, hazel eyes on me. "You're still here?"

"I'm like a bad penny," I said. "May I join you?"

She hesitated a moment, then rolled her eyes and nodded slightly. "Just stay on your end of the couch. I control the remote."

I gave myself a mental high-five. "Your house, your pick." I wasn't going to watch whatever she put on anyway. I was going to watch her.

She'd matured over the last decade. Firefighting was demanding work and her body showed it—in the best way. She'd always been fit, but now her muscles were lean and tight. Her kaleidoscope eyes showed her maturity and, when she looked at me, cynicism. Did she still have that dimple in her right cheek when she smiled? Lately, I hadn't seen her do that too often around me—smile.

Again, my fault. And one I hoped to remedy soon.

"You're making me uncomfortable," she said. "Stop staring, or I'm kicking you out."

"Nice shirt," I said with a grin.

She glanced down as if she forgot what she had on and sucked in a breath. A crimson blush crept up her neck and face. So, she did remember.

"We were good together, Nicki," I said softly.

"And then we weren't." She sighed through her nose. "Listen, Marcus. I'm really not in the mood to rehash our past. Again. What's our next move with the arsonist?"

I pursed my lips, but let it go. I didn't want to annoy her to the point that she'd kick me out. Between last night's phone call and today, this was the most she'd talked to me in a long time.

Do. Not. Blow. It, Marcus.

"I still say we wait. It's been less than a day. He usually has a cooling off period between attacks anyway, right?"

She turned to face me on the couch, so close yet still so far away. Her forehead creased in thought. Damn, she was beautiful. Her angular nose, her high cheekbones, her long neck. She loved when I nibbled her collarbone. Would that still make her squirm and beg for more?

"Marcus?" she asked. Apparently, she needed a response. Shit.

"Sorry, I was spacing," I admitted. "Do you remember the

time we went to Baltimore?"

"Marcus…" Her voice held a warning.

"We went on the boat cruise around the harbor. You had your hair down and the breeze kept blowing it in my face. I think about that a lot. The way your hair felt on my skin."

The blush crept up her face again. She put a hand on her throat. So, I continued, "We kissed against the rail as the sun set. Until that older couple came and scolded us for being, and I quote, 'yucky.'"

A small smile tugged at the corner of her lips, and I caught a fleeting glimpse of her dimple.

I continued, "You told me you wanted to be a firefighter that day. I was so proud of you."

The light that adorned her face a moment ago faded. Shit. What had I said?

"I often wonder about that," she said. "Were you excited because I was following my dream? Or were you excited because my dream would help advance yours?"

I winced. "You really think that little of me?"

She cocked her head, raised an eyebrow. "Have you given me much choice?"

"One mistake, Nicki. Do I need to pay for that forever?" I asked, annoyance pricking at my resolve to be the very best version of me.

"A mistake?" she said on a surprised laugh. "That mistake almost cost me my placement in the academy. It almost destroyed my dream. It did destroy us."

"I said I was sorry. I'll say it again. A thousand times. I was selfish and stupid."

She huffed out a breath and set the wine glass on the coffee table. "You should've thought of that before you used a personal, confidential conversation to sell newspapers. You put yourself and your career over me. Over us."

"I know, Nicki. But that was so long ago. And now you're fire captain."

She shook her head with a rueful smile, standing to pace around the room. "Right. It all worked out in the end, so I should just forget about you betraying my trust, lying about it, and breaking my heart without a second glance."

I stood too, unable to mask my frustration much longer. I stepped up to her; she stood her ground. "It broke my heart too. Everything I've done since has been a path back to you."

She put her hands on her hips. "Forgive me if I don't believe you."

I threw my hands up. What did she want from me? "What else can I do? How can I convince you I've changed over the years? Tell me, Nicki. Tell me what to do."

"It's too little, too late, Marcus."

I couldn't accept that. Wouldn't. Nothing was ever finite. Her pulse throbbed in her neck; her breath was ragged. Anger, yes, but something else. She licked her lips. Her hand kept fluttering to her throat. When I touched her earlier, I felt the electricity, saw her eyes dilate. And to me that meant one thing.

Hope.

"Bullshit," I said, leaning in. Our faces were inches apart. I could count the freckles on her nose, see the flecks of gold in her blue-green eyes, feel the pull between us. Her eyes flicked to my lips and back again. Oh yes, I recognized desire and longing when I saw it.

"What would be the point?" she asked, her voice practically a whisper.

"This," I growled. And crushed her trembling lips with mine.

Chapter Four

Nicole

My whole body stilled the moment his lips touched mine. Then came alive again in a rush of heat and sparks. Desire overpowered resolve as I stepped into him, used my tongue to trace his lips, felt his arousal against my hip.

I slid my hands up his arms to grip his biceps as he erased the years between us and reminded my body exactly how combustible we were. His arms wrapped around me, engulfing me in his strong frame as his tongue explored my mouth. He growled, deep and animalistic, and my core clenched.

When he released my mouth, I sucked in oxygen, fueling the inferno between us instead of dousing it. He kissed along my jaw, down my neck. My knees wobbled when he reached the nook between my neck and shoulder. Marcus held me tighter.

"Nicki," he whispered against my skin. His voice was husky and thick, mirroring my own desire.

His hand slipped beneath my t-shirt, reigniting parts of me I thought were long dormant. None of my recent lovers even came close to awakening my body like Marcus. When he ground his erection against me, I realized how underrated hate-fucking was.

Passion burned at both ends after all. The buzzing in my body got louder.

His mouth stilled against my skin. I squirmed against him, wanting more but too proud to ask for it. He picked his head up.

"Do you hear that?" he asked.

The buzzing came again. Not from my body. My cell phone.

I peeled myself away from Marcus, adjusting my clothes as I checked the read-out.

Shit. Another fire.

"I've gotta go," I said, slipping into work mode. I shot off a quick text indicating I'd meet my team at the scene and hustled to the bedroom to change.

"Is it him? Is it our guy?" Marcus asked, following me up the stairs.

"Can't confirm," I said, shutting my bedroom door before he could follow me in.

"I'm coming with you," he shouted through the door.

I rolled my eyes as I pulled on jeans and a sports bra. I could argue with him, demand he stay here. Or better yet, go home. But he would only follow me anyway. I would save time and oxygen by letting him tag along. At least the fire was a distraction from the "What the fuck did I just do" wallow threatening beneath my surface.

When I was changed, I opened the door and marched past Marcus down the stairs. He stood at the top of the steps watching me.

"Well, you coming or not?" I asked. He scrambled after me.

I didn't even wait for him to close my truck door before taking off down the street.

"Where are we headed?" Marcus asked, making a big show out of buckling.

"Plug this in. Put it on the dash." I tossed him the portable emergency light.

"Are you avoiding my question?"

I took a deep breath. "I'm gonna need you not to freak out when we get there, okay?"

"Where are we headed, Nicki?" he asked again, the excitement drained from his voice.

I pointed to the building up the street. The building with the smokestack already rising. The building currently belching flames.

The build housing the *Mapleton Gazette* offices.

"Holy fuck." Marcus strained the seatbelt to look out the windshield.

"Guess our arsonist answered the article after all."

Somehow, I managed to keep Marcus from running into the burning building. I grabbed my turnout gear from the truck and, alongside my crew, battled the blaze. This was bigger and more destructive than before. Fire licked the façade through blown-out windows hungry for the oxygen outside. We threw enough water at it to fill a small lake. Our firebug had grown some balls. Either that or Marcus and I had really pissed him off.

"Cap, you've gotta see this!" Charlie called from inside the charred remains of the lobby when we finally beat it to submission.

I picked my way over the still smoldering debris to where he crouched. To most, what remained after a fire was hard to decipher.

Everything looked gray and brittle and gone. But walk through fire scenes long enough and the rise and fall of objects retained the shadowy shape of their former selves. There, the receptionist desk often piled high with messages, now piled high with ash and debris. There, the console table that once held a coffee machine and pamphlets for waiting guests, now a sagging heap on the floor.

And there, where Charlie crouched, the wire newsstand usually boasting the day's newspaper, now melted from the heat and taking its last bow.

But Charlie ignored the newsstand, an obvious source of fuel. Instead he pointed at a tell-tale melted puddle of wax on the ground.

"Dammit. It is him, isn't it," I said. We'd found a similar pile at all the other arson scenes. I stood and stepped back a little to survey the floor around the wax. Sure enough, a wide round stain created a circle around the candle wax. When we tested it, I knew it would be gasoline just like the other scenes.

"Dammit," I said again. I really wanted this to be unrelated to the article.

"There are at least three other spots like this around the room," Charlie said.

"Makes sense. Bigger room needs more accelerant to do maximum damage." I rolled my neck around to ease the headache settling there and nearly fell out of my boots when I looked at the ceiling.

"Holy shit."

"Whatcha got, Cap?" Charlie asked, looking up. His expression changed as he saw the small bit of rope still hanging from what was left of the drop ceiling. "Holy shit is right."

We'd seen something similar at the other scenes, but since

they were in uninhabited sheds or garages, a bit of rope hanging from the ceiling didn't seem out of place. In a newspaper office, however, they stood out like a nun in a strip club.

"Cut them down, carefully. Preserve them. I'm not sure we'll find anything, but it's worth a shot," I instructed and headed back out of the scene.

"Marcus!" I called. When he came within earshot, I asked, "Does the *Gazette* have anything hanging from the ceiling in the reception area?"

He furrowed his eyebrows, confused, "You mean like Halloween decorations or party streamers?"

"Anything. Was there anything there before you left today?"

"No. Not today. Why do you ask?" I could practically see him reaching for the pencil he always carried in his pocket. Panty-melting kiss or not, I still didn't fully trust him.

"I'm not at liberty to say," I said. I took off my helmet and jacket as I walked to the engine.

"Are you going to be long?" Marcus asked, following me. He lingered beside the engine truck looking a little like a lost puppy. I saw the concern etched in the creases of his forehead.

I put a hand on his arm. "No one got hurt. Most of the building is salvageable."

He covered my hand with his. "This is my fault though. For writing that article."

"Then I'm to blame too. I made you write it," I pointed out.

"But you didn't make me put in the personal attacks. I took it too far. Someone could have gotten seriously hurt."

"Marcus," I started, but he shook his head.

"Most of the *Gazette* staff are going to debrief at Champs," he said, pointing to the sports bar across the street. "We'll be there if you need more information."

I nodded, squeezed his arm then got ready to help with clean-up.

"Nicole," Marcus called. I turned to see him watching me, his eyes dark once again. "Come meet me regardless. We have unfinished business."

I didn't meet Marcus. I was exhausted by the time we'd finished at the scene and officially turned it over to the police. Not only that, but I wasn't sure I wanted to finish the "business" between me and Marcus.

I leaned against the side of the station shower, letting the water flow over my back and wash away the grime from the fire and the memory of Marcus's hands. God that kiss was hot. I could taste his need, feel his desire. Maybe he had missed me. Maybe he had changed.

Or maybe that was my libido clinging to hope? We'd been incendiary in the bedroom, Marcus and I. That was never the issue. Trust was the issue. Could I trust him again?

My naughty bits certainly wanted me to give him another chance. My core clenched when I saw his whisker burns on my neck. And now, as I ran my hands over my body to lather it with soap, parts of me wished it were his hands.

I shook my head to clear it. Oh no. I was not seriously

considering this. I vowed I would never forgive the untrustworthy, egotistical, selfish douche canoe. And even if we set the bed on fire, real relationships were more than sex.

And yet, his remorse and guilt for the fire today were sincere. And he didn't alter our plan for the article even though we disagreed on some of the content. He'd built a name for himself in his industry as someone with integrity and compassion.

"Ugh!" I groaned, scrubbing a hand over my face. "Damn you, Marcus."

Why couldn't he leave me alone? I was doing perfectly fine before he swaggered back into my life with his "I'm sorry"s and "I want you"s. Besides, my career was demanding, leaving little time for dating and relationships and intimacy. I didn't have time for a relationship at all, much less to recycle one with an ex. So, what was the point?

When I'd asked Marcus that earlier, he'd made his point loud and clear: it would be a shame to waste our chemistry; our bodies fit perfectly together.

A heat started in my pink parts at the memories—recent and past. I closed my eyes and leaned against the cool tile.

The seed of a thought grew under the nourishment of those memories. Who said anything about a relationship? Why couldn't Marcus and I heat up the sheets? We were two consenting adults. Very compatible consenting adults. I just had to be clear it was only a booty call. Wasn't that what Kennedy was suggesting with her cowboy comment earlier? At least I knew Marcus and I were great in bed, so it would be worth it.

I toweled off my hair and tried to decide if being a fuckbuddy was actually something I could do. I'd already kissed Marcus without feeling the need to call him a boyfriend. It might be fun. Shit, it *would* be fun. And just what I needed to de-stress from this serial arsonist business.

Because when I kissed him, the only blaze I thought of was us.

"Marcus. Earth to Marcus." Anderson Jacobs, sports editor at the Gazette and the closest thing I had to a work friend, snapped his fingers in my face.

I refocused my eyes on him and took a swig of my beer. "Sorry. Zoning." How had this day gone from amazing to shit storm all in the same hour? One minute I'm finally kissing Nicki again, and the next the newspaper goes up in flames. Literally.

"It's not your fault, man," he repeated, echoing Nicki's words from earlier. "No one got hurt."

I rolled my eyes. "Not physically. But the building is trash. It'll take some time to clean and refurbish."

"Come on. This isn't the first time you've had push back from a story. And it probably won't be the last."

"Push back is one thing. Setting a building on fire is another."

"We don't know for sure it's the arsonist anyway," Anderson said. "You did put some MO type stuff in your article. Could be a copycat."

I considered. Unlikely, but possible. "Maybe. It does seem a bit brash to go from unoccupied sheds to an office building. He just added a whole other set of charges by hitting an occupied building."

Anderson snapped his fingers. "What if it's Carol? She just got fired. Maybe she's using the arsonist to hide her revenge."

"Carol has grandchildren," I said.

"So does the BTK killer," Anderson pointed out.

I clinked his bottle with mine. "Touché."

"Lots of candles used. Did the fire captain say if they were all the same brand?" Anderson asked.

"Didn't say." I chuckled as my mind wandered. "What if it's some housewife with a failed candle MLM? She's just trying to get rid of her unused inventory."

Anderson smirked. "Kinda like a *Mommie Dearest* situation but with candles. No scented candles. No scented candles ever," he shouted in high-pitched voice. Several patrons turned to look at us.

Before I could respond, our chief editor wound his way through the crowd to our table with a "Oy, guys!"

"Any news?" Anderson asked as he approached. The other writers and staff members had peeled off and gone home a while ago. I lingered at the bar longer than I intended, hoping that Nicki would walk through the door to join me. I should've known better. I should've known she would freak about our kiss the second she had a chance to think about it.

Either that or she was pissed at me for provoking the arsonist. Either way, my chances of a repeat kiss were slim to none.

I braced myself for the wrath of Jim Johnston, our editor in chief and resident ball buster. I could count the times he turned his sharp tongue on me on one hand. And I'd like to keep the count there. I signaled to the bartender for another drink—for Jim, not me.

Instead, he surprised me by saying, "You really did it this

time, Ace." He looked down the bottle at me as he drank the beer the bartender placed in front of him. "You better turn this into a damn good story."

I blinked at him. "I'm sorry? You want me to write this? Me?"

"Yes, you. You started this. Just try not to burn down any more buildings, capiche?"

Well, shit. I smiled. "Yeah. I can do that. I'll write it up tonight."

"For the website only. We're going complete black out on print to really drive home the point of silencing the news. Our ratings are going to skyrocket!" He smiled broadly and a took a long swig of beer.

Anderson said to me, "You know Captain Hot Pants from the fire station, right? Maybe you can get an inside scoop into what happened."

I narrowed my eyes at him. Although he wasn't wrong, Nicki was hot, I didn't like that coming out of his mouth. "I'm not using my personal connection to get a story."

"Since when?" Anderson asked.

"It's perfect! The lead investigative journalist and the fire captain work together to catch an arsonist. I can see the headlines now. This is small town gold!" Jim said, running away with the idea. "See what you can get out of her."

"Guys, she's not gonna tell me anything different than she said at the press conference," I said. Although she did ask that weird question about things hanging from the ceiling. No mention of that at the press conference.

Jim pointed his finger at me with a smug smile. "I see your wheels turning. You already have something brewing. Go with it.

Trust your instinct. Let's get back at this guy for messing with our offices."

"Do we even know for sure it's the arsonist?" I asked, trying once again to divert attention away from using Nicki as a source. "Anderson and I were just rolling around the idea that it could be a copycat."

"No chance. Same MO," Jim said. "Wax and ropes."

Anderson laughed. "Sounds like a kink, not an arson."

"What about ropes?" I asked. Candles were old news, but ropes were new.

Jim's eyes sharpened. "Ropes hanging from the ceiling. Didn't your hot captain tell you that?"

"She mentioned something like that," I said slowly. If Jim knew, it wasn't a secret.

"Brilliant, actually," Jim said. "Or at least unique. The fire fighters can't figure out the connection." His eyes lit up with an idea. "We could use that as an engagement tool for the newspaper social media. Have people guess what it all means."

I considered and said, "Could work. Let me check with Nicki to make sure that won't hinder her investigation."

Jim's eyeballs bugged out. "I'm sorry. I must have heard you wrong. You want to *check* with Nicki *first*? We don't need her permission, in case you forgot the first amendment."

I backpedaled. "It's a courtesy. Or at least a head's up."

He narrowed his eyes at me and pointed his chubby finger in my chest. "I don't care how badly you want to get in her pants. Run the story how you see fit—no, how *I* see fit—or you're fired." He threw back the rest of his drink and stomped out the door.

I slapped a few twenties on the table and stood. "Can you give me a ride to my car?"

"Leaving already?" Anderson asked even though we were the only two still here from our original group.

"I have a story to write."

A few short minutes later, we pulled up in front of Nicki's house.

"When I asked if you knew the fire captain, I didn't think you knew the captain," Anderson said, reading the name on the mailbox.

I scowled at him. "It's not like that. We knew each other a life time ago. And we're working on catching the arsonist." I opened the door and got out.

"Sure," Anderson said, sticking his head out his open window. "If I were you, I'd forget the arsonist and work on catching her."

"That's the plan," I mumbled under my breath as he gave a little wave and drove off, leaving me standing on the curb contemplating whether to knock on Nicki's door again. I had great success with that choice earlier today. But all the windows were dark, and her curtains were drawn. She was probably in bed.

Great. Now I was thinking about Nicki in bed. Not helping my resolve to leave. Even though she didn't come to the bar tonight, or call or text me, she definitely felt something when we kissed. Even if it was lust or desire, I'd take it. I'd take anything I could get from her.

Because she'd kissed me back. Kissing her was like coming home. Like finally finding what I was craving. Like holding my future in my hands. And until she told me in no uncertain terms to fuck off for good, I was going to keep trying.

I knew I wouldn't sleep, not with thoughts of the fires—the real one and the one Nicki ignited in me—swirling around my brain. But I also knew I couldn't wake her up if I wanted to be on her good side. So I adjusted my jeans, tucked tail, and drove home to start writing the story of the newspaper office blaze.

An hour later, I smelled the smoke.

Chapter Six

Nicole

I heard Marcus start his car, saw the headlights illuminate the front of my house and then fade as he drove away. As often happened with Marcus, my emotions warred with themselves—equal parts disappointment and relief that he didn't try to come in. I'd gotten a text from him a few hours ago telling me they were still at Champs, but I hadn't responded.

I squeezed my eyes shut and wished I could go back to earlier this week when Marcus was an annoying yet fairly distant memory. To when I hadn't elicited his help, hadn't provoked the arsonist, hadn't agreed to dinner. Hadn't kissed him.

Although the kiss was really awesome.

I groaned and covered my head with my pillow. Was I seriously considering the friends with benefits scenario? Or really, the enemies with benefits scenario?

I called Kennedy. I needed some outside advice.

"I'm about to make a big mistake," I said when she answered.

"Did you buy that banana yellow leather jacket? We talked

about this, Nicki," she said.

I laughed. "No. It was sold out when I went back to get it."

"Thank Christ. So, what's the big mistake?" She gasped. "Don't tell me it has to do with Marcus."

"It… has to do with Marcus," I admitted.

"Nicki!"

"I know! But you haven't seen him over the last few days. He really does seem different and apologetic."

"Of course he's apologetic. You were the best thing to ever happen to him."

"We also may have kissed," I mumbled.

"I'm sorry. I think I just blacked out. Did you say you kissed him?"

"Technically, he kissed me. I just didn't pull away."

"Sounds like you already made the big mistake," she quipped.

"That was a little mistake. I'm thinking of a lot more than just kissing. God, Ken, it ignited all the fires in me. We were so freakin' good in the bedroom. It's just, I don't know… tempting," I said.

She was silent a moment. She knew my history with Marcus. Had seen the fallout after we broke up.

Finally, she sighed. "You are an independent, badass woman. And as much as I hate Marcus for what he did to you, if you say he's different, I believe you. Just make sure that's your head talking and not your wawaha."

I laughed. "My lady parts definitely have a horse in the race. In fact, they're pushing for a friends with benefits situation."

"If you can separate your libido from your emotions with him, I say get it girl. You've earned a good lay. At least this time you're going in with eyes as wide open as your legs."

I laughed. "Ew, but true. I'll hold him at arm's length. When we aren't in flagrante delicto, that is." I yawned. It was late. "Thanks, Kennedy. I'll let you go. Next time we talk you better have an update on your cowboy situation."

"From your lips to John Wayne's ears," she said and disconnected.

I settled back down into bed, trying not to think of what Marcus could do to my wawaha when my cell phone buzzed from the bedside table. My heart jumped a little. Had Marcus changed his mind about seeing me tonight? Did I want that? I reached out from under the pillow to check the screen.

Then bolted upright in bed and answered on speaker as I dressed. Another fire.

"Captain Flint. Talk to me," I said, pulling on a pair of pants.

"Two alarm. Private residence."

"Send the address. I'm on route in less than five," I instructed.

"Ten-four. Sorry to bother you at home, Cap, but you said you wanted to know about all fires until the serial is caught."

"That's right. I doubt this is our guy, but I'd like to be on scene just in case," I lied. I absolutely thought it was the arsonist.

"Engines in route. Sending the address now," dispatch confirmed then disconnected.

I programmed the address into my GPS as I shoved my feet into boots. First the newspaper offices. Now a private residence. If this was our arsonist, and I'd bet my mint condition Cal Ripken, Jr rookie card it was, he needed to be stopped. Like now. This was worse than escalating. Two fires in the same twenty-four hours. Two inhabited buildings.

I pulled up to the scene to see the engines already throwing water on the flames. I glanced around to assess the progress. Two fire companies, three engines, one ambulance, a dozen firefighters, an equal amount of spectators. Since the crews had the blaze under control, I walked to where the spectators were standing. Perhaps I'd get lucky with an eyewitness who saw someone weird in the neighborhood.

When the group came into focus through the smoke and engine lights, one face came to the forefront right away. I clenched my jaw and approached. Of course, Marcus would sniff out the story and be on scene even before me. He probably had a CB radio in his house like the ambulance chasers.

"Fancy finding you here. Were you sleeping in your car at the station waiting for another call to come in?" I said unable to control the snark in my voice.

He looked at me slowly, his eyes wide, face ashen. Soot marked his cheeks; ash littered his hair. His hand was bandaged. I noticed then that he wasn't actually with the crowd, but within the perimeter.

"Marcus?" I asked, placing a hand gently on his arm.

He gave me a rueful half-smile. "That's my house." We both looked at the quickly burning structure. "Or was my house."

"Oh, Marcus." Instinctively, I pulled him into my arms in a hug. He buried his face in the crook of my neck. I could feel him trembling slightly. "Thank God you got out okay."

He nodded, took a deep tremulous breath, and leaned back to

look at me. "Guess I pissed him off more than I thought."

"Tell me what happened."

He sighed. "I was upstairs in my office writing an article about the Gazette fire," he said. "I smelled smoke. I couldn't see anything out the office window, so I went downstairs. I burned my hand on the doorknob. My entire downstairs was filled with smoke." He coughed at the memory. "I ran out and called 911."

"You did the right thing. I'm glad you're okay. Did you notice anything unusual? See anyone lingering nearby to watch?" I asked.

He shook his head and coughed again.

"Marcus!" a man's voice bellowed from the crowd. "Holy shit, man."

"That's Jim, my editor," Marcus explained. I waved him under the perimeter tape to where we were standing.

"Jim, this is Captain Nicole Flint," Marcus said, introducing us.

"I've seen you at press conferences," I said, shaking his hand. He was always the one asking the asinine questions. He and my Chief would get along great.

"I appreciate your commitment to the story," Jim said, slapping Marcus on the back which caused another coughing fit. "But you didn't have to burn your own house down to sell newspapers." He laughed at his own joke.

"Hey, Cap!" Charlie called.

"Nice to meet you in person," I said to Jim. "Duty calls." I gave Marcus's arm another squeeze, then picked my way over to Charlie. He threw me my helmet and a coat, then lead me around to the back of the house where the scene had cooled.

"This was our point of entry and ignition," Charlie said. He pointed to the door. “It was open when we got here. Homeowner said he went out the front.” We moved inside. “Then, there’s this.”

Rope hanging from an upper cabinet above a puddle of candle wax.

“Shit,” I said.

“There’s another in the adjacent bathroom. And in the laundry room.” He pointed to each doorway.

“How’d he get in? How’d Marcus miss someone down here tying rope all over his house?” I asked to no one in particular.

Charlie shrugged. “Probably you should ask him.”

For an instant, I wondered if Marcus could be setting the fires. Maybe Jim’s comment wasn’t too far off the mark.

No. Marcus prized his possessions too much. He’d never burn down his own house. That was a little too extreme, even for him.

“We also found something odd outside,” Charlie said, moving back out onto the lawn. I followed him toward the fence line.

“Here. Could be nothing, but it seems out of place.” Charlie crouched down beside something bright in the grass.

I took a closer look. “Is that a balloon?”

“Looks like,” Charlie confirmed.

I used a nearby stick to move it. Sure enough, a children’s party balloon, yellow and unused, lay in the grass.

“Weird,” I said. Now I had even more questions for Marcus.

“Maybe we’re looking for a Party City employee,” Charlie said with a smirk.

“Or a balloon animal artist,” I said, playing along.

“Or a six-year-old.” We both looked at each other a moment,

grimacing.

"Nah," we said in unison.

"Not a child. They'd never be able to reach the ceiling to tie the ropes," Charlie said.

I stood. "No one else hears about the ropes or this balloon," I reminded Charlie. He mimed zipping his lips. "Tell the rest of the crew too."

When I reached Marcus, he stood alone, staring at the carcass of his once beautiful house. I stood beside him, listening to the murmur of the crowd behind us and the slight crackle of the last of the fire burning out.

"It's just stuff," he said, more to himself than to me. "Just stuff."

"Do you have a place to stay?" I asked.

He blinked at me like he hadn't even thought of it. "I guess I could stay at the hotel in town until I find a place to rent."

I wrinkled my nose. The hotel in town rented by the hour. "No one at the Gazette will put you up?"

He shrugged. "I'm not really on 'crash on your couch' terms with any of them."

I couldn't connect my brain to my mouth fast enough before I blurted, "Why don't you stay with me. I have a guest room."

His eyebrows shut up into his hairline. "Are you serious?"

Dammit. No going back now. I nodded. Kennedy was going to have an aneurysm when she heard about this.

"I'd really appreciate that. Thank you," he smiled one of his genuine smiles. Not the "I'm using this to manipulate you" smile or the "I've got you where I want you" smile. But a real, genuine "because I mean it" smile.

I smiled back. And marveled at the lack of panic and dread coursing through my veins. This was going to fine. Right?

Chapter Seven

Marcus

I couldn't sleep. I tried not to think about the fires. I could do nothing about those but pick up the pieces and try to rebuild. Use it as a personal vendetta against the asshole who set them. It was game on now. What more could he possibly do to get back at me for hurting his feelings in the newspaper? He'd already taken my house.

Nicole had been sure to lock up everything tight tonight and set her inner and outer cameras. If this pyro saw us together, he could come after Nicki next. I quoted her in the original article as well.

And she'd found something else. Something besides the ropes. The questions she asked me as we rode to her house were bizarre and vague. And I was apparently absolutely no help. I could feel her frustration with every one of my negative answers.

"Have you had a birthday party at your house recently?" *No.*

"Have any of your neighbors?" *Not that I know of.*

"Do you have anything hanging from your cabinets?" *No.*

"Do you keep rope in the house?" *No.*

"Does anyone have a key to your house?" *No.*

"Do you keep a spare?" *Only at the office.*

"Did you hear any noises in your kitchen?" *No.*

"Did you go into the kitchen when you returned home from Champs?" *No. Straight upstairs to write.*

...And try to forget about wanting you. I kept that to myself.

Wanting Nicki—the real reason I couldn't sleep. Watching her take charge at the scenes, handle the crew and those heavy hoses with ease, made me admire and desire her even more. Now I was laying mere feet away from her with just a stupid wall between us. I rolled over in bed, trying to get comfortable.

What did she sleep in? A nightgown? Shorts and tank? She used to sleep in my t-shirts. Or that damn Smokey the Bear shirt. Maybe I could sneak a peek into her room. Pretend to be looking for the bathroom but got turned around. One quick peek, just enough to fuel my dreams. It certainly beat tossing and turning all night.

I threw off the covers and tip-toed to the door—well, as much as any six-foot-two, one-hundred-seventy-pound man can tip-toe. No noise on the other side. And no time like the present. Chances were she wouldn't even wake up.

I creaked open the door slowly and stepped into the dark

hallway. And directly into Nicki.

"Oof," she said, steadying herself by grabbing my arms.

"What are you doing out here?" I asked, holding her elbows.

"What are *you* doing out here?" she shot back.

"Bathroom," we said together. Then laughed lightly. I loved her laugh. I loved her smile. I vowed to put it there more often. She looked up at me, and her eyes darkened. I was suddenly very aware of everywhere our bodies touched. Her fingers jumped on my arm; she felt it too.

I sucked in a breath and took a chance. "That's a lie. I planned on peeking in on you while you were sleeping."

She smirked and raised an eyebrow, much better than the slap I expected. "Creeper."

"I wanted to see what you were wearing," I explained.

"How cliché." She stepped back a fraction so I could see. An old college t-shirt, threadbare to the point of being almost see through, and short cotton shorts. Delicious.

She said, "Boring. Sorry."

"Far from boring, Nicki. You'd make a paper sack look good."

"Whatever," she said, but I could see the blush on her cheeks.

Since she didn't scream and run into the next room, I took another chance. Now or never. I brought her palm to my lips then moved them to the inside of her wrist. Her breath hitched; she didn't pull away. Or scratch my eyes out. I kissed up her arm and then, wrapping my other hand around her waist, gathered her to me and kissed her collarbone. She ran her hands up my bare torso, nails lightly scratching my skin, eliciting sparks all over. She gripped my shoulders and pressed harder against me, threading her legs with mine.

"I lied too," she whispered, her breath tickling my ear.

I pulled back a little to look at her. Her hazel eyes reflected my desire. "About what?"

"I was coming to find you. I couldn't sleep."

I smirked. "Did you want a bedtime story?"

"An interactive one," she teased, trailing a finger across my chest. She tracked it with her eyes, avoiding mine. "You could have been seriously hurt today. If you'd been sleeping…" her voice trailed off.

I lifted her chin with my finger. "But I wasn't. Thanks to you."

"To me? You said you were working?"

"Only because I couldn't get you out of my head. When Anderson dropped me off after Champs, I stood in front of your house vacillating between knocking or not. For an embarrassingly long time," I admitted.

She smiled. "I wasn't sleeping." She leaned up on her toes to kiss me lightly on the lips. Surprised, I barely kissed her back before she broke the connection. "I don't know what can happen between us, Marcus, but today made me realize life is too short not to try. If this is all just a ploy to get me back in bed, or to get a better story, I will annihilate you." She punctuated the last part by poking my chest with her finger.

I captured the offender and brought it to my lips. "I promise it isn't. Losing you was the biggest regret of my life. I'm only hoping for a second chance. A chance to prove I'm not quite the same selfish asshole from years ago."

"It's like after a fire. It burns hot and angry and passionate for a little while. Then, when it runs its course, we rebuild. And sometimes the rebuilding is even better than the original."

I couldn't wipe the shit-eating grin off my face. "I couldn't have said it better myself."

"Sometimes the fire destroys it beyond repair, though," she pointed out. My smile faltered a little, hope made a retreat. "But I'm willing to give it a shot."

"That's all I'm asking," I repeated.

She stepped into me and threaded her fingers in my hair. "Great. Now take me to bed before I change my mind."

She didn't have to ask me twice. I gripped her ass and lifted her. She wrapped her legs around my waist, rolling them slightly against my erection. I backed up into the guest room and placed her on the bed. Gripping the hem of her t-shirt, I slowly lifted it, allowing my knuckles to run lightly over her skin. She squirmed a little when I reached her ribs, then sighed as I brushed the outside curve of her breasts.

When her arms were free from the material, she reached for my boxers, running a finger under the elastic waistband. I shivered, and she laughed softly.

"Two can play the tickle game. Remember that," she said.

"Duly noted." I grabbed her wrist and placed her hand on my hard cock. "See what you do to me with just a kiss?"

She stroked me through my boxers. Once. Twice. Then moved her hand away and leaned back on the bed. I crawled over her, taking one of her already taut nipples in my mouth. I rolled it around with my tongue, savoring the moment I thought might never come.

She gripped my hair in her hands and tugged slightly. Obliging, I moved up her body to mold my lips to hers. She wrapped herself around me, arms and legs, and pressed me to her.

"I want to feel your weight on me," she said between kisses. "I want to know this is real."

I lifted her hips and pulled her shorts down with one hand then the other. She kicked them off and helped me remove my boxers as well. I teased her opening with the head of my dick, finding her wet and hot. For me. It was a powerful feeling. She shifted her hips so I slid ever so slightly inside. I groaned and, through a strength known only to the gods, moved away from her.

"Don't move," I said. I dug as quickly as I could for my wallet. When my rushing fingers finally found the condom, I returned to the bed.

"Let me," she said, taking the packet from my hands. Expertly, she rolled the condom down my shaft, protecting us both, and teasing me in the process. She helped guide me back to her.

"Nicki," I whispered, pressing my forehead to hers. "I've missed you so much."

Chapter Eight

Nicole

He kissed me as he entered me. Slow and sweet and familiar and new all at the same time. My body remembered him, opened for him, welcomed him. And as he started a slow, deliberate rhythm, I knew this was absolutely the right decision. Marcus could play my body like a musician studied in his craft.

There was something to be said about recycling lovers. There was no awkwardness, no getting to know our bodies, no stops and starts as we figured out what the other liked. Instead, just feeling and touch and taste and rhythm.

He lifted my hip to get a better angle, gripping my ass with his strong fingers, and I neared the edge. I honestly couldn't remember the last time a man made me come from missionary. It was probably Marcus.

He felt me clench around him, understood the changes in my breathing. "Yes, Nicki. Come for me."

I let myself go. Let myself feel all of him as he thrust one last time and joined me in oblivion. His muscles tightened under my fingers as I slowly reconnected with my body.

He lay over me, breathing heavily. I knew he'd get up in a

moment, discard the condom, and then come back to spoon me. Marcus may have been selfish in other areas of his life, but the bedroom wasn't one of them.

When we were settled in our spoon position—his one arm under the arch of my neck, his other draped over my waist—I couldn't help my smile. I also couldn't help how comfortable and right it felt being with Marcus.

"Thank you, Nicki. For taking a chance on me," he whispered into my hair.

I squeezed his hand. "Don't make me regret it."

"Never again," he said. I held onto that hope as we fell asleep.

The next morning, I awoke to the smell of coffee. Maybe having a roommate for a while wouldn't be so bad after all. I stretched, enjoying the soreness in my limbs and core from our love making the night before.

And in the middle of the night.

And a few hours ago.

But coffee reminded me I had work to do today. We had more pieces to the puzzle which meant the arsonist was getting sloppy. We were close.

I breathed in the smell of Marcus on my pillow one more time and then got up to dress for the day.

Marcus sat at the kitchen table reading the morning newspaper and sipping coffee.

"I'm surprised you're still here," I said, moving around the kitchen to make my own cup.

"Is that okay?" he asked, watching me over the top of the

paper. “I don’t really have anywhere else to go.”

“Sure. Make yourself at home. I need to head to the station. If you leave, lock up.” I reached up for a mug as his arms came around me. He nuzzled my neck.

“Last night was amazing, Nicki,” he said. “I meant what I said. I want you. All of you.”

“One step at a time,” I reminded him, though I turned to kiss him good morning.

We moved to the table to finish our coffee. I considered him closely while I mulled over the puzzle of the arsonist. Rope, candle wax, gasoline, a balloon.

Maybe a balloon, I amended. Marcus was no help when I asked him questions. He seemed more confused than anything else. Still, he was good at puzzles. It used to drive me crazy that he guessed the ending to every movie.

And he’d promised never to abuse my trust again. If this second chance was ever going to work between us, I had to give trust a chance. Especially if he lead us to the arsonist.

“Marcus. You said I could trust you, right?” I asked.

He lowered his paper. “Implicitly.”

“How can I be sure you aren’t using me to get a story?”

He smirked. “Because this time I used the story to get you. You still owe me a dinner date, by the way.”

“We’ll renegotiate later. I’m going to run something by you, but any new information stays between us, got it. Like for real this time.” He nodded, folded his hands on the table.

I took a deep breath and ran through the evidence. When I

finished, he sat for a moment mulling it over.

"The rope is directly over the candle wax? And the gas stain is surrounding it?" he asked. I nodded.

"Would a balloon burst in extreme heat?"

"Not even extreme heat. My nephew held a balloon too close to his candles one birthday, and it popped right in his poor little face," I said. Marcus raised his eyebrows and waited. Then it dawned on me. "OH! Fill a balloon with gasoline, hang it over the candle. It's a time delay."

He touched his nose. "And almost all the evidence burns up in the fire. Kinda genius in a way."

"Okay. Now we know how. We just need to find out who," I said.

"Anderson, the *Gazette* sports reporter, and I were speculating wildly at the bar yesterday. You know, the bar you didn't come to despite my very polite invitation."

I cocked my head at him. "After last night, you're going to give me shit for not wanting to go to a bar after battling a fire when I was already off shift?"

"Okay, fine. You get a pass this time. Anyway, we thought maybe it could be a housewife with extra candle inventory from a failed side hustle."

I tapped my finger to my lips. "I supposed a housewife could have access to all the materials. Especially balloons. Now to narrow that down from the sixty gazillion housewives in the area."

"It's not impossible."

I sighed. "The police have a potential eyewitness coming in to work with a sketch artist today. Apparently, this tipster saw someone filling a ridiculous amount of gas cans late one night. Hopefully that'll be the break we need."

I finished my coffee and got up to leave for work.

Marcus caught me by the door in an embrace. He kissed me, thoroughly.

"Don't linger too long at the station," he said. "If you need a lead, I suggest clowns."

I rolled my eyes. "I'll have the police round them all up. Marcus, none of that new information gets into a story, got it? I'm trying to trust you here."

"You can trust me."

That afternoon, I was combing the database for any similar MOs when Chief Finnegan burst into my office.

"Were you planning on leaking all the details?" he yelled, pacing, as best he could, around my small office.

"What are you talking about?" I asked.

"Damn it, Flint, this could give copycats some ideas. Not to mention all the armchair sleuths that think they have the answers. Our tip line is out of control. I should make you weed through the crazies." He ran a hand over his balding head.

"What are you talking about?" I asked again. A rock settled in my chest; I was having a hard time breathing.

He wouldn't.

"As if you didn't approve this little stunt today," he said. The chief took one look at my astonished face and added, "Check the Gazette website. It's top news."

With shaky fingers, I opened the website on my computer. The floor dropped out from under me when I read the headline: When

Does a Rope and Candle Equal Fire?

"That bastard," I whispered. He'd looked into my eyes and promised me he wouldn't use the information. And, like a desperate fool, I'd believed him.

"The comments are full of 'helpful' suggestions. I have a call in to Jim Johnston, but you need to put a leash on your journalist."

"Oh, I have more than a leash in mind for him," I snarled.

I was rummaging around in Nicki's fridge to see what I could make for lunch—bologna, yogurt cups, a few sad grapes—when I heard her truck screech into the driveway. I smiled. Maybe I'd skip lunch and go straight to dessert.

"Nicki! Great minds think a…" my voice trailed off when I saw the fury on her face. Her eyes hadn't flashed like that since she threw me out the last time.

"How could you?" she yelled through gritted teeth.

I held up my hands and backed up. "What did I do?"

"I can't believe I actually trusted you, you cocky, back-stabbing, selfish asshole!"

"Whoa! Can I at least know why I'm being berated?" What the hell had happened?

"I explicitly asked you not to leak the details we discussed this morning. Did you even wait until I left the driveway before you broke that promise? Were you disappointed last night when you had to lower yourself to fuck me again just to get your precious story?" She ended on a sob.

"No, no, no," I said. This wasn't happening. Not again. I

reached out to hold her, but she shrugged away from me.

"Don't you dare touch me," she said, swiping away her tears with the back of her hand.

"Nicki, I didn't leak any of the new information. I promised I wouldn't."

"You can't help yourself, can you? You're still standing here lying. Why are you even here? In my house. After what you did!" She turned to lean on the sink basin and look out at the yard. I could see her chest heaving as she sucked in air. I scrambled to fix whatever this was.

"Are you mad because I asked for help from the public? That was Jim's idea. I only put in the facts already out there—the candle, the rope, the serial nature."

She turned to look at me. "The rope, Marcus. No one knows about the rope except me, my crew, and you. After I trusted you enough to tell you this morning."

I shook my head. "No. Not true. I found out last night at Champs."

She blinked at me. Then narrowed her eyes. Back to angry. That was good. I could work with angry. Seeing her hurt ripped me apart.

"Which one of my guys told you?"

"None. It was Jim. He said you guys were stumped with the rope and wax connection. Like I said, he suggested the comments from the community."

"Jim Johnston, editor of the *Gazette*, told you about the rope," she repeated.

"Yeah. I figured you told him. Nicki, I swear to you, I wouldn't have used it if I didn't honestly believe that. I left out the balloon," I pointed out, my voice pleading. "And the theory we came up with this morning."

"You're not lying? Jim told you about the rope. Did he ask you to write about the arsons?"

"Not lying and yes, Jim assigned the arsons to me."

"Does he know about your spare house key at the office?" she asked.

"Yes. What are you suggesting?"

Her phone pinged, and her features switched from anger to work mode as she checked the screen.

"The sketch artist just finished. Look like anyone you know?" she asked, turning the phone to face me.

"Shit. It's Jim," I said.

"Yup." She grabbed my arm. "Come on."

The fall out was explosive and quick—the equivalent of a bomb going off in our smallish town. Not only did the police find all the evidence they needed in Jim's house, but once they arrested him, he sang like a canary. Apparently, his first fire was an accident. Then, when he saw an uptick in newspaper sales, he decided it was a great marketing technique.

Anderson and I sat in Champs watching the police search the *Gazette* offices across the street.

"I can't believe he torched our building," Anderson said. "Ballsy."

"And my house!" I said, throwing back the last of my beer. "Probably figured it would throw suspicion off him."

"Kinda worked," Anderson admitted. "I never in a million

years would have expected him."

I sensed Nicole before I saw her, her scent surrounded me. I turned and met her eye across the room, elated to see them devoid of her earlier anger.

"Can I talk to you?" she asked. "Alone?"

"Sure. Later Anderson." I threw some money on the bar and followed her outside to her truck. She looked beat. But beautiful.

"I wanted to apologize for accusing you earlier," she said, leaning back against the driver's door.

"Apology accepted," I said.

She looked up and let out a little laugh. "Just like that?"

"Just like that."

"Phew! I thought I'd have to tuck tail and take Kennedy up on her offer to move to the mountains and flirt with cowboys."

"Please don't. Listen, Nicki, I know I have to earn your trust."

"But I shouldn't have jumped to conclusions over a miscommunication," she said.

"Well, that miscommunication lead to the arrest of the arsonist," I reminded her.

She smirked. "True. Can I take you out to dinner to properly apologize?"

I stepped into her, cupping her chin in my hands. "I say, let's skip dinner and go straight to dessert."

She wrapped her arms around my neck. "I have been missing dessert lately."

She pressed her lips against mine. A simple gesture carried out by millions of couples around the world every day. But to me, it was incendiary.

Epilogue

Nicole

A few months later

"Well, it's official. We're living together," I said into the phone, looking around at my—I mean, our—newly configured bedroom.

Kennedy laughed in my ear. "That's not news, Nicki. You've been living together since the fire."

"That was supposed to be temporary. Now, it's official. I've given him half the closet in the master, we've converted the guest room into an office, and I changed the name on the mailbox."

"That does sound official. How are you feeling about that?" she asked.

"Actually, pretty good. Everything's been great so far. I'm slowly picking up the eggshells I've been walking on," I said. And realized I meant it. It was taking some time, but I was starting to trust Marcus again.

"Truth be told, I always thought you two were pretty great together. I'm seriously happy you found each other again."

"Cue the sappy music," I teased. "But enough about me. Tell

me about you. How's your Safe Farming campaign coming along?"

She sighed. "About as well as high heels in a barnyard. The ranchers are giving me quite the push back. Especially this one particularly cantankerous cowboy. Remember when you said you were about to make a big mistake with Marcus?"

"That mistake turned out to be the best decision in recent years," I said. Just thinking about our first night back together after the fire at his house sent tingles over my body. There had been many more nights just like that since. And hopefully many more to come.

"I'm not so lucky," Kennedy said. "Let me paint the scene: I met this super, hot cowboy at Stables, the local bar. His jeans fit perfectly; his smirk was devilish. And, Nicki, he could dance. So, I went home with him. I hadn't had a hook-up since I moved."

"And how was your first cowboy? Would you recommend him to a friend?" I asked.

"I don't remember!" she whined. "I remember him driving us to his cute, little cabin, then nothing. Not until I woke up the next morning and realized the hot cowboy was Brock McAllister."

"What's a Brock McAllister?"

"Only the most annoying, arrogant, self-righteous asshole this side of the mountains." She groaned. "Why do all the cute ones have to be stupid?"

I laughed. "Look on the bright side. If you don't remember the one-night stand, it couldn't have been that great, right?"

"I guess not. But guess whose family is the epitome of safe farming in this area? The one family I really need on my side to make this campaign work and not get fired?" she asked.

"I'm guessing the McAllisters."

"Bingo. Ugh, why does the universe hate me."

"Remember what you said to me? You are an independent badass woman who will not let one grumpy cowboy ruin your chances of success."

"He just makes me want to throat punch that smirk off his annoyingly chiseled face."

Marcus' voice from the hallway pulled my attention away from the bedroom. I walked to meet him.

To Kennedy, I said, "Don't resort to violence. I don't think that will help your 'be kind to animals' stance. Just do what I did to Marcus all those years: ignore him."

She snorted. "Great advice. Worked out super well for you."

I ran a hand up Marcus' chest. He dropped the box he was holding to grip my hip.

"Yes," I said. "Yes it did."

Get caught up on Nicole's friend Kennedy's romance and Karigan Hale's other romantic comedies in the About the Authors section at the end of the book.

ALASKA DAWN

LoLo Paige

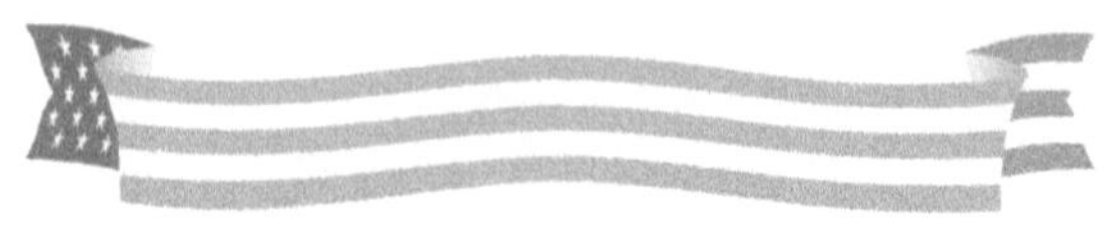

Ryan O'Connor's hotshot fire crew pulls out all the stops to save a trapped family in a Southern California firestorm. But when his crew is unable to reach them in time, Ryan considers the loss of lives a personal failure. He decides to apply and train with the Delta Force of wildland fire—the Alaska Smokejumpers. If Ryan can make it through the ball-busting training, his life will be set on a new trajectory…one that could lead him to the woman of his dreams.

Tara Waters loves being a wildland firefighter for the U.S. Forest Service in Missoula, Montana, and has worked hard to prove herself capable. But when the hunky Missoula smokejumper, Travis McGuire, aims his parachute at Tara, her worlds collide. Her father is against Tara dating any firefighter—especially smokejumpers. Others warn her she's setting herself up for heartbreak, but she can't resist when Travis shows her how hot and steamy a real wildfire can be…is he The One?

Fall in love with the brave men and women of Alaska's Wildland Firefighters in this smoking hot Prequel to *The Blazing Hearts Wildfire Series*.

Part I
Ryan's Night

The Mendocino Hotshots Crew Base, Stonyford, Northern California

Ryan O'Connor dragged himself through the door of the house he shared with three other wildland firefighters at his crew base in Stonyford. He shuffled his filthy boots down the hallway to his room and kicked open the door. The heavy fire pack slid from his shoulder to the floor. He gave it a pained look and let out a weary sigh. The springs on the mattress squeaked as he fell backwards onto his bed.

The Angelus San Bernardino Fire in Southern California that his Mendocino Hotshots crew had just demobilized from, was one of the worst he'd ever encountered. The Santa Ana winds had spun the inferno from a lightning strike on the San Bernardino Forest into hell on earth. Residents in the densely populated neighborhoods barely had time to evacuate their homes when the powerful, relentless winds plunged the hella firestorm into their midst. Both city fire and wildland firefighters had been powerless to stop the conflagration intent on destruction.

Ryan was thankful to be back in Northern California at his Mendocino Hotshots crew base in Stonyford. The base was within spitting distance of the six national forests in the surrounding area, and so far none had lit up yet this fire season, knock on wood. Lightning strikes were the culprits in this neck of the woods, but skies had been clear the past several weeks.

"I'm spent." Gunnar Alexanderson, Ryan's buddy and fellow crewmate shuffled in behind him and leaned on the doorway.

"Me too, bro," groaned out Ryan, his forearm over his face. His feet hung off the end of the bed and he didn't care. Hard to fit his six-foot-four frame on any bed he landed in, especially on the short cots at fire camp. He often wondered whether the fire cache warehouse got the memo that tall people fought fires too. He made a mental note to let them know.

"This SoCal fire sucked big time. The whole thing was a cluster fu—"

Ryan cut in, rubbing his eyes with his knuckles. "I know, bro. I know."

"You shower first. I need to be prone." Gunnar pushed off the doorway and lumbered across the hall to his room.

"Thanks." Ryan pushed to sit with great effort, his arm muscles shuddering from adrenalized over-exertion for the last seventy-two hours.

Ryan stripped off his blackened fire clothing and rubbed a hand over his stubble as he padded into the bathroom and ran the shower. He glanced in the mirror. Guilt and despair stared back at him, along with a host of other bullshit that goes with failing to save lives.

He stepped into the steamy shower and let the water beat on his sore, mangled body as the event played in his mind for the gazillionth time. It was the screaming that had brought him to his knees. And not a damn thing the Mendocino Hotshot crew could have done about it. They'd been busy laying hose, sawing trees, and chopping out the chaparral and eucalyptus to starve the ravenous firestorm of fuel—when they realized one hillside home still contained its residents. A family of five became trapped in a house and for the life of him, Ryan couldn't figure why they'd ignored the Go part of the Ready Set Go evacuation orders. He never questioned people's reasons for what they did or didn't do, but when it came to wildland fire in the rural-urban interface, where wildlands met city neighborhoods, *you don't question it when California law enforcement officers show up at your door telling you to get out NOW!*

It had all happened too quickly.

And it wasn't until after mop-up fifteen hours later, that the hotshot crew of twenty realized the extent of property loss and the lives that had gone down hours before.

"I'm done with motherfucking firefighting!" one of his crew had shouted, before breaking down and flinging his Pulaski, not giving a shit where it landed. "God, why didn't that family leave? *Why*?"

No one had an answer. Everyone had suffered their torment in silence, each dealing in his and her own way. Ryan and Gunnar, who normally teased and bantered with their crewmates—stayed silent for the remainder of their shift.

There was nothing to say.

Now that Ryan was alone to grasp the reality of not having saved the family, his eyes stung with salty tears. He squeezed them shut and gripped the shower nozzle with both hands, aiming his face at the spray to wash away what he was powerless to stop.

"Oh God…" He wept quietly, not wanting to be heard—for

that was a sign of weakness, he thought bitterly. Firefighters were tough. Strong. The stalwart, dependable force everyone looked up to and depended on each year when fiery shitstorms rained down on drought-stricken California.

What he couldn't rinse away was the agonizing guilt. He wished with all his heart that he could. Worst of all was recalling how his tough, thick-skinned crew boss had lost his shit when they couldn't retrieve the family from the burning house. All anyone could do was watch helplessly as the wildfire engulfed the home. When the crew was forced to retreat from the roaring flames, the last thing Ryan remembered was the screaming.

He let go of the shower nozzle and slid his back down the tile until he hit the shower floor. He brought his bunged-up knees to his chest and wrapped his arms around them. He blew out air and shoved the guilt and pain down to the basement of his heart. Pain that he knew would haunt him for the rest of his life.

Ryan did something he hadn't done in a long time.

He prayed.

Early the next morning, Ryan pulled up to crew headquarters in his old beat-up Mustang and switched off the ignition. The engine performed its prolonged shake, rattle, and roll before finally crapping out. He sat back and stared out the cracked windshield, while Gunnar sat quiet beside him in the passenger seat.

"Gunns, I've decided to resign from the crew." He fixed on a hillside of orange California poppies waving in the breeze.

Gunnar gave him a sharp look and his Norwegian accent thickened. "Never knew you to be a quitter."

"Not quitting firefighting exactly. I need to—I want to apply to jump school."

"What's the matter?" Gunnar made a sweeping gesture. "None of this is exciting enough for you? Or do you think you'll avoid seeing people die?"

Ryan flicked his eyes at him, then shook his head. "I've been thinking about it for a while."

"Why don't you return to helitack and rappel from helicopters to fight fire? Or did you not enjoy packing out heavy gear from remote locations? You'd still have to do that as a smokejumper."

Ryan shrugged. "Heli-rappelling was too hard on my body. And too loud. My ears rang for weeks from rotor noise, even with ear protection." Ryan and Gunnar had both retained their heli-rappel certification they'd trained for in Salmon, Idaho before joining the Mendocino Hotshots. Dangling from a rappel line below a *whump-whumping* chopper with intense rotor wash no longer appealed to him.

Gunnar guffawed. "As if squatting in an open door of a Twin Otter isn't loud enough for you? Smokejumping is the hardest of all on the body. You'll trash your knees, hips, and back. And that's if you don't impale yourself on a treetop after hurling your sorry ass out of a fast-moving plane with a shit-ton of weight."

"That's what the jump training is for. Gunns, this San Bernardino Fire kicked my ass. I don't mean physically, as much as mentally. I know I can do better, prove myself more capable. I think I can do that as a smokejumper."

"What do you mean, 'prove yourself?' More capable than what?" Gunns stared at him. "Listen to me. Rule number one—you can't save everyone in a wildland fire. You just can't. Especially when people don't evacuate, for whatever reason. You're beyond fucking capable, but you don't have to kill yourself to prove it. Those five people weren't your personal responsibility."

"Then whose were they? We should have been able to get them out," muttered Ryan, squinting at crewmates in yellow shirts sauntering into the building. "I couldn't climb that fucking hill fast enough."

Gunnar shook his head, exasperated. "None of us could. Look, you know they're going to drill us on the fatalities. Then offer us counseling. We'll have to prepare oral and written statements for the After-Action Reports."

Ryan's lips tightened in resignation. "I know."

Gunnar opened his door. "Time to go in and get it over with."

"Wait, just a second." Ryan leaned against his door. "I'm serious. I really have been thinking of applying to jump school in Redding. Yesterday just clinched my decision. I like our hotshot crew, but I need to do this." He squinted out the windshield, then back at his friend. "Gunns, do it with me. We'd have a blast. Come on, you talked me into joining the hotshots. So, let me talk you into jump school…I'm challenging you."

"Like what, to a duel?" quipped Gunnar. He hesitated, then tugged his door closed. "All right, I can see you're serious about this. It would suck without you on the hotshot crew." He gave him a lopsided smile. "And I've never been one to turn down a challenge."

"Does that mean you'll apply with me?"

"Let me think." Gunnar wrinkled his face. "Do I seriously want to trash my body?"

"You didn't fuck yourself up training and skiing for the Olympics, right?" Ryan smirked. "Too bad you missed the bronze by a nanosecond in your alpine ski event. Is that why you left Norway? So, they wouldn't put you in loser ski jail?"

Gunnar narrowed his eyes. "Thanks for rubbing it in, dickwad." He paused, looking out the windshield. "Technically, yes. I did abuse myself training for the winter Olympics. But that was a different kind of abuse."

"Sorry, didn't mean to salt your wound. But look at it this way. When you jump a fire, you'll hit the ground once at high velocity, as opposed to having bounced multiple times down an icy slope when you crash and burn at a hundred miles an hour." Ryan hoped Gunnar would do this next adventure with him. They'd been buddies since college at Humboldt, then both became wildland firefighters.

"Strange comparison, but okay." Gunnar let out a heavy sigh. "What the hell? I'll do it with you." He thought a minute. "I want you to promise no dating anyone on the team this time."

"After Amber, hell no. She's taken up acting in Redding." Ryan described his ex who had worked with him last season.

Gunnar's brows raised. "In Redding? Don't you go to L.A. for that?"

"Well...it's—it's a different kind of acting job. One where she works naked."

"Are you shitting me? She makes porno films?" Gunnar seemed incredulous. "Then again, no surprise there. She wasn't that modest at fire camp, as I recall."

"Guess she thought she was one of the guys," said Ryan dryly, envisioning the curvaceous, fit blonde, who he'd been attracted to on a superficial basis. "You know, with all her weight-lifting and body building."

"You fell for it, as I remember. Back when your brains lived in your pants."

Ryan held up a hand. "All right, all right, I screwed up. Not doing that again."

He recalled the tumultuous reasons why Amber had quit the crew. Once she and Ryan became romantically involved, it was awkward for crew morale. Most had turned a blind eye, but others thought Ryan and Amber would be too distracted to do their jobs. Ryan learned the hard way: *Never get involved with someone you work with—not in wildland fire.*

When their relationship soured, bickering had escalated into arguments that divided the entire crew. Amber quit, which was just as well. Her heart was never into firefighting anyway.

"Someday you'll meet a woman who understands you," said Gunnar. "Someone you can have an intelligent conversation with—and who likes to fly."

Ryan was glad he'd gotten his single engine private pilot's license while training to fight fire in California. He appreciated his friend's sentiment. "You think such a woman exists?"

"Don't worry, buddy. There's a woman out there for both of us."

Ryan shot him an amused look. "Hopefully, not the same woman. I'm not into throuples, bro. Especially with your sorry ass."

"So you're serious. We're doing this – all the training, the risking death, the jumping out of airplanes into burning forests, the giving up beer and women because you've gotta prove you're a superhero?"

Ryan admitted Gunnar had a point. He'd failed as a hotshotter, so maybe he could redeem himself as a smokejumper. He would atone, find a way to make things right. Prove to himself once again that he was a capable firefighter.

"Hell yes. Maybe we'll get assigned to Alaska. And maybe I'll meet a good woman there."

Gunnar snorted, "You are aware of the gorgeous, independent women in the Land of the Midnight Sun, right?" Gunnar thought a moment. "On the other hand, they're probably into skiing. I'll try to leave a few for you."

"Gee, thanks Gunns. How generous of you. I have to admit, a little smokejumper superhero status wouldn't hurt. Are you in?"

Gunnar gave him a lopsided grin. "What do you think? Does a moose shit in the woods?"

Part II

Tara's Dusk

Three years later. U.S. Forest Service, Missoula Ranger District, Missoula, Montana

Tara Waters couldn't take her eyes off the solidly built firefighter in a yellow Nomex shirt and green trousers, lecturing trainees about the dangers of erratic wildland fire behavior. Her gaze glued to him as he moved from the lectern to the white board, drawing fire scenarios and asking firefighters how they'd handle each situation.

"Miss Waters?"

Tara had been ogling him so intently, she didn't hear his question. All she could manage was, "Yes?"

"What would be your strategy?" his deep bass rumbled out as he swung a leg over the corner of a table, hand in his pants pocket.

"For...um…?" She shot her BFF Katy a what-the-heck-did-he-ask-me look.

Katy leaned sideways and whispered. "Flames running uphill toward structures."

"Oh." Tara nodded understanding. "Make sure your crew is

out of the fire's path as it runs uphill," she responded robotically.

He appeared amused. "Why?"

"Fires burn fastest moving uphill," she stated matter-of-factly, shrugging as if to say everyone knew that.

He stared at her a moment. "Why?"

"Because the angle of the flames pre-heats vegetation so it ignites faster."

A hum of approval. "You *were* paying attention."

"Of course, I was." Her gaze rested on the name tag above his shirt pocket. Travis. Her cheeks heated. To her dismay, they warmed every time he glanced in her direction for the remainder of the class.

When the fire refresher training ended for the day, Tara rose from her seat in the Missoula Ranger District conference room.

"See you tomorrow. Don't forget to study for my test," drawled Mr. Hot Firefighter, flashing her a panty-smoldering smile as he erased his fire scenarios from the white board.

"Sure thing." Her cheeks once again lit on fire as she wandered out the door and waited for Katy. They'd become fast friends when Tara joined the Missoula Ranger District fire crew a few years ago. Tara and Katy's first big fire was the Angelus San Bernardino Fire in Southern California—one of the worst in California history. And one that had influenced the direction of Tara's wildland firefighting career—she'd set her sights on becoming a hotshot firefighter. Hotshot crews responded to larger, high-priority fires to work the most dangerous parts of a fire. Hotshots were the elite ground crews—often referred to as the Army Rangers of wildland firefighting.

"Who's that Travis guy? No last name on his name tag," said

Tara with feigned indifference.

Katy swung her day pack onto one shoulder. "You didn't hear him introduce himself? You were so busy checking him out you didn't hear a word he said," she laughingly accused. "Travis McGuire, a smokejumper from the Missoula Smokejumper Base. Not bad, huh?" She led the way out to the parking lot.

"He must be new. He wasn't there when I temped at the base last winter." She tossed her waist-long, auburn hair over her shoulder, then poked her friend. "May I remind you, we're not here for booty call."

Katy laughed. "I know. But it's hard not to notice how easy on the eyes some of these wildland fire guys are. Plus, this one knows his stuff. He sure had you mesmerized."

"I was focused on what he was saying," lied Tara. She didn't sign up to fight wildland fire to flirt with the guys. But for some odd reason this one had her rapt attention.

"Yeah, right. Uh-huh." Katy gave her an eyeroll, then paused. "Have you ever envisioned how a guy makes love just by looking at him?"

Tara chuckled. "Sometimes, yeah."

Katy leaned toward her with a mischievous grin. "I bet this Travis guy screams his own name. I know several Missoula guys, and they aren't as fine looking as this one is."

"Just because a hot one appears on our radar doesn't mean we should hit on him. We're here to fight fire, remember?"

"God, Tara, you sound like your dad."

Tara gave herself an eyeroll. "He says it every time he sees me."

"I *know,* I've been with you when he does." Katy groaned out a sigh. "Your dad—bless his little heart—has no flipping idea what it's like for us. It's no different than being on a diet and someone offers you a donut…or worse, a hot fudge sundae." Katy groaned out a sigh. "But you're right. We shouldn't get our meat where we make our bread."

"You have such a way with words." Tara shook her head, amused.

"What can I say? I was born with class." Katy opened the door to her beat-up Subaru. "See you tomorrow for more fun and games." She climbed in and fired up the engine. The vehicle shuddered and knocked, but as Katy liked to say, "It gives my Subee character."

Tara waved goodbye to her friend. As she climbed into the driver's seat of her blue RAV4 Toyota, her eye caught movement.

Travis McGuire stepped from the building in an animated discussion with Tara's fifty-something crew boss, Jim Dolan. She skootched down in her seat, wondering what they were discussing.

McGuire really was fine eye candy. His dark, wavy hair had a persistent tousled look, and his yellow Nomex shirt was partially unbuttoned, revealing a black tee shirt that matched his hair. His wide shoulders and narrow waist accentuated his brawn. A firefighter's physique. She guessed him to be a few inches taller than her own five feet, eleven inches. Dimpled smile, angular jaw, rows of bright teeth—and those chocolate eyes made her blush whenever she looked at them.

Nope, he wasn't bad at all.

No sooner had refresher training ended, when Tara's crew got their first fire call early the next morning. Tara had easily passed her fitness capacity test, earning the red card qualification for another busy fire season. Each crew member had pack-tested to meet their arduous physical requirement of walking three miles under forty-five minutes with as much pack weight.

This year's predictive services at Boise's National Interagency Fire Center promised an above average fire season for the western states this summer. In other words, steady work for fire crews.

Tara rode in the crew van for a half an hour drive west of Missoula to the U.S. Forest Service, Ninemile Ranger District, where lightning had struck tinder-dry stands of Douglas Fir and lodgepole pine. The fire burned within three miles of the Ninemile Historic Remount Depot, which made this fire a high priority for suppression. On the drive out, Jim Dolan had explained how the remount depot had bred mules to help with fire suppression between the 1930s to 1960s, so protecting this historic ranger station was paramount.

The fire was some distance from the road where they parked,

so the crew hiked the three miles in single file to their work location. When they reached their site to establish a fireline, Jim briefed the crew on their initial attack plan. “Several smokejumpers jumped this fire at 3:00 a.m. this morning. We’re here to finish the fireline they started, as they move to the east flank to keep it from burning nearby ranches. Travis McGuire is the Incident Commander.”

Tara flicked her eyes up at her crew boss. "Travis McGuire?”

She must have sounded surprised because Jim gave her an odd look. “Yeah, why?”

Tara raised her brows, aiming for indifference. “No reason. Just curious. He was our instructor the last two days of refresher training.”

“I know. I arranged it.” Jim cocked a brow and gave her a look. “Just curious, huh?”

Tara ignored him and led off as the crew hiked to their position to dig fireline. They hiked up the mountain toward the thick plumes of gray smoke that stretched high into Montana’s big, blue sky. Each carried a Pulaski, their primary fire tool, consisting of a long-handled, two-headed axe and grub-hoe combination. Some carried chainsaws for cutting timber. Their objective was to create a fuel break—a fireline, to stop flames from progressing.

Jim fell into lockstep alongside Tara. “Keep in mind what your dad said about dating smokejumpers,” he said in his usual blunt manner. He was Dad’s closest friend after years of fighting fire together on the LoLo Interagency Hotshot Crew.

“Who said anything about dating smokejumpers?” she erupted, defensive. Her dad consistently warned her about dating firefighters, especially smokejumpers. In his opinion, they were notorious heartbreakers and therefore, forbidden fruit.

"I know that look." Jim narrowed his eyes. "I wasn't born yesterday."

"All right, already. I'm not interested in any smokejumpers. Satisfied?" she grumbled. "I don't troll for dates with Zulies."

"It's not me you need to worry about. It's your dad. He's only watching out for your best interest. Don't forget he was a hotshot and played that same game."

"And that's how he landed Mom. So why was that a bad thing? They were so much in love it should have been a romance novel." Her voice wiggled as she hiked upslope, stepping between downed timber that had succumbed to insects and disease. "Don't worry, Jim. I can handle myself."

"Uh-huh. Don't say I didn't warn you." Jim fell back to make sure the single file of twenty crew members kept moving.

The crew reached the staging area the smokejumpers had created. Tara and Katy spread out with the rest of their crew to dig a six-foot-wide fire break. Their mission was to clear all vegetation down to mineral soil a good distance in front of the fire to starve it of fuel. Other crew members sawed trees and large brush, to reduce the ladder fuels and prevent tree crowning, which spread fire faster than it could be contained.

Tara swung her Pulaski repeatedly to clear a wide swath, along with everyone else. Soon they had a solid fireline, joining the one the smokejumpers had established several hours before. Dolan told the crew to take a short break to eat some lunch.

Tara wiped sweat from her forehead, removed her red hardhat, and set it beside her. Eyeing the smoke from a safe distance, she sat on an old, weathered stump and tugged a turkey sandwich from its plastic bag. As she opened her mouth for a bite, a shadow fell over her. She paused to look up.

"Wondered if you'd be on this fire," rumbled the Incident Commander in his deep voice. Travis McGuire stood looking down at her, hands on his hips, a thousand times hotter than the fire they were fighting.

"Hello," she said, aiming for a casual tone. "So, you guys jumped this one."

Despite the soot covering his face and his fire shirt dark with ash and dirt, he still looked mother-freaking good. Some guys rocked their fire grunge, like movie stars. This one sure did.

"How's the containment line going?" he asked in a cheerful tone.

Why the heck do my cheeks heat up whenever he talks to me? Flustered, she tried to control it. "It's uh, going. How is it on your end?"

"We jumped it early this morning to stop it from burning up to the ridge. There's a historic lookout up there, the Lupine Mountain Lookout. Forest Service didn't want to lose it."

"You must have saved the day, or you wouldn't be so chipper," she volunteered.

"It's half contained. If wind behaves, we'll have 100% containment tonight."

"You sound confident." She hated herself for the coy look she gave him.

"I am." He took off his sunglasses and smiled. "As I'm sure you are."

She resolved not to let his gaze melt her. "I'm confident in my abilities," she said firmly, used to making such assertions in her mostly male work environment.

They locked gazes for what seemed a lifetime. Long enough so that Katy broke the silence and stood. "Got to go do some stuff. See you on the fireline." She winked at Tara and strode off, leaving Tara alone with this guy. She wasn't sure how to feel about it, but it couldn't be all that bad since her heart had ticked up to a healthy clip.

Travis took Katy's seat next to Tara. "So, this is what—your third fire season? Have you toured the Smokejumper Base yet?"

"No." The lie popped out of her mouth before she could stop it. She'd temped at the base for two short months last winter, before McGuire had arrived there. She paused, curious. "How do you know this is my third firefighting season?"

"I always check out my trainees—" He chuckled and stopped to correct himself. "I mean, my trainees' experience, so I can gauge what to cover in class." He pretended to be embarrassed, but somehow Tara didn't think he was. Embarrassment didn't fit this self-assured guy. He leaned in. "I can give you a private tour of the smokejumper base when we demobe from this fire."

She'd speculated he might offer and felt compelled to lie. No way would she disclose she'd had the run of the place during her brief office admin stint last winter.

"Ooh, a private tour after demobilization?" She pulled back from him in mock surprise. *Why not? What harm could there be in that?*

He laughed and lowered his voice. "But only if you'll have dinner with me."

Aha, he sweetened the deal.

"You're bribing me with food?" She sipped from her canteen.

She envisioned Dad admonishing her if she accepted. "Hmm. I've not been propositioned on a fire before. I'll have to think about it."

"What's to think about?" He stood and stretched. "We should be finished up here by tomorrow. How about day after tomorrow? That is, unless we're dispatched to another fire."

Tara couldn't think of a reason why she shouldn't. Since when did she do everything her dad told her to do? He hadn't wanted her to be a firefighter either. Besides, she and Travis didn't work together on the same crew or even in the same fire office, so no conflict there. McGuire may be the IC on this fire, but he wasn't her supervisor. What's the worst that could happen? They'd go out, and if they weren't into each other, they'd go their separate ways. No big deal, in her estimation. *Sure, I'll let him show me around.*

"All right. Talked me into it. Dinner and a tour, the day after tomorrow." She refused to obsess whether this was a bad lapse in judgment. Let the chips fall where they may. This was her life, not her legendary father, Steve Waters' life.

"It's a date, then." He put his sunglasses back on and strode off to check on the rest of the fire operation.

Tara's gaze glued to his receding backside, her mind reeling at what just happened. Here they were on the fireline and he casually hit on her during lunch. Not your normal workday.

Not normal. At. All.

Two days after the Ninemile Fire had been contained, McGuire was true to his word. Early one evening, he picked Tara up at her home in Pattee Canyon, a narrow, forested canyon southeast of town where she shared a two-story log home with her dad.

True to form, her dad wasn't thrilled with Tara dating a smokejumper. He'd roamed around the house after work with his mouth in a straight line, then sat in his recliner madly clicking TV channels. All he said to her as she was heading out the door was, "Don't make this a habit. And be careful." He'd lowered his reading glasses. "Or do we need the birds-and-bees talk?"

"Dad! Honestly! I'm pushing thirty. Are you kidding me?" She'd given him an eyeroll as she slammed the door.

McGuire drove her west of town to the Smokejumper Base and toured her around the mostly empty building. Most jumpers were either out on fires or retired in their quarters. Tara figured she deserved an Oscar for her acting like she'd never been inside the base. She pretended surprise at The Loft, the tall tower where the parachutes hung, ready for repacking. Travis explained that before the siren went off, the smokejumpers were organized into a specific order for boarding planes to jump fires. "For example, tomorrow I'm first man, first stick." He pointed to the jump roster. "I'll be staying close to base after tonight."

He escorted Tara from The Loft to the Ready Room, where smokejumpers kept their jumpsuits and other gear in their lockers, when they prepared to jump a fire.

"This is fascinating," said Tara, looking around. "I've always wondered what it was like in here." *I'm so going to hell for lying.*

He stepped over to an end locker and tapped his knuckles on it. "Pretty cool, huh? This one's mine."

She nodded, continuing her charade. "So where does everyone sleep?" She knew damn well where everyone slept and gave herself an internal eyeroll for her deceit.

He grinned. "You want to see my quarters?"

She flicked her eyes at him. "Uh, no, that's all right." Her cheeks ignited for the millionth time. "I was just curious."

He escorted her to a windowed door at the back of the main base and pointed at a nearby rectangular building. "There's our quarters. Close to the running track, weight room, and dining hall. And check out the tarmac and airport runways next to all of it. This is pretty much it except for our fire cache warehouse." He waved his hand in an off-handed gesture. "That's where we store a bunch of boring fire equipment."

"Not boring to me. I'm a fire nerd," she said, noting how McGuire's hair waved back on top and a random curl flopped over his forehead.

Tara had noticed two new women smokejumpers working in The Loft repairing chutes, and she had nothing but intense admiration for them, knowing the rigorous physical requirements for all smokejumpers. "Where do the female jumpers sleep?"

"On a separate wing in the same building. They have their own sleep quarters and shower facilities. Interested in jumping?" He gave her a perky smile.

She shook her head. "Nah, I'm good with being on a ground crew. Not a fan of jumping out of perfectly good airplanes."

He laughed. "That's understandable. It's not for everyone. Ready for some dinner?" He led her back out and they climbed into his Jeep. He pointed it toward The Steak Factory downtown, by the old railroad station.

After a delicious dinner of steak and prawns, Tara sat back studying Travis McGuire. The more she came to know him, the more attracted she became. "What landed you in Missoula?"

"I trained at the Smokejumper Base in McCall, Idaho, but always wanted to be a Zulie. Got my wish when I applied last year." He sat back, scrutinizing her. "What about you?"

She narrowed her eyes in a teasing manner. "Wait a minute. You said you checked out your trainees. I presume you have an idea of my fire experience."

A sheepish look crossed his face and he grinned. "Whoops, busted. I did glance at your overall work record but fill me in on the details."

Tara sipped her water. "I got on with the Missoula RD fire crew a few years ago. Last fire season when we were laid off, I took a part-time job for the winter at the Forest Service, Missoula Technology and Development Center, so I could work on my classes at U of M for my master's degree. Then I got back on my crew again this summer." She artfully skipped over her temp stint at the

Smokejumper Base.

"What's your degree in?"

"Wildland fire science." She smiled at him. "No surprise there."

"That's great. Before you know it, you'll shoot up to the management ranks as a muckety-muck in the Washington Office."

Tara laughed. "Not interested. I like Montana. Grew up here."

He told her about the fires he'd worked as a hotshot and the smokejumpers he'd met on those fires. "The Alaska Smokejumpers were a good crew. Got to know a few after fighting fire with them in Colorado and Oregon. They're the ones who who talked me into jump school." He drank the last of his ice water, his gaze focused on her. "What was the worst fire you've ever worked?"

Tara heaved out a sigh. "The Angelus San Bernardino Fire in Southern California a few years ago. It was my first out of state project fire, where I was one of thirty-nine hundred firefighters. We were positioned in the mountains, to keep flames from reaching cell towers and radio antennae sites, when the Santa Ana winds blew it up and the whole thing descended into chaos." Tara squeezed the bridge of her nose with her thumb and forefinger, recalling the stress of that awful day. "We heard hotshot crews on the radio, everyone yelling and shouting. They sounded frantic and panicky—trying to get people out of their homes."

Travis gave her an empathetic look. "Glad I missed that one. Good thing you made it out safely."

"We helped the overall suppression effort protecting the antennae sites, but…" Tara trailed off and looked up at him. "I want to be where the action is—where I can make more of a difference. Ever since listening to the hotshot crews that day, I've wanted to work on one." She gave him a shy look. "I've decided to apply to the LoLo Interagency Hotshot Crew next summer."

He nodded. "They're great to work with. You'll have a good experience." Travis regarded her with what she sensed was respect and admiration. She liked to think so, anyway.

"I know. My dad and my crew boss worked for them years ago."

After they left the restaurant, Travis drove her home. They sat in his Jeep with the engine idling. Tara's dad peeked out the window and she knew he wasn't happy. He didn't trust any firefighter with his only daughter. In his view, single smokejumpers had a love 'em and leave 'em mentality.

"I had a good time tonight," said Tara, her hand on the door handle. Her dad shot another impatient grimace out the window.

"Me too. Let's do it again." McGuire nodded at the house. "Is that your dad?"

"Yeah." Tara did an eyeroll toward the house. "He still thinks I'm thirteen. He's been stuck in a time warp since the 1970s and believes I shouldn't date until I'm thirty."

"No shit?" chortled McGuire. She loved the sound of his laugh. "Helicopter parent, huh?" He flashed her an understanding grin. "I get that, with a beauty like you for a daughter. Everyone knows about the legendary Steve Waters, hotshot extraordinaire. Don't think I want to mess with him."

"He is a tad protective. His bite is worse than his bark, so there's that. I'd better go in." She reached across, extending her hand. "Thanks again for the fun evening."

He took her hand and squeezed it. "I enjoyed myself."

Neither made a move beyond the handshake and that was fine

by Tara. She didn't want to rush anything. Not while her heart was confused about getting involved with firefighters.

Especially with a hotter than hell smokejumper, named Travis McGuire.

Tara didn't see McGuire again for eight weeks. Montana's extended drought exacerbated the multitude of lightning strikes during June and July, sending all wildland fire resources into emergency response at a frantic pace. No sooner had crews responded to one fire, when another ignited with a higher priority for suppression.

Tara's crew had dispatched from one fire to the next, for four weeks straight. She earned hazard duty pay when on direct attack with uncontrolled blazes. Federal firefighter pay was low compared to state firefighter paychecks, so most worked as many hours as they could. After four weeks, the crew needed a rest.

Missoula smokejumpers had been dispatched throughout the fiery Pacific Northwest and Tara lost track of which fires McGuire had jumped. She'd been too busy and exhausted to track him down. Besides, they hardly knew each other after only one date. Calling him felt uncomfortable, like she was chasing him. That wasn't the message she wanted to send. She wasn't sure what the heck message she wanted to send, but not that one. Maybe it was a one-time thing with McGuire. No doubt he was chased by women everywhere he went.

On a Friday in mid-August, after demob'ing from a fire, the Missoula crew's transport van rolled to a stop in front of the district office. Everyone grabbed their smoke-drenched fire packs and piled out of the van. As Tara trudged to her small SUV, she fished out her cell phone. Up popped a voice message from her dad, welcoming her home. Another popped up from Travis McGuire and she tapped it to listen. *"Heard your crew demob'ed. Want to get together? Call me."*

Tara's heart skipped a beat at the sound of his low, sexy voice. Her first impulse was to call him back, but she paused, her finger hovering over his number. For gosh sakes, control yourself. At least wait until you get home.

She peeled from the parking lot and beelined toward Pattee Canyon Road. She drove the two miles and turned right, onto a gravel road that led to the driveway of the log home her dad had built for her mom twenty-five years ago.

Steve Waters straightened his large frame and waved to his daughter from his riding lawn mower. Tara had always thought of her dad as handsome. Yet, judging by how women in general responded to him, they regarded him like one of those hot movie-star, silver fox guys. He was just as ripped as his younger counterparts at the Missoula City FD.

Tara pulled up to the four-car garage that housed both their vehicles, including Steve's two sports cars. One was his prized muscle car, a 1971 Ford Mustang Mach 1, that he bragged could hit sixty miles per hour in 6.5 seconds. The other was a red-and-white, 80s Corvette that Tara's mom drove until ovarian cancer claimed her life. Steve kept Lucinda's car spotless and shined it even when it sparkled, while listening to her favorite playlist with the Eagles, Chicago, and Creedence Clearwater Revival. Included in her playlist was the Mission Mountain Woodband from the 1970s, later renamed Montana. In 1987, the band died in a plane crash near Flathead Lake. From the time she was little, her parents had talked about the band as if they'd been family.

One of Mom's favorite songs blared as Tara guided her Toyota into the open space inside the garage. She crawled out, tugged the grimy pack from her SUV, and rested it on the concrete.

Steve pulled up and powered down the mower, wiping his brow with a bandana he fished from his pocket. "You were out a long time. Good to be home?" He swung his legs off and walked inside the garage to hug her.

"Yeah." Tara hugged him and broke free to turn down his music. "Hey Pops, great music, but are you deaf?"

He skated over her comment. "You could use a shower. You stink like you ate, slept, and breathed fire." He scanned her head to toe. "And you made it back in one piece."

"Of course, I did." She smiled at him. "Those torturous mountains you forced me to climb with all those heavy rocks paid off big time."

"Good to hear." He shrugged. "Since I couldn't talk you out of firefighting, figured I'd help you survive it." He motioned at the wash machine. "You know the drill. Unpack and remove your fire clothes out here. Don't want it stinking up the house."

He tousled her hair like he had since she was six. She'd twisted it into a messy ponytail, and it was snarled with soot, ash, and eagle nests, for all she knew.

"You had some calls on the land line," he said in a gruff tone.

"That smokejumper you went out with. You two have a thing going on?"

"Dad! No, we only went out once. We haven't seen each other all summer. How could we have a thing going?" She was impatient with Steve's unyielding, negative stance on jumpers, but at the moment she was too wiped out to get into it with him.

"Teriyaki chicken is on the grill. After your shower, you can fill me in on your fiery adventures." He grinned and picked up a spatula. "And I'll fill you in on mine."

"Okay, Dad." She motioned him to leave. "Make yourself scarce so I can undress." She unlaced her boots, tugged them off, and peeled off her stinky socks. Her sooty fire clothes were next and she stripped them off and stuffed them into the wash machine. She closed the lid, wincing at the popped blisters on her toes.

Tara tramped upstairs to her room and removed the rest of her clothes. She stepped into the shower and let the spray massage her backside. "Ohhh God…" she moaned, ducking under the hot water. She tugged off her hair tie and let her tangled, stinking hair fall around her. The water massaged her itchy scalp, and she examined her feet to see how dark the water was that swirled the drain. It was nearly black. No surprise. Her last shower was a week ago at a project fire camp on the Nez Perce Forest.

She shampooed her hair several times to remove the grit, then applied a hot oil treatment to her thick locks. She followed up with a healthy conditioner. When she stepped out and dried herself off, she worked an essential coconut oil into her hair that masked the lingering smoke smell.

Tara hurried so she could call McGuire before heading down to eat with Dad. She was surprised that he'd called the house phone and wondered how he got the number. Wrapped in a soft towel, she fell across her bed and tapped his number. Took a while before he answered. He sounded groggy.

"Travis?" she said hesitantly. "It's Tara. You know, Tara Waters."

"'Bout time you called." His low voice sounded relaxed. Sexy.

"Sorry if I woke you. How long have you been back?"

"Since this morning. Have two days off and asked to be put at the bottom of the jump list after fighting fire for eight straight weeks." He let out a sigh. "How about you? When did you demobe?"

"A little bit ago. Got your messages. How'd you get our home number?"

"Dolan. Damn near had to bribe him. Like he didn't trust me or something."

"Oh." *Great. Now my crew boss knows I'm dating Travis. So much for privacy.*

He yawned. "Are you off tomorrow?"

"Yes." The inside of her chest fluttered.

"Want to float the Blackfoot? Do some fishing?"

She perked up. "Sure. I love running that river. Do you have a boat?"

"Six-man raft. Pick you up in the morning, say nine?"

Tara's thoughts flashed to her dad and wondered how Steve would receive this information. The heck with it. She had her own life to live the way she chose to live it.

"Nine sounds great. I'll be ready."

The first order of business was to deposit one vehicle at the Blackfoot River takeout point, four miles downstream from the start location at a campground. McGuire followed Tara in her SUV and she parked her Toyota at the takeout and climbed into his Jeep for the ride to the campground.

"Here we are, back in the woods. We must be gluttons for punishment," joked Tara, assessing the fire fuel loads along the river, mainly Douglas fir and lodgepole pine. Ever since she began studying and working with wildfire, she couldn't pass a landscape without assessing its proclivity to burn.

"At least we'll be cooler on the river," responded McGuire, parking his Jeep. "It's supposed to hit triple digits this afternoon."

They untied the raft from the top of his Jeep and carried the inflated boat down to the riverbank. From under her sunglasses, Tara noted how McGuire's biceps bunched and his shoulder muscles worked as he readied the raft. This was her first good look at his partially bared physique in the sleeveless muscle-tee. Her mouth fell open in a *holy freaking shit!*

She snapped her mouth closed as he slipped on a tan fly-fishing vest, loaded with an array of colorful flies. She figured he tied his own; most guys did in this neck of the woods.

McGuire held the raft while Tara climbed in. She took the center bench next to the oars and motioned to the seat in front of her. "I always row when Dad and I float the river so he can fly fish. I know where to navigate to get you to the good trout holes." Besides, she thought. *This way I can ogle him. All. Day. Long.*

"Sounds good." McGuire shoved them off, climbed in with his fly rod, and took the bench facing her.

Tara guided them to the center of the lazy river, scanning for hazards, like rocks and sweepers, trees that have fallen into the waterway. The Blackfoot was a much-romanticized river, with a book or two written about it and even a movie, *A River Runs Through It*. Tara grew up watching it on their VCR and later on DVD, as a cult movie with her mom and dad. They loved fishing the Blackfoot.

Tara's mom had perfected her fly casting to the point where she'd become legendary in Missoula's wildland firefighting circles. Steve used to brag about his wife's fly-fishing ability, catching more fish than he did. When her dad hosted barbecues, Lucinda would demonstrate her technique in their spacious yard, giving pointers to the LoLo Hotshot crew, and talking about which flies lured the monster fish, depending on what was hatching on the river. She'd taught Tara how to fly fish, but Tara lost interest when she discovered boys in middle school.

Before leaving this morning, Tara had put on her bikini under her clothes. It was already hot, so she removed her U of M hoodie and stuffed it into her day pack. She looked up to see McGuire's sunglasses trained on her. She liked how he was looking at her—

much different than how he'd looked at her in her firefighting gear. Her blue silk bikini top was modest by swimsuit standards, but she more than filled it out.

She decided to leave her shorts on. A little skin was okay, but she didn't know McGuire well enough and still felt shy around him. Maybe she was daunted by his insane good looks and easy, confident manner. He liked who he was, and she admired that in people.

McGuire fiddled with his fly reel as the hot August sun beat down. "You're close to your dad, aren't you?" He glanced up at her.

Tara nodded. "I'm an only kid. We got super close after Mom died."

"Sorry for your loss. Dolan told me about it when he mentioned he'd fought fire with your dad. I was never close to mine. He cheated on my mom, so she left him and took me with her. Didn't see him much after that."

"Geez, that sucks. Do you see him now?"

"Only when I visit him in Colorado."

"Is that where you're from?"

"Grew up in Longmont. Then graduated from University of Colorado in Boulder."

"What made you want to jump smoke?"

"The challenge and adventure of it." His gaze rested on her a moment before he finished rigging his fly rod and began casting. He gave her a crooked smile. "Don't worry. I won't snag you."

"Thanks for that. Not a fan of plucking fish hooks from my body." Tara glanced from left to right, expertly guiding the raft between two large boulders. She loved the sound of the water as it purled around the rocks and eddied.

Tara loved watching a good fly caster and McGuire was good.

He turned to the side, pulled out some line, and with a forward motion, flew his line out in front. When it straightened, he whipped his hand back, the fly on the end snapping back and soaring overhead, behind him. He flipped it forward and settled the fly lightly on the water's surface, as a live caddis fly would land.

Snap! A sizeable trout snatched it. McGuire reeled, but the fish got off when he brought it close. "Shit! Did you see the size of that rainbow?"

"I'm still blown away by how fast he scarfed your fly." Tara laughed. "You're really good at this. My mom would be impressed." She explained to Travis about her mother's fly-fishing prowess.

"Wish I could have known her," he said, reeling in his line. "Do you want to cast?"

She shook her head. "Nah. That's my mom and dad's thing. Not mine."

The afternoon floated by with small talk as she navigated, and Travis fished. He caught two more nice-sized rainbows by the time Tara spotted their takeout point. She steered them to the riverbank, where they unloaded their stuff, then took out the raft and deflated it. They joked and laughed as they folded it and tied it to the top of Tara's SUV with multiple bungee cords.

They'd each had a couple beers on their float down the lazy river, and coupled with the warm sun, Tara had a slight buzz. "Let's sit down a minute," she suggested, pulling her water bottle from her pack, and unscrewing the lid.

McGuire plopped down on the grassy riverbank and Tara sunk down next to him.

"Thanks for today. A much-needed break from all things fire." He slipped his arm around her shoulders and goosebumps rose on her arms, despite the heat. "You're an expert at river running."

"Thanks. I do my best." She smiled.

Tara retrieved cheese and crackers and set to work making cracker sandwiches. When she offered him one, McGuire leaned in and pressed his lips to hers in a light, lingering kiss. She tasted beer mixed with the brownies she'd made before bed last night.

He lifted away and stroked a tendril of hair that fell from her messy bun. "Is there anyone I should be concerned about besides your dad?" He took the cheese and crackers from her hand and popped them in his mouth.

"What do you mean?"

"Anyone else that would object to my dating you?" His solemn look made her smile.

She thought a minute. "Maybe the Lolo Hotshots."

He pulled back startled. "What, like you dated the entire crew? So, you're one of *those* women?" he teased.

She laughed. "Ha, no, they're protective of me because Dad used to work with them. We still spend holidays and birthdays together. They're family, like having a bunch of aunts and uncles."

"Glad you told me that. I'll make sure I tread lightly."

"How do you plan to do that?" She gave him a seductive look.

"You tell me." He removed his sunglasses and pulled her close. His mouth covered hers and she became lightheaded when he rubbed her bare back and deepened the kiss. The murmuring river and the slight breeze in the treetops faded, as she lost herself in him.

When his hand paused at the clasp of her bikini top, she tensed.

A car door slammed, and kids ran down the path to the

riverbank and picked up rocks to toss.

McGuire broke the kiss and Tara opened her eyes. "We're officially dating. I don't kiss just any guy like that."

"I hope not. Now that I've snagged you without a hook." He stood and offered her his hand. "Let's grab a pizza on our way home."

She squeezed his hand. "Pepperoni."

Tara still reeled big time from his kiss. Her body tingled as she started her Toyota and drove them to get McGuire's car upstream. Before he got out, he leaned across. "I need one for the road."

She met him halfway and they swished tongues in a lingering kiss before he climbed out.

Tara liked this new guy in her life. He was a breath of fresh air; someone she wanted to spend time with. Not to mention he was hot as hell. Back when they'd walked around the Smokejumper Base, Tara had inwardly compared him to the wall photos of other jumpers. No one came close to McGuire's striking looks and splendid brawn. She couldn't believe that *she* had snagged *him*—without even casting.

But deep down she knew many would judge, especially Dad and Jim Dolan. Which made McGuire even more alluring—like a bad boy. That excited her more than anything. From what she knew of McGuire so far, he was far from it. So, let everyone else think the opposite.

She liked that even better.

Toward the end of fire season, another flurry of thunderstorms rolled across the Rockies, unleashing a swarm of lightning strikes upon unsuspecting trees. And where there's lightning, there's fire.

Tara dispatched with her crew, this time to central and eastern Montana, where wind was a constant. She stayed at a project fire camp for two weeks near Red Lodge, where they used the Red Lodge ski building as the Incident Command center. These fires burned fast and hot, a wind-driven conflagration that kept Tara busy for twelve-to-fourteen-hour shifts, all the way until the end of September.

She'd received a few texts from Travis, before he jumped fires in Idaho and Colorado. His last text was from Oregon, after the west coast had undergone triple-digit temperatures:

Can't wait to see you again.

Tara texted back:

Me too! along with a heart emoji.

On the last day of the season during the first week of October, Tara turned in her fire tools and Nomex shirt and pants, well-worn and not as bright as when they were issued at the beginning of the fire season.

She'd applied to work part time at MTDC but didn't have to report until November. *I have three weeks off!* Her head filled with all kinds of ways to spend her time. Front and center were thoughts of how she'd spend time with a certain smokejumper.

Travis had been gone on fire assignments all over The West, and she hadn't seen him since their float down the Blackfoot. She enjoyed naughty thoughts about the six-foot-tall smokejumper with the charismatic smile and dark curly locks she fantasized running her fingers through.

Her first week of freedom she lounged around, catching up on movies and binging on TV series. She read a few books while her dad worked the day shift. He'd asked her to figure out which trees to cut to create a defensible space around their log home now that the fire season had wound down. They'd talked about doing it at the beginning of summer and neither of them got around to it.

Finally, on a crisp fall afternoon, Tara assessed their property with a spray can of paint and sprayed an orange 'X' on the conifers that needed to go. Especially ones that had dried out close to the house, stressed from the extended drought. Dad had ordered her not to chainsaw anything unless he was home to be her spotter.

As she stepped toward a towering lodgepole pine to determine whether it was a 'keep' tree, her cell sounded with the song, *Burn, Baby Burn.* She fished it from her pocket, grinned at the Caller ID, and answered.

"You're back!" she smiled into the phone.

"Hi beautiful. Got in this morning from Southern California."

A top popped on a beverage can.

"Having a brew already? It's not five o'clock yet," she teased.

"It's sparkling water. Busy tonight?"

"Not anymore." *Honestly, I should play a little hard to get.* She gave herself an eyeroll. "I mean, I hadn't made any plans."

"Dinner and a movie? It's too chilly for a river float."

Tara laughed. "Come on, Travis. Where's that Big Sky heartiness?"

"Left it in California with the ungodly heat. Glad to be home."

"I'd love dinner. How about I pick you up this time?" The last thing Tara wanted was a run-in with her dad about going out with McGuire. It was easier to say she was going out with friends and was the designated driver.

"Sure," he said easily. "How about six?"

"It's a date," said Tara. "See you at six outside your quarters."

She hated lying to Dad. Up until now, they'd had an up front and honest relationship, and she wanted to keep it that way. At the same time, she wanted the freedom to date who she wanted. Dad hadn't mentioned McGuire lately. Out of sight, out of mind.

Tara abandoned her defensible space project and scooted inside to take a shower. If she hurried, she could be gone before Dad came home from work. Avoid any hassle. She finished showering and worked at the speed of light to get ready. She wore a forest green, form fitting cardigan and skinny jeans, and let her long, red hair air dry. She loosely curled a few strands on the sides with her curling iron.

She'd dreamed about Travis during their long separations and each time her dreams had become increasingly erotic. She'd fantasized making love with him in all kinds of exotic places.

As she pulled up to the Smokejumper Base, she steadied her gaze on his luscious form. He looked like a movie star stepping off a set after a day of shooting a smokejumper movie. She almost crashed into him as she wheeled close to the curb, and he jumped back in comical surprise.

Tara laughed as he swung open the passenger door. She was so excited to see him she scrambled out and rounded the SUV to give him a full-on embrace, in front of God and everyone. A few heads turned, but she didn't give a flip who saw her hug and kiss him like he was the last man on earth. "I've missed you! Geez, it's been so long," she gushed.

"It has. Thought about you and wondered which fires you were on." He lifted her hand and kissed it.

"Our crew is done for the season. I've already applied for the Lolo Hotshots next year." She beamed at him. "And guess what? I don't start at MTDC until November."

"Really?" He tugged her close. "In that case, let's go somewhere. Just the two of us."

"I would love that! What do you have in mind?"

"How about The Edgewater? Dinner and…maybe stay the night?"

She shot him a startled look. "You mean tonight? Staying together—like in the same room?"

He laughed. "No, in separate rooms," he teased. "Yeah, in the same room. But only if you want to."

"Hmm, I'll have to think about that."

"No, you won't."

Her insides turned to goo when he planted a soft kiss on her parted lips. Forbidden fruit be damned—she wanted him.

"You're right. I won't," she squeaked out, gazing into his dark, chocolate eyes.

She was more than ready to know Travis McGuire just a little bit better.

Tara waited until her dad was in bed before calling to say she wouldn't be home tonight. She knew her call would go to voice mail, and she hesitated before lying about where she was staying—with Katy. She hated lying to Dad—but when Travis had sprung this invitation, all her reasoning combusted, and she'd melted like a flaming marshmallow.

After a light dinner at The Edgewater Restaurant, they stopped at the reception counter and checked into a room. Tara glanced nervously around, hoping no one in their fire world would spot them. She didn't want word to get back to Jim Dolan, who would tell Dad. She fiercely guarded her privacy when it came to Travis.

"King bed or two queens?" asked the clerk, directing her question to Travis. She glanced at Tara, then back at Travis.

"King," he said, winking at Tara.

She hoped the heat in her cheeks wasn't obvious. She'd never done anything like this—gone to a hotel with a guy. It dawned on her they were doing this with the objective to have sex, and her stomach squeezed.

The hotel clerk handed Travis the key cards to their room, and they ambled down a long corridor. He inserted the key card into a door near the end. It opened into a room that overlooked the Clark

Fork River.

Tara walked inside and Travis followed her in and closed the door. She turned to him. “I’ve never done anything like this.”

He rested his hands on her shoulders. “We won’t do anything you aren’t comfortable with. If you want to watch TV or just talk, that’s fine by me. I want you to myself longer than a few hours at a time. Which is all we’ve had for the last—how many months?”

“Five. Five months since the day you walked into my fire refresher training class.” She smiled.

“Every time I jumped a fire, I thought of you. You’re the kind of woman a guy doesn’t forget.” He stroked her hair.

“Can you please hold me for a while? I just want you to hold me.” She turned her head to the side and rested it on his shoulder.

His arms came around her and he nuzzled her hair. They stood quiet holding each other for a long while. Travis broke the silence. “Want to go out on the deck and watch the river?”

“Sure.”

He took her by the hand to the small private deck that overlooked the slow waters of the Clark Fork. The sun had disappeared over the mountains, sending pink and orange streaks across the Missoula valley, where scattered maple tree leaves had turned a neon yellow and orange. “This reminds me of when we floated the Blackfoot.”

“That was a good day. Even though I lost that blue ribbon trout,” he said, brushing back her hair to kiss her, sending electric pulses to all her nerve endings.

She could stand out here and kiss him all night. But it was time to turn her erotic dreams into reality. “It’s chilly out here. Let’s go in." She longed for him to hold her again.

They went inside and Tara headed for the bed. She rolled to her side and gazed up at him, moving her palm over the space next to her. "Come here, McGuire. Tell me about the fires you jumped."

He seized the invitation and slid onto the bed, facing her. "Well, one fire had whorls that were pretty scary on the Oregon Deschutes fires." He lifted her hand and kissed her palm.

Electricity shot through her. "So, uh, what did you do?" Her breath caught when he leaned in, brushed her hair back, and kissed her neck.

His lips moved against her neck. "We jumped a mile from it…misjudged the fire behavior…" He kissed his way down her neck and eased her sweater off one shoulder. Kissed it.

She did a quick inhale and rolled onto her back. "Then what?" she whispered.

Travis unbuttoned her cardigan while kissing her throat. "We gathered our chutes…" He eased a bra strap from one shoulder. Kissed it. "…and ran like hell…"

"And you got away so you could return to me." She tugged his head up so she could kiss him full on the lips. He took her mouth and plunged his tongue inside hers, hungry for her. She ached deep down inside for him as she brushed her hands over his shoulder and along his bicep. He opened her sweater and kissed the tops of her breasts.

Her breath came fast. "We need to get down to business," she murmured, pushing him off her. She undid her jeans and wriggled out of them while he tugged his off. He unclasped her bra and eased it off, then tugged off his briefs. The more he unwrapped himself, the more beautiful he became.

Travis pulled back the bed covers and they slipped between the soft sheets, all warm and cozy in the crisp autumn evening. They explored one another, gliding palms over bare skin. Tara couldn't get over how exquisite and firm his abdomen and back muscles felt. Turned her on even more.

"You're so soft," he whispered in her ear, then kissed it. He ran his tongue around it, which sent her flying off to space.

"Make love to me." How could something others considered wrong feel so damn good? Wrong by everyone's standards but hers.

She was shy about touching him, but he took care of that by touching her first. She tensed, not yet used to his touch, but her want of him took over. She massaged him, then guided him inside of her.

"Wait a second," he cautioned, backing out. He unrolled a condom onto himself.

He moved inside her, and they rocked gently together. Long and slow. Passionate. He felt so good she wanted this to last forever. She couldn't hold herself back—couldn't control her need to have all of him inside of her. She rushed headlong into her peak and let out a moan that went on so long she startled herself.

"Oh baby, I'm right there with you," panted Travis, as he hit his and cried out her name. He stopped moving and stayed on top of her, their hearts thumping together a zillion beats per minute.

She loved his heart thumping against hers. This was right. It had to be.

He's The One, she thought, holding back happy tears. He

really is.

He's The One.

November and December were a blur. Here it was Christmastime and Tara hadn't any shopping done. Travis had spent November jumping fires in California and Arizona. December was the first time they'd had uninterrupted time together. Tara worked part time during the week while finishing up her classes and spent evenings at the library working on her master's thesis.

On the weekends, Travis worked ski patrol at Snow Bowl, north of town. Tara loved downhill skiing but wasn't as expert on the moguls like Travis. His legs were rubber bands, so pliable, as they bounced up and down as he aggressively took on the advanced mogul runs. She loved the graceful way he plied the slopes. He didn't seem the least intimidated by anything. Bold. Fearless. And that made her hot for him all over again.

Tara had put herself on birth control after that first night at The Edgewater. After their first five months of sporadic dating, December felt like they were getting to know each other all over again.

Steve Waters still disapproved of their involvement, but Travis worked hard to win Tara's dad over. He'd come to the house and talk firefighting and that helped, but Steve's adamant determination to keep that chip on his shoulder irritated Tara. Instead, she felt a wedge growing between them that distressed her.

"Your insistence on seeing that smokejumper won't end well. Break it off before you get hurt," he'd say to her on occasion.

"His name is Travis, Dad. Please stop obsessing about him. He's a good person. He wouldn't do anything to hurt me." *How many times must I say this?*

"Guard your heart. I don't trust him," he'd say, as if it were some sort of premonition. But at least Dad didn't argue as much as he had in the beginning.

She hoped she was wearing him down.

The Forest Service manned a visitor center at Lolo Pass on winter weekends for cross-country skiers, forty-seven miles from town. Tara had signed up as a volunteer to work on Christmas Eve, stay the night at the cabin, and drive home Christmas Day. When she'd signed up back in September, she'd planned for Dad to go with her as he always had. Tara and her parents spent every Christmas Eve cross-country skiing at Lolo Pass, from the time she was old enough to ski, at three years old. When Mom passed away, Tara and Steve continued the family tradition.

For the first time ever, Dad declined to ski this year. He claimed his arthritis had kicked in and he didn't feel up to it. At first Tara was alarmed, but when Jim Dolan invited Steve and a few wildland fire buddies over for a Christmas poker game, she figured he'd be fine.

So, she invited Travis.

He drove his Jeep with four-wheel drive, because as luck would have it, it had snowed a foot during the night, with no signs of letting up. Climbing the snowy pass wasn't an issue for traction as much as it was for visibility. It took twice the normal time to drive the forty-seven miles south of town up Highway 93, then on Highway 12 to the Montana-Idaho border. Snowplows labored in the heavy snow when they arrived, carving a path around the visitor's center, and plowing the parking lot.

Tara hopped out of the Jeep, flush with excitement. "The skiing will be fantastic with all this snow!" She repeatedly clapped her mittens together with a dull thud.

Travis laughed. "Look at you, you're like a little kid." He released the ski holders on top of the Jeep and lifted their cross-country skis off the roof rack.

"You're going to love this." She inserted the key in the lock to the visitor's center and held the door open for Travis, who gave her a fast peck on the lips on his way inside. "I have to stay here until five p.m. Go ski the trails and I'll catch up to you when I'm done. We can ski into a hot spring later for a soak. I brought head lamps." She offered him one and set her pack behind a wood counter.

"I'll take you up on that." Travis took the headlamp and suited up to take on the trails. "Snow is deep up here. We'll have to break trail."

She handed him a trail map and showed him which trail to take. "Don't get lost, McGuire. Cell phones don't work up here."

"I'm a smokejumper and a ski patrol guy. Trust me, I won't get lost."

"Okay. See you later, Hot Stuff." Tara looked up to see a family of four come in as Travis left. She took out the Forest Service brochures with the trail maps and lined them out on where to go.

The rest of the day brought a steady stream of skiers into the visitor's center, and soon it was time to close the doors for the day. She couldn't wait to get out on the trails and ski with Travis. After closing, she pushed through the deep snow to the cabin, behind the visitor's center in the snow-laden pines. She suited up and snapped on her skis, then set off on the trail she'd shown Travis.

She swished along, loving the stillness and the quiet. The snow made everything feel magical. She pushed her skis, breaking trail where snow was deepest. She noted fresh tracks. Travis must be ahead of her. This trail ended at the hot springs and that's why she told him to follow it.

Tara broke out of the trees into a small clearing and saw steam rising. The hot springs. Travis was nowhere in sight.

That's strange, thought Tara. *I know I told him to take this trail.*

She called out. "Travis? Are you here?"

Silence. A slight breeze dumped snow on her from a bough above. She brushed it off her face. "Travis? Where are you? Answer me!" Tara didn't like the unsettled knocking in her chest. *Where the heck did he go?* Maybe he took a wrong turn someplace. She hesitated, then turned around. She flipped on her headlamp. Darkness dropped fast without her realizing it.

Tara skied as fast as she dared. The woods felt eerie in her anxious state, even with the snow brightening both sides of the ski trail. Every so often she called out for Travis.

No answer.

When she reached the visitor center half an hour later, she unsnapped her skis and slogged through the snow to the cabin. She went inside and everything was as she'd left it. Fear clenched her chest. *What if something happened to Travis?*

She raced outside and looked wildly around in the dark. She walked to the visitor's center and scoured the parking lot. No sign of him.

Shit.

Tara snapped on her skis and got back on the trail to the hot springs. She blew through the snow as fast as she could, working arms and legs in a fast-paced rhythm. Her lungs nearly burst as she broke free from the narrow trail in the towering, snow-covered pines. Her headlamp showed steam rising. The hot springs.

She spotted a beam of light.

"Tara!" McGuire called out.

Thank God. Relief flooded her, upon hearing his voice. She glided forward and her beam of light shone on Travis, standing on his skis, smiling at her.

"McGuire! Where the hell were you? I've been looking all over the place."

"Got off the trail somehow when it got dark. Had to backtrack." He skied to her, then unsnapped his skis and put his arms around her. "Sorry I worried you."

Her uneasy concern must have been evident, judging by how hard he hugged her. She swallowed a lump in her throat. "I never thought—when I couldn't find you, I guess I panicked—the thought of losing you—" she choked on her words.

"Losing me? Ohh, baby." His empathetic tone comforted her. He lifted her chin and kissed the tears that fell on her cheeks. "Does this mean what I think it does?"

She only looked at him, unable to form the words she wanted

to say…afraid to say them.

"In that case, take off your skis," he ordered.

"What? Why?" she stuttered.

The black of night muddied his movements as he skillfully stabbed her ski clasp and snapped it open to release her foot. He did the same to her other ski. "Step over here." The beam from his headlamp bobbed as he led her by the hand.

When she followed him to the steaming pool of water, he turned off his headlamp and knelt on one knee in the snow. "This is as good a time as any."

Before she could react, he held out a small white box. "Tara Waters, soon to be a hotshot firefighter…will you marry me?"

The words shocked her senses and her mind reeled. *Did he just say that?*

She pulled off a mitten and flipped the box open. Bright snow lit the diamond just enough to sparkle it, even in the dark. "Oh my gosh, this is beautiful, Trav! Did you plan this?"

He laughed. "Sort of. I planned to ask you next to a roaring fire, followed by me making mad, passionate love to you in the cabin." The way the shadows fell on his face as he looked up at her made her fall head over heels in love all over again.

Tara honest-to-God didn't know what to say. She stood gawking at the ring, open-mouthed as she catapulted over the Big Dipper in the night sky.

Travis looked up at her. "Are you going to keep me kneeling in the snow? You haven't answered my question."

She plummeted back to earth. "Yes, yes, I want to marry you!"

"Hoping you'd say that." He closed the ring box and stuck it in his coat pocket. "I'll hang onto this until we're back in the cabin.

Then I'll make it official."

Her heart imploded into a million pieces as he rose to give her a panty-vaporizing kiss that buckled her knees. He broke the kiss and nipped her lower one. "Let's go. I'll race you." He snapped on his skis.

"You're on." Tara had never skied so fast in her life. Tonight—this time, this place, this smokejumper—she would freeze-frame in her mind.

Forever.

The following May, Tara graduated with her master's degree and Travis made love to her that night in her black graduation gown, hood, and sash. Earlier, Dad threw a huge party at the house that seemed to draw every available firefighter, both city and wildland fire. And everyone put cards with money into Tara's hardhat.

"I'm rich!" she announced gleefully, dancing around after sharing a bottle of champagne with Travis at the party.

As spring led to summer, Tara and Travis spent June through August reluctantly apart, working fires in different western states. Tara kept in touch by texting him, but service was spotty, and most of the time she was lucky to have one or two bars of shitty cell service.

When Tara discovered they were both in town on Travis' thirty-third birthday, she had the delicious idea to get the same room at The Edgewater as they had a year ago. She wanted to give Travis a special birthday gift—an all-night sex fest, since they hadn't been together much this summer. It was the twenty-fifth of August, and by wonderful coincidence, both of their work schedules meshed on this hot August night.

Travis still lived in shared quarters at the Smokejumper Base, and Tara stayed with her dad. She and Travis had discussed moving in together, but Tara was reluctant to leave her father all alone—she couldn't bring herself to move out.

While Dad tolerated Travis, he still hadn't warmed to Tara marrying him. To his credit, he'd mostly kept his mouth shut and only spoke up when she and Travis had arguments. They were rare, but intense—because of the pressures and schedules of their firefighting jobs, and the travel required to do them.

When Tara closed the hotel room door after they'd checked in, she turned around and leaned against the door. Travis wasted no time and covered her mouth with a penetrating kiss. She felt his need and her want of him met that need. The two of them clawed at each other's clothes.

"Oh God," moaned Travis, when he saw her naked in the moonlight, as it streamed through the window. He devoured every inch of her, running his palms over her body and kissing her until she ordered him to get inside of her.

He complied, and it didn't take long for both to reach their peaks to nirvana. Tara first, then Travis. Afterwards, they rolled onto their backs, collecting their breath, their skin glistening in the moonlight. After a while the moon disappeared, and distant thunder rumbled.

Tara leaned over him, running her palms tenderly over his pecs and rippled abs. "I love being with you," she said softly.

"Me too." He enfolded her in his arms and held her until they fell asleep.

A crack of thunder startled them awake. Tara sat up, squinting, then rose to open the door to the small deck next to the rushing river. Lightning lit the sky southeast of town, and thunder instantly snapped. A severe storm cut loose overhead as neon lavender lit the skies.

Travis joined her on the deck as a bolt of lightning struck Mount Sentinel and tell-tale smoke shot up in rapid response. "Ignition, dammit," he muttered. He ducked inside, struggling into his t-shirt and pants. He turned on his phone and sure enough, it lit up like fireworks. *"FIRE CALL!"*

"Got to go, babe. Sentinel isn't the only strike. Blue Mountain and the Rattlesnake have been hit. You'll have to drive me to the base," he said, scrambling for his overnight bag. He gave her a quick peck on the cheek.

"At least we had *some* time together." Tara tossed on her sundress and sandals, gathered her stuff, and followed Travis out the door. They bolted for her SUV, and Tara broke every speed limit through the pounding rain out to the base. When she pulled up, Travis leaned across for a quick kiss. "Love you, babe. See you after." Before she could respond, he was out, slammed the door, and he was gone.

"Love you too!" she called after him. She lifted her phone: Three p.m. Suddenly it vibrated and lit up. Jim Dolan calling. Great, she had to report for a fire call.

She tapped it. "Hi Jim. I'm at the Smokejumper Base and have to go home to gear up before I can get there," she pushed out in one breath. She shifted the SUV into park, with the engine idling.

Silence on the phone. "You're all right," said Jim, sounding relieved.

"Yes, I'm fine. Why?" A chill raced up her spine.

"So, you weren't in the house. Tara, it's Steve—your dad…" His voice muffled as he trailed off.

"What Jim? What? Is he with you?"

"Tara, you need to drive here to my house. Now." His voice sounded odd.

"Jim, don't fuck with me. Where's Dad?"

"Lightning struck Pattee Canyon. It all went up fast—before anyone could do anything—"

She cut him off. "Are jumpers or crews there? Talk to me, Jim." She couldn't control the tremor in her voice.

"Tara—your house is gone. Steve—Steve…was inside. No time to get out. A neighbor tried to get him—it went too fucking fast."

"No, Jim! You're lying—it can't be real…" screamed Tara, disbelieving. This can't be happening.

His voice broke. "I wish I were lying…"

"Stop it Jim, this is nothing to joke about." Tara had witnessed Jim's pranks and teasing in the past, but this was no time for such foolishness.

"Chrissakes Tara, I'm not joking. Get over to my house. Now!"

No-o-o-o!" She flung open the car door and tried to run back to the smokejumper quarters. She didn't make it—instead, she doubled over and collapsed to the sidewalk, phone flying from her grip. The crushing pain of sudden loss swallowed her. "Not Dad!

He's a firefighter, Oh God…oh God oh God no-o-o-o!"

"Tara! Tara!" called out Jim from her phone as she writhed on the pavement, raindrops pelting her, drowning her in torment.

A whirring plane engine drowned everything out as a Twin Otter lifted off in the pounding rain and disappeared into black clouds.

"Travis! No, come back! Please, please, you can't leave now, you can't!" she sobbed, utterly helpless on the sidewalk, paralyzed with pain and grief. Rage rose inside her like bile, and she let out an agonized wail. "I hate fricking fire! It steals everyone from me!" She curled into a fetal position on her side and howled into the saturated wind. "Why? Why? Why…?"

Suddenly, a pair of hands lifted her from the wet pavement and carried her to a waiting vehicle, wipers going and rain dimming the headlights. Someone talked to her and wrapped a blanket around her drenched, trembling body and settled her into a back seat. A woman climbed in and put an arm around her.

"We're taking you to Jim Dolan's house. We'll make sure your car gets there too. You're in no shape to drive," the woman said, gently brushing back long tendrils stuck to Tara's cheeks.

Tara turned to the woman in a smokejumper t-shirt. "What happened? Can someone please tell me what happened?"

"Jim will explain," was all she said.

Tara stared at blurry lights as they passed into the university district and stopped on McCleod Street. Dolan's house. Her world had become grotesquely surreal, like she was watching herself and everything else from a distance.

Jim met them at the curb and helped Tara from the car. "Thank you," she said numbly to the woman who gave her a hug, ducked in the vehicle, and it pulled away.

"Say it isn't true. Tell me Dad is okay. Damn it, Jim, say it!" She searched his face, hungry for the words: *Steve is all right. Your dad is okay.*

But it was not to be. All she saw was pain and anguish on his face, as he enveloped her in a hug.

Her mind desperately groped for logic, an explanation. But the cold bitter truth was, she'd had sex with Travis the one time her father had needed her—and she hadn't been there.

"I should have stayed home…he'd be alive, oh God Jim, I could have saved him! I could have gotten him out. And I didn't—cut the—fucking trees!" Tara choked out between sobs. "I didn't cut the trees and they torched the house. It's all my fault, all my fault, I didn't—"

"Stop it, Tara!" Jim gripped her shoulders and gave her a slight shake. "Nothing you could do—nothing anyone could do. Sometimes fire just fucking wins…" he moaned, trailing off. His head fell forward, and his shoulders shook as he wept.

Tara had never seen him cry. She pulled him to her and clung to him and they cried…and cried…and cried. Two souls. Two firefighters—one wracked with unrelenting guilt and unbearable loss; the other, grieving a hundred thousand wonderful things Steve Waters would never get to do again.

Each agonizing they would have given anything to prevent Steve's death. Loving father. Best friend. Devoted husband. Dedicated firefighter. Courageous hero—a man who'd loved his wife and daughter more than life itself.

A man who'd lost his life to the one commanding force he'd valiantly battled hundreds of times. The force they had all battled and fought, sometimes winning, sometimes losing.

Fire.

Tara sat back in the pew, fixated on the small pine box resting on a tall table at the front of St. Francis church. Still in denial that it contained the remains of Steve Waters—what few remains had been found. *I should have cut the damn trees. I'm so sorry, Dad, it's my fault. I didn't cut the trees...*

The modest pine box was fitting for a man who'd loved the woods and his beloved Rocky Mountains. Jim Dolan had fashioned the box from Dad's favorite pine, a Douglas Fir that miraculously hadn't been destroyed by the fire.

Tara was inconsolable. *Dad is dead.* Didn't the world know she was hurting? How can everyone go about their lives as if nothing had happened? Didn't people care?

Travis had demob'ed in time to attend the service. He strode in, wearing a suit and sat in the front row seat Tara had saved for him. She hadn't seen him since the tragic fire and though he looked a million in the dark suit, he seemed alien to her.

"Trav, I needed you—you flew off…and I needed you—" She couldn't let go of the image imprinted on her mind—his jump plane taking off as she learned of her father's death, crumpling alone on the hard, wet pavement. It was all she remembered from that horrible night.

At least Travis was here now. He was the only stability she had left.

"I know, babe. I'm here now. I'm so sorry I left that night. I didn't know…" He cradled her head to his chest and stroked her as she clutched his strong arms.

She lifted her head to look at him. "Trav, I should have stayed home that night." Her voice shook. "I could have gotten him out. He'd be alive now."

"Don't say that. It wasn't your fault. You could have died in that fire too," he said firmly. He lifted her chin. "Look at me. Don't blame yourself."

"Dad and I were always going to cut those stupid trees next to the house. How ironic is *that?* We're firefighters for chrissakes. We preach about defensible space. And we didn't cut our own flipping trees."

She was all cried out. She couldn't squeeze out another tear if her life depended on it, but the pain in her chest was merciless. "The fire torched the second story first. It burned so hot they only found his bone fragments. He just—vaporized."

Travis spoke softly in a low, steady voice. "I'll help you through this, Babe. Don't blame yourself. Don't go down that road. It's a losing battle, don't fucking do it."

She lifted her chin, looking at him with trust in her eyes. "Thank you for being here."

"Wouldn't have it any other way." He kept his arm around her, and she leaned into him for strength.

Looking around at the other faces almost undid her. Every

wildland firefighter that had worked with her dad, as well as those who hadn't, stood in unison to pay their respects. The LoLo Interagency Hotshots, along with other U.S. Forest Service firefighters, stood straight and tall in their yellow Nomex shirts and green pants, hands clasping wrists. They filled one side of St. Francis church, occupying row after row of pews. The Missoula city fire department filled the other side in their dress uniforms.

When the funeral ended, Travis took Tara's elbow and urged her to stand. She smoothed the wrinkles in her black silk dress with an out of body sensation, as if someone else stood in the black dress and peep-toe heels. She remembered the last time she'd worn black stilettos. *Mom's funeral.*

Her brain fogged with the realization that she was an orphan.

Travis guided her to the front of the church. She'd requested to carry the pine box from the church to the base and had stubbornly argued with the clergy about it. She won out because she was her father's daughter.

Travis lifted the box and handed it to her. She wrapped her arms around it and with downcast eyes, she proceeded down the center aisle, followed by her smokejumper. Everyone else filed out to drive to the jump base, where a separate firefighter memorial service was scheduled for Steve Cornelius Waters.

The sun bore down on this last day of August as she stepped toward Travis' Jeep. No one should have to say a final goodbye on such a beautiful day. Tara didn't remember the drive to the base. She numbly got out and followed Travis inside.

She used to like fire. And liked fighting it. Now she hated its evil destruction—how it robbed everything of life. She'd always braced herself for Dad to die firefighting—but never in his own house fire.

Familiar faces smiled as Travis led her to the front row of a huge roomful of chairs. She was blown away by the number of people there to pay last respects. The city fire folks lined the walls as the wildland firefighters filled the chairs, in deference to the thirty years of firefighting Steve Waters had spent with the U.S. Forest Service.

Tara squeezed Travis' hand as Dad's previous supervisors got up and talked about his illustrious and brave career in wildland firefighting and how he'd turned down job offers to move up into the ranks of ops chief and management. He'd refused, not because he didn't think he could handle the responsibility, but because he loved his boots on the ground.

Jim Dolan took the podium and Tara locked gazes with him. The sound of Jim's voice sent Tara back to happier times. Like when they'd hike the surrounding mountains to get Tara into shape to apply for the handline fire crew with the Missoula Ranger District. Dad couldn't talk her out of wildland firefighting. Jim told him to give up trying to stop her—she was hellbent to do it anyway. Together they'd hike steep slopes with rocks in her pack, to the point she'd cry and beg him to lighten her load.

"Suck it up. You won't have a choice in a bad fire situation," Dad would bark at her. "There's no crying in firefighting!"

Jim talked about how he'd sneak his bandana to Tara so she could wipe her tears as she struggled on, mean-faced, taking those last agonizing steps up the damn mountain. Then, Jim told a funny story about a fire he and Steve fought on the Idaho Panhandle. On their hike out after a fire fight, they'd encountered a group of ladies skinny-dipping in a lake and Steve threatened to steal their clothes.

Jim had the room howling with laughter by the end of it.

Jim settled into a soliloquy about how he met Steve Waters. "We served in Viet Nam together and afterward we got on with the Lolo Interagency Hotshots. Steve taught fire science at the University of Montana, where he met the love of his life, Lucinda. When she died, Steve asked me to be Tara's legal guardian in the event something happened to him." He flicked his eyes up at Tara. "Although Tara is now a responsible adult…right, Tara?" He gave her his stink eye that sent a titter around the room. "I won't forget my promise to Steve to keep an eye on her. That is, if she behaves herself with that smokejumper of hers."

A rumble of laughter circulated the room and Tara placed a palm on her chest to let Jim know she appreciated his sentiment.

Jim didn't talk about how Dad didn't approve of her relationship with Travis, and that suited Tara just fine. *Come to think of it, there's nothing to stop me from marrying him now,* she thought. Subconsciously, she'd delayed the wedding because of Dad's disapproval.

Jim ended his talk and introduced the city fire battalion chief, who talked about Steve's years fighting fire with the city fire department. When the battalion chief finished, he approached Tara with her dad's fire helmet and offered it to her.

"Steve Waters was legendary in the department. I entrust his helmet to you with honor and respect." He stepped back and dipped his chin, with a fist on his heart.

Bagpipes played *Amazing Grace* and Tara fought for composure as she accepted the helmet. She trembled and her chest heaved. Travis gripped her shoulder and squeezed it tight.

When the song ended, a U.S. Army man in dark, military dress stepped to the microphone. “Steve Waters was an aviation warrant officer pilot in Viet Nam for several years in the late 60s.” He went on to talk about her dad’s service time in the U.S. Army as a helicopter pilot and how many lives he’d saved. When he concluded, he marched forward and stood rigid in front of Tara.

“Miss Waters. On behalf of the President of the United States, the U.S. Army, and a grateful nation, please accept this flag as a symbol of our appreciation for your loved one’s honorable and faithful service.”

“Thank you,” she mumbled. The red, white, and blue blurred as she placed her palms on either side to accept the triangular flag. She pressed it to her chest.

The officer saluted her and stepped back.

Jim announced for everyone to step outside for the final, traditional sendoff. First the wildland firefighter sendoff, then city fire. Not many firefighters had such a combination at a funeral and Tara knew how special this was.

Once people had assembled on the tarmac, Jim stepped over to Tara and flicked his eyes at Travis. “Me and McGuire arranged a special flyover for Steve. He wasn’t a smokejumper, but his exceptional fire career and his time as a chopper pilot in Vietnam warrants one. So, I pulled some strings with fire aviation.” He winked and smiled at her.

Tara hugged him. “Thanks, Jim, I appreciate it. And I know dad would.”

Jim turned away, his aviator shades shielding his eyes she

knew were filled with emotion.

Tara lifted Travis' hand and kissed it. "Thank you."

Travis nodded, his face solemn as he pulled her in tight.

She heard them before she saw them. The sound of aerial firefighting. The distinct, metallic *whup-whup* of rotor blades chopping the air. Everyone's heads tilted up.

Three red-and-white, Bell 205 helicopters came thundering from the west, in a perfect side-by-side formation. As they approached the crowd, one lifted away in a missing-man formation in an aerial salute. Tara glimpsed Jim, his mouth in a straight line, gazing up at the choppers. She saw a wet cheek and he swiped at it, unable to mask his own heartbreak.

As the rotor aircraft faded, a loud siren echoed throughout the base. The sound bounced off the tarmac and adjacent runways for several seconds, then faded.

"Final fire call for Steven Cornelius Waters," announced Jim over the sound system. "Rest in peace."

A woman in a U.S. Army dress uniform stood at the edge of the runway and faced west. She lifted a bugle to her lips and played *Taps*.

This undid Tara. The finality of it all hit home, slamming her chest against her spine.

She choked back a sob, summoned every ounce of self-control she had, and forced back the flood of tears…because Steve Waters always said…

There's no crying in firefighting.

"It's the first of October already. We need to set a date for our wedding," said Tara, as she chomped on toast in the kitchen of the small apartment she now shared with Travis. "And we need to talk about what'll happen—you know, after we're married."

Travis told her the last time he'd come home that he thought Tara should stop firefighting. They'd argued about it. Frankly, Tara had been surprised that he'd suggested it. He knew she was working on her master's degree in fire science. Did he expect her to quit firefighting to be a housewife? She hadn't planned on ending her fire career once she was married. With Travis gone on extended duty, it had been impossible to discuss much of anything.

And Dad was no longer around to talk about things. She knew what he would say though…*don't let anyone else tell you what you should do with your life.*

Travis sat bare-chested at the kitchen table with his bedhead of dark, tousled curls. She loved how his chest and abdomen were like two side-by-side mountain ranges, from his glorious pecs on down to that sumptuous V that disappeared into his sweatpants.

He looked up from tapping a phone text. "First, get over here, so I can adore you. Then we'll talk."

She laughed and stepped over to him, tuning into his heat.

"You're so damn sexy." He looked up at her like a ravenous man about to devour steak and eggs. He set his phone on the table and stood, sliding his hand under her robe.

She lifted her face as his lips sought hers. He finished the kiss and lifted her onto the kitchen table. She ran her fingertips up and down his muscled back when his phone sounded a siren notification.

"Oh no," she groaned, darting a glance at the table. *Fire Call.*

Travis tapped his phone and read the text. "California's exploded and they need all resources." He gave her a quick kiss and lifted off, then rushed to the bedroom where he kept his fire pack on the ready.

Disappointed, she pushed off the kitchen table and padded down the hallway, following him. She hadn't realized how heavily she'd leaned on him these past few months. Dad had left her life but thank God Travis had entered it. The only problem was that he was always gone.

He emerged from the bedroom decked out in his Nomex and slung his tied-together boots around his neck as he rocketed for the door. Tara met him there and he gave her a fast kiss.

"See you when I demobe." There was his beguiling smile that had melted her from day one.

"Be safe, McGuire. Hit your jump spot." She lifted herself to give him another fast kiss. "We'll decide a wedding date when you get back."

"Copy that, hot woman." He pointed at her. "Behave yourself."

"Aw, that's no fun." She gave him a wink and then he was

gone.

Tara picked up her cell and texted Katy. "Let's go shopping. You need to help me pick out a wedding dress." A pang jabbed her, knowing her father would never see her in it.

But she couldn't wait to be Mrs. Travis McGuire…a smokejumper's wife.

And that alone helped to heal her grieving, guilt-ridden heart.

Eight months later. The Copper Peak Fire in western Montana

Tara had never seen a firenado incinerate a house like a nuclear-powered blast.

Until today. She prayed she never would again.

It wasn't her job to question whether the hand of God had hurled an apocalyptic firebrand, or whether the devil's finger had whirled stormy air into a fire vortex, inhaling oxygen and exhaling acrid smoke. Her job was to fight the damn wildfire. The storm had fueled it with seventy mile-per-hour winds and spit lightning into the forest like a dragon drunk with power.

Tara stood two blocks from the main road leading into a subdivision near the southern edge of Butte, Montana. She squinted at the flames engulfing the one-story home. Dry stands of lodgepole pine and Douglas fir trees lured the hungry flames. The sound of crackling branches and popping needles echoed as sweet-smelling pine, honeysuckle, and sagebrush blended into the sharp reek of burning timber.

She spotted movement on the front porch of the burning

house. Her spine numbed.

An elderly man with a walker stumbled down the porch steps. No! He didn't have a snowball's chance in hell to outrun the charging flames blitzing through crown after crown of towering trees.

"Dammit, someone didn't evacuate! Where's the city fire department?" Tara shot a distressed glance at the only road leading into this neighborhood, then back at her boss, Jim Dolan.

Jim barked into his hand-held radio. "Missoula crew needs backup and fast. We can't hold it away from the houses. We'll lose the entire subdivision if we don't get an engine in here now!"

A deep voice on his radio responded back.

Jim's expression mirrored the dread clutching Tara's chest. "They'll get an engine here when they can free one up."

"There's no time! We have to get him *now.*" She lowered her goggles over her eyes. Flop sweat dripped down the lenses. Tara had never left anyone helpless and wasn't about to start now.

"I'll get him. I can do it." She took off and sprinted toward the man. *Legs, don't fail me now.*

"Tara, not enough time!" her boss yelled. "Get the hell back here. I'm ordering you!"

Resin snapped and tree trunks burst as if dynamited. Pine needles glowed red and crackled. Brown smoke spun to black, as flames rushed at the besieged homeowner.

Intense heat bit through Tara's flame-resistant, Nomex shirt and pants, scorching her chest and legs. She floundered through tumbleweed, tripping on rocks, and weaving around torched lodgepole pine. She tugged her orange neckerchief over her nose, willing herself to reach this man.

She pushed harder, faster. Fifty yards left, almost there…twenty-five…*I've got this.*

Smoke billowed and she lost sight of him. She skidded to a halt, her eyes piercing the smoke, frantically searching. When the smoke thinned, she caught a glimpse of him collapsed on the ground. He raised an outstretched arm. *He sees me!*

A sudden wind gust lunged a wall of flame forward, pitching fireballs bigger than anything she'd ever seen. Flames danced in front of the porch and the imperiled man disappeared inside a blanket of orange. If he screamed, Tara couldn't hear it. The fire robbed the air of sound except for its own tornadic roar. A scream lodged in her throat, searing it.

Somewhere, a nearby car gas tank exploded, causing her heart to stutter. She stumbled backward and hit the ground.

Tara choked back nausea as revulsion gripped her. Her body numbed despite the unforgiving heat. She couldn't will herself to stand. Her muscles wouldn't work. Paralyzed, she sat on the ground, glued to the unburnt green, transfixed by smoke and flame.

"Get out of there!" yelled a gruff voice as something slammed against her. Strong arms locked around her abdomen, lifting her, dragging her back.

She struggled for a grip on the moment, wriggling to free herself from the vise grip. "Let go!"

"Wait till the flame front passes," a deep voice pressed.

Internal hysteria seized her, and her breathing became sporadic and ragged. "I couldn't get him—"

"Nothing you could do," said the deep voice. The arms restricting her released. A firefighter stepped around her and rested gloved hands on her shoulders. His once yellow shirt was sooty with grime, matching hers.

"Look at me."

She locked onto the taller firefighter's big blue eyes, an oasis in the orange and red chaos.

"I can't—can't breathe…" She couldn't inhale without coughing. Her mouth tasted like cinders and her stomach's contents still wanted out. She hated her confusion, her lack of control.

The man lifted Tara's filthy goggles onto her hardhat and brushed back the escaped mass of hair away from her face. He placed a firm hand under her arm to support her. "Look at me. Inhale…exhale...you're going to be okay."

She focused on the gritty face looking down at hers. "Shouldn't have stopped me," she croaked, planting her boots apart for stability.

"You were in danger. I had to get you out."

"He was a dad…a grandpa…" she choked out, erupting into a coughing fit. The image of the man engulfed by flame had etched itself inside her head. She wanted to run screaming across the burnt black to erase it… *because you never run into the green. You could die.*

She almost had.

"He wasn't yours to save."

"Who are you, God? I can take care of myself." She gritted her teeth and stepped back.

The stranger let go of her shoulders and opened a water canteen, holding it out to her. "Take a sip."

"Thanks." She gulped greedily, then splashed water on her face. Her heart still knocked from the turbo injection of adrenaline.

"Sorry about the God comment," she mumbled.

He gave her a dimpled smile. "No worries. You could have died with the homeowner. What's your name?"

"Tara." It came out angry and she didn't care. She swayed, then steadied herself. She raised her hands in front of her and squeezed her eyes closed. "Give me a minute. Where's the—where are we?" *Don't lose it. Not here, not now.*

"In the black. Out of harm's way." He pushed his goggles up onto his hardhat, revealing white circles around the pools of blue. Ash and grit streaked his neck and clung to the stubble on his rugged face.

He snapped his fingers. "Tara, look at me. You're safe. You'll be okay."

"But *he* isn't." She could hold back the tears, but not the tremor in her voice.

"You did what you could. Compartmentalize. Focus on the job." His deep baritone offered her a lifeline. It steadied her.

"Working on it." She eyed the flames moving away from them, her breathing still ragged.

He fixed his gaze on her and held it there. "Slow your breath. You'll hyperventilate."

She saw empathy in his eyes. "Okay, dammit. I *am*." She sucked in smoke-tainted air and blew it out, battling for normalcy. There was nothing normal about seeing a person burn to death and failing to prevent it.

Jim made his way to them and peered at Tara. "You okay?"

"Yes." *No.* She was still trying to figure how the fire reached the old man before she did. That was not supposed to happen.

Jim nodded at the firefighter. "O'Connor, thanks for helping out."

O'Connor smiled at Tara's boss. "Hey, Jim. Came around a building and saw her close to the flames." He motioned at her. "She's dazed, but okay."

Jim spat on the ground. "She tried to get a homeowner out. Did you see him?"

"No, just saw her on the ground in front of the flames. She seemed to be in shock," said O'Connor.

Tara snapped her brows together. "Hello, don't talk about me like I'm not here."

"Sorry, I'm explaining to your crew boss—"

"I can explain it myself, thanks." She forced a quick smile at O'Connor.

Jim shot her a look and shifted his long-handled Pulaski to extend his hand to the firefighter. "Appreciate your helping out."

O'Connor shook it. "No worries. Glad I was close enough to assist. I'm sure you've heard this hellcat's running and we've lost containment. The Incident Commander ordered crews to retreat. He'll hit her hard from the air."

Tara sized up his confident, easy manner. He'd brought calm to her storm. She was thankful but too shook up to form the words. In fact she was trembling.

"Caught it on the radio. We're moving out now." Jim looked from O'Connor to Tara.

"I need to find my smokejumper crew," said O'Connor. "Don't envy you having to do an AAR for the line of duty death of the homeowner."

"Yeah, I've done After Action Reviews. They aren't fun, but

necessary for lessons learned," replied Jim.

"Our jump crew will be doing a close-out with Travis McGuire as the incident commander," said O'Connor. "I'll inform him about the fatality unless you want to since a member of your crew was involved."

Jim's gray mustache became a straight line. "I'll take care of it. You know McGuire?"

O'Connor nodded. "We jumped a few fires together in Colorado and Oregon."

Tara gave O'Connor a double take at the mention of Travis, but she didn't let him see her grimace. The last thing she wanted was her freaking personal life colliding with her job. *Of course, this guy knew Travis. They're both in the fraternal brotherhood.*

Fire was a small world.

"Smokejumpers are the superheroes of wildfire," said Tara with a wry smile. "I've always thought part of your standard issue should be red capes with an "S" on your jump suits."

O'Connor's face softened into another dimpled smile. "You're back in action now." He hoisted a chainsaw to his shoulder as if it were made of aluminum foil.

"I was never out of the action." She squinted up at him. Despite the dirt and soot streaking his face, she noted a blue-eyed charm, accentuated by a lot of bright, white teeth.

O'Connor stared at her a moment. "I'm glad you're all right. Remember your ten standard firefighting orders." He turned to her boss. "Good to see you, Jim." He tugged his hardhat with thumb and forefinger as he strode off across the black.

"I'll do that," she hollered to his retreating backside. She rolled her eyes at his subtle reminder of the ten commandments of wildland firefighting she could recite forward and backward. She was aware of the one she'd violated, attempting to save a life: *Base all actions on current and expected behavior of the fire.*

"Hey, O'Connor, wait a minute." Jim glanced at Tara before trotting after O'Connor for a private conversation. He gesticulated as he spoke, the way he always did, then pointed in her direction.

O'Connor looked back at her, nodding. Jim patted his shoulder and O'Connor lifted a hand to her and vanished into the smoke.

"What did you say to him?" She hadn't screwed up deciding to go after the trapped homeowner. She screwed up by not being fast enough.

"I thanked him for helping you." Jim shot her a grim look. He took off his hard hat, revealing a tousled crop of silver. "Still okay?"

She gave him a mechanical nod. She was anything but okay.

"I told you to fall back. You went anyway." His steely gray eyes pierced her.

"A life was at stake—"

"*Two* lives were at stake, dammit!" shouted Jim, slamming his hard hat to the ground. He stared at it a moment, his mouth in a straight line. "We'll talk later," he muttered. He bent to pick up his hat and stomped off.

"Missoula Crew, retreat to the safety zone!" Jim called out, leading the crew at a fast clip. Everyone fell into single file, following him through the burnt black.

Shit. Jim was pissed. Tara blinked back the pressure building behind her eyes. *No crying in firefighting*, Dad always said. And by God she wouldn't. She wasn't weak. And she would prove herself capable once again—not only to herself but to Jim and her crew. She'd let Jim down today—but worse than that, she'd let herself down. What good was she if she couldn't save a life?

Unfortunately, Tara knew the drill. Jim would place her on administrative leave, routine protocol for a line of duty death. He could terminate her for ignoring a direct order, despite the fact she'd risked her life to save another. Not only had she failed, but she'd also landed in deep shit for trying.

She would do it again in a heartbeat. But there would be a cost—and now she feared how the veritable Pulaski would fall.

After her crew hiked a few miles from the fire to their camp site, Tara headed to her tent.

Jim caught up to her before she ducked inside. "Tara, wait a moment. Need to talk to you." He led her away for privacy. "Listen…sorry I came down on you so hard. But you almost got yourself killed."

She grimaced. "Not saving the homeowner wasn't in the cards, Jim." The dull ache in her chest turned into a sharp pang.

"You did what you had to but went against my orders." His jaw twitched.

She looked him in the eye. "You know I don't have a habit of not following orders. Please give me the benefit of the doubt on what happened today."

"Here's the thing." He shifted his weight to his other foot. "I've been thinking you need a break…to help you move on. You and I both know why you ran toward that fire to save the homeowner. Even with impossible odds."

She stiffened, irritated that he knew her so well. "I *have* moved on."

He stared off in the distance and shifted his weight again. "The agency will advise administrative leave and counseling after the line of duty death today. Lord knows a reprimand or suspension won't do a damn bit of good for you."

She shook her head. "Sorry you think that I messed up. But the way I see it, I had no choice." She stared at wispy layers of leftover smoke hovering over the Rockies.

"Off the record, I understand. But I think you should take the admin leave."

Her eyes pleaded with him. "No. I need the money. I need to keep working."

He bent to pick a blade of grass and fiddled with it as he spoke. "Figured you'd say that. I have a deal for you. I won't make a federal case of you ignoring my directive and I'll agree to you staying on the job if you agree to get counseling. But not here."

"Then where?"

"Alaska has requested resources. Fires have ramped up in the Interior."

She gulped. "Oh, come on. Please don't ship me to a miserable outback for trying to save a life—"

"—and nearly losing your own." His jaw jerked harder. "You thought saving that old man would make up for not saving your dad."

His words carved a hole in her chest and she fought to control the quiver in her voice. "So what if I did?"

"Hear me out. Alaska can use your skills. You're trained and disciplined. Change will do you good. A different place helps after losing a loved one. I'm doing you a solid here."

Her voice rose. "Alaska? No, please. Let me stay to get on the Lolo Interagency Hotshot crew. I already meet their fitness requirements but can't do it from five thousand miles away." She waved her hand in a northerly direction.

"Twenty-five hundred miles, give or take," he corrected. "Look, I've known you since you were in diapers, when me and your dad worked on the Lolo Hotshots. Saving the world won't bring him back. I promised him I'd look out for you." He stared at her a long moment. "I don't break promises."

"Is this the boss talking or the family friend talking?"

"Both."

"I take it I don't have a choice." She fought the pressure behind her eyes as her world crashed and burned yet again. He was pulling her off assignment and sending her to Alaska, effectively ending her chances of getting into the Lolo Hotshots!

"Speaking as your boss, no. You don't have a choice. I'm reassigning you to the Bureau of Land Management Alaska Fire Service for a sixty-day detail."

The sky and trees twisted as her vision blurred. "AFS? You can't be serious."

"As a family friend, I hope you accept this reassignment. And as your boss, you'd be well advised to take it. I'll Skype you into the After-Action Review meeting from Fairbanks. The higher-ups will want your statement about the fatality." He removed his hardhat and rubbed his forehead.

"Come on, Jim. Get me on the Lolo Hotshots instead," pleaded Tara.

Jim held up his hands to placate her. "Sometimes life smacks us on the head with signs. Today you had one. I hope you pay attention. It's hard to heal from a line of duty death on top of a family loss. I'll arrange for you to get counseling in Alaska."

"I'll arrange it myself," she muttered, turning away. She'd be damned if he'd see her cry.

"Make sure you do. I'm demob'ing you from the Copper Peak Fire as of zero seven hundred tomorrow morning. Go home and pack. Alaska Fire Service is top notch. You'll be in capable hands."

"Please don't demobilize me." She emphasized each word, hoping he'd cave.

He let out a tired sigh. "Your flight leaves for Fairbanks at zero nine hundred, day after tomorrow," he called over his shoulder. "Be on it!"

His boots crunched on the gravel road as he walked back to the men's encampment.

"Wonderful. Just wonderful," she sputtered, her heart thudding. *I'm being sent to the godforsaken tundra. I may as well be on a spaceship to Mars.*

The moon vanished behind the drifting haze as night settled in, leaving her in the dark. Today was a freaking sign? Of *what*? Fighting fire in Alaska wasn't at all what she wanted. Jim knew what her career goals were. How could he do this?

Her friend Katy sauntered over. "What was that all about?"

"Jim reassigned me to freaking bum-screw Alaska." She spit the words like bullets. "He thinks I need a change. Did I seem like I lost my shit today?" Tara had proven herself a competent firefighter on this wildland fire crew. But now she wasn't so sure.

"I thought you held it together, considering. Can he reassign you if you don't want to go?"

"He just did. As of zero nine hundred the day after tomorrow, I'm out of here."

"Alaska. The last wild place. A friend in dispatch said a load of calendar-worthy Alaskan smokejumpers worked this fire. And I do mean *calendar* worthy, Tara." She laughed.

Tara flashed back to the one she met today. "Nope. Forget it. You know how I feel about smokejumpers." She huffed out air.

"Travis was a douche, but not all of them are. The one who helped you today seemed like an okay guy."

Something stabbed Tara's chest. "I wasn't nice to him. I was pissed and embarrassed he had to help me. It's awful seeing someone die. And I just sat on the ground like an idiot…" She choked on her words.

Katy hugged her. "You did the best you could. Go to Alaska. Take a shitload of bug dope and don't get eaten by a Griz when you go pee." She unzipped her tent and grinned at Tara. "As we all know, that's when the bears show up."

"Right. I'll do my time up there fighting fire and then come home. See you in a couple months."

"Be safe up there. Keep in touch." Katy ducked inside her tent.

"Okay. Keep me filled in on Montana's fires." Tara crawled inside her own tent, her head pounding.

She coaxed her down filled sleeping bag from the nylon sack, shook it, and let it settle on the tent floor. Sitting on her bag, she tugged off her boots and socks. Her back muscles tingled, and her joints ached. Thank God that Alaskan smokejumper showed up when he did—what was his name again—right, O'Connor. If their paths ever cross again, she'll remember to thank O'Connor for helping her.

She thought of one good thing about going to the Great Alone, as poet Robert Service had referred to Alaska—there'd be no constant reminders of her dad…or Travis.

"Alaska. Oh God…" she groaned, squeezing the bridge of her nose with thumb and forefinger. All she wanted was to belong, to have family again. When Dad and Jim worked on the Lolo Hotshots everyone celebrated holidays and birthdays together, like a close-knit family. How could she get on the hotshots from middle-of-nowhere Alaska?

Two thoughts plagued her as she drifted to sleep. Never again would anyone on her watch die in a fire.

And never again would she fall for another smokejumper.

I always get burned.

Ryan stepped through the woods to join his jump crew, feeling like he'd been smacked by a planeload of retardant. *Damn.* That woman had kahunas. Dolan had reamed her a new one for her recklessness, but hell, if Ryan had been in her boots, he would have done what she did. *When a life is at stake, you don't blink—you go after it.*

As dangerous as it was, he admired her for trying to save the poor guy. Said a lot about her character.

Five years ago, the lives lost on his watch had messed him up. His need for atonement had led him to beat the shit out of himself by training to be a smokejumper. He'd worked like a dog to train and qualify. It was no walk in the park. Even some of the U.S. Marines who had applied said the training kicked their ass.

Every other day he'd wanted to quit.

After making it through jump school in Redding, Ryan and Gunnar both applied for a transfer to the Alaska Smokejumper base. First, they'd had to pass the more rigorous physical fitness requirements: Sixty sit-ups, thirty-five pushups, and ten pullups as fast as possible; run 1.5 miles in less than nine and one-half minutes, or three miles in less than twenty-two and a half minutes—plus carry a one hundred ten-pound pack for three miles in less than fifty-five minutes. And that's not counting the ninety pounds of jump gear.

Wildland fire in Alaska was unforgiving, just like anyplace else—*if you can't do the fitness in the time allowed, you may not survive when that fire takes a run at you.* That was enough motivation for Ryan. That and the fact that smokejumpers carried a mystique in wildland fire that nobody else could touch. It made him feel good that he'd proven himself more capable since that awful day on the Angelus San Bernardino Fire five years ago.

On that first leap out of the Sherpa, he'd held his breath until his parachute opened. And every jump since, his heart always pounded until his chute deployed. Preparing to jump from a plane taught him focus and to be very much in the moment.

He'd endured, stuck it out—and was damn glad he did. His first adrenalized jump on a runaway fire in Alaska's Interior had been worth every second of the grueling physical training and harrowing practice jumps. He'd trained enough that now it was second nature. He'd bonded with his Alaskan smokejumper crew of trustworthy, hard-working people. He'd become grounded in their integrity, undaunted by fear, and the enormous sense of responsibility each smokejumper had for one another.

Because of their hard and fast response to remote wildfires, Alaska smokejumpers were in high demand to assist with lower forty-eight fires. Ryan was one of fifteen Alaska Smokejumpers that had been sent to help with Montana's blowup of two hundred thousand acres burning on five national forests. The Copper Peak Fire on the Beaverhead-Deerlodge National Forest had been one of the worst.

Gunnar raised a hand in greeting as Ryan arrived at the jumpers agreed-upon meeting place in Fleecer Meadows, next to a dude ranch, a healthy distance from the Copper Peak Fire. "About time you got here. What took you so long?"

His voice shook Ryan from his reverie. "Stopped to lend a hand to a local crew."

"Oh yeah? What's the skinny?" asked Gunnar, holding out a can of sparkling water. "The ranch cook brought us some cold drinks. Catch." He tossed the can to Ryan.

"Thanks." Ryan caught it and plopped down on a cargo box. He popped the top, guzzled the whole thing, and burped. "Ooh, that tastes good. We lost containment on this side of the fire."

"Yeah. Heard about that. And heard there was a casualty."

Ryan nodded. "I was there right after it happened. A firefighter tried saving a homeowner who hadn't evacuated."

Gunnar waited expectantly. "And?"

"She ran like hell into advancing flames to get the guy but couldn't reach him in time."

Gunnar raised his brows. "She?"

"Yeah. I happened upon her sitting in the path of a running

flame front. She was freaked out. I had to get her out of there."

"What did you do?"

"Dropped my gear and dragged her to safety into the black. She was none too happy."

An incredulous expression crossed Gunnar's face. "She was pissed that you saved her?"

"Mostly embarrassed I had to help her." Ryan shook his head, recalling Tara's situation. "She was traumatized after seeing the guy burn to death." Tara's plight reminded him of his own experience. He glanced down at the number "5" with the five angel wings he'd tattooed on his forearm—so he would always remember.

Gunnar whistled. "Oh man, that sucks."

"Tara took it really hard. Her crew boss chewed her out for endangering her life."

"Tara? You know her name?" Gunnar grinned. "You don't waste time, do you?"

Ryan gave him a peeved look. "It wasn't like that, Dickwad. I had to calm her down. Her big green eyes were—she was—she was—" he almost said she was a beauty, but he caught himself. "She was extremely upset."

"Ah, I get it," said Gunnar with a smug tone. "Green eyes, huh? I take it this woman made an impression on you."

Ryan's head snapped up. "What *she* did was impressive. Not how she looked."

"I didn't say anything about how she looked, bro. You did." Gunnar downed the rest of his sparking water. "Why do I have the feeling there's something more?"

"Nothing more," lied Ryan. "Just my observations, that's all."

"Well, don't get your hopes up to see her again. McGuire radioed and he's demob'ing us. We're on a flight back to Fairbanks the day after tomorrow."

Ryan let out a sigh. "Yeah, you're right, as usual." Although it wouldn't break his heart if he bumped into the auburn-haired firefighter again before he caught the plane back home to the Alaska Fire Service in Fairbanks.

"We don't have time for women, remember? Plus, you resolved not to hit on firefighters after what happened in California." Gunnar slapped his arm. "Glad you learned your lesson buddy. Come on, let's pack up our gear and GTFO of here."

Ryan knew Gunns was right. That's exactly what he'd told himself on his hike over here. No smokejumper had time for women. Ryan certainly didn't. Definitely not for women who wielded Pulaskis, no matter how good they felt to hold. And definitely not Tara Waters. For a fleeting moment he'd had his hands on her, his arms around her, peering into those wild, emerald eyes as he tried to calm her. He'd sensed her physical strength while holding onto her and noted the mass of auburn hair that fell in a tangled knot from under her hardhat.

He'd caught the astonished look on her face when he mentioned Travis McGuire, though she'd tried to hide it. Something was going on there. Ryan didn't know what; but no matter what her deal was with a fellow smokejumper and the incident commander of this fire, *she was most definitely one hundred percent hands off.*

Their job was done here. They were going home to Alaska. He could leave all that had transpired here behind him. He could put her out of his mind…but it wouldn't be easy.

What he hadn't counted on was the raving beauty under all that soot and grime.

What he hadn't counted on was Tara Waters.

The thing that had impressed him the most—she had risked her life to save another. And that spoke volumes. There weren't many female firefighters.

But this one was the stuff of legend.

If you want to find out what happens between Tara, Ryan, and Travis, don't skip the About the Authors section at the end of the book where you'll find everything you need to know.

BROKEN PROMISES

LC Taylor

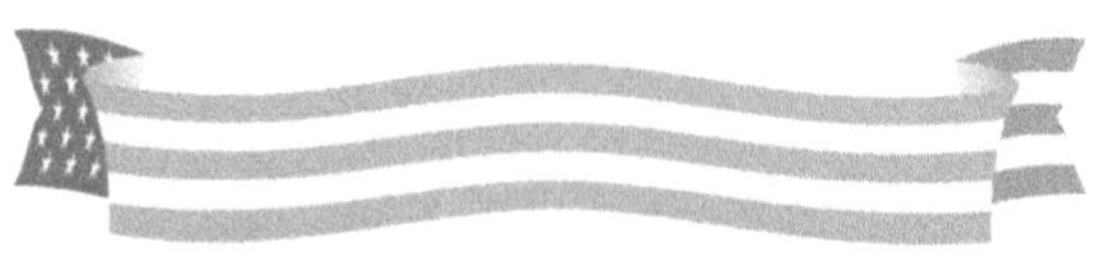

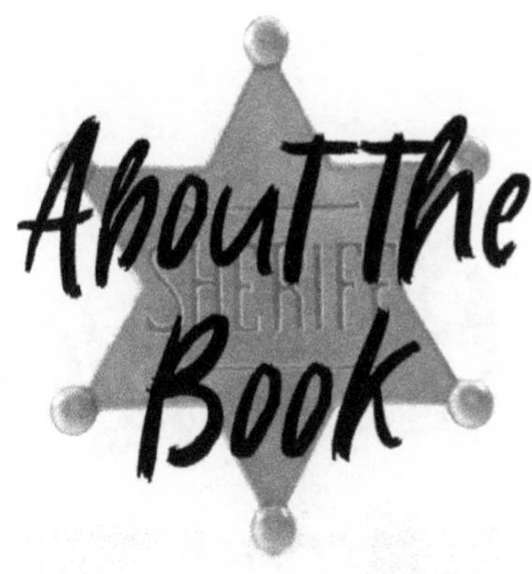

The hardest part of loss is learning to give your whole heart a second time.

Kerrigan Walker's whole life changed on 9/11 when he lost his wife and committed himself to the Marines. Burned out and retired, he's returned home to Alabama and joined his best friend's sheriff department. He wasn't looking for love until he met Lorelei.

This wasn't how Lorelei envisioned her life going. With the loss of her husband overseas last year, she's been left with an empty house, greedy in-laws who demand his life insurance money, and a town where no one knows her name. A chance encounter with Officer Kerrigan Walker changes all of that.

Will these two wounded souls finally find the connection they need or will the grief of the past be too much to overcome?

Prologue

Kerrigan

September 11th, 2001

It had been a normal day at the Pentagon—until it wasn't. In an instant, everything can change. Life is filled with unknowns you can't attempt to plan for. And even though you do everything to be prepared… it isn't always enough.

I knew the moment the alert went out, something was wrong. At twenty-one, my senses were finely tuned in detecting out of ordinary occurrences. This was one of those moments. As I stood there watching in shock as my gut coiled with fear. It was the first time I felt afraid. An emotion I hadn't felt since joining the Army three years ago—but now it ransacked my body. I fired a quick text to my wife, Kara, asking her to be careful. She was a civilian paramedic stationed just outside the Pentagon. With everything going on, I knew she was probably on standby somewhere in the city.

I watched on one of the mounted televisions as the first plane barreled into the North Tower of the World Trade Center, imploding it from the inside out. I wanted to believe it was a tragic accident, but then I heard it. There was a report coming in of another hijacking. The entire Pentagon went on high alert, and I scrambled to get everyone out. The second plane struck the South Tower—and it was only 9:05 in the morning.

I rushed through the hallways, urging others to leave when the sky rained hell fire onto us as a third plane crashed into the building. Smoke and ash filled the southwest side of the building as flames licked the cinder walls. My nose burned from the smell of Jet Fuel as it filled the corridors of my workplace. The utter devastation nearly froze me in place as I scanned the rooms. I'd done my time overseas when I first enlisted with the Marines at eighteen, but nothing prepared me for this. As a Military Police officer, I was sworn to protect and serve others. Today proved how difficult doing my job was going to be.

"Sergeant Walker," I cut my head in the voice's direction. Even over the roar of the fire, I could hear someone screaming for me.

My face contorted with concern when I spotted the Command Sergeant Major. He was carrying a woman in his arms toward me. We got her outside to the grass, where hundreds of others were lying in wait for help. I closed my eyes and even though the acrid smell burned my lungs—I forced myself to inhale a deep breath. This was shear madness. Chaos was around every corner as the Command Sergeant and I hurried through the debris, searching for anyone who needed our help. It felt like a never-ending battle—one we couldn't win no matter what we did.

As I made it out onto the lawn, I paused and took in the sight. A jet airliner rested on what used to be the southwest corner of the prestigious Pentagon. The morning sky was no longer blue. Instead, it was filled with thick black smoke, coating the warm summer air in a pungent fog. As much as I wanted to stop from the exhaustion threatening to push me over, I couldn't.

Not now. Not when so many people were still inside. I helped my friend and fellow Marine retrieve as many survivors from the building as possible. Even after a massive explosion detonated inside, we continued to work simultaneously for what felt like hours, but the harsh reality was it had only been one.

Time seemed to play on a loop until finally I couldn't keep going any more. My body ached from the physical exertion I'd put it through. Scanning the surrounding grounds, I saw several military personnel looking just as worn down as me. Bracing my hands against my knees, I allowed myself to think of my wife.

Fear punched me in the gut as I realized she was probably here, assisting with rescue. I moved through the yard, scanning faces as I went. I fingered the cell phone tucked inside my cargo pants and pulled it out. The last text Kara sent me was right after the second tower had been struck. She warned me to do the same and told me she loved me. Pressing the icon for her contact, I lifted the phone to my ear and listened. It immediately went to voicemail.

"Kara. Baby, it's me. Call me when you get this." I disconnected and sent her a text. I knew she was probably busy, but I couldn't shake the feeling something was wrong. I checked the areas I could access, praying I'd find her among the other military personnel. But luck was not on my side and finding Kara was proving to be like finding a needle in a haystack.

The sun was finally setting, causing the sky to take on an eerie vibe. The fire was out, but smoke continued to billow into the tainted air. My stomach tightened as I took in the casualties of today's events. The ground was littered with the wounded waiting to be assessed. But what really got me. What really made my throat burn with bile was all the dead that laid before me. Bodies were laid out on the Pentagon grounds, covered in sheets. There were so many that didn't survive today's terrorist attack—and the ones that did would never be the same. Me included.

As I sat down in the grass, I kept my head on swivel. I still hadn't heard from Kara, and now my phone was dead inside my pocket. If I just sit here, maybe she'll find me. I stood when I saw the fire chief from Kara's station cutting across the parking lot. He'd spotted me and immediately made a beeline towards me.

"Kerrigan." He blew out a breath. "Have you heard from Kara?"

I furrowed my brows and clenched my jaw. "What do you mean? Haven't you been in contact with her?"

"No. Once the plane crashed, all hell broke loose. I know she and her partner were in the area and were first to respond, but dispatch hasn't been able to raise them since."

"Fuck." I pushed my fingers through my hair. "You're sure she was here?"

"Yes."

"I'll go look for her. Meet me back here in thirty minutes. Maybe one of us will have come across her by then."

"Ok." The chief took off in the opposite direction.

I pushed through the chaos I was feeling inside and started looking for my wife. Coming up empty-handed, I headed back to the rendezvous spot to meet the Chief. Maybe he had better luck and Kara would be there, too. I paced the grass, scorching a path from my constant motion.

"Kerrigan."

I glanced toward the Chief who was moving toward me, my best friend, Hayward, following behind him. Even from the distance, I could tell something was wrong. Hayward's body was tense, and his jaw was set in a grimace. My head shook, even before he made it all the way to me.

"No." I refused to let him speak, afraid of what he was going to say.

"Kerrigan." Hayward's voice cracked as his eyes welled with tears. "I'm so sorry." He paused, trying to get his emotions in check. "She was inside the building when the plane exploded for the second time."

"No." I cried out. "You're wrong." I pointed my finger into his chest and bit back a sob. "Please. She can't be in there, Hayward. She can't be."

His arms wrapped around my shoulders as he pulled me into an embrace. This couldn't be happening. My wife couldn't have been inside. But as he spoke his next words, I already knew. Kara had made the ultimate sacrifice, leaving me alone on this earth without her.

"I'm sorry, Kerrigan. Kara's gone."

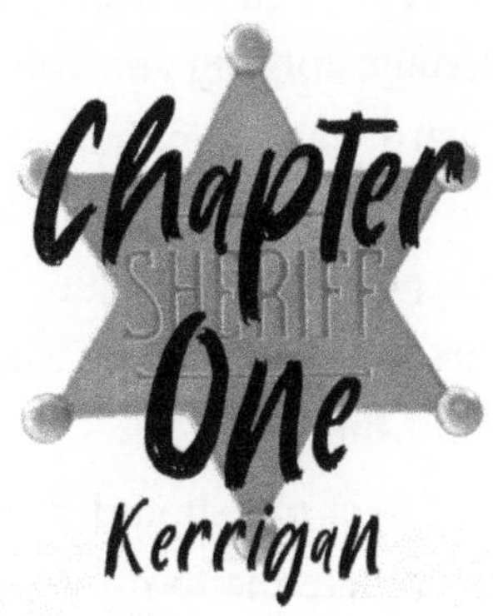

Twenty Years Later

They say time heals all wounds. Well, I can tell you they're full of shit. Time heals nothing. It only allows scars to form. Scars you'll carry with you until your time runs out. I wish my time was over, but it's not. And as I stand here staring at the sign for my new normal, I had to laugh.

For the last twenty years, the military has owned me. That's a harsh statement. They didn't own me. No… I gave myself to them willingly in hopes it would numb the pain. A pain they unknowingly caused me. But after several tours overseas and countless hours battling the rage inside my chest, I left the Marines. It was long overdue, and the truth I was told to go. After a massive breakdown, they urged me to retire. Battling my demons had finally taken its toll. And honestly, at the pace I was going, I'm lucky to have even made it this far.

At almost forty-one years old, I had nothing to show for my life. Which is how I ended up here—my hometown, Crossroads, Alabama. The man I called my best friend, who I shortly after basic training had learned was also from my hometown, begged me to come work for him.

Hayward Cross had been with me from the start. We'd been deployed many times together, forging an even stronger bond than most Marines have. Hayward was older than me, but we became close. He was with me the day I married Kara, and the day I buried her. He had enough of the military and got out, leaving me to fend for myself. Now, five years later, he was the Sheriff of our tiny town. And I was going to work for him.

I slung my duffle bag over my shoulder and climbed the steps to the glass doors that would take me to my new start. It was odd being out of my BDU's and not hearing a noisy military base. Perhaps in time I would get used to the lack of commotion.

The cold air brushed against my skin as I tugged the door open and stepped inside. For a small department, the building looked modern. I could tell they had renovated it since the last time I'd seen it. A half wall with plexiglass separating the lobby from the office on the opposite side filled most of the room. I tossed my bag into a vacant chair and headed to the window. An older woman with dark-rimmed glasses sat behind the small opening on the phone. She held her finger up in a motion asking me to wait. I forced a smile and tipped my head in acknowledgment.

"Sorry about that. Can I help you?"

"Yes, ma'am. I'm here to see Sheriff Cross. I'm Kerrigan Walker."

"Oh. Mr. Walker. He's expecting you." She pushed up from her seat and hurried to the locked entry. Pushing it open, she waved me toward her. "Come on. I'll show you to his office."

After retrieving my bag, I followed the woman down a long hallway. Several officers greeted me with a wave as I passed by them. Suffice to say, this department was welcoming so far.

"As I live and breathe. Holy shit. Is that Kerrigan Walker, I, see?"

The unmistakable sound of my past rushed in. I turned to find Brady Moore filling the hallway. I shook my head in disbelief. "Brady. What the hell are you doing here?"

"You haven't seen me in nearly five years and that's what you lead off with? When I got out of the Marines, I had nowhere to go. Hayward offered me a job—and here I am." He laughed as he approached me and the receptionist. "I see Betty is taking care of you." He winked at the older woman, causing her to blush. "Betty my dear. You gotta watch out for this crazy motherfucker." He slapped his palm against my back.

"Brady." I growled his name in warning. He'd always been the joker when we were deployed together, but I didn't want this woman to think I was a troublemaker. "Don't be telling this woman any of your lies. I'm sure they know by now you're full of shit."

Betty covered her mouth to stifle a giggle. "We do. I assure you. Mr. Walker." She schooled her expression and glared at him. "Don't you have some paperwork to do? Maybe you should get your ass out on the road and leave us alone. Chief is waiting on Mr. Walker, and I need to get back up front."

Brady threw his hands up in submission and smiled. "Yes ma'am. Kerrigan, find me later. We have some catching up to do."

I tipped my head and watched as he headed down the hall toward a door marked patrol. "Come on, Mr. Walker. Let's get you to the Sheriff."

"Thank you, Betty. And please, call me Kerrigan."

I stepped inside the room and was immediately thrown off

kilter by the man standing before me. A thousand memories rushed through my mind. Some were good, and some… were not. Hayward had been there during the darkest hour of my life. He'd helped picked up the pieces of what remained when my world was shattered into a thousand fragments of bitterness and regret. His knowing expression made me pause in the doorway.

"Kerrigan." He sighed. "I'm glad you're here." Hayward smirked at the elderly woman. "Betty, thank you for showing him back. Please hold my calls."

"Yes Sheriff. Welcome aboard, Mr. Walker."

"Thank you, ma'am."

I watched as she exited the room and closed the door. Taking a deep breath, I turned to face my longtime friend. He looked exactly as I remembered. Five years hadn't changed him any. Other than the slight gray at his temples, Hayward looked the same.

My chest constricted with guilt as I looked him over. After he left the corps, I didn't reach out to him as often as I should've. Part of that was the pain I wanted to hide from everyone—Hayward could always see the smoke screen I tried to put up.

"How long have you been back?" Hayward pulled me into an embrace and patted my back before pulling away. I watched as he rounded his desk and sat down. He leaned back in his chair and waited for me to respond.

"This morning."

"Have you seen your mom?" Hayward cocked his eyebrow at me in question.

She was my next stop. I wanted to square away my job first, before heading to my childhood home. My mom was all I had left of my family, and while I hated being home, seeing her again would be good.

"Nope. Going there after I square this away with you."

He pursed his lips and shifted nervously in his chair. "What about—"

I cut him off by holding up my hand. "Don't. That's not up for discussion." It was the reason I hesitated coming back to Crossroads. This place didn't just hold memories of my childhood—it held memories of her… Kara.

Kara and I dated throughout high school. When I joined the Marines, we continued our relationship long distance. Once I was stationed in D.C., Kara joined me and became a paramedic. We were married just under two years before our time was cut short. The last time I was home, it was to say goodbye to her. I hadn't been to her grave since.

"Fine. For now, Kerrigan." Hayward pulled out some paperwork and slid it across the desk. "Fill these out and then I'll show you where to get fitted for your uniform. I'm putting you on nights, seeing as I need a supervisor covering that shift."

"Supervisor?" I blinked in confusion.

"Yes. Supervisor. You left the Marines as a staff sergeant in the military police. Did you really think I was going to start you off at the bottom?"

"Won't the others be pissed at that? I'm the newbie." I ran my hand down the back of my neck.

"I don't give a fuck. I'm the Sheriff here. If I had someone ready for the position, I'd have already put them in it. Besides." He stood and moved toward the door. "My deputy chief agreed you're the best person for the job. Come on. I'll introduce you to him and get you squared away with your equipment."

I followed behind him as the reality of my new life was hitting. No longer a Marine and alone at forty-one left me feeling hollow. It was easy to ignore the loneliness of not having Kara when I was overseas. But now, I wasn't so sure.

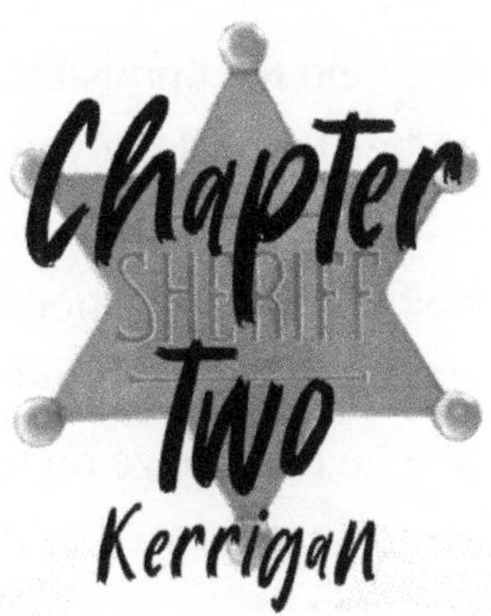

"Let me fix you some lunch." My mother's voice filled the kitchen. Since coming home, she'd been feeding me every day before going to work. And in the two months I'd been back, I was sure I'd put on ten pounds. She patted the chair at the table and smiled. "Sit and tell me how it's going."

"Mom, you're going to make me need new uniforms if you keep feeding me like this." I seated myself and propped my arms against the top. "Works good." I smiled down at the plate she put in front of me. If there was one thing I missed while in the service, it was her cooking.

"I'm glad you're home, baby boy." She patted my hand and continued wiping down the counters. "But I'm worried about you."

"Worried?" I paused my bite, the sandwich hanging midair as I waited for her to elaborate.

"Yes. All you do is work. When are you going to take some time to get out and meet some people?"

I knew what she was asking and as much as I hated to disappoint her, I sure as hell wasn't in a place to meet new people. I honestly didn't think I would ever be.

"I'm not really looking to meet anyone."

"Kerrigan." Her voice held the unmistakable tone of sadness. "She wouldn't want you to be alone. Have you even been to see her grave?"

"Mom. Please." I took a bite of my food and chewed. My eyes burned with emotions—emotions I refused to let surface.

"I'm just saying." She held her gaze on me. "You need to let her go. Going by might help you. Please? For me? I'd like to see you happy before I die, Kerrigan."

I closed my eyes and swallowed. I hated my misery was causing her pain too. But the thought of letting go of that part of my past was too hard. "I'll think about it." It was all I could promise her right then.

After disposing of my trash and washing my plate, I adjusted my gun belt and headed out. The perk of working at the Sheriff's department was the take home car. Actually, it was an SUV. Hayward decided SUVs were a better choice for the department, considering our surroundings.

Crossroads might have been small, but we had a lot to offer. With a national forest on one side of the town and a lake on the other, people had plenty to do. A set of railroad tracks cut through the center of town, giving it a down-home vibe. We had two schools—an elementary and high school that sat on the same plot of land. My high school memories trickled in as I started my car and backed out. Fisting the radio in my hand, I pressed it to my mouth and spoke.

"Dispatch. Log unit 202 in service." I hung the mic back on

the dashboard.

Sometimes I went into the station before going 10-8, but today I didn't feel like being around many people. The solitude of my car let my mind sort out the lingering thoughts or guilt I'd woken with. Today was not a day I wanted to be bothered—in fact, I'd contemplated calling in sick. Every year on this day, I struggled to function. It didn't take long for my peace to be disrupted. I'd been dispatched to a two-car accident near the train tracks. The fire department was already on scene and requesting us to expedite our arrival.

Flicking the blue lights on, I navigated my SUV as quickly as I could to their location. When I arrived, I was shocked at the severity of the collision. One car was toppled on its side, covering the tracks. I immediately radioed Dispatch.

"Unit 202 to dispatch."

"Unit 202, go ahead." The radio barked.

"Dispatch, notify the railroad a car is on the tracks. Fire is on scene trying to extricate the driver."

"10-4. 202."

I climbed from the front seat and slammed my door—that's when I heard them. A firefighter was wrestling with who I assumed was the other driver.

"Need some help?" I approached them slowly, assessing the situation.

"Yes. This bozo was the other driver, and he's trying to leave." The man wearing full turnout gear grumbled.

"Sir. I'm Sergeant Walker. Can you tell me what happened?"

"Yeah." He slurred as he continued to struggle against the

firefighter. "I am trying to leave."

The smell of whiskey wafted through the air. It was like the man had bathed in a bottle of liquor before getting into his car.

"Sir, have you been drinking?" I already knew the answer but had to ask anyway.

"Yep." His head bobbed as he swayed on his feet.

"Alright then. I'm going to give you a ride down to the station. Are you in need of medical help?"

"I ain't going with you nowhere." He took a step away from the firefighter and swung at me.

With barely any effort, I grabbed his arm and flung him to the ground. I pressed my knee into his back and pulled out my cuffs.

"Sit still." I manhandled him, as I secured the cuff on his wrists. "I'm placing you under arrest for driving while intoxicated. You have the right to remain silent. Anything you say can and will be used against you in a court of law. You have the right to an attorney. If you cannot afford an attorney, one will be appointed for you. Do you have any questions?" I jerked him from the ground and helped him stand.

"Fuck you." He groaned as I half-drug, half-walked him to my car. After searching his pockets and ensuring he wasn't holding any weapons or drugs, I secured him in the backseat of my patrol unit.

"Thanks for getting here so fast." The firefighter who had been holding down approached me. "I'm Chase Galloway. I don't think we've met." He stuck his hand out in greeting.

As I shook his hand, I introduced myself. I still hadn't made it by their station—partly because it reminded me too much of what I'd lost. "I'm Sergeant Walker—Kerrigan Walker." I forced a smile.

"Glad to meet you. I've heard a lot about you from Brady."

"Shit. Don't believe anything that bone head says. He's a shit stirrer." I laughed.

"A bunch of us are meeting at Vickery's tomorrow at seven. You should join us." He seemed sincere when he threw out the invite.

Vickery's was the local bar and hangout. Rumor had it the owner's daughter was now the owner and made some pleasant changes. I hadn't ventured out yet, so I hadn't seen it for myself. My mom's plea popped into my head. Making her worry was not something I wanted to do, so with apprehension, I agreed to join them.

"Sure. I'm off tomorrow, anyway. I'll stop by. In the meantime." I pulled open my driver's door and climbed in. "I should get this drunk to jail."

Chase nodded in agreement and waved as I closed the door and pulled out. The drunk had passed out in the backseat, so he was oblivious to everything going on. The jailers were going to have a heyday messing with him.

After dropping him off and finishing up the paperwork, I headed out. My vehicle seemed to have a mind of its own, because I pulled into the cemetery even though I'd told myself I wasn't going to. I sat inside the car, staring at the rows of headstones. It wasn't supposed to be like this. Kara and I had plans for our life. And losing her had me refusing to move on with them. I pushed open my door and took a deep breath. The warm summer air filled my lungs as I closed my eyes. I wanted to hold her in my arms—but that would never happen again.

Finally, mustering the courage, I headed to her final resting place. It was obvious someone had been to visit her recently as there were fresh flowers on her tombstone. I ran my hand across the smooth granite surface and inhaled.

"Hey Kara." I swallowed the pain down and willed myself to keep talking. Every breath I took burned inside me, igniting the anger I held onto. "I miss you, baby. I'm back home now. The Marines told me it was time to go. After you left me, I jumped at every opportunity to be deployed overseas. It was the only way I could keep the memories and pain at bay. But I'm here now. And you're everywhere I look. I don't know if I can do this, Kara. You're supposed to be here with me. That's what we planned, remember?"

I pinched the bridge of my nose and sighed. "I'm sorry I haven't come sooner. Being here is too painful. Why'd you go inside the building? If you'd just stayed outside, you'd be here." I tilted my head to the sky and screamed. "Fuck. I have to go. I'll be back, baby—even though coming here makes me feel hopeless. Staying away lets me pretend you're not dead. I love you, Kara."

I turned and started back to my car. As I was cutting down the path, my eyes caught sight of a woman leaning over a tombstone. Her body was shaking from the sobs I could hear from where I was standing. Not wanting to leave someone in distress, I made my way toward her.

"Excuse me, ma'am?" I stepped beside her. "Are you alright?"

The air caught in my lungs when she looked up and met my gaze. Despite her reddened eyes, this woman was breathtakingly beautiful. Her long black hair fluttered in the slight breeze framing her face. Her eyes were a deep blue, almost gray-blue color that held a multitude of emotion behind them. She was kneeling on the ground with her upper body draped over the top of the cement marker. I watched as she righted herself up and sat back on her butt.

"Oh god." She closed her eyes and grimaced. "I didn't think anyone was here. You must think I'm a lunatic." She covered her face with her hands and sighed.

"Are you ok?" I asked again, concern plaguing my body.

"What?" She looked up again, this time taking in my uniform. "Shit. Did someone call the sheriff's department on me?" Her head swiveled around as though she were looking for another onlooker.

"No. I was here and saw you crying."

"You were here?" She blinked in surprise. "Oh, you mean visiting a grave?"

"Yes." I gritted out through my clenched jaw. Reaching my hand out to her, I offered to help her up. "Let me help you."

As soon as her hand slipped in mine, a strange sensation traveled the length of my arm. It was like tiny pinpricks of electricity danced across my flesh. She must have felt it too, because she jerked her hand from mine and took a step back.

"I'm fine. Thanks for checking."

My eyes tracked the tombstone and froze. "Who was he?" I nodded toward the cement stone. It was clearly a man's grave, and someone who'd been in the military based on the verbiage written beneath his name.

"My husband." She closed her eyes and fought the tears pooling in her lids. "He was killed in combat a year ago. Today was not a good day for me—I'm not usually this hysterical."

My eyes flicked over to hers. I fought the demons inside me, willing them to stay buried while I stood before her. "I understand."

I forced out the words.

"What about you?" She fidgeted with her hands in front of her. "Who were you visiting?"

"My wife." I barely recognized my voice.

"It's hard, isn't it?" She bent down and picked up her bag. "Letting them go. I didn't think our life together would end so soon, but here I am. And here you are."

"My wife died in 9-11."

The woman sucked in a breath. "I'm sorry. I know how you feel. They were taken from us without a genuine reason. I'll never have answers, I guess. And that makes it harder to let go."

I followed behind her as she walked toward the parking lot. We were both still hurting from a loss that neither could explain. I hated to see her in pain and wanted to tug her into my arms. That thought was alarming to me. In all the years Kara had been dead, no woman had ever elicited those types of thoughts.

"If you're going to be alright, I should get back on the road."

"Right." She nodded absent minded. "Thanks again, um—" she paused. "I didn't get your name."

"It's Sergeant Walker." I held her gaze as I gave her my name.

"Sergeant Walker," she repeated back. "Well, be safe out there." I watched as she climbed into her car and started to shut the door.

"Wait." I grabbed the door, keeping it open. "What's your name?"

"Lorelei." She gave me a half-smile as she tugged her door from my hands and pulled it shut.

I stepped back and watched as she put her car in reverse and backed out. Her eyes held my gaze as she stopped and eased forward. The unspoken words were disconcerting to me, leaving me to feel vulnerable. My gaze followed her out of the parking lot and watched until she disappeared from my line of sight.

Something happened. Something I didn't quite understand. Either way, I it didn't matter. I wasn't ready to pursue a woman, and from the looks of her—she wasn't ready to be pursued.

I hurried to my SUV and climbed inside. I'd barely made inside when dispatch gave me another call. As I headed toward the domestic, thoughts of Lorelei swam on the surface of my thoughts. I didn't even know her last name, but something about her had me wish I'd asked.

Shaking the bizarre thoughts from my head, I focused on the call I was enroute too. For the first time since Kara's death, I felt an attraction to another woman. The realization hit me like a bolt of lightning. Was I ready to date again? My gut coiled with guilt when I thought about another woman. For that, I pushed the beautiful woman out of my mind just as I pulled into the driveway of my call.

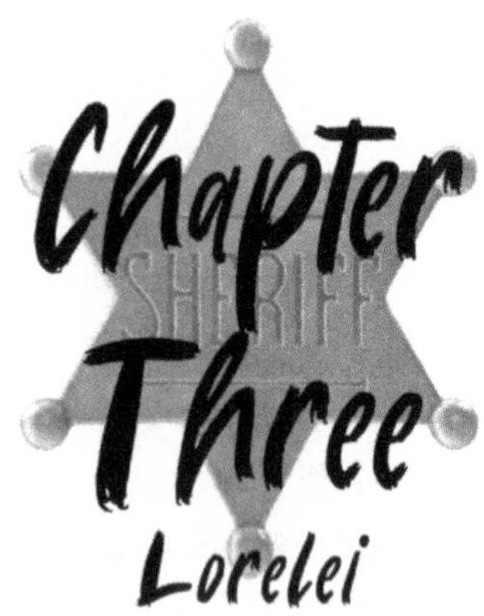

How embarrassing. I'd completely lost it at Gavin's graveside. It'd been a year since I'd buried him in the ground, and not a day goes by that I struggle to put one foot in front of the other. Today was one of the worst. I'd just come from the attorney's office again and was feeling over-emotional. His family insists he wanted them to have his life insurance money. Ever since he died, it's been one fight after another. His sister and brother have been the worst. Threatening me with lawsuits and even bodily harm, they refuse to let up.

The truth is, I'd give it all away if I could just hold Gavin one more time. He lost his life serving our country and left me a widow at thirty-one. We'd just spoke and decided we would try for children when he was stateside. We never got the chance. Instead, I spent what should have been his homecoming planning a funeral.

I hated living here. The only reason I came back was to be close to him—even if it was his grave. There was nothing in this town for me other than the ghost of my husband. And stupid as it may be, that was enough.

I cut the engine of my car off and laid my head against the steering wheel. The humiliation of being found draped over my husband's gravestone was still fresh. The strange thing was, I couldn't get Sergeant Walker out of my head. He appeared to be just as broken as I was, even though his wife died twenty years ago. It made me wonder how old Sergeant Walker was. Not that it mattered. Getting involved with someone wasn't on my radar—even if he was good looking.

The summer air warmed my skin as I stepped out of my car. When I moved here, I lucked up and found a small house I could afford. I didn't just lose Gavin when he died—all the military benefits disappeared along with our future. It was gut-wrenching pain when the military officials told me I would have to move off base. Starting over hurts like a knife to the gut.

I climbed the steps to the place I called home. Only I didn't feel at home anywhere without Gavin. The door snapped shut behind me as I tossed my keys onto the entry table. My purse hit the wooden floors with a heavy thud as I let it slide down my shoulder. An emptiness I'd come to accept swirled around me like a fog threatening to swallow me whole. Like every other day, I collapsed onto the couch. My arms wrapped around my knees as I laid there, looking at the mantle.

Gavin's picture stared back at me from the last framed portrait we'd taken together. Ten years I loved him. Ten years I stood by and watched him head off into the dangerous world he loved so much.

I wanted to scream and shout. But it was useless. Gavin was gone, and he took my heart with him. The sound of my cell phone ringing in the foyer forced me to get up. My purse sat mocking me on the floor as I fished out the device. Of course, it was the one person I didn't want to hear from—Gavin's sister. I swiped the call button and pressed it to my ear.

"What do you want Linda?" I grumbled into the phone.

"That's a friendly way to greet your sister-in-law." Her sarcastic tone wasn't hard to miss. "Anyway," she continued. "Have you reconsidered our request?"

"What request? The one where you demanded part of your brother's life insurance? No. I haven't reconsidered. He left that to me, Linda. And if I could give it back to have him here again, I would."

"If that's how you feel then giving us our share shouldn't be a big deal."

If I could have reached through the phone and slapped her, I would have done it. The nerve of them, thinking they deserved Gavin's money. They never came around when he was alive, and certainly didn't help with the funeral. Giving them money was the last thing I ever planned to do.

"Stop calling me. Tell your brother and mom the same thing. We are no longer family, and I don't owe you anything."

"You're going to regret this, Lorelei."

"I'm not scared of you, Linda. If you want to take this to court, have at it. But you'll lose and look like a greedy bitch." I sighed as I shook my head in disgust.

"We'll see about that. Just remember you did this to yourself."

With that, Linda hung up. I stared at the screen, wondering what she meant. I was tired of dealing with them and felt like being in the town made it worse. A part of me wondered if I should just leave Crossroads. But the guilt of leaving Gavin behind like that was too much. My visit with him today had been especially difficult. Rarely did I lose my shit like that anymore, but dealing with his family had pushed me to my breaking point.

Immediately visions of the handsome Sergeant Walker trickled into my thoughts, filling me with an emotion I couldn't decipher. Gavin had been the only man I'd been attracted to—but meeting the hunky deputy had thrown my emotions for a loop. My reaction to him was a complete shock, considering it'd only been a year since Gavin died. Being attracted to another man left me feeling guilty. Turning on the shower, I stripped my clothes and stepped beneath the hot spray of water. All I wanted to do was wash away the feeling of betrayal.

By the time I emerged, my skin was red from my attempt to wash away the guilt I was harboring. After eating dinner, I found myself snuggled under my covers. It was early, but having no one special in my life, this was how my days went. Maybe tomorrow I'd get a part-time job to keep me busy—Gavin had left me with enough money, so I didn't have to work. But having all this idle time enabled my depression.

I climbed into bed. My thoughts were muddled with memories of Gavin. But there, entwined with his memory, was a new one. One I wasn't sure what to do with.

Vickery's bar was loud and busting at the seams with patrons. As soon as I walked into the bar, I spotted him. Chase was seated at a high-top table closer to the restrooms. Unsure if I'd made the right decision to come, I headed to the bar. Liquid courage was a necessity if I was going to put up with being around people. I saddled onto a stool and turned my body to watch the place. My nerves were all over the place. An attractive woman slid in beside me, her body brushing against mine when she did.

"Oh. Sorry." She chuckled when she realized what she'd done. "I don't think I've ever seen you around. Are you new to town?"

"Yes and no. I grew up here, but just home from the Marines."

She pressed her palm to my forearm and grinned. I was used to women throwing themselves at me, but I'd always ignored them. My heart was blackened, and I had nothing to offer a woman unless it was just sex. It was easy to detach myself from the emotional side of fucking someone. Unfortunately, women weren’t so gifted. And looking at the way she was staring at me, I knew what she wanted.

"Are you here with anyone?" She held my gaze, waiting for a

response.

"Just my buddies over there." I pointed toward Chase. A couple more guys had arrived and were sitting with him. Chase tossed his head up in a silent greeting. I threw down a few bills and stood. "Have a good night." The burn of her gaze seared into the back of my shirt.

From the looks of her, I was doubtful anyone had turned her down. Chase was laughing as I approached the group.

"You pissed her off." He continued to chuckle. "Probably wise, since she's a badge bunny. I'm pretty sure she's slept with half of the fire department and sheriff's department."

I shuddered to think why someone like her was opening her legs for any man in a uniform. There was no way I'd stick my dick in a woman who'd been passed around by the men I worked with. The server brought over a pitcher of beer and set it in the center of the table.

"Walker." Brady plopped into a seat opposite me and grinned. "Glad to see you out and about."

"Felt it was time to see how everyone lived outside of work." I sipped my beer, my eyes watching the surrounding people.

"I saw that badge bunny hitting on you. You gonna take her up on her offer?"

My eyes narrowed at him for a moment. "I'd rather my dick not fall off. Seems she's been passed around by a few of you."

"Not to me." Brady threw his hands up in defense.

"That's because you have the hots for the bartender. What was her name again?" Chase peered toward the bar and laughed. "Mia, right?"

"Fuck off, Chase."

The bartender was a cute little thing. She had long blond hair that she kept pulled into a tight ponytail. She was, at most, five foot three, but even with her short height, she had curves that made her fuckable.

"Why haven't you asked her out yet?" Chase continued.

"She's not interested." Brady swigged his beer and glared at Chase.

"Well, I think maybe Kerrigan should ask her out. He needs to get laid."

Brady shot me the deadliest look I'd ever seen. "Whoa. I'm not asking her out. Calm down." I threw my hands up in a mock defense. "But based on your reaction, I'm going to say Chase is right. You like her."

"It doesn't matter. She turned me down." His shoulders sunk as he leaned his head back.

"A woman that turned you down is a woman worth fighting for." I tapped my fist on the table and stood. "I think I've had enough socializing tonight. I'll catch you guys later."

"Seriously Kerrigan?" Brady groaned. "You've been here what, thirty minutes?"

Closing my eyes, I inhaled. "I'm just not feeling it. Ok? This is the first time I've been out in a social setting since my wife died. So, forgive me for not being more receptive. Maybe next time I'll feel better about it, but for now, I'm going home."

Chase gave me a solemn look of understanding. "Damn, Walker. I didn’t know you were a widower. If I had, I wouldn’t have made you come."

"It's fine Chase. She's been gone a long time, but some things are just too difficult."

I turned and walked away before any of them could respond. As though I was being pulled toward the cemetery, my truck pulled down the long gravel entrance and I parked closer to Kara's grave. The sky was black, except for the glow of the moon and some stars. There was no other light.

As I walked toward her tombstone, I caught movement out of my peripheral vision. Lorelei was sitting down in the grass by her husband's grave. My feet stilled as I stopped and watched her. She wasn't hysterical this time, but obviously here for a reason. Torn with what to do, I closed my eyes and let the night air fill my lungs. Would I be betraying Kara if I went over to see Lorelei? Deciding to take a chance, I altered my course and headed toward her.

The moonlight cast a beautiful glow around her as she leaned with her back against the cement marker. Her long black hair hung over her shoulder, grazing the top of her breast. She didn't hear my approach, which concerned me. If it had been someone else, she could have been seriously hurt.

"Lorelei." I kneeled in front of her and ran my hand over her leg.

She jumped at the sudden weight on her thigh. "What the hell are you doing?" Lorelei jerked her leg back and glared at me. "Jesus Christ. You scared the crap out of me."

"I was worried about you. You really shouldn't be out here at night by yourself. And definitely not sleeping."

I held my hand out to her. "Let me help you up."

Lorelei stared at my hand for a few seconds, but finally

slipped her palm into mine. I tugged her off the grass and steadied her on her feet. Even in the dark, I could tell she had been crying. Something passed over her face when she realized we were still holding hands.

"Sorry." She jerked her palm from mine. "Why are you here at night?"

"Same reason I suspect you are. It's been twenty years since she died, yet I can't seem to move past the hurt. Why don't we get out of here and grab a cup of coffee?"

"You want to have coffee with me?" Lorelei tilted her head, mulling over my request.

"Yes." I blew out the breath I was holding. "It would be nice to talk to someone who understands the pain. Not to mention I'm attracted to you, and I don't know what to do with those feelings."

Lorelei picked up her bag and sighed. "I don't feel like being around people, Sergeant Walker."

"Kerrigan."

"What?" Her head snapped back to look at me.

"Call me Kerrigan. We can go somewhere that isn't crowded. Please?"

There was no way I could explain why I was practically begging her to have coffee with me—I just knew I needed her to say yes. There was something going on between us, and I needed to figure out what. Since losing Kara, no other woman had made me feel the way I do when I'm near Lorelei. I wanted to believe it was because she was dealing with similar emotions, and that's why I felt a connection to her. But deep down, I knew it was more—and that scared me.

"I'm probably going to regret this, but why don't you come to my place. I'd rather not be anywhere public. I can barely control my emotions on a normal day and if you're wanting to talk about feelings, I guarantee I'll be a hot mess."

"Ok." I couldn’t believe she suggested her place. "I'll follow you there."

I followed her to her car and made sure she got there safely. Once she had locked her door and cranked the engine, I hurried to mine. As we pulled out of the cemetery, I sent a silent prayer to Kara. The guilt was still there, but beneath that was something else. Something I wasn’t prepared for.

What the hell was I doing? I'd just invited Kerrigan to my house for coffee. A man who was making me feel things I wasn't ready to acknowledge. My husband had only been dead for a year. Moving on with someone new this soon seemed wrong. Despite that, I couldn't deny the attraction I had for him. And based on what he said at my husband's graveside, he felt it too.

The headlights of his truck flashed in my rearview mirror as he pulled into my driveway behind me. My body shook with nerves as I climbed out and headed toward the front door. Kerrigan stood behind me as I unlocked the door and stepped inside.

"This is it. It's not much, but its home—kind of. Have a seat in there and I'll grab us drinks. You still want coffee or something stronger?"

"I'll have whatever you're having." Kerrigan scanned the inside of my living room.

I watched as he stepped close to the mantel and fingered the folded flag and photo I had perched there. "That was two years ago. It's the last photo I took with him before he was deployed."

Kerrigan turned to face me. "I'm sorry for your loss, Lorelei.

Should I go? Is this too much for you?"

"What?" I blinked in confusion. "It's hard, but I want you to stay. Let me grab those drinks so we can talk."

I hurried into the kitchen and pulled down two glasses. Forgoing the coffee, I grabbed my whiskey. This conversation was going to require more than caffeine. When I stepped back into the living room, I found Kerrigan sitting on the couch with his head buried in his hands.

"Are you alright being here?"

His head snapped up. "I'm good. No—" he sighed, "That's a lie. I'm here because I want to be, but I'm far from good. But I suspect you understand that better than anyone."

"Yeah. I do. Hope whiskey is alright. I felt this conversation would need a bit more liquid courage than coffee could provide."

His eyes widened in surprise. "I didn't take you for a whiskey drinker."

I set the glass down and perched myself on the couch beside him. My feet were tucked beneath me, causing my knees to brush against his thigh. It was the first time I could really look at him.

He had been wearing his uniform the first time we met, but even under the polyester I could tell he was fit. Having him sit here dressed in blue jeans and a fitted tee told me I had been right. He was a lot taller than me, closer to six-one or six-two, if I were guessing. He had muscular arms that seemed to stretch the fabric tight around his biceps. His broad shoulders held up his gorgeous face. Kerrigan had a neatly trimmed goatee that framed his full lips. But the part I couldn't stop looking at where his eyes. They're a deep chestnut brown color that seemed to hold a lot of emotion behind them. It was like I was staring into a reflection of my sorrow.

"You don't know me. But I think that's about to change." I took a sip of my drink. "You say you're confused. Well, so am I. My husband has only been dead a year. Having these feelings for someone else has me feeling conflicted. And not that I am trying to lessen your pain when I say this." I took a breath and continued. "Your wife has been dead for a lot longer. Most people would assume you'd moved on by now."

Kerrigan reached out and brushed a loose strand of hair out of my face. "They are all shocked I am still holding on to her memory as hard as I am. The day I ran into you at the cemetery, something changed. I love Kara. I always will. But for the first time in a long time, you made me feel like trying again."

"Can you tell me about her?" I watched as Kerrigan swallowed down the amber liquid. The muscles in his neck tensed as he took a deep breath. "You don't have to if it's too hard."

"No." He pressed his hand to my knee. His fingers trailed along the skin that was exposed. "I want to tell you, Lorelei. If this could be something more, then you deserve to hear all my demons—good or bad. But will you tell me about him when I'm done?" His eyes glanced toward the photo of me and Gavin. I nodded, waiting for him to begin his story.

"Kara and I dated throughout high school. When I joined the Marines, we continued our relationship long distance. Once I was stationed in D.C., Kara joined me and became a paramedic. We were married just under two years before our time was cut short. She was the light of my life, Lorelei. And any woman who becomes involved with me needs to understand a part of my heart will always belong to her. I've avoided relationships for that reason—plus I'm afraid I'll forget her if I start over. It's already started. I remember the big moments, but the little things… they're slipping away. Kara had this way about her that could put a smile on your face. She was silly and lovable."

"Did you see her the day it happened?"

Kerrigan squeezed his eyes shut and leaned his head against the couch. "No. She was a paramedic and was on shift the night before. Like the firefighters, she did a twenty-four-hour rotation. She should have been getting off the morning before all hell broke loose. That wasn't Kara. I knew when the alerts started pouring in, my wife would be in the thick of things. I'd tried to call her so many times that morning. And when I saw the fire chief walking with my best friend toward me, I knew. Hayward looked just as broken as he told me she was gone. I remember little after that."

"Hayward Cross? The sheriff?"

"Yeah. The sheriff. He became my best friend when I joined up. He was there the day I married Kara, and the day I buried her. He was in the core with me until he came home and ran for sheriff here. I stayed in, using my deployment to mask the pain. But even that caught up to me. The Marines gently suggested I retire—so I did, and Hayward gave me a place to land."

"You're from Crossroads? Isn't it hard being here? I don't know if being surrounded by my past would help me heal. This isn't my hometown, but it's where Gavin wanted to be buried. Since I didn't want to be away from him, I moved to be close."

"The memories aren't as suffocating as I thought they would be. I haven't run into Kara's parents yet. I'm not sure they even know

I'm back—my mom certainly hasn't told them."

"I bet your mom is glad you are home. What about your dad?"

"He died when I was in high school. Heart Attack."

"I'm sorry. I lost my mom ten years ago to cancer. My dad died a year later. They were so in love I think her death was more than his heart could take."

"I know how he felt. There was a time when I didn't think I would survive without Kara. But I got up and put one foot in front of the other. She wouldn't have wanted me to stop existing. Knowing her, she'd want me to be happy. And that leads me to my current predicament."

He looked me in the eye. "I haven't been able to get you out of my mind since we met. At first, I thought it was because we shared a connection through our loses, but after seeing you in the moonlight, I knew it was more. I like you, Lorelei, more than I care to admit right now. I know you're probably not in a place to deal with that truth, but I needed to be honest with you. I'm scared of what this means after all this time. Just know, there's no pressure on you to reciprocate right now. I'd settle for just being friends for now." He smiled and traced his thumb along my kneecap. "Alright. Enough about me, tell me about Gavin."

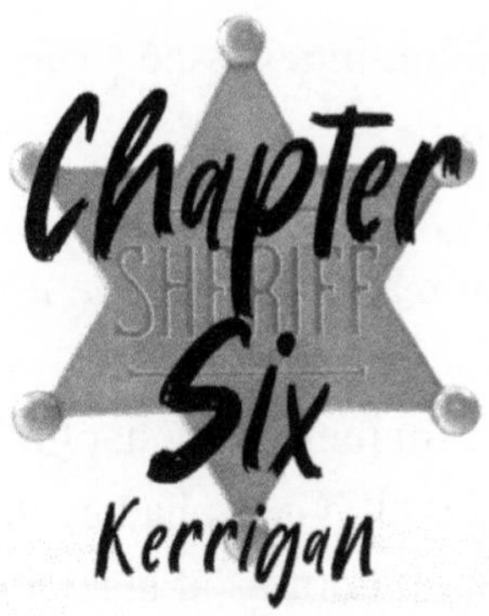

Maybe I shouldn't have told her everything. But getting it all off my chest made me feel lighter than I had in years. Giving her time to gather her thoughts, I simply watched her. She was beautiful. And so unlike Kara. Where Kara was blonde, Lorelei had dark brown, almost black hair. Lorelei had eyes that were a deep blue, almost gray-blue color. Kara's had been green. Kara was almost as tall as I was, but Lorelei—I could tuck her against me perfectly. There was a considerable age gap between us, but it didn't seem to bother her, and I didn't care.

"Gavin and I met while I was in college. He was on leave and out with friends at a local bar in Atlanta. That's where I'm from, by the way." She forced a smile. "We hit it off and spent every day together until he was due to return to his assignment. For two weeks it was only him and me. The day he left, he promised his heart to me. We worked out the logistics of a long-distance relationship and agreed to make it work. And we did. When I finally graduated two years later, I moved to be with him. He had been stationed in Texas, making the move easier. We got engaged a year later, and we were married the next year. His family was pissed because we eloped.

Gavin knew I didn’t want to do a big wedding—with both of my parents gone. It didn’t feel right.”

I nodded for her to continue as she seemed almost uncertain if she was talking too much.

“Anyway, we move a lot the first three years of our marriage, but I didn’t care. I love him and would have followed him anywhere. We had a great ten years together, even if half of them were spent apart. I'll never forget the moment the Chaplin knocked on my door. The look on his face said it all. Gavin had been killed in a roadside bombing and wasn’t coming home—at least not the way I was expecting him to. That was a year ago. I've spent the last twelve months trying to remember our last conversation. Did I tell him I loved him? I can't remember. And that's the part that sucks the most."

I didn’t hesitate. I reached out and pulled her into my arms. This beautiful woman was broken like me. She harbored guilt for things she shouldn’t. But like her, I understood. Both of us lost someone suddenly, leaving us with hurt and unanswered questions. Questions we would never have answers to.

"What would Gavin say to you if he could see you one last time?"

"He'd tell me to move on. He always put my happiness first. But it's hard, you know? And you're not alone in your feelings, Kerrigan. I don't understand it, but I have feelings for you too. It's crazy right? We've just met, and I feel like I've known you a lot longer."

"It's not crazy. Sometimes people come into your life, and they were meant for you. I think that's what's happening with us. Like I said, I'm good at being your friend—for now. And maybe down the road we can be more."

I watched as a myriad of emotions crossed over her face. For me, this was the start of what I had been holding out for. Someone who would accept my past and not hold it against me. The more I sat there holding Lorelei, I knew she was that person for me.

"I'm tired of hurting." She whispered against my chest.

"Kara used to tell me if you stumble, make it part of the dance. We've both stumbled, Lorelei. Now we need to make it part of the dance. Our history is part of who we are. And I'm pretty sure it's what will make our next relationships strong. Knowing what we do about loss, we will give everything to living in the present with someone else."

"I just want to feel again." She shifted against me, her palm pressed against my abdomen as she looked at my face.

"What are you asking me, Lorelei?" My heart raced beneath her touch.

"Maybe it's too fast. Maybe I'll regret it tomorrow, but right now I want you to help me remember what it feels like to be touched. Gavin and I hadn't been together in over a year before he died. His deployment made sure of that. I'm scared to death I won't feel that way again, because I'm already forgetting."

My breath hitched as I sucked air in through my nose. I searched her face for the truth in her words, shocked to find desire hidden beneath the confusion and guilt.

Not wasting another moment, I laced my fingers through her hair and pulled her lips to mine. It was unlike anything I'd prepared myself for. Electricity sparked between us as she opened to me, giving me silent permission to take what I wanted.

And I did. I slipped my tongue in her mouth and took

everything she was giving. Lorelei shifted her body so she was straddling my legs. Her hands wrapped around my neck as she arched her body into mine. Her fiery center radiated its warmth against my growing erection. She fit perfectly against me.

"Lorelei." I groaned. "Are you sure about this?"

"Yes. Please." She rubbed her pussy against my jeans again. The dress she wore had ridden up her thighs, exposing the lace panties covering her center.

"You need to understand something. If we do this, it changes everything. I don't think you're ready for that." I brushed her hair away from her face.

"Why can't it just be sex?"

"Because you're the first woman I've wanted more from since Kara. This means something to me."

She froze above me, searching my eyes as she pondered my words. "I want you, Kerrigan. I can't explain it, nor do I understand how I can be moving on this fast. I love Gavin. Just as you love Kara. But they're gone and we're here. Gavin might have died only a year ago, but the truth that I have to accept is I hadn't seen him for a year before that. Video chats and phone calls were all I had—and until this moment, I hadn't realized how lonely I was."

"What are you saying?" I held her gaze.

"I'm saying I want to try with you. And I'd say let's take it slow, but I really need you inside me. The rest we can figure out later."

"Ok." I leaned forward and kissed her lips. "But we aren't fucking on your couch." I stood, taking her with me. Her legs wrapped around my body as I started down the hallway. "Which one is your bedroom?"

"Second door." Her lips fastened to my neck as I walked us into her room.

Kicking the door shut, I tossed her to the bed. Lorelei watched with hooded eyes as I stripped my shirt off and tossed it to the floor. She sat up on her knees and pressed her palms against my chest. I grabbed the hem of her dress and pulled it over her body.

"Fuck you're gorgeous." I hissed.

She was wearing a white lace bra that did little to hide her plump breasts. Her pink nipples showed through the material, begging for me to taste them. So, I did. I leaned down and fastened my mouth over the material and sucked. Lorelei moaned at the sensation of my lips against her skin.

"This has to go." I flicked the clasp of her bra and pushed the material down. "Perfect." My palm cupped her breast as I swirled my tongue around her nipple. "Lay back, baby."

I nuzzled her back, helping her adjust her legs. I gripped her ankles and pulled her to the edge. Immediately, I covered her body with mine and showered her flesh with kisses. Her hands burrowed into my hair as I moved down the length of her body. My hands held onto her hips as I pressed kisses to the inside of her thigh. The sounds she was making drove me wild with desire. Needing to taste her, I eased her panties off, exposing the spot I wanted to bury my tongue.

Her pussy glistened as I swiped my finger through her folds. "You're so fucking wet." Lorelei moaned as I pushed my finger inside her channel. She was tighter than I expected, which made my cock pulse beneath my zipper.

Not able to withstand another minute without tasting her, I

pressed my face between her legs. She let out a little yelp when I thrust my tongue between her folds. Lorelei pushed her hips into me, giving me more access to take what was now mine. I latched onto her clit and sucked it into my mouth. Her body tensed and she shook.

"That's it, baby. Let go."

And boy, did she. Lorelei screamed out in ecstasy as her orgasm washed over her. I wasted no time stripping off my pants and plunging into her. Her body contorted with the invasion of my cock. "You, ok? Did I hurt you?"

"No." She wiggled her hips as she locked her legs around my back. "But I need you to move, now."

I withdrew my cock slightly, then slammed back inside her. Her cries were like music to my ears. It drove me wild, urging me to fuck her without abandon. Our bodies move in perfect harmony and in that moment the only thing that existed was the two of us. Our pasts and present collided in an explosive union that rocked me to the core. And as I stroked my cock through her folds, I fell a little harder for her.

"That's it, baby. Squeeze my cock."

"Kerrigan." She whispered between thrusts. "I'm going to come."

I adjusted my position and drilled into her. The tip of my cock struck against her g-spot with each pump of my hips. Her walls quivered around my shaft as she let go. Hearing my name on her lips as she came around me was torture—but in the best possible way.

When she stopped shuddering, I rolled us over, forcing her to ride me. "I want to watch your tits bounce when you come undone for me, baby."

Lorelei seated herself over my shaft and leaned back. The angle she was riding me was going to push me over the edge quick and I needed her there with me. The pad of my thumb pressed into her swollen nub. She bucked and rocked faster, my dick moving inside her with each movement.

"I'm going to come, Lorelei. Come with me."

I swirled my thumb across her clit, coaxing one more orgasm from her. Her walls clamped down as my cock swelled and exploded inside her. Her pussy milked me for every drop as I pumped into her from below, riding out my release. When she had nothing left to give, Lorelei collapsed against my chest.

"Wow." Her breath tickled my skin.

"You can say that again." I rolled to my side, taking her with me. My cock slipped out, the evidence of our coupling dripping down her thighs. "Shit, Lorelei, I forgot a condom.'"

She glanced down and shrugged. "I'm on the pill. Are you clean? Do I need to worry you just gave me something?"

I laughed. "No, baby. I haven't been with a woman for a long time. Plus, I got tested before leaving the Marines. I'm clean."

"Me too. I mean I'm clean. I've never had sex without protection."

"Not even with your husband?"

The minute the words were out of my mouth, I regretted them. I could see the guilt mirroring in her eyes as she shook her head no.

"Hey. Don't do that. We did nothing wrong. I think we both agree our former spouses would want us to be happy."

"I know." She closed her eyes and took a deep breath. "I was just thinking about how Gavin was adamant to wear one. He didn't want kids, so he wanted to ensure there were no mishaps."

"You didn't want kids?" My throat constricted. Kara and I had talked about starting a family the week before she died. Kids were something I had wanted back then, and now—laying here with Lorelei, that desire had returned.

"I did. He didn't. I hoped when he slowed down his deployments he would change his mind, but we never got that chance. What about you?"

"Kara and I talked about starting a family. But then she died, and I pushed that out of my mind. Until you, I hadn't considered kids as part of my future. Hell, I'm almost forty-one. Speaking of which, does my age bother you?"

"Shouldn't I be asking that question? Maybe my age is a problem for you. I am ten years younger." She bit her lip.

"Fuck no. I'd be proud to tell everyone you 're mine." I closed my eyes. "When you're ready for that. Sorry. I'm getting ahead of myself."

"Stop apologizing. I won't lie and say I don't feel guilty about what we did, because I do. But beyond the guilt, I have feelings for you. Feelings I want to explore—slowly."

"Slow it is." I tucked her against my side and hugged her. "I should go."

"Will you stay with me?" Lorelei looked into my eyes. "I don't want to be alone tonight."

I reached over and turned off the bedside lamp that had been on. After pulling the covers over our bodies, I rolled her to her side and spooned her. I couldn't deny she fit perfectly in my arms as I laid there listening to her breathe. Lorelei was the first woman I willingly spent the night with since Kara. And as scary as it was, I loved it.

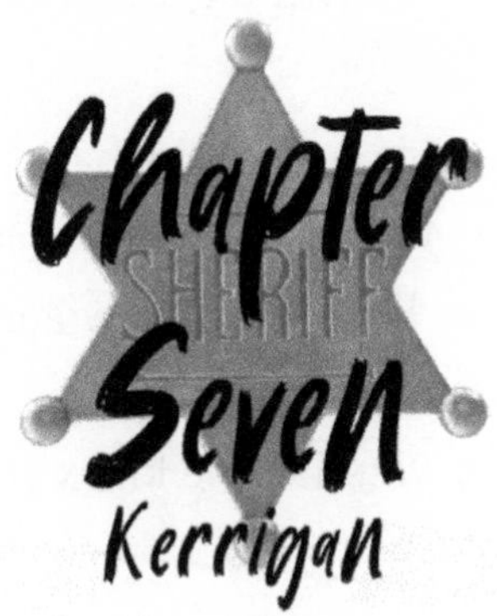

It had been three days since I held Lorelei in my arms. Waking up with her the next day was perfect in every way. And after making love to her two more times, I kissed her goodbye and left. We'd been talking or texting every day since. It's crazy how someone I'd just met had me feeling emotions I thought I'd never feel again. Glancing down at my phone, I couldn't suppress the smile while reading her latest text.

Lorelei: Looking forward to our date tonight.

I fired off a response, grinning like a teenage boy.

Me: Same here. I'm glad we're taking a chance on each other.

Call you when I'm on my way?

Lorelei: Yes. Be safe. Can't wait to see you. Xo

"Hey man, Chief's looking for you before you head out." Brady grinned as he stopped me in the station's hallway. "What's got you smiling? Did you finally get laid?" He huffed a laugh.

"Can't a guy smile?" I shrugged, avoiding the conversation I knew he wanted to hear.

"Sure. But you're not known for that. What gives?"

"I met a woman."

Brady slapped his palm against my back. "I knew it. About time, brother. You deserve to be happy. Do I know her?"

"No. I don't think so. But it's still new and we both have some things to work out—but I really like her."

"Man, I'm happy for you. Let me know if you need anything, ok. We got your back, Kerrigan."

"Thanks."

When I got to Haywards's office, I wasn't expecting to who was waiting for me. Hayward shot me a sympathetic look and shrugged.

"Kerrigan. I tried your house first. But your mother said you were on duty. The chief was kind enough to call you in here. How are you?"

A flood of emotion poured in, nearly knocking me off my feet. Here, standing in front of me, was Kara's mom. She was a mirror image of the woman I lost, which is why I had avoided contact with her. Seeing her face was a painful reminder of what I lost.

"Why are you here, Kelly?"

Hayward stood and moved around the desk. "I'm going to step out and give you two a few minutes alone." He squeezed my shoulder and excused himself from the room.

The tension was so thick you could have cut it with a knife. I hadn't meant to be callous to her, but seeing her made the pain resurface.

"I have some things that belonged to Kara that she would want you to have."

I watched in horror as Kelly placed a bag on the table. She tugged out a photo album and handed it to me. When I opened it, I was nearly knocked over with grief. Picture after picture filled the pages of the two of us in high school. It was clear from the photographs we were in love.

"I thought you'd want that. But this is what I really brought to give you." She fished out a box and held it in her hand. "It came in the mail a few weeks after her funeral. I've held on to it all this time, waiting for the right time to give it to you. When I heard through the grapevine, you were here in town, I knew it was time."

She shoved the tiny container into my hand and patted my arm. "She loved you more than life itself." Kelly started toward the office door and paused. "Don't be a stranger, Kerrigan. We miss you, too."

I stared down at my hand. Why now? I was just starting to let go and live. But if what I thought was in this box, I didn’t know if I would survive seeing it. My eyes closed as I willed myself to be strong enough. The photos were hard enough, but that was so long ago, it wasn’t nearly as painful as I suspected this would be.

The door opened, and I vaguely heard Hayward's voice behind me as I eased off the top and stared at the contents inside. A broken sob escaped past my lips as I slipped the one thing that would bring me to my knees from the box. My fingers wrapped around it as I fell to my knees. Hayward was there in an instant.

"Fuck." He wrapped his arm around me. "I got you buddy. It's ok. Let it all out."

"No." I pushed off my knees and jerked back. "I can't be here, Hay. I need to go." I shoved it in my pocket and grabbed the door handle.

"Let me take you home. You shouldn't be driving like this."

I silently nodded and hurried out the door. Several people watched me pass by. My face did little to hide the pain I was feeling. Hayward climbed in behind the steering wheel and cranked the engine.

"Don't let this set you back, Kerrigan. These last few days I got to see the old Kerrigan—and I suspect it's because of the woman you've found. You can't let this come between you and the future you deserve."

"I can't think about Lorelei right now. This." I held up the reminder of what I promised to Kara between us. "Is a sign I am betraying the promise I made to love her forever. Getting involved with Lorelei was a mistake."

"You don't really believe that, do you?"

"I don't know anything anymore."

"Call her, Kerrigan. She can help you work through this."

"Thanks for the ride." I slipped out of the passenger seat, ignoring his suggestion, and hurried inside.

I wasn't surprised to find my mother waiting when I got inside.

"She found you." She sighed. "I didn't want her to go to your job, because I knew this would happen. What did she give you?"

I held it up. "A reminder of why getting involved with anyone is a mistake."

"A mistake?" She blinked. "Are you an idiot? Kerrigan—Kara wouldn't want you to die alone. She'd be happy for you and

Lorelei."

"I can't do this, mom. Not now. I need to be alone."

"Don't make a mistake, baby. I know you're hurting right now, but that woman made you smile. If you walk away now, you'll regret it. Kara is your past—it's time to let her go."

I slammed my door shut, cutting off anymore words from my mother. My fist clutched the tiny reminder in my palm as I sat on the bed. I was supposed to pick up Lorelei in twenty minutes, and I couldn't bring myself to move. My phone vibrated against my leg. When I pulled it from my pocket, I wasn't surprised to see it was Lorelei. I was late for my date with her based on the time my phone read. Opening her message, I cringed.

Lorelei: Hey are you ok? You were supposed to be here already.

My mom pushed open the door and saw me staring at my phone. "Did you call her?"

"No."

"I hope you know what you're doing. You might be throwing away the one chance you have at starting over. And for what? A stupid ring? You need to tell her, Kerrigan."

I knew she was right. But I couldn't face her right now. Not with the suffocating emotions I was feeling right now. I rolled the reason for my guilt around in my palm. Pinching it between my fingers, I held it up in front of me. " This symbolized forever. How am I supposed to look at this, while giving my heart to another?"

"I don't know, Honey. But Kara is dead, and you finally have a chance at starting over. Ignoring her is a big mistake."

"Maybe. But seeing this hurts." I pulled open my nightstand. Giving her wedding ring one last glance, I tossed it inside and closed the drawer.

The expression of my mom had cut me to the core. It was a mixture of sadness and disappointment. I'd lost Kara all those years ago, and this reminder of her death scorched my soul in ways I wasn't prepared for.

My phone rang, startling me out of my self-pity. Lorelei's face filled my screen. I glanced up at my mom and flashed the screen to her. She simply shook her head and walked out. It rang several times, then stopped. Another text message pinged.

Lorelei: I know you're not at work. I called and talked to the Chief. He said you weren't there. What's happening Kerrigan?

I didn't reply. I *couldn't.* What would I say? Oh yeah. My dead wife's mother brought me her wedding ring, and it fucked me up. Sorry. I can't talk. Even saying that in my head made me feel worse. The guilt of wanting Lorelei was like a dagger to my heart. And I wanted her—like I had wanted Kara when I met her. But this was more than I could handle. Shutting her out was best for both of us. I'd only wind up hurting her when she learned I couldn't let go of my past life.

Her face filled the screen again. Was I right to do this? Emotions I thought I'd reserved for Kara lingered in my chest as I stared at Lorelei's image. One swipe to the right and I could hear her voice. But in doing that, was I diminishing the importance of what I had with Kara?

I knew either choice I made would leave me with pain. Kara was my past and Lorelei, my future. My thumb hovered over the button for a moment. Swallowing the bile burning my throat, I closed my eyes and sent a silent prayer to the heaven as I made my choice.

A choice that would change *everything.*

"I'm so sorry, baby."

Want to know what choice Kerrigan made?

The story continues in Broken Vows, Crossroads Heroes Book 1. Stop by the About the Authors section at the end of the book to learn more.

AN IRRESISTIBLE SPARK

Samantha Thomas

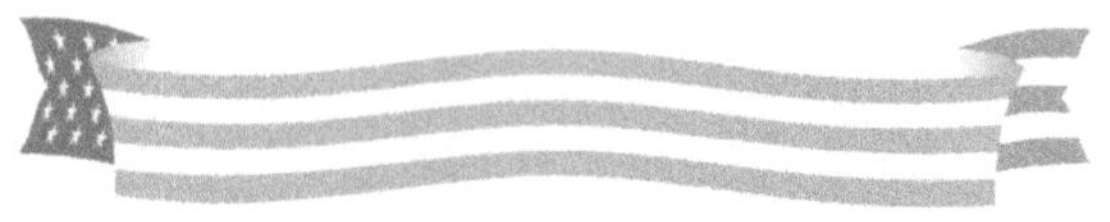

Police Officer Cassie Peck is starting in a division with a new lease on life now that her divorce is final. She is sure, she is done with uniformed men for good.

New Battalion Chief Chris Mackie never thought he was going to find a woman who loved him for his heart and not his occupation.

Sparks fly after an accidental cuffing, and an intentional fire, have Cassie and Mackie working together to catch an arsonist.

She's been burned before, but now they're caught by a fire they can't put out in this sweet, clean romance.

Cassie was resisting the urge to press down on the non-existent gas pedal on her passenger side of the patrol car.

"Can you pick it up a little, Frank?"

"Take it easy, Peck. Where's the fire?" Frank started laughing at his own joke. It quickly turned into a hacking cough.

"Serves you right," said Cassie, thumping her partner on the back.

Breath back, Frank replied, "Relax, the cowboys are already there. Waving and taking pictures with the adoring crowds, I'm sure. I don't need to get into an accident rushing to a scene that's under control."

Cassie took another deep cleansing breath and smoothed back the wayward curls of her curly blonde hair. Breathe in, breathe out. She found she'd been doing that a lot lately. Her yoga instructor thought it would help her learn to relax. Cassie hadn't seen any proof of that yet.

It wasn't Frank's fault, and the reality was he was probably right. They weren't the first unit on the scene, so there was no reason to go flying around corners. Moderation just wasn't her thing.

Impatient, and restless had been showing up on her reports since pre-school. She was working on it, but it wasn't an overnight fix.

Being partnered with Frank Murphy was either going to be a blessing or a curse. The old guy was only nine months away from retirement. He had a spotless record and was intent on keeping it that way. By the book, follow the rules and no showboating. Leave the Hollywood moves for the firefighters. His only job was to get everyone home safely.

After four years of marriage to a glory seeking detective who couldn't follow the one basic rule of fidelity, she should be appreciative of Frank's pace. She was certainly done with charismatic charmers who thought that a winning smile absolved them of any wrongdoing. Now, she needed to take her own pace down a notch.

With the divorce final, and a few favors called in, Cassie made her transfer to a new precinct two weeks ago. The further away she was from East Division and her ex, the better off they would both be. She was going to have to prove herself all over again, but it was still worth it.

She looked over as Frank carefully put on his signal and made a left turn. She took another deep breath. She was definitely being tested.

As they approached the scene, Cassie saw Frank was right, and the fire looked to be under control. It must have been called in pretty quickly from the time it started. Another police unit was already there. Thank goodness for small mercies. The shop was part of a strip mall in the neighborhood, and the damage didn't look too bad. Hopefully the owners would be back on their feet and open soon. Small businesses had already taken some hard hits in this current economy, something like this could be the final nail in the coffin for some.

Frank unexpectedly turned down a side street leading to the back alley between the strip mall and a row of houses.

“Where are we going?” asked Cassie.

“Since you’re all fired up like a racehorse, I figured we’d do a little drive around back. See if anything sticks out,” replied Frank.

“You’re too good to me, Frank,” said Cassie.

“I know.”

This was the fourth fire in this neighborhood in as many weeks. Arson was suspected, but it was hard to tell if it was one person responsible or several. General consensus was that they had a serial arsonist on their hands. The fires had been fairly small so far, and no lives had been lost. But that could easily change.

Cassie wanted to get her hands on the person who was starting these fires. The damage fire can do is absolutely horrendous, she’d seen it first-hand in past calls. Fire doesn’t care what it’s burning. Forest, homes, or people, the flames will eat it all with the same fervor. Most arsonists escalate, it was only a matter of time before someone got hurt. They needed to find the person responsible, sooner rather than later.

Cruising down the back alley, something white flashed, catching Cassie’s eye. There were hardly any fences between the yards, it was a series of hedges and bush.

“Whoa, whoa, slow down.” Who’d have thought she ever be saying that to Frank? “You see that?”

“Nope,” Frank replied, but he slowed the unit right down.

“Over there.” Cassie pointed towards a house down the alley.

She saw it again. “I’m getting out.” She didn’t wait for a

response or for Frank to come to a complete stop.

She saw the movement of white again. This time it was attached to a man, and he was now one house closer to the scene.

Carefully moving along the hedges, that divided the property lines, Cassie got closer while remaining out of sight. She was able to see him clearly now, while still staying hidden. Tall, dark hair covered in a baseball cap, he looked fit. His muscled back straining against a tight, white sweaty t-shirt, and long legs encased in track pants.

Nice. Muscle bound athlete out for a little jog, with a dash of arson. The press was going to love this.

As the man moved the branches of the bush before him, Cassie caught a glimpse of the muted red of a gas can. She ducked down as he lifted his head to look around. Was he hiding it, or grabbing it? She couldn't tell. She did know that there was no way he was going to get away with it. Frank would be happy to have a solid win under his belt his last few months too. This guy was almost making it too easy.

With his back still facing her, Cassie called out. 'Show me your hands."

The man was still looking down. He didn't even acknowledge Cassie. Her dislike increased.

"Police. I said show me your hands and stand up very slowly."

Still nothing. He was almost twenty feet away.

"Last chance, pal. Stand and put your hands up slowly."

Then man finally stood up, but to her shock he didn't even turn around. He broke into a run and was heading straight for the scene of his crime.

"Oh no you don't, big guy," muttered Cassie under her breath.

She immediately took off after him. His legs were almost twice as long as hers, but Cassie had always been fast, and she'd missed her workout this morning. She was ready to go, and this guy wasn't getting away.

Cassie was easily gaining on him. It was like he wasn't even trying to get away. Just before he rounded the corner of the next house, she launched herself at his back. Target hit, they both went crashing to the ground. He was quick, and flipped her over on her back, yelling, "What are you doing?"

With adrenaline still coursing through her veins, years of judo kicked in and before he knew it the outraged man was flat on his back, his tapered waist squeezed firmly between her thighs. Between martial arts and a few years on the cheerleading squad back in high school, Cassie had thighs of steel. This jerk wasn't going anywhere. She could feel the strength of his body beneath hers, but then he completely stopped struggling. Her brown eyes narrowed in on his green, framed by long soot-colored lashes. The kind women pay a lot of money to replicate.

The corner of his eyes crinkled as he spoke, "Officer. As enjoyable as this may be, do you plan on getting off me anytime soon?" The man seemed to be confident and accepting for a guy who'd just been caught. "Can I at least take my ear buds out?" He slowly pointed one finger towards his ears.

Now up close, Cassie could see the earbuds tucked in and hidden by a mess of hair. He'd lost his baseball cap in their fall to the ground. *Oh no!* No wonder he didn't hear her when she called. How had she missed that? It was that mop of hair. But earbuds still didn't explain what he was doing here, or the gas cans.

She pulled the buds from each ear and then in one swift move jumped up and off the man, stepping back and motioned for him to get up. “Get up.”

“Yes, Ma’am.” The man was all smiles now. “I’m afraid it won’t be as impressive as that, when I do it.”

Cassie gave a quick disgusted snort. “Just get up.”

As he stood, she took another step back. He was well over six feet, and even at a respectful five foot eight, she didn’t feel like having to crane her neck to look up to him. It was hard not to notice he was in great shape and had a face that could turn a few heads. The kind of guy who knew he was attractive and likely used it to his advantage. He probably thought that slightly lopsided, boyish smile was going to get him out of this too. He had no idea how wrong he was.

After wiping escaping tendrils from her forehead, she placed one hand on her right hip, at the ready and took a wide stance. “Care to explain, what exactly it is you are doing back here?”

The man shrugged. “I live here. Well, not right here, around here.”

“Sure, you do. I do too, we’re neighbors,” Cassie shot back. She didn’t know why she was engaging like this with him.

“You definitely don’t live around here.”

“What makes you so sure about that?”

“Officer, if you lived anywhere near me, I’d remember.”

He shot her another winning smile. Perfect white teeth, and full, smooth lips, came at her full force. This guy must really think he's something.

"You're not as cute as you think you are buddy."

"But you still think I'm cute?"

Was this guy for real? He'd been caught red-handed. Why do attractive men think they can get away with anything? She saw him with the gas cans, and he was chatting like they were on a first date. Cassie didn't know exactly how, but he was definitely involved, and she wasn't letting him go until she got some answers.

"I think you're an idiot, but what I think doesn't really matter. You're in a lot of trouble here. I want to know what you were doing with those gas cans." Cassie could see Frank getting out of the car and walking towards them.

"Listen, I'm not saying I'm opposed to you trying out your cuffs on me—"

"Wow, never heard that one before." Cassie gave him a hard thin-lipped grin.

"You don't want to do this…" he looked at the patch on her uniform. "Officer Peck."

"I've never wanted to do something more," assured Cassie.

"Now that's what I like to hear," grinned the man. He was absolutely unrepentant. She was not going to fall for another pretty face.

Cassie was ready to knock that smug smile off his face. "Shut it, Casanova. Turn around."

The man quietly complied as Cassie put on the handcuffs.

Frank joined them, and both men looked each other up and down. Faces neutral.

"There's two gas cans over there in the bush," motioned

Cassie. "That's where I caught him poking around."

Frank looked over to where Cassie had pointed then back to her and the suspect. "I see you got the cuffs on him and everything." Then Frank started to laugh. "You took him down hard."

The man, jut out his chin in Frank's direction. "Keep it up there, chuckles and you'll be—"

Cassie yanked on the man's elbow. "A little respect, pal."

Frank, now coughing, waved away her demand of the man. "That's okay, Peck. Mackie here is probably a little cranky from all the steroids."

Mackie gave Frank a derisive once over. "It's called exercise, Frank. You should try it sometime."

"No time, Mackie, we work on our shifts."

A sinking feeling hit Cassie in the pit of her stomach. She knew that she'd screwed up, the question was how badly. These two obviously knew each other, and their teasing interaction with an underlying hint of animosity, almost guaranteed she'd bagged herself a firefighter.

She started to uncuff him. "You could have said something."

"I did."

"Something helpful, not obnoxious."

Frank was patting his vest and pockets, looking for something. "You're lucky I don't have my phone on me Mackie. This one would be on the Wall of Shame for sure."

"You're not helping me here, Frank," said Cassie.

"Ah, don't worry," reassured her partner. "I woulda cuffed him too."

Rubbing his wrists, Mackie held out a hand to Cassie. "Chris

Mackie. I'm at Station 13 and I do in fact, live in this neighborhood."

Cassie hesitated for a moment, then took his hand. "Cassie Peck, obviously embarrassed."

She wanted to curl up and disappear. Eight shifts in and she had already made a fool of herself. It didn't help that the brash firefighter was still looking at her with twinkling green eyes. This was not the foot she hoped to start on.

"To be fair, you couldn't have known."

"You didn't answer, but I should have seen the earbuds."

"I was out for a run." He pointed to his discarded earbuds in the grass. "May I."

Cassie bent down and grabbed them, holding them out, it was the closest she was coming to an apology. She still wasn't sure if she liked this Mackie or not.

He took them from her, his fingertips lingering on her palm, longer than necessary. She felt a shiver run across her skin. He watched her reaction and raised a brow. "Thank you."

Mackie turned back to Frank. "I'm off, but when I heard the sirens, I had to come check it out. Figured I'd do a quick look around. Glad I did. There are two five-gallon plastic cans over there, empty. I didn't touch or move them. I doubt the homeowner's keeping them in the bush."

"I'll go take a look, and leave you kids to sort this out." Frank headed towards the cans, still laughing, leaving Cassie alone with Mackie.

"Any chance we can keep this between us." She wasn't going to beg, but it was worth a shot to ask. "I really don't need your Chief to know."

Mackie cocked his head to the side. "Even if I were to say yes, there's no way that Murphy is keeping his mouth shut."

She shook her head. "I'll worry about Frank. Do I need to worry about you too?"

"How about we discuss it over drinks?" asked Mackie.

Cassie shook her head in disbelief. Momentarily at a loss for words. "Are you blackmailing me? Drinks for your silence."

For the first time, Mackie didn't seem so confident. "Easy now, I didn't mean anything by it."

He probably didn't. She was still smarting from the embarrassment of her actions, and the fact that he was so attractive wasn't helping. Cassie took another deep breath.

"No, that's on me. I'm not exactly showing my best side here."

He tilted his head, "Doesn't really look like you have a bad one from here. Although, you may need to fix that hair. Our little wrestling match has you flouting regulation." He reached out to brush a curl from the side of her face.

At his words, Cassie broke eye contact and instinctively put her hands to her hair and blushed. She'd been trying to grow it out, and it was the stage where it was more often a tangled mess than styled. An exorbitant amount of product was usually the only thing keeping the blonde disaster in its bun. The fact that Mackie felt the need to point it out was almost as embarrassing as how it had become undone. That had to be why her cheek was so heated. There was no way it could be from his brief gentle touch.

"I should really chop it off." Why was she talking to a man she had almost arrested about hair decisions?

Mackie frowned, “Don’t you dare. I like it. Suits you.” He cocked his head again as he looked at her. “A little wild.”

“What makes you think I’m wild?” asked Cassie. Apparently, her mouth had decided to start flirting.

“Well, that takedown wasn’t exactly, by the book.” He gave her a sexy wink, and Cassie wondered if it was a move he had practiced for hours in the mirror.

This time it was Cassie that smiled. “What takedown? I don’t recall anything like that. If there was, I’m sure Frank would have had a photo of it.”

“Alright, if that’s the way you want to play it.” He gave her another playful grin.

“So, you won’t tell your Chief and the rest of the station?”

“My lips are sealed.”

Cassie wished he hadn’t referenced his lips; it was taking all control not to look at them as it was. Needed to get herself out of this dangerous liaison, she thrust out her hand. “Thanks, Mack—”

“Chief!”

Two firefighters came around the corner of the strip mall towards them. Cassie looked from the uniformed men to Mackie and yanked back her hand. At least he had the decency to look a little ashamed.

She leaned towards him and looked up into wide green eyes. He’d been caught and he knew it. No sparkles, now that he had been busted.

“You’re a real piece of work, Chief.”

She didn’t wait for a response. She marched off toward Frank, wishing she'd hit Mackie a whole lot harder when she'd taken him down. What had she been thinking, flirting with a fire eating playboy? Another lesson learned.

Cassie was going to swear off men forever.

"Was it something I said?" asked Dalton.

"Usually is," said Rhys, giving Dalton a quick slap to the back of his helmet.

Mackie watched as the retreating figure of Officer Cassie Peck stomped away and wondered what caused him to act the way he did. He was acting like the young fools back at the firehouse. Especially the two that had just ratted him out.

"You didn't help." Mackie gave both men a glare over his shoulder.

Dalton gave an approving look Cassie's way. "Looks good from here. Who is she?"

"Have some class. And who she is, is none of your business." Mackie didn't know why he was so irritated by Dalton's words, and suddenly so protective of a woman he had just met. A woman who thought he was a criminal up until a few minutes ago. A woman with unruly hair, he wanted to… What was wrong with him? Clenching his jaw, he turned to face his men.

Both firefighters straightened up and Mackie watched in

irritation as they gave each other a wink. "Sorry, Chief."

"Yeah, Anyway, what are we looking at here?"

Mackie didn't want to talk about Cassie, and he sure didn't want these two talking about her either. And he really didn't like the way Dalton was looking at her. Not that it should have mattered. He had known her a whole ten minutes, and in that time, she had knocked him to the ground, cuffed him, and even after recognizing her mistake, she didn't apologize. Then when he'd forgotten to tell her one little thing, she'd told him off. Not exactly a great start.

He should be chalking this up to a rough morning and walking away, yet here he was wondering if he should run after her. Cassie was the exact opposite of every single woman he'd ever dated, right down to those brown eyes and unruly blonde curls she thought she braided and sprayed down. So, why was he still thinking about her?

Dalton and Rhys gave him a rundown of the scene, but since he was off, Mackie figured it was better to get home and let the boys get back to work. He would be at the station soon enough.

Cassie wasn't the only mystery he wanted to solve. They needed to find out who was setting these fires. He was hoping that the gas cans he found, could be of some help. It wasn't really his job, but this was his community. The Office of Fire Investigation would be taking the case from the detective soon, but Mackie was worried. He'd never seen an arsonist, that given enough time, didn't escalate his crimes. It was only a matter of when.

There was no obvious suspect, and the targets all seemed random. From few park fires to a local business, there was already escalation. The only thing that was similar was that gasoline was being used as an accelerant. It didn't seem like whoever was doing this really knew what they were doing. In some ways that made them all the more dangerous.

The timing was also a concern. Once a week wasn't much time between events, and that worried Mackie even more. Who knew when the next one would be? He had a bad feeling it was going to be sooner than they expected.

Jogging back to his place, Mackie decided to leave one earbud out. He should have done that earlier. He knew better, and it would have saved both Cassie and him the embarrassment. Not that he minded completely. She'd caught him off guard when she managed to flip him on his back. It was an impressive move. He could feel the strength in her legs, and he decided stop moving and enjoy the view. He was glad he hadn't shared that thought with Cassie. If he was looking for a chance with the lovely Officer Peck, he was going to have to up his game. This was not a woman impressed by his uniform, she wore her own.

Mackie was greeted at the door, by his black lab Molly. Normally she would run with him, but she'd gotten into a tussle with some bramble bushes out back and was still healing from an infection on her leg. Molly thought she was good to go, but Mackie wanted to wait a few more days to be sure.

Molly was the closest thing to a wife, that Mackie wanted. She was patient and forgiving, and didn't mind if he wasn't home for supper, as long as she got hers. In his line of work, relationships were tough to keep. Molly was perfect. If he'd had a tough call, he could tell her everything, or if it was too much to even speak of, she would curl in close and share the silence.

Scratching beneath Molly's ears on the couch, Cassie once again, popped into Mackie's head. He looked over to the empty seat on the other side of Molly and wondered what it would be like to have someone there. For some reason, when he did, he could only picture the red-cheeked face of Officer Cassie Peck.

"I don't know, girl. I think I may have hit my head a lot harder than I thought."

Molly looked up as he spoke. "I know. It's supposed to be just me and you. That was the deal, right?"

The lab cocked her head to the side, waiting.

Mackie gave her head a hard rub. "Ah, don't worry, girl. It's fine. Maybe a date or two. If she's willing to talk to me again. Enough to get her out of my head. Then we'll both move on."

Molly settled her head back down in his lap.

"That's right. I don't need anything more than this."

Mackie let out a deep sigh, then Molly did then same.

Who was he kidding? The problem was he could never find someone who could look past the uniform. To see him as a whole man, not only the guy who runs in when others run out and poses with puppies for calendars. To know that some days his heart is broken by the calls he takes, and that his hurt can sometimes affect the ones he loves.

So, he'd given up and kept his dating life casual. That seemed to be working, until today. Mackie never thought that falling hard for someone would be so literal, but here he was. Still thinking about a woman, who he had ticked off within moments of meeting her and was unlikely to ever give him the time of day.

Mackie chuckled to himself. What Officer Cassie Peck didn't know was how much he loved a challenge. She thought it was over.

But for Mackie it had just begun.

After passing off the gas cans from the morning fire to the detective in charge of the case Cassie and Frank had a relatively quiet day, which made Frank very happy. Sitting on a bench in the locker room, she watched as Frank hummed to himself.

He stopped and turned to Cassie.

"One more down." Frank licked his figure and drew a one in the air, in front of his locker.

"Are you going to count every single day, Frank?" sighed Cassie.

"Darn, right I am," he nodded. "Each day is one day closer to retirement. Me, boat, pole. The fish don't even matter. I don't care if I ever catch anything again. I'll leave that to you kids."

"Speak for yourself. I'd like to catch whoever's starting those fires." Cassie shook her head. "I hate knowing there's going to be another call because of the same guy."

"Well, you sure came close today, Peck." Frank's laugh started to turn into a wheeze. He shook his head. "I just wish I had a picture. Pride of the 13, taken down and cuffed."

Cassie pressed her lips together and crossed her arms, staring at Frank.

"What?" His look of innocence was almost comical.

"Are you planning on letting this drop anytime soon?"

Frank gave her a big grin. "Not likely, but it's not really teasing you, Peck. I just like to see those cowboys taken down a notch once in a while. He's still new to the position, but Mackie's the bright shining star of Station 13, that's how he got to be Chief so quick."

"I thought he looked young for the job," mused Cassie.

"Yup. And no strings to the brass. He's just that good. I actually really like the guy. Not that I'd ever say it to his face. So, I'm going to savor this moment for a little while longer if you don't mind."

"If that's what floats your boat," replied Cassie, as Frank went back to humming.

Of course, he had to be good at his job. Guys with that kind of confidence always were. Probably had it easy his whole life. Pretty face, and a body like that makes this journey through life a whole lot easier. He's probably been a step ahead in everything he'd ever done. Just like her ex. Seriously, how did she keep bumping into to these guys.

As she grabbed her bag to leave, Frank called out. "Hey, kid. Why don't you meet us at Brews tonight? Let me buy you a drink. I owe you one for the entertainment today."

"Nah, I'm good, thanks." All Cassie wanted to do was have a nice hot shower, and maybe read a couple chapters of her new book before hitting the sack. She wanted to read about a sweet blonde-haired hero, so she could get the vision of a certain, muscle bound, dark-haired Battalion Chief out of her mind. Book boyfriends, that was where it was at. A noisy bar filled with cops and firefighters was the last place she wanted to be.

"Ah, come on, Peck. Do an old man a solid. Besides, you need to get to know some of the others around here. Don't be the snotty new kid."

He wasn't wrong. Cassie had almost gone out of her way not to make friends. She didn't want to end up in the same situation as she'd been in East Division with her ex. She didn't want to become a pariah either. An hour at Brews probably wouldn't hurt.

"One drink."

Frank slapped his knee. "Sold!"

At least her partner was happy.

Cassie was about to open the door, when their Sergeant, Dani Kim, stuck her head in.

"Frank, you, still good for the school thing tomorrow?"

"You bet, Sarge. Looking forward to it."

Sergeant Kim gave then both a nod and disappeared.

Cassie opened her hands in question, "Ah, when were you telling me?"

Frank shrugged. "You know now. You're riding with Martinovic tomorrow. I'm on kindergarten duty. I'll miss that the most. One of the few places where the whole room still thinks you're the good guy."

Cassie loved the school and community outreach as well. Kids were so excited and filled with questions. It was usually a great reminder, why they did the job. There was never a shortage of volunteers for those days.

"Lucky," said Cassie.

"Well, maybe you'll get lucky too, and Martinovic will let you drive with that lead foot of yours." laughed Frank.

Cassie rolled, her eyes. "See you tonight, Frank." She could hear him wheezing at his joke, as she walked out the door.

She checked her phone. If she grabbed a bite to eat now, she might have enough time to get a short run in and maybe even a quick nap. She was still a little wired from the day, especially after her morning run in with Chief Chris Mackie.

It was really starting to bother her how his irritating face, with his 'aw shucks' smile kept popping into her mind. The guy was exactly like all the others. Charming, attractive, and thought they could do no wrong. Even when they are caught. Seriously, she made a fool of herself, the guy could have told her he was the Battalion Chief.

Of course, it had been her error that had set the whole thing in motion. It wasn't exactly like he had lied. Maybe it wasn't fair to compare all guys against her ex, but she'd been burned by a handsome face before, and the wound was still a little fresh.

Vietnamese take out in one hand, with the other Cassie slid her key into her apartment door. She hesitated for a moment then went in. She didn't know why she still expected to hear the sounds of Max running to the door.

Max was the only thing she missed from her marriage to Brad. The border collie was a better companion to her than Brad had ever been. He'd belonged to her ex before they were married, so there was no way, he was giving him up. There were a few nights, that as she slept alone in her new apartment, she contemplated kidnapping Max, but by morning she came to her senses and realized that Max didn't need to be in the middle of their battle. Didn't make the ache of missing him any less, especially after a rough day.

Cassie sat down at the old wooden kitchen table. Eating her supper, she looked around the small space. She sighed as she saw her reflection in the mirror across the room, alone at the table eating takeout. It wasn't the life she'd dreamed of.

Most of her furniture was mismatched. Cassie knew she wouldn't be featured in any home magazines any time soon, unless it was a before picture. She tamped down the bitterness that bubbled up. She knew it wasn't much and that she was starting over, but money in the bank was more important than fancy end tables, and she finally had that. It was all hers, and she didn't need to worry that it would suddenly disappear, because Brad was paying off a secret credit card to hide his hotel bills. She would get where she needed to go, and it would be on her terms.

Cassie was finally in charge of her own life, and even despite the little mishap this morning, she was still feeling pretty good.

She tapped her phone. There was still lots of time before heading to Brews, but the nap would have to wait. Quick run, shower, one drink, then home. She should be in bed by 11pm.

By morning she would be refreshed, and all thoughts of Chief Chris Mackie should be long gone.

Cassie nodded across the crowd to Frank. Thank goodness the entrance to Brews was higher than the floor of the bar. The place was packed. It would have been hard to see him without the extra height. He was sidled up to the bar with a two other cops from the precinct. He waved her over.

Pointing at bottles lined up behind the bar, he asked, "What'll you have. This ones on me."

"Wow, Cassie, you got Frank buying drinks? What happened on your shift today? Catch him robbing a bank or something?" Megan Hurst was another officer at their precinct. She'd been one of the first people to reach out when Cassie arrived. The friendly woman had been on the job for a few years longer than Cassie, but it seemed like it was much longer as she came from a family of cops. Multiple generations. Her youngest brother had become a firefighter, but Megan joked that they still loved him anyway.

Cassie shook her head. "I'm amazed Frank hasn't spilled the beans, already."

"You wound me, Peck. My lips have been sealed." Frank ran a

finger across his lips and pretending to throw away a key.

"Yeah, right, front desk sure knew." Cassie wasn't even mad. The story was obviously bringing Frank some joy.

Frank grinned. "Well, mostly sealed."

"Are we going to hear this story or what?" Darian James had previously partnered with Frank and so far, he was one of the nicest guys she'd met at the precinct. How guys like that were single made no sense, while the players, made out like bandits. "If Frank's willing to part with his cash, it must be good."

"You're making too much out of it." Cassie shrugged. "There was a small mix-up this morning, and I may have ended up cuffing, Battalion Chief Mackie from Station 13."

Jaws dropped on both Megan and Darian.

"What?"

Frank broke in, "Come on, Peck. Don't hold back the best part."

"They get the point, Frank," said Cassie.

Frank turned to back to the other two officers. "She took him out." He shook his head with the memory. "It was beautiful. Mackie was out for a jog, and came by the scene, he was poking around out back and looking all kinds of sketchy." Frank gave Cassie a pat on her shoulder. "Peck here thought she'd ask a few questions. Mackie refused to turn around and then took off running." Frank started laughing and holding his chest with one hand. "Peck threw herself at Mackie while he was running away. BAM!" Frank smashed his fist into his palm. "Square in the back. Mackie went down like a sack of potatoes. Beautiful. Just beautiful." Frank finished by pretending to wipe a tear from his eye.

Cassie watched as Megan and Darian laughed at Frank's

retelling. This story was going to get bigger and bigger over time. There was no way she'd be able to keep it under wraps. She been hoping it would die a quiet death, but that didn't seem like it was going to happen. Wishful thinking wasn't going to get her through this one.

"Alright, alright, I think I'll take that beer now," said Cassie.

Beer in hand, the four of them chatted about their shift, and upcoming plans. Frank held most of the conversation with his dreams for his retirement. Megan had dreams of a beach getaway for the summer and Darian wasn't planning much past the next few weeks.

Cassie was nursing her drink, as she checked out Brews, and she could see the appeal of the place. There were pictures all over the walls of celebrating the lives of first responders, with the exception of one wall near the back. She now knew what 'Wall of Shame' Frank had been talking about, and was even more thankful, that he hadn't had his phone on him.

They talked for about an hour, but Cassie was getting tired, and although the company was nice, but she wanted to get home.

She was about to say goodbye, when Frank, who was facing the door, threw out a bark of laughter. Whacking Cassie on the arm, he pointed to the entrance. "Look who the cat dragged in."

It couldn't be.

Cassie slowly turned around to see none other than Battalion Chief Chris Mackie walk in, a couple swaggering firefighters behind him. There was a bunch of giggles and sighs from a nearby table of young women. Cassie could hear Megan sighing at the reaction. "Those foolish girls have no idea."

"Bunch of cowboys. I'm telling ya," scoffed Frank as she

watched the firefighters making their grand entrance.

Cassie ducked her head, hoping to avoid making eye contact, as Mackie and his crew confidently surveyed the crowd. The last thing she needed was another run in with Chief Perfect.

Unfortunately, the temptation was too strong, and her curiosity won over. The moment Cassie lifted her eyes, they locked on his. His green on her brown, sending a tingle straight down to her toes. Before she could stop it, her traitorous mouth smiled. Cassie was furious with her body's reaction.

He lifted both brows at her and gave her a lopsided grin.

It wasn't going to work. Well, maybe on the table next to them, but definitely not her. Her mind was stronger than her heart, and she would not be taken in. This was a road she had been down before and had no interest in repeating the trip.

Not wanting to get caught up, in any potential back and forth banter, where flirting led to an exchange of numbers, Cassie quickly said goodbye to the group. Ignoring their cries of 'coward,' she took the furthest route around the bar and Mackie and made her getaway.

She was halfway down the street to her car when she heard someone call out.

"Peck." She didn't turn around. "Cassie."

She kept walking, pretending she couldn't hear him.

"I know you can hear me. You don't have any earbuds in."

A smile hit her lips before she could stop it from forming. His footsteps got closer.

"Slow down, Officer Cassie Peck, we don't want a repeat of what happened this morning."

Cassie stopped, wiped the smile from her face and swung

around. “What do you want?”

Mackie halted in his tracks, looking a little surprised that she had turned around so quickly. Was he prepared to chase her all the way down the street? “Well, to start with I wanted to say I was sorry.”

Cassie stared at him. He looked adorably sincere, but she wasn’t going to give an inch. He was probably expecting her to tell him, not to worry and then fawn all over him. He was going to have to sweat it out a little longer than that. Even if it was her that really needed to apologize.

Since she wasn’t filling the silence, he did. “Did you want to apologize to me?”

What? The nerve of this guy. Cassie actually had planned on apologizing eventually, but now that he was telling her she had to, there was no way, it was going to happen.

She narrowed her eyes at him and placed both hands on her hips. “And what exactly am I apologizing for?”

Mackie raised both brows. “It was you, who jumped me. An innocent man, I might add.”

“I was doing my job.” Cassie took a few steps closer to Mackie and jabbed a finger in his direction. “You looked suspicious, you were near a crime scene, and you ran.”

“I had earbuds in! I couldn’t hear you, maybe you should have been louder.” His self-righteous tone had her ready to spit. She was about to let him have it, when he held up both hands, holding back her onslaught.

“Okay, stop. I came out here to apologize, not to fight with you," said Mackie.

"I don't think you're very good at it."

He shrugged. "Fair enough. But at least I'm trying here. You could do the same."

He was right. She was being unnecessarily petty. Cassie had no idea why this man was affecting her this way. Normally she could brush these guys off no problem. What was so different about this one?

"Fine. Try again."

"Try what."

"Apologizing."

Mackie shook his head, and a dimpled smile came her way. "Alright. Officer Cassie Peck, I humbly ask you to forgive me for my behavior today."

"You should have told me you were Battalion Chief," said Cassie.

"I should have," replied an earnest Mackie.

How was she supposed to stay mad at that? She had to give him some credit for at least coming after her to apologize. Most guys would have made it their mission to make sure she was embarrassed by what happened. He wasn't doing that. It was obvious he meant it, and if she didn't forgive him, she was definitely the jerk. She was going to have to give in, at least a little.

"I may have overreacted," conceded Cassie.

Mackie didn't say anything. If he was expecting more, then he would be waiting a while.

He gave a low chuckle and then he looked back at the bar, then back to Cassie. "Do you want to come back to Brews? Play some darts or something?"

He looked so hopeful, that Cassie almost caved. Almost. "I'm good thanks."

Mackie gave her that boyish grin. "Do you think that now you've forgiven me, you might agree to drinks one day."

He was incorrigible. Absolutely no shame, and for some sure to be regrettable reason, she found herself liking him, a little more with each moment that passed.

"All things are possible there, cowboy. How about you take the win for today and leave it at that?"

"You realize that's a yes in my book, Cassie Peck."

"I know you think it's a yes," she smiled and shook her head.

Mackie tilted his head gave a soft smile. "Unless you would like me to walk you to your car, I'm going to leave while my foot remains outside my mouth."

"Smart move, Mackie. And I'm fine to walk."

"Alright." He gave her a wink and then walked back to the bar.

It took all his self-control not to turn around and get one last glimpse of Cassie. Those soft curls wrapped around her face, begging for him to swirl them around his finger. She definitely had him spinning, and he wasn't even sure if she liked him.

Absolutely no interest in staying at Brews with Cassie gone, Mackie shared a drink with the crew and then begged off. They would have more fun if he wasn't there anyway.

He'd only made Battalion Chief a few months ago, but even in that short time there was a shift in how his team saw him. Mackie expected and accepted that fact, but it did mean most nights were spent with Molly.

It wouldn't hurt to get a decent sleep at home. He'd volunteered to chat with the kids at one of the nearby schools for career day. It was always a good opportunity for the children to meet some of their local first responders. It was one of his favorite parts of the job. Usually in the weeks following, they would have families of the children visiting the station. It was a morale boost for everyone.

He was met at the door by Molly and for some strange reason thought of Cassie and wondered if she liked dogs. He laughed at himself for even thinking it, as he'd just gotten himself removed from 'total jerk' zone. He still hadn't convinced her to go out with him. He had a lot of work to do if he wanted Cassie to meet Molly.

Mackie looked down at his dog and scratched her in her favorite spot beneath her ear. "Who couldn't love you, hey girl. And if they don't love you, we don't want them."

Mackie really hoped Cassie liked dogs.

Martinovic wasn't a bad guy, but only three hours in, Cassie was surprised to find herself missing Frank, and his fishing stories. Officer Nick Martinovic had non-stop tales to tell of his newly discovered love for beekeeping and his prowess in day trading. He was oddly able to combine the two subjects. He wasn't overly concerned about her participation while he talked. Cassie quickly realized why he was considered a bit of a floater in the department. One shift was more than enough.

"I want to go check something out," said Cassie.

Martinovic nodded then continued talking about the importance of a good quality queen catcher if you wanted to separate the queen from the hive for a while. Cassie soon tuned him out and hoped Frank was enjoying himself today.

Cassie wanted to drive back to the strip mall. When they got there, the windows of the business were now covered with plywood, but there was a homemade sign on the sidewalk out front, declaring 'Reopening Soon!' It appeared to be a massage therapy clinic. Cassie hoped the owner was right and they would be able to open their doors to the clinic soon.

She pulled into an empty space and took in the scene.

Asking Martinovic for a few minutes, Cassie got out of the patrol car. She was looking around at the other stores and the neighborhood, when she saw a slim man at the edge of the parking lot, taking pictures. She waved in his direction, and although he startled, he waved back, but he didn't leave.

Cassie walked over to the man. "Hello! How are you today, Sir?"

The man cleared his throat and slid his phone back into his pocket. "Hi there, Officer."

"You from around here?" asked Cassie.

Something was off with this guy. He looked harmless in his clean jeans and collared shirt. His salt and pepper hair was trimmed in a crew cut, exposing surprisingly big ears, but nothing really out of the ordinary. Cassie didn't know what was bothering her, but something about the way his eyes kept shifting to the boarded-up massage clinic bothered her.

The man noticeably swallowed before he answered. "My wife…she uh…she works here. She owns the paint studio over there."

Cassie looked to where the man was pointing. There was a cute little shop with pictures covering the front window, advertising adult paint nights, several doors down from the clinic.

"Lucky it wasn't her place," said Cassie.

"Yeah. Thought I would take some pictures. Pretty crazy stuff." The man seemed more comfortable now. Maybe she was wrong. Lots of people are fascinated by fire. If his wife's place was so close, it wasn't completely out of the ordinary to be taking an interest.

"You around when it happened?" asked Cassie.

The man quickly shook his head, "No, no. We don't live in this neighborhood. I'm usually away for work, anyway."

"Ah," replied Cassie. She was about to let him go, when he asked an odd question that didn't sit right with her.

"Do you think that he will really reopen that place? Or will insurance pay it out? The fire department got here pretty quick, so that made a difference. If the fire had been bigger, then it would have been destroyed, for sure. Right?"

Cassie felt the hairs on the back of her neck stand up and looked over to the clinic, and then back to the man who was now back to fidgeting. "Not really my jurisdiction, Sir. Looks like they're hoping to. Why do you ask?"

Nervous laughter bubbled up from the man, and he waved her question away. "No. No reason, just curious." He glanced toward a silver sedan with bright orange and yellow sunshine sticker on the back bumper, that was parked further down the road, away from the parking lot. "I should get going. I told my wife I would take a few pictures and be back." He gave her a brief smile, and then turned, heading back to his car.

"Sure. Take care, Sir." Cassie called after the man, watching him as he walked away.

Weird. Not everyone was comfortable around cops, but it was more than that with this guy.

She had a feeling, and she knew where she needed to go.

Mackie was sorting through paperwork, when there was a

knock at his office door.

"Yeah." Mackie called out, and to his surprise it was Cassie.

He jumped up, smashing his thighs on his desk, causing the firefighting bobble-head on his desk to begin bouncing up and down. He saw her mouth twitch at the sight and brown eyes quickly take in the rest of his office. He wondered how many conclusions Cassie had already jumped to about him, as he offered her a seat.

"To what do I owe the pleasure?" grinned Mackie. "I can only hope you couldn't wait to see me again."

He watched as Cassie shook her head and rolled her eyes at his words, but he didn't miss the little smile that touched her lips.

"Business. For now," replied Cassie.

Mackie's day was just getting better and better. With a visit from Cassie to start his morning, and a group of kindergarten kids to finish his day, he was feeling pretty good.

"For now, hey? Then let's get that business out of the way. How can I help?"

Cassie hesitated, like she wasn't quite sure what to say. After what appeared to be a brief inward debate she spoke. "It might be nothing, but since you live in the area, I thought I would ask."

"About?" asked Mackie, and placing both hands on his desk he leaned in. He could smell a faint hint of cinnamon coming from Cassie. He had to push the alluring aroma from his mind. He had no idea where this was going, but Cassie seemed pretty serious, and he wanted her to know he was listening.

"My partner and I were over at the scene from yesterday." She gave him another soft smile. "Our scene."

His heart leapt at her description. *Focus Mackie, play it cool.* This was not the moment to throw out another poorly timed invitation for drinks. He wisely kept his mouth shut, Cassie continued to speak.

"I spoke with a guy there today. It was weird. Not sure if it's anything, but I figured, I would throw it past you."

"What happened," asked Mackie.

"He was taking pictures. Said he didn't live there but his wife owned the paint studio in the strip mall. He was acting nervous, but it wasn't until he asked me about insurance, that things really felt off."

"Why was he asking a cop about insurance," asked Mackie. "No offense."

"None taken, it didn't make any sense to me either. He also seemed curious about your station's response time to the fire." Cassie shrugged. "Anyway, it didn't sit right with me. So, I thought I'd bring it to you."

Mackie leaned back in his chair. He agreed with Cassie, the whole interaction seemed off. Often firebugs went back to the scene of their crimes. If this guy had been responsible, maybe he was trying to get some pictures of his handiwork.

"I'm glad you did. Sounds off to me too. Any chance if you saw this guy again you could pick him out."

Cassie gave him a questioning look. "I would hope so. Wouldn't be much good at my job, if I couldn't."

Mackie smiled back at Cassie. "Should I be apologizing again?"

She waved him away. "I think we have all of those out of the way. We're good."

"Great. Can I show you some pictures? I always have someone take pictures at every call. The other chiefs have also adopted the habit. You never know when you might need them."

He started to pull up the files on his computer. If this guy was on scene at any of the other fires, then Cassie might be able to point him out, and then might finally have a decent lead for the Fire Investigator.

"Come around and take a look."

Cassie walked behind his desk, and standing at his shoulder, she silently watched as Mackie clicked through scene photos. The smell of cinnamon was stronger now, and despite the gravity of what they were doing, Mackie found himself wondering if her lips tasted as good as she smelled. Mentally shaking the thought from his mind, he refocused his efforts on the pictures.

They had already been through the first park fire, and no sign of the man Cassie had talked to. It was halfway into the second playground fire that she pointed at the screen.

"There. Right there. That's him." She was indicating to a figure off to the side of the crowd of young mothers and parents in the photo. "Him. No way, to miss those ears. Have you seen him before?"

"Never. But you said he didn't live in the neighborhood."

Cassie excitedly slapped his desktop with both hands. "Yeah, exactly, so, what's he doing hanging out at a playground, in a community he doesn't live in? He also said he didn't come around the area often. He was usually away for work."

Mackie let out a low whistle. "Holy buckets, Cassie, you may have just found our guy."

"Holy buckets?" Cassie looked at him, with a funny smile on her face.

"You obviously didn't grow up in my house. You never knew

when my mother was listening," explained Mackie. Even as a grown man, he dared not curse as he never knew when his mother might show up with a bar of soap. Kids these days had no idea.

"That's actually pretty adorable," laughed Cassie.

"I'm glad you think so, because it's a source of great amusement here at the firehouse," replied Mackie.

"I need to pass this on to the Fire Investigator's office." Mackie stood up quickly and as Cassie stepped back in response, she caught the back of her heel on the corner of his desk. She was about to fall back, when Mackie snaked out an arm and brought her into his body. She hit his chest with a thump and an exhalation of breath.

He looked down, at the deep brown eyes that were looking up into his. Then for the first time, he noticed the soft dusting of freckles across her forehead. He couldn't let her go, and she wasn't moving.

"Is this payback for yesterday?" Cassie's question almost a whisper.

The way she was staring at him, Mackie had to bite his lip to prevent himself from kissing her. She felt so right in his arms, and the cinnamon was intoxicating.

"No point in revenge for something that may be the best thing that's ever happened to me." Mackie was finding it harder and harder to resist the urge to taste Cassie's bowed lips.

She closed her eyes, and just as he was about to give in to his desire, there was a knock at the door.

"Chief?"

Dalton. That guy may be one of the best guys to have at your side on a call, but he had the absolute worst timing.

Cassie and Mackie broke apart, and Cassie quickly moved toward the door of his office, smoothing her uniform and her hair as she walked.

She opened the door, and a slack jawed Dalton, stared at Cassie and then winced when he saw the look on Mackie's face.

"I can come back," said Dalton.

"No need," Cassie sidestepped around the interrupting firefighter. "I got what I came here for." She shot a sassy smile Mackie's way, and soon Dalton was left alone standing in the doorway.

"Sorry, Chief. I—"

"What is it? It had better be important," growled Mackie. He knew he wasn't being fair but having Cassie in his arms and then suddenly ripped away, made him a special kind of ornery.

Dalton, cleared his throat then spoke, "Lunch is up."

"Get out!" yelled Mackie.

Unless it was a tray full of cinnamon buns, the last thing he was thinking about right now, was food.

Cassie wasn't missing Martinovic, but she was definitely missing driving.

She and Frank had a busy morning with an ugly domestic violence call, and an interesting ride with a seven-year-old pickpocket, who on her ride back home, was explaining she had been watching an old movie called Oliver! at her grandmother's house and wanted to see if she could be as good as the pick pocketing street urchins of London. She was not, and her poor mother was horrified to know what her young daughter was up to, while supposedly under the watchful eye of her teenage brother.

"Just a quick drive by, Frank. It's quiet right now, we're in the area, and we have time."

Cassie had been trying to convince her partner to swing by the strip mall in hopes of bumping into the suspicious man from yesterday. Frank figured the case was out of their hands and wasn't interested in sticking his nose where it didn't belong. Cassie felt otherwise.

"I think you're getting a little obsessed with this case, Peck. Or is it a particular firefighting poster boy, that's got you all worked up?" She could feel her partner giving her a look, but she refused to meet his eyes. Any answer she gave would be fodder for Frank, so she wasn't even going to try.

"Up and down the street and alley. That's it. He's either there or his not, and I leave it alone for the rest of the week," bargained Cassie.

"Week?" Frank gave her withering glare. "Why don't I believe that? If you can promise to drop it for the rest of the shift, we'll go."

'Done!" Cassie gently punched Frank in the arm and laughed. "You're getting soft in your old age, Frank. You should have held out for the week."

"Yeah, yeah, tell me about it." Frank carefully pulled into traffic and made his way toward Mackie's neighborhood.

Cassie could feel her pulse quicken and her insides were almost vibrating. Frank would call her high strung, but this was something different.

She'd lain awake last night going over her contact with the man she now believed to be the suspect in the arsons in Mackie's neighborhood. Rolling it over in her mind, she didn't know if it was the way he looked when he mentioned his wife, or the anger that was initially hidden by his nervousness as he asked if 'he' will reopen. If the clinic owner was around Cassie was hoping he might have some answers. She felt it deep in her bones that something was going to happen.

As they got closer, Cassie noticed the same silver sedan that the suspect had gotten into yesterday parked out on the street. This time it was further down, but the same bright sunshine sticker was on the bumper. There was no doubt it was the same car.

"Frank, look," Cassie pointed towards the parked vehicle. It's that guy's car. The same guy from yesterday."

Cassie was pulling the plates as they pulled up alongside the car. No one was inside, so, Frank turned and went into the alley between the strip mall and the houses where she had first met Mackie.

That was when they first saw the smoke.

"Call it in." Frank, stepped on the gas and sped down the alleyway. The senior officer was all business now.

He parked away from the scene and both of them rushed from the patrol car. The back door to the paint studio was open and the unmistakable smell of fuel was hanging in the air.

Frank edged towards the side of the door, and looked in. "I can't see all the way in, stay here."

There was no chance Cassie was leaving her partner to go in alone. Not only could the arsonist still be inside, but Frank had no idea what he was walking into.

"We both go!" shouted Cassie, and she followed Frank inside.

"You're a terrible listener, Peck." Frank called back, as he held his elbow to his face, trying to protect himself from the smoke that was turning from brown to black, as it began to swirl around them.

They were about to enter the main studio, that could be seen from the front windows, when Frank, suddenly stumbled back, a large red welt, staining his forehead. Trying to soften his fall, both Cassie and Frank fell back, as a man ran past down the hall and out the back door.

"Frank!" Cassie shook her partner's shoulder. "You good?"

The wound looked angry, but not deep, Frank nodded. "I'm fine. Go after him." Frank wheezed. "Go!"

Cassie hesitated, and Frank pushed her from his side, so she did as she was told. Frank only had to get down the hall. The fire was now burning in the main studio, and one side room, but he still had a clear exit.

Jumping to her feet, Cassie made sure Frank was back on his feet and following behind, before she ran down the hallway, out the back door and hot on the heels of their suspect. It might have taken her longer to track him down, but the idiot had decided to wear a bright orange shirt, and he stuck out like a sore thumb, among the green of the hedges he was running between. He was trying to make it to his car, there was absolutely no way she would let that happen.

She unleashed the adrenaline she'd been holding back. Her fury at her partner's injury, and the knowledge that if she didn't give it her all, this piece of dirt might get away, spurred her on. Cassie easily gained ground on the fleeing man, he now knew he was being chased, but his panic wasn't his friend. As she got closer, she thought she might be able to grab him to take him down, but the fool tripped over his own feet, and fed himself about twelve inches of asphalt.

Cassie looked down at the bloody sniveling mess at her feet and shook her head. The man had completely given up. He was sobbing as he tried to explain that his wife had been having an affair with the clinic owner. H only wanted to get the insurance money for the studio and then divorce her.

Shaking her head at the disaster the man had created for himself, Cassie noticed he was holding one of his front teeth in his hand as she hauled him to his feet.

After cuffing him and reading him his rights, Cassie did a quick assessment of his injuries. Other than some facial road rash, a broken tooth, and a broken spirit, the man was going to survive.

How he handled jail, would be a whole different matter.

Looking toward the strip mall, Cassie noticed that the black smoke was now billowing high above the stores. Pulling the arsonist along with her she made double time down the alley. Cassie felt a sinking feeling when she couldn't see Frank in the alley. He had been right behind her. She was about to call him name when an explosion rocked the studio.

Cassie hauled the man down to the ground with her. She could hear sirens in the distance. Looking around she saw a chain link fence surrounding a dumpster. Cuffing the still wailing arsonist to the fence Cassie took off down the alley to find Frank.

The backdoor to the studio was still wide open, and Cassie looked around for Frank, calling his name. There was no reason for him to have gone back inside, and certainly not alone.

Fighting the smoke, she stepped inside the shop, calling out for her missing partner. "Frank!" It was hard to hear, the fired seemed to suck the sound from the air. "Frank." Cassie screamed, then coughed as she swallowed the smoke.

"Peck!"

"Frank!" She took another step into smoke, her eyes burning from the heat.

"Get out of here!" yelled Frank.

Cassie could finally see her partner through the smoke. He was caught, beneath a cabinet, that must have blown through one of the side rooms. Exploded aerosol cans were everywhere. The entire place was an accelerant. Why had Frank gone back in? She could faintly hear the sirens, as they made their way closer.

The air was acrid and thick, so Cassie began to crawl towards her fallen partner, fighting the smoke and obstacles in her way.

"Go back!" Frank strained against the cupboard that was holding him down. "This place is going to blow!"

If Frank thought Cassie was going to leave him to burn to death in this place, he had no idea who his partner really was. This was one order she was never going to follow. Ignoring his protest, she continued.

Finally reaching him, she looked down to see his face. He was now bleeding from his injury, but it was legs that were pinned beneath the heavy cupboard. Thankfully they didn't look broken, just caught.

Cassie tried to lift it, but it was wedged tight in the hallway. She could see the room it had come from, and there were more aerosol cans and canisters that had yet to explode from the heat. If she didn't get Frank out of here, they were both going to be in trouble.

She shoved her shoulder beneath the corner of the cupboard. "Can you push with me?" She was less than a foot from Frank's face, but the fire was so loud, she had to shout.

His arms were free, and they both began to push. She had to get Frank free. There was no other option.

They both screamed as they tried to move the heavy piece. Another small explosion went off and Cassie threw herself over Frank's exposed neck and head as another spray can narrowly missed them.

She looked down at Frank, and she could see the tears that formed in his eyes. "I told you to go back, kid."

Cassie grabbed Frank's face. "I never should have left you. We leave together. Partners. We leave together."

Mackie knew he was breaking protocol, but when he recognized Cassie's patrol car outback, and when Rhys pointed out there was a guy cuffed near the dumpster, he quickly put it all together.

If Cassie and Frank weren't outside, that meant there was only one place they could be, and that was inside. Mackie had been in a lot of fires in his time, but knowing that Cassie was in there, sucked the oxygen from his lungs in a way he had never felt before.

The front of the studio was engulfed in flames. Everything the fire touched, lit like dry kindling. The heat was incredible. Refusing to fixate on the worst-case scenario, he set his team to work, and despite legitimate protests, he followed Dalton in through the back.

He found them quicker than he expected. He quickly gave thanks for how small the studio was.

Cassie was covering Frank, using her body as a shield, as cans from a side room were exploding. Dalton didn't hesitate, he pulled back on Cassie's legs, dragging her away from Frank's body, as Cassie fought to hold on to Frank.

Once Dalton had a firm grip on Cassie, he passed her to Mackie, who scooped her up in his arms and ran out the door.

"Frank!" shouted Cassie.

"Dalton has him."

Cassie shook her head violently, "No, he's stuck."

Mackie, put Cassie down and grabbed her hands with his. "Look at me, Cassie. We got him. Frank is going to be okay. Trust me. We got him." She needed to believe him. She needed to know if was going to be okay.

She stared back, her face smeared and dirty from the smoke, and nodded. “I trust you.”

Mackie held her head next to his chest and wrapped his arms around her. “Thank you.”

He could have held her there forever, but the paramedics were waiting to check her over.

“Let’s get you looked at,” said Mackie, as he guided Cassie over to the ambulance, her eyes still glued to the back door of the studio.

They hadn’t even started taking vitals, when Dalton came out, his arm around a walking and wheezing Frank. Mackie heard Cassie’s cry of relief, and as Frank walked over to the other ambulance, he gave Cassie a head shake, then a thumbs up.

He didn’t dare say it to Cassie, but it was a near miracle.

Cassie about to sit back when she whipped her head around to Mackie. “The guy. I got him. He’s over by the dumpster—”

Mackie placed his hand in Cassie’s and squeezed. “Relax, your guys have him in custody now.”

Cassie’s shoulders sagged and she leaned back against the door of the ambulance. She seemed to finally be taking it all in. “Good.” She took another deep breath and closed her eyes. “Good.”

She opened her eyes and looked at Mackie. “It is the same guy, right? The one with the ears?”

He couldn’t help but give her a little poke. “Those ears were almost the only way to tell. You’re going to have to stop jumping people. Poor guy’s face looks pretty rough. I’m glad you and I landed on grass.”

For a moment she looked confused, but then she started to

smile. “Not me. He tripped over his feet all by himself.”

One of the paramedics passed him some water, and Mackie held it out to Cassie. She went to take it, then pulled her hand back.

“Wait. Does this count as having drinks?” He could see the twinkle in her brown eyes and started to laugh. “If this is how I have to get you to agree, then yeah, this is us having drinks.”

Cassie took the bottle from his hand and took a drink. Mackie pushed back an ash covered tendril from her forehead. He could see her blush even with the dirt on her face.

“Now that this is official, how about you start calling me Chris?” Mackie wanted to hear his given name from her lips. She wasn’t another one of the guys, she was so much more.

“Chris.” Cassie gave him a sweet smile as she said his name once more. “Chris…Hmm, sounds…right.”

Mackie smiled down at the brave, beautiful woman before him. “It sure does.”

Cassie looked up at him and smiled. “You know, I didn’t expect you to smell like burnt toast on our first date.”

Mackie shook his head, “Neither did I, but what’s funny is you still smell like cinnamon.”

Cassie laughed, “Cinnamon hearts. A whole bag each shift. Frank and I are addicted.” Then she shrugged. “You’re lucky, last week it was garlic sticks. Enjoy it while you can.”

He ran his finger down her cheek and bent forward to gently kiss her forehead. “I’m so glad you’re okay.”

Cassie turned her head and whispered. “I said, enjoy it while you can, Chief.”

Mackie didn’t need to be told twice. Capturing Cassie’s lips in his, he couldn’t be sure if it was the heat of the fire, or the burning in his heart that warmed him to his very core. As he drew back, he stared deep into the eyes of this unexpected treasure he had found in Cassie, and knew that opposites don't just attract, they ignite.

You can learn more about Samantha Thomas's sweet romances in the About the Authors section at the end of the book.

SAMPLED

Carina Alyce

Behaving herself has always been Vandy Patel's way. Her path is clear – she's going to be an accountant just like her parents planned for her. That was until she met Royce on summer vacation, and she starts to question who she is and what she truly wants.

This past year has not been Firefighter Royce Murphy's best. He was avoiding women until Vandy landed in his arms, and he can't resist sampling her delicious taste. They know they don't have a future – or will they decide it might be worth taking a huge risk?

Enjoy in Sampled – part of the MetroGen Universe where the women are strong, the guys are brave, and the scenes are steamy – all written by an actual doctor.

SAMPLED

Sampled: Adjective. 1. To have inferred the behavior of a whole batch or population by studying a representative subse*t*

Netter's Medical Dictionary for Health Professionals

If you want to get away from your parents on your twenty-first birthday, tell them you're visiting a responsible friend. A solid pre-med friend would never help you get all slutted up and take you to a sake bar/dance club.

'Slutted up' wasn't quite true. Like the good girls they were, they followed the Beyonce rules of sexy. Skimpy top or skimpy bottom, but not both.

Hence, on her twenty-first birthday, University of Chicago senior-to-be Vandy Patel wore a skin-tight, fluorescent-pink, long sleeve top with a micro mini.

And also her first thong.

That might have been violating all sorts of Tiger Mom rules, but too bad. Tiger Mom was Korean, not Indian, and honestly, Indian moms were far more intimately acquainted with tigers.

Genetics or something, right. Vandy's med student brother Raj would know that, or her engineer sister, Aparna.

Who cared, because Vandy was ordering her first drink.

She'd worked her way to the front of the bar, and when she got there she realized she had no idea what to order. "I want a…"

The bartender, who wore a kimono but was decidedly not Japanese, waited a couple seconds and then turned her eyes to a different customer.

"Oh, damn it," she swore.

"Order Ginjo," a man next to her said.

She turned to say something back and stopped with her mouth open. White guy, green eyes, red hair past his collar. Muscles. Freckles. Worse, did he have a tattoo?

He glanced at her uncertainly. "You okay?"

"Yes-yes. I am. I just never had sake before," she stammered. His blue suit jacket brought out light flecks in his irises.

"Why don't we fix that?"

"I've never ordered before. It's my twenty-first birthday." Now she sounded lame.

"It's best to buy the bottle." He waved the bartender over and paid for a bottle of sake with two cups.

"I need two more cups," she interrupted. "I'm here with two girlfriends."

He nodded, and Vandy resisted smirking at the bartender.

See, hot guy in his half unbuttoned white dress shirt wanted 'Vandy with a V, not an M.'

She grabbed the two cups the bartender set down and led him through the crowd back to the side tables. It was more difficult than she expected because the dance floor had gotten busier. Luckily, he had a solid six inches on her and shielded her from the worst of the jostling.

Anna and Tara were quite surprised by her new company.

"This is…" Vandy realized she didn't know his name.

"Royce," he politely supplied. "I was giving the birthday girl a hand. Is it really her birthday?"

"Of course it's my birthday. You think I'm pretending?" Vandy said, slightly affronted.

"I can't say since you're a pretty girl." Royce set out the cups on their table.

Tara, Anna's friend from Case Western University, sniggered, "I absolutely did that at Friendly's when I turned twelve. You got a free sundae."

Vandy's mom, Dr. Sonal Patel, would have been unbelievably embarrassed if Vandy had ever pulled something like that. However, since he called her pretty, she might reconsider. "I don't need to pretend. It's my real birthday."

"Here's my present, birthday girl. Don't forget to pour for each other," Royce offered gallantly and moved to leave with his cup.

"Stay," Anna stopped him. She pointed to the chair next to Vandy. "You paid for it. You should at least try it. Teach her how it's done. It is her first time."

Vandy flashed a scowl at Anna. They'd gone to high school in Charlottesville together but ended up at different colleges. She wore a little green dress that nearly violated Beyonce's rules, and she had more than a little mischief behind her smile.

"Can't refuse that." Royce sat down, and his gaze dropped when his leg brushed Vandy's.

His eyes flashed with something Vandy didn't quite recognize.

She burned too hot and too cold at the same time. Part of her brain urged her to drape her knee over his.

Which she did not obey.

They both reached for the bottle at the same time and his fingers covered hers.

Calluses. This man worked for a living. What did he do, with his tribal tattoos peeking out of his cuffs and twisting up his wrist.

He didn't move his hand right away and caressed the top of hers with his thumb.

She'd thought trying out college guys had taught her about lust and passion. This didn't even compare. He wasn't a boy who stayed up reading Fundamentals of Microeconomics and whined about his stock portfolio.

Royce poured the three of them glasses and passed the bottle back to her. She remembered not to stare at his lips and poured his cup.

She picked up her glass and said, "Bottoms up."

He put a hand on her wrist to stop her. "No. Sake is meant to be sipped. It's not a shot. And it's stronger than wine, so unless you want it to knock you on your cute little birthday girl ass, sip it."

She nervously licked her lips. She took back everything she thought before. She was totally staring at his lips. His behavior wasn't any better because his hand released her after a solid ten seconds while he stared back.

After taking a sip of the sake, which tasted relatively sweet, she found her tongue. "So, do you live around here?"

"Cleveland born and bred," he said. "You ladies?"

"Anna and I go to Case. She's visiting from University of

Chicago," Tara said.

"Chicago?"

"Yeah. I'm an accounting student." Vandy tried to sip her sake again without slurping.

"I was kind of surprised she got a whole week off to visit me. She took classes the past two summers, and she's an intern at KPMG," Anna added.

Vandy would have kicked her for making her sound boring if her knee hadn't bumped into Royce's.

"What do you do? Tara asked at the same time Anna said, "What are you doing here tonight?"

"Hanging out with friends from work." Royce set his cup down and aimed his next words at Vandy. "Would you like to dance with me?"

She must of have heard that wrong. He wanted to dance with her?

Vandy didn't move until Anna nudged her with a foot under the table, missing Royce's leg completely. "She'd love to dance."

Unable to think in sentences, Vandy tried to wiggle off the chair without losing her skirt. Royce helped her up with his hands gripping her hips. She froze for a second as he headed to the dance floor without checking on her.

Probably because normal girls didn't turn into mumbling zombies.

Anna, who had been her best friend in high school, shoved her in the direction of the dance floor. "He's into you. Go get it!"

Successfully not tripping over her three-inch strappy heels,

Vandy made it to the dance floor.

Within three seconds, a few things were clear. Royce was a passable dancer. Vandy was not. She gave him her best smile and almost cracked her head on his chin.

Obviously she should have been taking ballet classes rather than going to national honor society classes and oboe lessons. When her mother sent her to swim lessons because 'drowning is a leading cause of death under the age of twenty,' she should have considered that dance floor humiliation was a leading cause of social death.

Less weekends studying and more time going out might have prevented this too.

"Sorry," she mumbled. Her hands fluttered in weird directions as she failed to locate the beat.

"Try this. Lean back and stop thinking." Completely ignoring the actual music, he twirled her around to press his chest to her back. He swayed back and forth, and she felt some of her tension ease.

He was much larger than her, firmer, muscled and, oh my god, was that his cock? Could she think about his cock? Did she do that to him?

Experimentally, she thrust her butt against that spot, and his hands caught her hips. She froze again, but he bent his head down and kissed her by her ear.

Unfamiliar need rushed through her. The heat of him, the darkness, she wanted his hands on her. She was hot, bothered, and wishing they were alone. What would it be like to get the way too short skirt off and feel him for real?

She ignored her mother's constant refrain of 'a good Indian girl is judged by how she behaves.'

Royce's hands guided her right back to what she'd been doing, and he whispered, "What's your name, birthday girl?"

Feeling daring, she tried an experimental hip wiggle. "Vandy. Vandy Patel. Like Mandy with a V."

He matched her movements, "Vandy. If you keep doing that, I might have very bad thoughts about you."

Did bad thoughts include naked thoughts? She had plenty of those. "I – I – I…"

The music faded away, and he stopped dancing. "Don't worry, Vandy. I won't take your halo. Though your phone number would be nice."

"I'm only here for a week," Vandy said and instantly regretted it. A hot guy who admitted having sexy thoughts about her asked for her number. She sounded like a complete goody-two-shoes.

He didn't react. "I see. Let me take you back to your friends. Have a happy birthday."

She followed him back to the girls, cursing very loudly in her head. Way to torpedo things. In the first ten minutes of meeting him, she'd proven to be a novice drinker, dancer, and flirtee. Great.

Her friends weren't alone, though.

"These are Royce's friends. Did you know they were Cleveland firefighters?" Anna's words ended in an exultant note, pointing to two guys with way too many muscles.

"We saw you dancing it up with our Royce," one guy said, with Tara hanging on him.

Royce stopped short, looking considerably less excited to see his friends than Vandy would have expected. "It was one dance."

The second guy almost mocked. "You stopped at one dance?"

"As I was saying, it's Vandy's twenty-first birthday," Tara said helpfully. “Royce bought us sake. Want to join us?”

“Murphy was showing Mandy a good time?” the first guy said, like it was an odd occurrence.

“She’s visiting for a week from college.” Royce, whose last name must have been Murphy, partially blocked her from his friends.

“You don’t even need a week. You gonna make Mandy's twenty-first birthday memorable? Give her an adventure?” the second guy shouldered past Royce and gave Vandy a head-to-toe visual assessment.

"She's not interested, Jon,” Royce said, while it seemed that *Royce* wasn’t interested.

"What twenty-one-year-old doesn't want an adventure?" Jon said, having finished his assessment. “Mandy’s dressed for it.”

"She doesn't seem to like the adventuring type," Royce said and took half a step away from her.

Definitely not what she wanted. "I am the adventuring type,” she lied.

Royce's green eyes seemed shadowed with doubt. "Really?

"Really." Vandy hated how her face felt hot.

"Any tattoos?" His gaze skimmed down her sleeves to her short skirt.

"Zero."

"Felonies?"

"None." She kept her chin up. It was her twenty-first birthday, and this man screamed adventure.

"Misdemeanors? Shoplifting?" He took that step back toward her and hooked a finger on the boat neck of her shirt. "Even if you didn't get caught."

"Never. Accountants need clean records," she gasped. His heat radiated through her skin. Here he talked about how she DIDN'T want adventure and yet he seemed not to be able to back down.

"Streaking? Skinny dipping?" Royce slid his hand down her back to her waist.

"No." Vandy faced him, almost in his embrace.

"Ever had a one-night stand?" he asked.

She licked her lips, wanting to lick his. Everything else faded away except him.

Jon less than helpfully ruined their moment. "You're barking up the wrong tree. She's probably a virgin."

Royce started to step away again, and she stopped him by laying her brown hand on top of that vine tattoo on his freckled forearm. "Not a chance. It is college."

Losing her virginity at the end of freshman year to a friend of a friend after an accounting exam had been disappointing. Vandy had tried it out with a couple more guys, but they had been equally underwhelming.

But the way her body hummed suggested a night with him would be very different than a quickie in a dorm room.

"Sounds perfect for you. Take Casey's truck if you're sober enough to drive. It should be fully loaded after Casey's last time." Jon took a set of keys from the first firefighter. "It's about time you had some fucking fun and got your cherry popped."

"What does that mean?" Vandy asked.

"You'll have to find out if you're up for an adventure," Royce said, giving her a seductive grin at last.

That decided her. "I'm in."

He reached around her hip, pulled her phone out of her pocket, activated the camera, and took a picture of himself. "Send that to your friends."

"They need that?"

"Don't want your friends to worry when you leave with me."

"I thought I was being adventurous?"

"No reason to be dumb. My brother's a cop." He brought his lips close to hers. "And I promise any DNA will be willingly given."

She opened her mouth and thought better of it. He confused her with his combination of hot and cold, danger and caution. He acted like he wanted her to come with him but didn't.

Screw it. It was her birthday. She stood on her tip toes and kissed him.

Those hard tattooed arms enclosed her with an unyielding grip as he kissed her back. He tasted like sake. Sweet, heady, and boiling. She wanted to climb onto his body, grip him with everything she had.

When she pulled away, she could hear cheers from his friends. Vandy, feeling bold, said, "Fuck them. It's my birthday, and adventure can be my present this week."

She couldn't quite read the expression on his face, but he definitely looked hungry. He took the keys, and she followed him out. Anna and Tara gave her very enthusiastic thumbs ups before chatting up his firefighter friends.

When they got in the truck, Vandy wasn't sure how to feel. She may have just agreed to a one-night stand. “Where we going?”

“On an adventure. Not to the red room of pain.” He put the truck in gear.

"Red room of pain?"

"You know… *Fifty Shades of Gray*. The movie. It was a book first," he pointed out, "and fanfic before that."

"I didn't read it. I heard it sucked," Vandy said, trying and failing to sound more edgy.

"That’s the point. Hide it under another book cover. Pretend you were reading something intellectual. What do you do for fun?"

"Study. Chat with my friends. I'm doing an internship in an accounting firm this summer, so I work events with them."

"That’s a lot of things you do for other people. What do you do for you?"

"I exercise. I swim. We have a really nice pool at the college and the firm has a gym. Hey, don't judge me. What do you do for fun other than firefighting and sake tasting?"

"I taught myself to play the ukulele. And I sing with it. I think I want oboe lessons even though I can sing while playing it."

"You want to play the oboe? I played that in middle school band. Back when I had braces and a perm. And I can't believe I said that out loud." Vandy covered her mouth as if her crooked teeth and fried hair could come back.

He laughed, "Why?"

"Because I'm driving to parts unknown with a hot guy on an adventure, and I told him about my crossbite and Cheetah Girls phase. "

"If I didn't want you to talk, I wouldn't be talking to you. And you don't seem like a badge bunny."

"What's a badge bunny?"

"You don't need to worry about it. You're not a badge bunny."

"Tell me or I'll Google it." She waved her phone with mock threat.

"Badge bunnies are people who have sex with firefighters because they're firefighters. They'll sleep with any firefighter they can find. They're not particular."

A completely ridiculous wave of jealousy swept over her. "You know badge bunnies?"

"I can't say I 'know' the badge bunnies, but I've seen them."

"'Seen them' or slept with them?" Vandy's nerves were on edge now. She'd known Royce for at best an hour, and she was irrationally angry about anyone he'd been with before.

Irrational didn't even describe it. Crazy. Insane. Pathologically jealous for no stupid reason.

"I don't sleep with badge bunnies." His answer came short and clipped.

"Then why did your firefighting buddies say… and why are you with me?" Her emotions went on full spin cycle. Jealous, needy, horny. He liked her enough to leave with her, but the way his guy friends acted…

"My friends have big mouths and think a dick in any chick equates happiness. It doesn't." He parked with unnecessary force in an empty parking lot. "I just didn't want my job to be the thing that made you interested. We're here."

"Where is here? And does this mean we aren't going to—" Her

black hair had to be redder than his.

"Open the glove compartment and take out what you find there." Royce took a blanket out from behind his seat.

She obeyed and a wide array of condoms fell into her lap. "So 'yes' on the sex thing?"

"We’re having an adventure." He dropped his suit jacket on the driver’s seat before opening her door. He offered her his hand.

She considered it.

Royce waited. "I won't make you do anything you don't want to." He scrunched up his face and dropped his voice. "Come with me if you want to live."

"Are we going somewhere dangerous?"

"It's from *Terminator.* I guess you haven't seen it. We're at Edgewood Park Beach."

That decided her. She took his hand and made sure to lean into him. Her breasts pressed into his solid chest, and she felt that weird electric shock of her nipples hardening. She let her legs straddle one of his.

He closed the door and pressed her against the truck, letting the hard planes of his muscles push back. Royce's face was inches from hers, and she could actually feel his heartbeat increase against her breasts. His hand cupped her butt and lifted her up against a bulge down by his crotch.

"What are we doing here?" she whispered, the cool night air refusing to enter her lungs.

He gave her a wide grin full of wicked temptation. "We're

going skinny dipping."

This was not how Royce Murphy had planned his night. He'd planned to go out with his friends from Firehouse 19, get quietly drunk, and then go home to revel in his aloneness with his cat.

He had not expected to be sober with a plan to get a hot girl naked.

Vandy had seemed so disappointed about not getting to order a drink that he'd helped her out. And within the first couple minutes he had discerned a few informative tidbits.

She was inexperienced and somewhat naïve, whereas he had become so jaded he was almost unrecognizable from who he'd been at her age. They had nothing in common since she was an accounting student at a top university, and he hadn't even taken a single college class.

And his body gave exactly zero fucks about that because it wanted her naked and beneath him.

"I'm really not a virgin. Really. I really like sex," she said, following him across the soft sand. He'd have believed her more if she hadn't said it with all the enthusiasm of someone getting their tooth pulled.

"Then your first skinny-dipping shouldn't be a problem." Royce spread the blanket out near the water and set the condoms on it. He started rolling up his shirt and was gratified to hear her quick intake of breath. The past six months of running and weightlifting had paid off in a six pack.

He'd stripped down to his boxers when she said, "You're serious about skinny dipping."

"I'm going skinny-dipping, with or without you."

"We won't get arrested. Will we?" she asked.

"I can't promise anything, but public nudity is more of a problem when the beach is crowded." He indicated the deserted beach.

"Oh." Her hands went to the zip on her tiny excuse for a skirt. She had it partway down, revealing the edge of a thong, before she repeated, "We won't be arrested?"

"It's a risk you'll have to take." Vandy's expression was so tense he took pity on her. "The police usually have bigger problems. I worked the hypothermia tent during February's Polar Plunge. They didn't arrest the people who ran into the lake naked."

With that reassurance, her skirt and top came off in rapid succession. The bright pink bits of lace pretending to be a bra did very little to hide her excitement. She might not have been aware, but her nipples were hard points. They'd been just like that while they were dancing, and only her nervousness kept him from pursuing anything beyond a phone number.

For him, it was a big step.

However, his dick responded in the most appropriate fashion.

"Are you a virgin?" she asked just as he hooked his thumbs on his waistband. Her gaze was drawn to his hard-on slowly emerging from its prison.

He smirked when her eyes grew to the size of saucers as he casually stepped out of his boxers. "Definitely not."

She bit her lip and unclasped her bra. Now he was the one staring at her dark skin and even darker nipples. His dick twitched again because it knew what it wanted. This past year had left it more than lonely.

Royce's recent policy of keeping his distance from women typically prevented this kind of encounter. While he hadn't been actively searching for this, if she was offering, he'd be taking. The long-denied beast inside of him growled with salivating hunger.

"What did they mean about popping your cherry?" She took a tentative step or two forward. He didn't move, allowing her to approach him. With a few more steps, she was trembling slightly and resting her smooth belly against the tip of his cock.

That felt way too good on the sensitive tip. His blood roared in his ears. She made it worse because she placed her hands on his length and began to stroke.

Fuck that felt too good. "Because I was a one-woman man. Engaged," he admitted. Though right now he couldn't even bring up his ex's face. Vandy's hot hands were blanking every memory.

Then she dropped to her knees and took him in her mouth.

His hands were already in her long black hair, guiding her. She made up for her inexperience with enthusiasm. "Holy fuck, Vandy. Focus on the tip."

Perhaps she was a little bit less innocent than he thought because she complied without hesitation. Or she learned fast, because she didn't hesitate to follow his lead when he showed her how to pull and stroke his sac.

He was going to cum in her mouth if she didn't stop soon. He gave her one strangled warning. "Spit, swallow, or pearl necklace?"

"Pearl necklace?" She sat back on her heels, her hand working the shaft.

"In your mouth or on your chest." Royce hoped his words didn't come out as a growl.

"Oh," she tilted her head up to stare into his eyes and pointed his cock at her breasts.

That was enough because he came with a loud groan, emptying himself. His white seed sprayed across her pert tits, his heart pounding wildly.

He opened his eyes, which he hadn't remembered closing. She was examining the white resting on the upper slopes, and she swiped a finger in it… and put it in her mouth.

"Huh, I've never done that before." She smiled with what he imagined to be a dizzying dose of feminine power. "I think I like it."

Royce gave her a hand up, bringing her to her feet. "Which part?"

"I've never finished a guy like that. Usually we'd mess around, maybe I'd do a little down there, and then we'd…"

"Screw?" He went with a gentler version of the preferred word.

"Pretty much. It was always disappointing… I thought it had to be me. And now…" She averted her eyes, instead looking at the pale beads clinging to her bare breasts.

"Now you feel horny as fuck and wish you could do

something about it?"

"Yes," she squeaked.

He captured her mouth with his, inhaling her novel taste. She answered by writhing her body against his, bouncing up and down on his thigh. He could already tell how wet she was.

Wet and about to get wetter.

"Take those off. Time to wash up." He helped her out of her thong, and she unhesitatingly followed him into the warm July water.

Fortunately, she hadn't exaggerated her ability to swim because it made it easier to 'wash' her off. He swiped her breasts clean before sucking each tip into his mouth. Vandy purred and moaned and pulled on his hair. He brought her higher and higher, pushing her pleasure points.

She arched backward, giving his hand access to the black curls covering her folds. He kept suckling as he got one finger between her legs. She was hot and tight, stoking his lust.

And even better, she was very responsive.

So responsive. No faking, no posturing, no pretending. Completely unrestrained, because she had no clue how good it could be when done right.

Sure, he didn't know her, and she didn't know him, but he'd promised adventure, and she'd given him her trust.

And he'd prove himself worthy even if it was only for tonight.

When his fingers found her clit, he grinned at the sound of her hiss. She mumbled something; it sounded like begging for more, so he didn't stop. He felt her tense, and this time he pulled back long enough to watch pleasure rush over her.

Magnificent. He had a beautiful naked woman in his arms on a moonlit night coming down from one hell of an orgasm.

Then she went limp, and he dove to catch her before she went under the water.

"You okay?" He pulled her fully against him.

She draped her head on his shoulder. "It's another first. I've never done that without batteries."

"Did I outperform your vibrator?"

"Way ahead." She peeked down, noticing his cock stir from its position trapped between their bodies. "But I need more."

He sucked on her lip for a second. "Why? You just came."

"Because I know there's more. And if you can do that to me, I want everything."

"You want me inside." He shifted her hips to let the head of his cock tease her opening. "You want me to show you how good it can be, birthday girl. So greedy."

He squeezed one of her nipples, twisting it slightly, making her moan. "Please, Royce."

As if a man would ever be able to resist that. He carried her back to the blanket and laid her down on her back. "I'm definitely not done cleaning you up. And once I get you clean, I'll get you all dirty again."

He didn't give her time to think because he put on a condom and got between her legs.

Not the way she expected, because he put his head between her legs and said, “Lay back.”

He licked her from top to bottom, listening to her purrs and whimpers. Vandy was a huge fan of the way he twisted his tongue inside her slit and then back up to her clit. He was never going to get her clean because, as planned, she got wetter and hotter with every motion. She kept thrashing so he gripped her legs to keep her wide open to his mouth. She went rigid in a wordless scream, right on the cusp of a second orgasm.

"You ready, birthday girl? Your hole is dripping wet and empty. Tell me what you need." Royce accompanied his words with more attention to her slick bud.

"Royce, I need you. Inside me. Please."

"Like this?" He scooted up and slid the first inch inside her grasping channel. It strained his control, but he'd had plenty of practice lately.

She shook and raked him with her short sensible nails. "Stop fucking with me, Royce!"

He shoved home, letting her take his full length, which was by no means small. Her eyes crossed for half a second as she adjusted to his invasion. Royce gripped her knees, widening them to drive deeper, and dropped his mouth to hers. She met his kiss with a desperation of her own, moving with him instinctively, matching his rhythm in a way she hadn't on the dance floor.

There wasn't much room for thought when it went to all sensation. Her heat, the close fit of her channel, the taste of her lips and skin. Though his control frayed, he needed her to come first. Whatever asshole hadn't treated her like the perfection she was needed to be replaced with him. He could make it good enough for both of them that nothing remained.

One flick over her clit as he plunged in the furthest yet was enough. She spasmed and he paused, wanting to see her come undone again, under him, because of him. It was as gorgeous as the first time, but she wasn't the only the one who needed to forget the past.

He waited for the last twitch before he thrust a few more times and let go, his orgasm practically blowing his head open.

A few minutes later, he rolled them over and found her covering his face and top of his chest with kisses.

His buddies at the firehouse had told him what he should do now—compliment her and pay her cab fare.

But that wasn't who he was, and hoped he'd never be.

Instead, he asked her, the second woman he'd ever slept with, one question. "Want to go back to my place?"

Vandy woke up late Monday morning with two beautiful green-eyed redheads.

The first redhead yawned and stretched from her spot on the bed. She fluffed her hair and licked her lips before giving Vandy a self-satisfied smirk.

"Meow."

The ginger cat jumped off the bed, and Royce also stretched. Unlike his cat, he curled back around her and kissed her naked shoulder, right above a love bite she'd acquired overnight.

After their little foray on the beach, they'd reached his apartment. Rather than go to sleep, they had spent several hours exploring each other. He had done… things to her that she'd heard about but never believed were true. Hopefully she'd given as good as she got. At least he'd called her name more than once when he'd had her in ever position she'd imagined and some she hadn't.

A weird beeping noise came from outside of the room. "What's that?"

"Umm, I don't know." He nuzzled her shoulder. "Phone or

something."

Vandy checked the clock and sat straight up. "It's two in the afternoon!"

She jumped right out of bed and remembered her nakedness. Her clothes were nowhere to be found, though there were six—six?—condom wrappers on the floor. Trying to cover her breasts and her vagina with two arms didn't seem possible. "Where are my clothes? My parents have to be freaking out."

Royce looked thoroughly amused by this. "You think there's anything left of them?"

He had banged her against the front door the minute they'd entered. It had been awesome, but he might have ripped her miniskirt. And her panties.

Then they'd done body shots and shared a cup of sake ' in honor of their first meeting.' And then disposed of her bra and shirt on his table.

"I can't be naked!" she spun around in a circle fruitlessly hoping to find a whole piece of her clothing.

"Why not?" Royce got out of bed, and she forgot her search to gape at his body.

Yep, he was even better naked. He had multiple languages written across his chest, including the ever-familiar Sanskrit OM. His back had a fire ax stretching shoulder to shoulder—now accompanied by several bite marks that she might have given. There was also a dragon, a robot, and a cat that looked rather suspiciously like the one that shared his apartment. The phrase 'True allegiance is only given willingly' was written on his shoulder and his chest.

The splendor of his tattoos in no way took away from the sculpture of muscles that made this man. The red hair went down his chest, pointed to his happy trail, and outlined the base of his cock to great effect. That particular cock hardened under her gaze, sending shivers down her spine. Royce loved it when she got on her knees and traced the veins along the shaft. Once she got him riled up, he'd—

"Vandy?" He advanced on her, and she felt her brain melting because her body suggested she let him bend her over the bed.

The beeping continued, reminding her of the original problem. "My phone. I need it. And clothes."

"If you insist." He took a Firehouse 19 shirt out of his dresser and handed it to her. She resisted the temptation to climb on him. The fabric brushed her nipples, which gave her a slight twinge. He raised his eyebrows and fixed his eyes on the hard points sticking out of the t-shirt.

"Aren't you getting dressed?"

"Why? It's my house, and I won't be at work until Wednesday. I can lounge around like this as much as I want."

"But you have to leave sometime. Get food. Study. Exercise."

"I could, but I don't have to. I'm an adult. Me and Eowyn can hang out by ourselves and order takeout." He pronounced the cat's name with an odd emphasis.

"EoWin?"

"Eowyn. Like A-O-Win. Riders of Rohan? Fights the Nazgul?"

"*Game of Thrones?*"

He walked by her and pointed to a spot on the massive bookshelf that encompassed his entire hallway.

"You have *Nietzsche, Kant, Schopenhauer, A Game of Thrones, Fifty Shades of Grey, the Kama Sutra, The Chronicles of*

Prydain . . ." She tilted her head to the indicated book. "*The Two Towers?* What's that?"

"The middle book in *The Lord of the Rings*. Has the Riders of Rohan." That didn't mean much to her. "Fantasy classics. Swords, the One Ring. Orlando Bloom?"

"Does he date Katy Perry?"

"What exactly do you do all day?"

"I work. With numbers. And get coffee. And do math. And more math."

"Eowyn is chewing on your purse." He pointed to the living room.

Eowyn, the cat from a book she'd never read, had to be chased away from her purse. Her phone only had one bar left of battery, hence the odd sound of her dying text reminder. It was Anna checking on her status and sharing the cover story she'd told Vandy's mom.

Vandy had conveniently forgotten her charger and would be spending the next few days at Anna's.

"Feel better?" he asked, quietly getting out food from his fridge, still naked.

"Yeah, gotta send a few texts. Go get a charger. See my parents."

"I have a charger." He pointed to the wall and poured Cinnamon Toast Crunch into a bowl and topped it off with a sprinkling of Special K. "Why don't you eat first?"

"I guess I could." She plugged in her phone next to an empty space on the wall where it looked like a picture had once hung. She sat down and would have asked about it, but he passed her the bowl.

"This is breakfast?"

"Or lunch. Your parents'll be worried about you?"

That made her sound like a baby, not a grown woman who'd spent a wild night having dirty sex. "Not yet. Anna made excuses for me. They're already at the hospital. They're doctors at MetroGen."

"Do they expect you back?"

"I guess not. As long as I check in, I should be fine, but I should go." It dawned on her what he was suggesting—she didn't have to leave.

"If you want. Or you could stay here and do nothing." He helped himself to her cereal. "I only have one bowl."

"This is my cereal now." She pulled her bowl back, and it tipped onto her borrowed shirt.

"That shirt's dirty." His voice dropped a pitch, and she sensed sex awareness sweeping over her. "You need a shower."

Less than a minute later, they were both in the shower, and Eowyn the cat made herself comfortable on the milk-covered shirt.

Sneaking around turned out to be a lot of damn fun, and so did watching TV and reading books all day. From the moment she'd met him on Sunday night, Royce had showed her nothing except fun. In the moments between romps in his bed – or floor – or shower, he'd made microwave popcorn and introduced her to mindless action movies or read her sections of *Fifty Shades of Grey* out loud.

Yet somehow, he managed to leave Wednesday morning around 7:00 a.m.

At least that's what his note said. He also left her a key.

Good thing because she'd run out of excuses to be 'staying at Anna's.' A few texts later, she had arranged meeting her parents at the hospital for lunch. That should keep them off the scent.

At least she hoped. She'd never done it before, so hopefully they wouldn't suspect anything.

Vandy passed the hospital front desk and headed to the attending lounge. Raj wasn't allowed in since it was off limits to third year medical students, and her mom wanted to avoid the suggestion of nepotism.

As if there weren't a few hundred Patels in the hospital

already. No one was likely to realize Raj Patel was their son, but her mom wouldn't budge.

"What are you wearing?" Dr. Sonal Patel wrinkled her nose while escorting Vandy into the well-appointed seat area.

"I didn't pack that many clothes." Vandy hoped that excuse flew. She'd stopped at her parents' empty house and ransacked her luggage to find a long-sleeved maroon T-shirt in University of Chicago colors. Otherwise her mom would have noticed the bite marks.

"Eat. Eat. Eat. They can't have real Gujarati in your dining hall." Her mom had already set out plates of dal bhat shak rotli (lentils, rice, curry, and flat bread). Raj probably had a whole freezer of it, and Vandy didn't mention that Chicago had a million Indian restaurants. "Are you having a good time with Anna? She's such a nice girl."

"Yes, she said she got early admission to Cleveland College of Medicine." Vandy stuck to topics that would interest her mother.

"But she didn't get into University of Chicago, which is why she's at Case. I can't wait till you do your master's program," her mom said, her accent rising and falling depending on the topic. "Things are going well at your internship, yes?

Vandy nodded unenthusiastically. "Things are great."

It wasn't exactly a lie. She was a glorified secretary working long hours, fetching coffee, filing forms.

"I'll have an MD, a PhD, and an CPA-MBA. Sapna is going to be so jealous."

"Doesn't Aunt Sapna's son work on Wall Street?" Vandy tried to remember her older cousin. "Isn't he engaged?"

"Not anymore. He got rid of that blonde around Holi, and

Sapna is over the moon. She has a list of eligible good Gujarati women longer than my arm."

Vandy tried not to choke on a mouthful of curry. Couldn't her cousin have broken up on a day different than on Holi, the spring festival of love? Any time marriage came up, there was only one way it would go. Her mom would believe it was fated for him to find new love, which therefore meant Vandy could use some fate in the love and marriage department. "Isn't it a little early to start dating? Weren't he and his fiancé together for years?"

"It's never too early. Don't frown." She pointed at Vandy's forehead. "No wrinkles. Is that Anna's makeup? When you wear that much mascara, people will think you're hiding an alcohol or drug problem."

"It's my makeup. It's in style." Vandy refused to glance at her reflection.

"If it gets smeared, you'll look like one my patients after a bender. What do you think, honey? Does she look like an alcoholic or a drug addict?"

"Mom!" Vandy did glance around this time, but no one else in the lounge batted an eye.

"What?" Dr. Rishaan Patel sat up from where he had been eating his dal bhat and making notes on a long list of patient names.

"Her makeup. Alcoholic or drug addict?"

"She does not look like an alcoholic. Or a drug addict. They have more marks in their arms," her father said absently.

"Every day I listen to their parents," her mother complained. "'My son is living in my basement smoking pot and drinking beer. He doesn't have a job, unless it's having sex with random women.

He's got his fifth STD, and I can't get him off my insurance."

"She should start charging him for rent," her dad said practically.

"I doubt it. Then she'll complain about the money he spent on tattoos. No wonder those women's blood pressures are out of control." Sonal waved her fork at Rishaan. "I am so glad my daughters will never do anything like that to me. Accountant with a CPA-MBA has such a nice ring. Safe and successful woman you will be, and still so young at twenty-four."

"Great." Vandy had missed out on a lot of fun because she'd taken overloads and two full summer semesters to earn the 150 hours to sit for the CPA exam at graduation next summer. Then she'd start Chicago's two-year MBA program.

"Then it's time for a good man… or maybe before. I'd like him to be Gujararit, but I will settle for Punjabi or even a Sikh if you make the Dean's list." Her mother finished her bowl.

Dr. Patel's portable hospital phone rang. He listened, gave a few orders, and hung up. "I hate July. So many new interns. And the medical students. Raj better not be like one of these know-nothings."

"Raj is on renal service this month. According to his text messages, the dialysis machines are fascinating," her mother added. "Not that I see him because I must keep my distance to show no favoritism."

In the past, Vandy would have been mostly at ease with this type of convo. Today, however, she felt like she'd been hatched in the wrong nest. She wanted to get away.

Even better. Get away, do nothing all day except read actual paper books, and wait for Royce to get home so she could have random sex with a guy that she hardly knew. Her mom would definitely disapprove of her Irish tattooed firefighter who stayed in bed on his off days.

With the number of orgasms Royce had given her, she could totally understand how women would visit him if he lived in his mom's basement. Her mother probably would not.

Time to make an escape. "Well, Anna and I are going to go to the Cleveland Museum of Art. Soak up some culture."

"Have fun. Remember, stay hydrated and wear your sunscreen. Skin cancer is no joke. That t-shirt doesn't have UPF." Her hospital phone rang, and Vandy took the distraction to clean up like a good daughter.

She had everything packed in the metal tiffin and was making her way out when her mom waved her back down.

"Please deliver that to Raj. I just texted him. He should be coming by the staff elevators any minute."

"Why?"

"Because I can't be seen with him. And he's post call. He needs food. Can you drop him off at home?"

"His apartment?"

"No, at home. He should be in a real bed post call, not whatever bed the pre-furnished medical housing provides."

"Got it." Vandy fled before she got more jobs or more questions.

She stood for ten minutes by the staff elevators, waiting for her brother to come down. He'd missed her birthday dinner.

Normally she'd have been impatient, but where else did she have to be? Netflix and books by somebody named Tolkien at

Royce's would still be there in an hour.

She mentally bopped back and forth between how Royce might feel if she answered his door tomorrow naked or if reading those books naked was weird—which made her almost miss seeing Raj.

"Raj?" she called after he walked right past her.

He turned around and blinked once. "Vandy?"

"Mom gave me dal bhat and told me to drive you to their house." She bent down and hefted the metal tiffin, a combination of a bucket, a cooler, and a mess kit in one.

"I can drive myself to my apartment just fine," Raj said. "She still pretending she doesn't know me while I'm here?"

"Yes, followed by full mother hen when you're out."

"I know. You're the third person she's sent to try to drive me back home post-call. I'm fine."

"She'll ask." They started toward the parking garage. Raj had lost some weight since she'd seen him last. He seemed older and almost taller than he had in the winter when she's been home for a visit.

"Then lie to her and say I had a slow call night and I got plenty of sleep."

Vandy stopped. Had those words just come out of her perfect brother's mouth? They hadn't seen each other much since he'd chosen to go to University of Pennsylvania after high school. "You want me to lie?"

"Make something up." He continued walking. "It shouldn't be

that difficult for you."

"What does that mean?"

"You know how Mom texts constantly? She told me you're staying at Anna's."

"So?"

Raj pushed the edge of her t-shirt down to her collarbone. "Did Anna give you that hickey?"

She pulled her shirt back up. "Hey!"

"You shouldn't have bent down. You think I can't tell someone's banging my sister."

"Raj! People can hear you."

"It's a hospital. If you aren't bleeding to death, no one cares." He crossed his arms over his chest. "You want me to keep my mouth shut?"

"Yes! I'm not banging anyone."

"Sure you aren't. Patients lie to med students constantly. You aren't even in the top ten. I'll make a trade. I won't out you to Mom or Dad, and you tell them I slept fine on my slow call night. Tell them I said Mom's cooking was delicious."

"You don't want it?"

"I am capable of microwaving my own from the two freezers worth she gave me. If you keep the tiffin, she won't have an excuse to force me to stop by their house to drop it off."

"I had no idea."

"It's called living your life." Raj grinned. "White guy, isn't it?"

Vandy rolled her eyes. "I'm not telling."

He did a celebratory dance. "Another one bites the dust.

Welcome to the club, little sis."

"What! You're with someone?"

"Not right now. The only White girl I spend time with is my teammate Nora, and she's way more likely to murder me than sleep with me." He flashed her a picture of three medical students on his phone—Raj, a White woman, and an African American man.

"Isn't a team usually four people?"

"Yeah, but Clint never showed up. His parents forced him to go to medical school, so he keeps finding ways to not finish. Don't tell Mom. She'll worry I'm violating the 80-hour work week. His call nights get covered so I only sleep here once every four nights instead of once every three."

"Is that why there's no girl?"

"There's no girl because I'm busy becoming a doctor. No free time for fun. Like you can talk Ms. 'My daughter makes me so proud she's getting two sets of letters. CPA-MBA. Be still my Indian heart.'"

"I see why Nora wants to murder you. Bye, big brother."

"Stay hydrated. Use protection. STDs are real." Raj sounded exactly like their mother for a second.

It appeared lineup would start late on Thursday morning. The outgoing shift from Firehouse 19 was sleeping in, and the next shift hadn't shown.

Unless they were the members of the dynamic duo of Royce Murphy and Casey Jensen on the Medic ambulance.

"How long do you think you can hide?" Casey asked. Royce had volunteered them for the Medic yesterday morning and had done his best to stay outside of the firehouse for the shift.

"I'm not hiding," Royce said. By mutual accord, they went to the Engine and started checking the hoses.

Per his routine for the last six months, Royce had arrived early for his shift at Firehouse 19 yesterday. The captain was notoriously easy going about line-up, so Royce liked to come in, work out, and do an equipment check on the outgoing shift. Actual line-up usually occurred closer to ten instead of nine on most days.

"You checked your phone every ten minutes, and you had that goofy smile between calls," Casey said, folding the hose.

"I get texts."

"She's still at your place, isn't she?" Casey and Royce had

been paired together for the past year because Casey was actually punctual.

"So what? I just… I just couldn't. Didn't you see your last one more than once?" Royce remembered going to Firehouse 15's rookie graduation party where Casey had left with one of the rare female firefighters.

"Three drunk nights without sleeping over don't count." Casey re-rolled the hose.

"See, more than once. It's something," Royce said and pointed to the crew quarters off the garage. "How long do you think they're going to sleep?"

Firehouse 19 had been called in support of an overnight fire in Battalion 2. As usual, Medic with Casey and Royce had beaten the Engine and Ladder to the scene by almost ten minutes. They'd ferried 10's Lieutenant and rookie to MetroGen hospital after they got hit by some rafters. The rest of 19 stayed to start overhaul before collapsing into bed.

"Not long enough for you to escape," Casey warned him.

"Sex doesn't have to be random. I'm not attached. She's really nice. A workaholic, but nice."

"No one wants to nurse you through another heartbreak."

"I'm fine," he said. "My heart wasn't that broken."

"Right. Drinking alone. Getting a ton of tats. Taking stupid risks like going into buildings without air or your partner?"

"That only happened once," Royce disagreed. "You know why I went in. I had to save that kid."

Firehouse 19 had been slow to respond to a fire call. As they were deploying, Royce had seen a kid trapped inside the building. He'd abandoned his position in Medic and ran into the building first without air. Casey had followed him.

He should have gotten written up. But, according to the captain, escaping death by an inch was as good as a mile.

Casey nodded, “I don't know why you're still here. Take the lieutenant’s exam.”

“Why don't you? You're older than me and more experienced.” Royce had this argument with Casey and his brother Shane regularly.

“I don't need to stretch my wings. I've only been here for two years, unlike your six. You've never been in another station. If you wanted to fix this screwed up one, be a lieutenant somewhere else and then come back.”

“I don't know. I might not be ready.”

“You were ready to leave a year ago. Her dumping your stupid ass can’t be the reason you stay here bored.”

An odd metallic screech came from the Medic radio, but he swore he heard the words ‘over, dispatch, over.’

Royce ran over to the ambulance and hopped into the driver's seat. He checked the radio and discovered it was still set on the tactical channel. They were receiving the transmissions from a scene meant for the dispatch center.

A woman's voice was asking for help, using appropriate radio terminology. Royce checked the computer and tried to figure out which scene was in progress. “Who do you think it is?”

“It's Firehouse 15. It's her voice.” Royce understood that there was only one ‘her’ Casey would know from Firehouse 15, his previous hook-up.

Royce did a quick calculation. He’d subbed in at 15, which is how they’d ended up at the rookie graduation party. Firehouse 15 was super punctual, therefore their fresh shift was the one calling for help.

He lifted the radio. “Copy, 15. This is Medic 19. Over?”

No one responded.

He tried a different tack. “Dispatch. Do you read? This is Medic 19. Over?”

“Dispatch might be down. Let me get the lieutenant.” Casey headed to the crew quarters and woke the lieutenant.

The lieutenant growled, “There isn’t an actual call from Dispatch. We don't drive around the city willy-nilly like a newsie with his first police scanner. We wait until we're called. It's not even our battalion."

“I think we should—" Royce protested.

“We’ll go when Dispatch calls us.” The lieutenant headed back to his quarters.

“But Dispatch goes down all the time."

"Then when you’re lieutenant, you can make a decision to provide aid when Dispatch doesn't call you. Let me sleep another thirty minutes or until Dispatch actually calls me." The lieutenant shut his door firmly.

"He's wrong and I'm right. Firehouse 15 needs help," Royce said.

"Gonna disobey him?"

Royce set his teeth. "No. But I feel like opening the barn doors and sitting inside the Medic with the engine on. Just in case."

"I guess you need a partner." Casey climbed into the passenger seat.

"It'd be nice."

Royce tried rousing Dispatch again but heard nothing. Tense minutes ticked by as he waited, wondering what was going on over at that scene.

The commotion with the lieutenant had roused the rest of the team, and the incoming shift started to arrive. When they saw Royce refused to leave Medic, they ferried him coffee and bagels instead.

Line-up was delayed anyway because the lieutenant took his extra thirty minutes of sleep very seriously.

Then the klaxon went off. Dispatch was calling for Medic, Ladder, and Engine from 19 to respond to a call because Firehouse 15 was in trouble.

Royce gunned it out the open doors before Casey even confirmed their reception.

Newly promoted Battalion Chief Haskell was more than happy to see the speedy arrival of Medic 19. Royce felt his jaw drop at the unbelievable sight in front of him.

The scene involved a fire engine crashed into a garage. The garage had burst into flames on top of the fire engine, and the team from Firehouse 10 needed more water.

With the weather close to ninety degrees, the battalion chief put them on setting up rehydration stations for the firefighters. Fifty pounds of turnout gear got pretty hot.

Lieutenant Pickford, the battalion chief's aide, said. "Where is the rest of 19?"

"On their way. ETA five—six minutes. New shift settling in," Royce said and wrote their names on the accountability list.

"You're from yesterday's shift," the battalion chief noted.

"Why are you still working?"

"We heard a distress call from 15. We tried Dispatch so we stayed to monitor the radio." Casey helpfully omitted the general tardiness of their firehouse.

Chief Haskell wasn't fooled. "Firehouse 19 was at the other fire last night. Pickford, keep an eye on them."

Pickford waited for his boss to move out of earshot. "I want to know if whoever arrives from 19 is the new shift or the old. I'm not going to let anybody fuck up the boss's first day on the job. Got it?"

"Got it," Casey said.

"You set up rehab here. I want you to monitor for dehydration, heat stroke, and heat exhaustion. As soon as another medic comes, you're off."

As they set up, Royce couldn't help but wish he had that kind of decisive leadership.

Or that he was any kind of leader.

Royce had caught a three hour cat nap at the firehouse before he headed home.

The text messages from Vandy indicated that she was still at his place. She'd sent a couple photos of herself and Eowyn snuggling on the couch with half his bookshelf.

She bounded to the door when he knocked and gave him a bright smile. Even better, she was wearing his t-shirt and boxers. "Welcome home."

"Sorry I'm late. The incoming shift was a little late and then there was a crashed fire truck."

"Wow, that sounds bad." She let him in.

"Or a regular day. Did you clean in here?" The apartment was cleaner than usual. But not excessively clean. "What were you doing while I was gone?

"The usual. Snuck into my parents' house to get clothes and saw them in person at the hospital. After hearing how important it is that I become a hard-working CPA, I came back here and did hardly any work. I watched a bunch of movies and read a book or seven. Did you know that someone turned one short book *The Hobbit* into like three movies??"

"Did you like them better than *Terminato*r?" he asked. He'd shown her the first two Terminators to introduce her to real action movies.

"No, the third movie had a goat chase on ice. It wasn't in the book. I started reading the next books, and they have movies too. I didn't know that Viggo Mortensen used to be super hot."

"Did you cook?" His coffee table had a place setting and something that looked like rice and vegetables on the plate.

"No. It's dal bhat—Indian comfort food. Mom tried to force it on my brother Raj, the med student. He didn't want it, so we get to pretend he ate it to keep her happy." She pointed to a pile of books she had unearthed from somewhere. "Are you studying for the lieutenant's exam?"

"No," he said, trying to ignore the books.

"Really? Because there's like a study schedule clipped to them…"

"No," he repeated. "You were the busy little bee, weren't

you?"

"This place is empty except for books, a cat, and a ukulele. You have a box of empty picture frames. I thought about putting this one in a frame." She showed him an old picture from over a year ago. "Is this your brother?"

"No, it's me, that was a while ago." He kept his response vague. Back then he'd had zero tattoos and a shaved head.

For someone who claimed to do nothing, she had done quite a lot, but she also seemed to be having the time of her life.

"Oh. Are you like anti-photo frame? Isn't that Amish? Or was it Feng Shui?"

"I got rid of the pictures of my fiancée," he said.

She bit her lip adorably. "Sorry. I've just never been in like a dating relationship, so I don't know what I'm supposed to do. Am I too much?"

"You're doing fine." He grabbed her hips and kissed her to shut her up. It worked like a charm, because she melted underneath his mouth.

When he let her breathe again, she was almost putty in his hands, but she soldiered onward. "I had this whole plan about going out tonight. I was going to make reservations. I'm only in town till Saturday.

"Stop planning," he said. Touching her felt good, and he didn't want to think about the future or the past. "Live in the now. Have your adventures."

She helped him take her t-shirt off, and she was beautifully bare underneath. "I'm having an amazing time."

"Good. Now get your ass to the bedroom, and I'll make it even better."

"I can't believe I'm doing this," Vandy exclaimed Friday night, her last full day in Cleveland. Tomorrow she'd share a lunch at the hospital with her parents, say good-bye to Royce, and hop on the late flight to Chicago.

"Don't think, just do," Royce encouraged her and took her hand.

Vandy stepped onto the stage clad in her bra and a tight new mini skirt. Wolf whistles greeted them from the crowd.

"Here's Royce and Mandy singing *Light My Candl*e from *Rent*," the Emcee announced.

For her final adventure, he had taken her to karaoke, musical theater style, at Cleveland's Cherries Lesbian Bar. The rules were simple, you could sing from any musical you wanted but you had to be in character. And she had somehow agreed to be the stripper Mimi singing to the doomed musician Roger.

It was humiliating, embarrassing, and quite a fucking adventure.

The song called for them to sing to each other as they pretended to resist their attraction. Or so Royce said since musical theater was low on her list of movies to watch.

She was supposed to be the seductress, but Royce was seducing her again. The spotlight's glanced off his tattoos, each word familiar, as was the texture of his skin.

Then his eyes flashed when he sang a line about a girl he used to know. She wondered who he was thinking about then.

Fiancée or her. She hoped it was her.

So she changed the words a little at the end, wishing this wouldn't end. She was supposed to dance away, but she kept getting closer. "They call me Vandy."

"Kiss her!" the front row of lesbians called.

Royce didn't hesitate to obey. And the kiss was crazy good.

They climbed down and ended up sitting at a table next to a Black guy and a blonde, a rare straight couple in the bar.

"Good work," the woman said. "Your pitch wasn't that bad."

"I can only imagine how terrible music class has to be for you," the man laughed. "I'm Michael, and this is Angela. She's a teacher, just move here to Cleveland."

"Hey, I'm Vandy, and that is a great dress," Vandy said. Angela didn't look much older than her, and she was wearing a short number that emphasized her boobs. Vandy prepared to be jealous, but Royce hardly glanced at Angela.

Angela, the schoolteacher, smiled, "Half of your dress forgot to be here. But you stayed in character."

"Extra points for staying in character," Michael said, and, like Royce, he only had eyes for his date.

"I'm Royce, not Roger. What are you singing?"

"Nothing. Didn't come here for the music." Michael said. He

and Royce shared some type of mysterious masculine communication that she didn't quite get. “And here’s our food.”

“I feel like I need to use the little boy’s room. Then you need to powder your nose.” Royce excused them and walked to the back of the club.

As if powder fit in her tiny micro purse. It had just enough space for her phone, some cash, and her ID.

The bathrooms were neither male nor female. They were just bathrooms.

“Do you have to go to the bathroom?” Vandy whispered.

He gave her an incredulous look and led her to the last unoccupied stall against the wall. Then he kicked the door closed behind them. “Not exactly.”

Royce pounced on her, kissing her again. His hands caressed her breasts, which gave her that shivery desperate hungry feeling—a continuation of what she’d craved on stage.

“New adventure?” she asked.

He'd unzipped his jeans and put on a condom. She let him lift her against the wall and push his cock inside her. “Definitely.” He kept one hand over her mouth as he sucked her tits and banged her.

Thus, Vandy got her very, very dirty, adventurous initiation to bathroom sex.

Rumor was that sex would get boring someday. Vandy had a difficult time believing it because every time they did this it just felt so fucking good.

Fifteen minutes later, they were at the front tables ordering food. Michael and Angela were long gone, and they had missed a group of women performing Sweeney Todd.

The food had arrived when someone made a gagging noise

next to them and collapsed. Vandy stared in surprise, unsure of what to do.

Royce sprang into action and tried to perform the Heimlich on the woman. “See anything come out?”

“Nothing. I don’t see anything.”

“Is she blue?” Royce tried another squeeze on the woman’s abdomen from behind.

“I can’t tell!” Vandy said. The stage lights made it difficult to tell what color anything was.

The lady went completely limp. Royce rolled her over and felt for a pulse. “Fuck, lost the pulse.”

Vandy was terrified. This was definitely a job for her parents or Raj.

“Call 911. Get me the AED.” He started doing CPR on the woman’s chest and called out the the milling bystanders. “It’s the blinking box by the bathroom.”

As Vandy explained the situation to the 911 operator, the crowd grew, watching Royce do chest compressions. He was pumping his arms very fast, and it looked very tiring.

“What can I do? Anything else? Anything else?” Vandy offered, wanting to be less useless than the bystanders.

“I need a second person to switch out with me. Can you do chest compressions?”

“No, I think I can do the breathing thing though.” She put her hand over the woman’s nose and said, “What do I do now?”

“When I count to thirty, you breathe once.”

She obeyed and said, “Royce, air is moving. Are you sure she choked on something?"

He was focused on the person who dropped off the yellow box with the AED. "Open it up, attach the pads," Royce ordered her.

"To what?"

"It plugs into the machine, and the pads go on her chest." Royce said, breathless from the compressions.

She held the pads in her hands. "Do I put them on through her shirt?"

"Hang on." Roland ripped the shirt down the center. "Oh no."

"What?"

"Medical alert tag." He lifted a silver necklace off the woman's chest. "Peanut allergy." He checked her pockets and purse. "No EpiPen."

"Someone must have one. Anybody here have an EpiPen? Anyone?" Vandy called to the crowd.

The crowd of useless bystanders stood around acting useless. She saw a subtle change in Royce's eyes. They went from merely desperate to hopeless.

Then she did something she never imagined herself doing. She channeled her mother.

"You! You help him do CPR. Switch out with him." She grabbed the nearest woman who looked like she had any muscle.

She ran to the side of the stage and took the stairs two at a time. Vandy grabbed the microphone away from a woman dressed as Dorothy who had stopped singing Somewhere Over the Rainbow during the commotion.

"Anyone with an EpiPen immediately report to the front tables. This is an emergency. Repeat. Anyone with an EpiPen. We need an EpiPen now. Report to the front tables."

She repeated that four more times before running back down to the floor. More people were gathering so she had to shove her way through them. It took her what felt like an infinitely long time to reach the center.

She got there in time to see Royce stab the woman's leg with what she assumed must be an EpiPen. Three pens sat next to him, so her message must have worked.

The crowd murmured expectantly, and nothing happened.

She dropped onto her knees next to him. "How we doing?"

"No pulse. No shock," he said, face bleak and frustrated. "Where the hell is a Medic? If it's my fucking station being late again, I'll be pissed."

She picked up another EpiPen and handed it to him. "Use another one."

"Another one?" he asked.

"What's it going to do—kill her twice?"

He jammed the second pen into a different leg.

Tense seconds passed, and the woman made a gasping noise.

"She's alive!" Vandy yelled.

Then they heard the sirens in the distance. Their patient was breathing easily with her color much improved by the time the ambulance arrived. Royce stayed by the woman's side the whole time. He explained the situation to the two business-like women in paramedic uniforms. They said something to him that seemed to annoy him before they wheeled the patient off.

"You okay?" Vandy asked, having followed the group out to

the ambulance.

"Yeah, it's fine. They reminded me I should've checked for the medical alert bracelet sooner."

"Well, they are paramedics. They probably have more experience or something."

"They called me out for skipping the steps. The ABCDE's of basic life-saving skills. I never checked her airway until you did. Then I waited too long for Disability and Exposure." Royce watched them pull away, his eyes hooded.

"So, you study. You have the books for it."

He spun to face her. "What do you mean by that?"

"If you were unprepared, you should study."

"You think I don't study?" Royce sounded odd.

"The books had dust on them. Your firehouse doesn't seem the best run one either, so you aren't exactly challenging yourself." Vandy heard the words coming out of her mouth but would have sworn she heard her mother.

"You don't know anything about what I do," his voice cracked with unfamiliar anger.

She sputtered back, "It's not that big of a deal. Just study. Or take another class, or apply yourself better. Being a lieutenant might be a good idea."

"Oh, you're giving ME career advice? Let me give some back then. Tell your parents you don't want to be an accountant!"

"What does this have to do with me?" she said, stunned by his reaction.

"Vandy, if we're going to talk about the real world, then I've heard you mention loving numbers and loving being an accountant zero times. I have heard you whine about your parents and celebrate not having them lord over every minute of your free time."

"My relationship with my parents isn't the business of some guy I met this week." How dare he make assumptions like that.

"Exactly, then my meathead tattooed ways aren't your problem either."

"I didn't say that! You aren't a meathead. You read Nietzsche!" She was angry and hurt and pissed now.

"Yeah, which is why you've been lying to your parents about getting your brains fucked out by a blue-collar schmuck—a loser who doesn't apply himself."

"I never said that. This thing between us…" She could see this becoming an avalanche, and she didn't know how to stop it.

"What thing between us? Fucking me for a whole week doesn't mean you know me!"

"Why would I? You never tell me about yourself. Anytime I try to get to know you, you strip me naked!" she retorted with growing fury.

"And you loved it. Look, Vandy with a V and not an M, you're with me because you wanted to be rode hard and put away wet." He spun on his heel and turned away.

"So that's it!" She reeled from the abruptness of how this had spiraled out of control in exactly three minutes.

"That's all this ever was. One week. You had it. It's over." He flagged down a passing cab and handed the driver a wad of cash. "Please take her back to her real life."

Before she could say more, he disappeared into the faceless parade of people passing by, silent witnesses to the death of a summer fling.

Vandy stopped to get coffee at the Panera nearby MetroGen before meeting her parents for their good-bye lunch. She'd spent the night at Anna's—finally—and slept terribly. She kept reliving the night over and over again. Anna, good friend that she was, had not asked any questions.

"Here's your regular, Dr. Perkins." The clerk handed the blonde woman in front of her a soup and half a sandwich.

Vandy almost fell over when the doctor turned around. “Angela?”

The blonde from last night had confusion on her face. "Yes, and you are?"

"Vandy from karaoke yesterday. You aren't a teacher?”

Angela sidled away from the counter. “Oh… that.”

"Your date said you were an elementary school teacher." Vandy wasn't giving up.

Dr. Perkins blushed, "I'm not. Michael thinks I am."

"You're lying to him?" Vandy asked.

“Not on purpose. There was a little mix-up about my job, and I didn't correct him. He's an accountant so I don't think he'd understand."

The same clerk handed Vandy her coffee as that hit a little too close to home. "There's nothing wrong with being an accountant."

"If that's what you want. While I'm sure it's stressful in its own way, it's safe. No one's life is on the line. Simple, non-complex," Dr. Perkins said.

"But what happens when he finds out?" Vandy couldn't stop asking these far too personal questions of a total stranger.

Angela smiled sadly, "What was always going to happen. I end up alone, but at least I'm true to myself."

"So why do it?"

"Because I wanted to be fun, even if it's not who I am."

"I just found out I liked fun. And karaoke, and tons of other stuff I never did before. Am I addicted to fun?"

Dr. Perkins apparently understood this was really about Vandy's problems. "Is fun hard drugs, prostitution, illicit sex, or anything illegal?"

"Fun's telling my parents I'm at the art museum when I'm in bed with a cute guy I met on vacation. Fun's watching terrible movies and hanging out reading books – actual books on paper."

"Congratulations, I diagnose you with college-student-itis. You aren't addicted to fun; you're figuring out who you are."

"It's not the guy?" Vandy hadn't been ready to consider that.

"Would you still love the books and movies if the guy disappeared? Are you enjoying all that stuff because of him or because you're letting yourself do those things?"

Vandy opened her mouth and closed it. “I don't know.”

"That's the beauty of being your age. Figure out who you are and what you want, and not for a guy," said Perkins couldn't have been even ten years older than Vandy. She gave Vandy a sly look, "Not for your parents, either."

"How do you know when you've made the right choice?"

Perkins shook her head. "No one can answer that except you. And that will be three hundred dollars."

"It will?" Vandy blinked hard.

"No, I just always wanted to say that."

"Oh. Well, I hope you and accountant guy get it to work when you figure out who you are."

"I know who I am. Best of luck on figuring out who you are,” Angela said and walked off.

This was definitely a new thing for Vandy—to interrogate and seek advice from random strangers. But maybe that was who Vandy really was…

She looked at her phone and made a decision. Her parents could have lunch by themselves.

Vandy sent him a text asking to talk at his place.

Royce texted his permission, feeling a little guilty about how hard he'd come down on her last night.

Okay, he'd completely over-reacted, and she deserved some closure.

Still, the outcome had always been a foregone conclusion.

When she came by at three pm, they stood on opposite sides of his living room. Poor Eowyn was confused, they'd never spent time apart.

She wasn't alone, because Vandy said, "What did I do wrong? Is this my fault? Did I ruin us?"

He shook his head. "Us was ending today no matter what. And I was ruined way before you met me."

"What do you mean?"

Time to absolve her. "I was engaged to my high school girlfriend. We lived together, and I helped put her through college. I trusted her with everything—my bank account, the lease of this apartment. She had a job lined up in Cincinnati after graduation last year. I was going to take the lieutenant exam that summer and transfer there."

"You never took the exam," she observed.

"The day she graduated, she left me a note. She'd been cheating on me for a year. She'd found a real man with ambition who 'applied himself.'"

"Oh my god." Vandy covered her mouth, having recognized the phrase that set him off.

"She cleaned out my bank account rather than paying our rent and threw away all the overdue notices. Since I was mid-transfer, I didn't have a job in Cleveland or Cinci. I holed up in here with Eowyn for weeks. I was about to be evicted when my brother found out from a friend in the police department. He paid off what he could and told my team at 19. They passed the hat and paid the rest. My captain 'lost' my transfer, so I was never unemployed."

He skipped how he'd destroyed every single thing Alyson'd ever touched, including every plate and dish.

It took her only a few seconds to digest all of that. "That's why you stay at your firehouse. Because of the people. True allegiance is only given willingly," she recited the words he wore on his skin, a quote from *The Chronicles of Prydain*, which she likely hadn't read yet.

"Exactly. Ever since then I haven't been willing to put myself out there." He sighed and made an admission. "You were a good thing for me. It was nice to have someone who cared—who wanted me to be more. I'm going to apply for lieutenant and take those oboe lessons."

She sniffled. "I feel so lame right now. Me and my stupid problem of not knowing what I want, when you went through hell…

I like you. But my life, my future, are in Chicago. Though I don't even know if I want that future anymore."

Crying women all always got to him. Before he thought about it, his arms were around her, and he was smoothing back her hair. "Then change majors. Do you want to be doctor like your brother?"

"No idea. Totally clueless. I've been so focused on school and achieving that I never asked the question. I've never hung out in bed just reading books that don't do something. I read all the *The Lord of the Rings* books and the three *Fifty Shades of Grey* books."

He couldn't help but admire how industrious she was that she'd found reading two thousand pages in a week and watching twenty hours of movies relaxing. "You don't have to know yet. That's the job of college, right? Find what you want. It's not comfortable, for sure, but it is an adventure."

She pressed her head into his chest, right over his heart. "I didn't think it would hurt this much. This is the opposite of comfortable."

"Do you want to be comfortable?"

"I don't know anymore. When I stole the microphone, I felt different. Like I was flying, like I was someone else. And I think I want that…"

"That's something at least." He rubbed her back gently, parts of him relaxing. Other parts were not responding in the same way.

"I know one thing." She leaned forward and kissed his mouth. "Our last kiss cannot be while I was having sex with you in a bathroom at a club."

"Vandy…" Royce was wavering. They were supposed to be saying goodbye, getting closure.

"I did something cliche and rebellious. I skipped lunch with my parents today and got a tattoo instead," she whispered conspiratorially. "It's in a secret spot. My flight leaves in three hours."

Music to his ears, because twenty seconds later they were naked in his bed, and he had her nipple in his mouth, loving the way she moaned.

His fingers found a bandage on her left hip by her bikini line. He peeled it back and saw a small black glyph.

He paused because it was vaguely familiar. "*The Lord of the Rings*? Elvish?"

"Sindar Elvish for 'loved.'" She trembled in his arms for the last word. "I wanted it to mean something, even if it just means it to me."

She wasn't talking solely about the tattoo.

He kissed her lips, holding back his own feelings. "It means something to me."

"Even if this is goodbye." A tear formed in the corner of her eye.

He wiped it away. "It's not goodbye as long as you're in Ohio."

"Good. You can drive me to the airport." She kissed him and gave herself over to him.

Vandy sat waiting to board her flight to Chicago, trying not to cry. They'd stayed in bed until the last possible moment, and he'd kissed her at the security line. It made her want to cancel her flight and stay another day.

Or forever.

But that wouldn't do. She had a life in Chicago. An internship and a degree or two to finish.

She was fine.

Fine was relative because she couldn't stop texting Royce.

V: So, you haven't cut your hair for a year?

R: Nope.

Two photos popped up, the one she'd found and a current one where he was gloriously tattooed and shirtless.

"Ma'am, boarding." A helpful airline employee smiled knowingly at her phone screen.

Vandy gave her a dirty look and saved the photos to her phone before deleting the message. She could drool over Royce's hotness and relive her memories later.

Or maybe when she sat down.

Screw it. She could be weak.

She flicked her screen back on as she walked down the tunnel to the plane and started a new convo.

V: I could kiss you everywhere. I wish we could still see each other.

This texting was addicting. Did breaking up only count after she left Ohio air space? Or landed in Chicago?

R: Send me a photo.

She glanced around. No one was in her row. She took a quick snapshot of her boobs still in the bra and hit 'send.' Her face wasn't in it, that was okay, right?

Her phone beeped as a new photo loaded.

And holy fuck that was a photo of her brother and his medical student team.

R: Are we playing Game of Thrones? Busted. <3 Raj

Vandy hadn't realized until that moment that she needed more friends whose names started with R to fill the space between Raj and Royce.

V: You are the worst brother on the planet.

Raj: Or the best. You two ended stuff?

V: I live in Chicago. Duh.

Raj: If you can't survive on zoom and phone sex alone, there's an overnight Amtrak between Cleveland and Chicago. If you set up a Paypal account, Mom and Dad will never know. Check it out.

She quickly skimmed the suggested website. With creative

class scheduling, she could spend two to three days at a time in Cleveland easily.

V: Crap. You are the best brother. How do you know this?

Raj: I met a blonde from Chi-town at an AMA conference during Med 1. It didn't last, but it was fun. You owe me.

She started a new text message string—to Royce, not Raj this time.

V: Can I have your email?

To: Rmurpheee1997@gmail.com

From: VandywithaVnotM@gmail.com

I get that this was supposed to be over, but I'm not sure I'm ready for that. Can we still see each other?

I know it's a big ask with me being clueless about relationships and life in general, and you with the evil-stealing ex stuff… but I don't want to let go of what could be a very good thing just because of distance.

True allegiance is only given willingly, and you have mine. Come on a new adventure with me?

-Vandy

She attached a screenshot of the Amtrak schedule and

calendar.

To: VandywithaVnotM@gmail.com

From: Rmurpheee1997@gmail.com

Allegiance is given willingly in return.

I'll see you at 9am on 8/14. Pack nothing. You won't need clothes.

-Royce

Vandy thought about texting Raj back to thank him but decided against it. He had his life and she had hers. It was best to hide all evidence of their conversation—and her boobs.

As she deleted his text messages, she noted that the African American guy in the photo looked a little like not-school-teacher-Angela's date to karaoke. That wasn't possible though because he was an accountant.

Besides, what were the odds that they'd both lied to each other about their jobs? That was just ridiculous.

What wasn't ridiculous was ordering paperback books to be delivered to her apartment. *The Chronicles of Prydain* sounded like an excellent place to start. It looked like there was a box set. . .

And then she'd open that PayPal account to buy train tickets for her next adventure.

Weeks later…

Coffee before clinic was a great team building exercise for third-year medical students.

Nora, however, was quite busy stacking review articles in Michael Harper's arms. "Just some light reading."

Michael smiled and fake staggered under the weight of the paperwork. "Light reading, huh?"

The few doctors in scrubs ahead of them made him guess it had been a busy night somewhere since this was when the overnight shifts from the ICU signed out.

He miscalculated the movement of the line and accidentally collided with one of the two female physicians in front of him.

The doctor bounced off him, spilling coffee everywhere.

"I am so sorry, ma'am," Michael apologized for the deluge of coffee and medical articles all over the fallen doctor.

Then he looked down at his victim.

Impossible.

Angela.

In green scrubs and a long white coat.

She stared at him. He stared at her. He tried to comprehend the words emblazoned on her stained white coat. 'Dr. Angela Perkins, Interventional Cardiology.'

That was not a kindergarten teacher. That was a highly trained medical professional.

Neither of them moved, stunned into frozen silence. Nora took action. "We're sorry, Doctor. Old man Harper here. Raj, napkins." He scrambled to follow her order.

"I'm fine," Dr. Angela Perkins sounded dazed. Michael tried to give her a hand up, and she recoiled with the same disdain one would give a tarantula.

"I'm sorry," Michael mumbled, unsure of what to do or say upon discovering the identity of his recent date.

"Angela, are you okay?" the other doctor asked Dr. Perkins.

"I'm fine." Dr. Perkins stood up and read his badge in an unfamiliar tone. "Thank you, Medical-Student Harper, for your offer of assistance. Mistakes happen." She blanked her shock from her features and addressed the rest of his team, taking their proffered napkins. "Thank you, Patel and Borenstein."

"At least let us buy you new coffee," Raj offered quickly.

"It was quite the jolt as it was. I'll go get new scrubs. I'm post-call so I'll be off tonight." Dr. Perkins looked anywhere but at

Michael.

“We're outpatient family med. We don't get off until six or seven,” Michael answered. That was obviously a message for him.

“She wasn't talking to you,” Nora said. “We're sorry, ma'am. We'll get out of your way and very sorry about your clothes.” She signaled Raj who grabbed the papers off the floor and helped propel Michael down the hallway.

Michael had no choice but to go.

Need to more drama and forbidden love at MetroGen Hospital? The About the Author section at the end of the book has more info than the medical school library.

LOVE ON CALL

Karigan Hale

Marian, the sarcastic manager of a Costco, tries out the Cloud 9 dating app against her will. Lightning strikes when she connects with Trevor, a male ER nurse, who's been striking out on the app for reasons he doesn't quite understand. Despite an initial, mutual attraction, a series of cock-blockable events threatens to end this relationship before it begins.

Will the Cloud 9 dating app prove successful in this match?

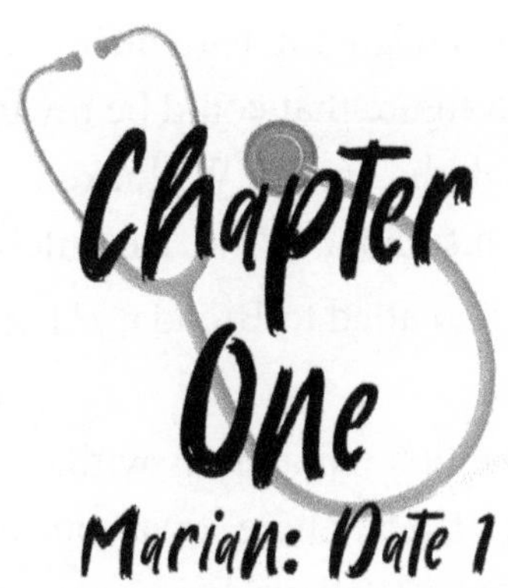

Chapter One

Marian: Date 1

Another Friday night. Another dive bar. Another first date. My finger hovered over the delete button of the Cloud 9 dating app on my phone. I'd threatened to delete this thing at least a bajillion times since I set up my profile last month. How I had let Essix, known to everyone except her grandmother as Six and my soon to be ex best friend, talk me into it in the first place remained a mystery.

As did my current date. According to his profile, and the few messages we'd exchanged before setting up this failed meet and greet, Trevor was in the medical field (vague), liked hiking in the mountains (cliché), and always let the girl choose the movie (pedantic). But he was cute in a boy next door meets Zac Efron kind of way, his name didn't appear on any sex offender registries, and he didn't send me a dick pic. Three checks in the pro column. So, I agreed to meet him at a centrally located adult beverage establishment full of people, liquid courage, and escape routes. As any twenty-first century single woman would do.

I was now a few sips away from finishing my drink and walking out the door. I'd been stepped on, stepped around, and sat down, but never stood up on one of these Cloud 9 hook-ups. I guess there was a first time for everything.

I signaled to Brendan, the bartender, for my tab, paltry though it was, when I saw a figure that could be my time-impaired date weaving through the crowd. We locked eyes. He smiled broadly and waved his phone at me. Definitely Trevor.

"Never mind," I called to Brendan. "I see my, uh, friend, now."

Yes, I was on a first name basis with the bartender. That was how many first dates I'd had here. I was one date away from Brendan thinking I was a sex worker meeting clients here.

"I'd make him pay for that one for making you wait," Brendan said with a smirk.

"I'll see how it goes first," I said.

Trevor, wearing a polo shirt, nicely fitted jeans, and an apologetic smile, pushed his way beside me at the bar.

"Sorry I'm late. Thanks for waiting," he said in a deep baritone I was not expecting. Like I said, boy next door—as in lanky, wholesome, and kind of a nerd. His voice, though, brought to mind melted chocolate and Randy Travis. Intrigue replaced annoyance. I was instantly attracted.

I held out my hand for him to shake. His was warm and smooth. The boy had big paws.

"You got here just in time. I was about to leave," I said.

"I'm glad you didn't. Can I get you another?" He pointed to my empty glass.

"Yes, please. Chardonnay." He ordered a Mich Ultra for himself. Good start. Bud Light would go in the con column on whether there would be a second date. I'm not a snob, but seriously...

When our drinks arrived, we settled into the typical first date stuff: a little personal information, dotted with some life highlights or funny anecdotes, and sprinkled with flirty compliments and heated stares. His eyes, an interesting mix of blue and gray that I'd never seen before, distracted me while his voice lulled me into submission. I could've cared less what he was saying as long as he kept talking. Hell, he could be reading Kim Kardashian's Twitter feed, and I'd be here for it.

"Are you sure you aren't a singer?" I asked, letting my fingers brush his arm. "Your voice is amazing."

He chuckled. "Nope. Not a singer. No one wants to hear that."

"What do you do for a living? Specifically. Your profile says 'medical field.'"

His dimpled smile faltered a fraction. I heard the record screech on our wedding march. Uh-oh. A million scenarios flitted through my brain in a second as he hesitated.

He's lying and not in medicine at all.

He's the guy who gives lethal injections at the penitentiary.

He's a traveling doctor and only in town for tonight.

He's a dentist.

Or worse—a podiatrist, looking at people's hammertoes or picking their cracked heel skin all day. And I'd shaken his hand.

I grimaced and shuddered. Then tried to fix my face.

He jutted his chin out and held my gaze. Here it comes. I braced myself for a conversation full of toe fungus.

"I'm a nurse," he said. "The ER charge nurse at Holy Cross

Hospital actually."

Before I could stop it, a small laugh escaped my mouth. Not because his profession was funny. Only because I was so relieved.

His eyebrows slammed together as his glass slammed the counter. "You think a male nurse is funny?"

"Oh no. Absolutely not—" I started to explain, my face heating in embarrassment.

He interrupted, his eyes now glacial, "Because I'll have you know that we work twice as hard as the doctors. Especially in the ER. I mean, yesterday I had to remove maggots from a severely infected pressure ulcer. You think a doctor could handle that? And being the head nurse has its own extra set of stressors."

"You misunderstood. Being a nurse is totally admirable," I tried again.

He didn't seem to be listening. "As if being a Costco store manager is so demanding."

Okay, Mr. Sensitivity went a bit too far by throwing my career into the mix. Still, it was my goof originally, so I attempted some levity. "It's demanding in its own way. I had to remove maggots from a shipment of strawberries the other day."

"Hardly the same thing."

My patience ended before his eye roll did. I slapped a twenty on the bar. "Well, I was having a nice time. If you would listen, you'd realize I have no problem with male nurses. It sounds to me like you're the one with the issue. If you decide to get to your handsome head out of your ridiculously perky ass long enough to stop jumping to conclusions, message me. Otherwise, good luck and God bless."

I turned on my heel, ignoring his stunned expression,

and stomped out of the bar, not expecting to hear from him again.

Which was a shame because I kinda had a thing for men in uniform.

Chapter Two

Trevor: Date 1

What just happened? She'd stolen my exit. After she laughed at me.

I knew things were going too well. I don't usually date red heads, but Marian's was more of a muted copper and framed her heart-shaped face in perfect layers. I recognized her the second I saw her sitting at the bar—major plus for her. Too often these first dates emphasized the overuse of photo filters. But not Marian. Light makeup, bright smile, great tits. Check, check, check.

I was getting serious interested vibes—not quite "take me home and ravage me now" vibes, but definitely "make out with me while we wait for a ride share" vibes. Then she laughed at my profession. And accused me of being sensitive about it.

Being a nurse was not a laughing matter. You'd think in the twenty-first century where gender was a spectrum, nursing wouldn't still be gender-bent. Apparently, I was wrong.

Again. And left alone at a bar.

Again.

Maybe I should lie about my career. List axe grinding or something equally as ridiculous. Most of these connections didn't end up moving past a few dates anyway, so what was the harm?

I added another twenty to Marian's and texted Rob, my best friend, while I walked out to catch an Uber.

Me: Another bust another night alone.

Rob: Sorry, man. Was she a dog?

Me: The opposite. Gorgeous, into me, then poof.

Rob: Don't tell me you got all butt hurt about being a nurse again.

Me: ???

Rob: Copy paste from your last date.

Me: Not my fault people think male nurses are funny.

I got no reply, so I checked the Uber app. Two minutes away. My phone buzzed again.

Rob calling...

"What?" I asked. "I'm outside waiting for my Uber."

"You need to get over yourself," Rob said, crunching on something into my ear.

"She laughed at me when I told her I was a nurse," I explained. "Actually laughed."

"Tell me exactly," he demanded.

"Only if you stop eating in my ear. You know I hate that shit." I heard the bag crumple, and Rob swallow.

"Hit me with it," he said.

I replayed the night for him in fast-forward. The way Marian's dress dipped and flared in all the right places, her flirty smiles, our constant touching. I left out the part about the little fires her fingers started each time they settled on my bare skin. With Rob, more emphasis on her banging figure and less on the way her easy laugh settled into my chest.

"I had second base on lock. At least." A small embellishment; doesn't ruin the story. "Then she laughed at me."

"What did she say after you inevitably put up your defenses?" he asked.

"She tried to make excuses." I said. My Uber pulled up then. I checked the license against my phone and got in.

"And did you listen to her explanation?"

"Rob, she tried to equate removing maggots from a person to removing them from bad strawberries."

"Just so I'm clear. You got mad at her for allegedly mocking your career, so you responded by mocking hers."

That shut me up. "Not exactly," I back-pedaled.

"Yes, exactly. What did she say before she walked out?"

"How did you know she walked out?" I asked, scowling at the Uber driver who flicked his eyes to me in the rear-view mirror. Mind your business, asshole.

"Because that's exactly what I would have done! Now tell me what she said."

I sighed and replayed the conversation. "Something to the effect of not jumping to conclusions and to message her if I got my head out of my ass," I mumbled.

Rob laughed. I refrained, barely, from hanging up on him.

“Why am I even listening to you? You’re chronically single too,” I said.

"Chronically single on purpose. That doesn’t mean I sleep

alone." I groaned, he continued, "And she is correct. But she also left the door open, so you must have done something right."

"She did call my ass perky," I said. "I think that's a compliment."

"Message her right now and apologize. Grovel if you have to," he suggested. "If she's as hot as you describe her, you'd be an idiot to let her go."

"She was hot. Like if Emma Stone had tits hot."

"Then why are you still on the phone with me?"
He disconnected.

"If I had a girl like Emma Stone, I'd let her laugh at me all day long," the driver quipped as he dropped me off in front of my apartment.

I gave him three stars before opening the dating app to message Marian.

Me: If I told you I was dropped on my head as a baby, would you forgive me?

No immediate response. She might still be on the road. Or she already deleted me. The little bubble with her profile picture moved under my message. I waited a beat. When nothing popped up. I tried again.

Me: I am sorry for acting like a 💩.

Marian: I'm sorry for my initial reaction. Your career is not funny. From the look on your face, I thought the worst.

It was a relieved laugh.

Me: What'd you think I would say?

Marian: Taxidermist. Grave robber. Podiatrist.

Me: Yikes. Nope, none of those.

Marian: Hence the relieved laugh.

Me: I had a great time tonight. Until that asshole freaked out and ruined it.

Marian: Me too.

Me: You really think my ass is perky?

Marian: Caught that did you?

Me: I'd love to see your beautiful smile again in person. Can we start over?

...

Me: Please? I love Costco. Buy all my bulk products there

Marian: Okay. One more chance.

Me: You won't regret it.

We set up a time to meet at a local walking trail. Classic second date location destined not to fail.

I gave myself a mental high-five and a pep talk about cooling it on the nervous energy. I wanted this next date to go well.

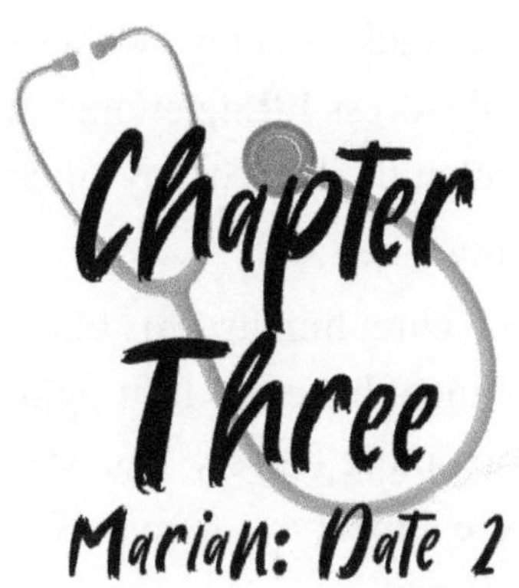

I'm not usually in the business of giving second chances, but I couldn't get the cadence of his voice out of my head. And those eyes. I've heard of eye candy, but this was like eye crack. I needed to see them again. Yesterday, I actually caught myself trying to find something that matched the color. Impossible so far.

Besides, I got it. Being a male in a female dominated profession came with some jokes and less than savory reactions. Most of my counterparts were male. Each rung on the corporate ladder came with more male genitalia to navigate around. I was near the top, so it was a regular sausage party at managerial meetings.

Trevor's dimpled smile greeted me as I approached the pavilion where we'd agreed to meet. On time today. Good start. I returned his smile and meant it.

"Thanks for agreeing to meet me again," he said in his hypnotic voice, taking my hand in his and giving it a little squeeze. "I left my neurotic evil twin at home this time."

"Good to hear it. If I can manage to have normal reactions to information, we'll get along fine."

His eyes turned to smoke as they swept over my fitted dress. I gave him a little twirl, the dress lifting enough to show off more of my thigh and the cut-out at the base of my spine.

"You look amazing," he said.

I made a show of sizing him up. His blue button down was the perfect shade to compliment his eyes. It fit tight around his shoulders and chest, then more loosely around his tapered waist. In my kitten heels, we were almost eye to eye. He was sexy, but not in an in-your-face kind of way.

"You're not too shabby yourself," I teased.

"I'll take it. Shall we walk?" He gestured for me to lead the way onto the wooden foot bridge that circled a large pond. As I walked passed, he placed a hand on my lower back causing a shiver to run all the way up my spine and heat to settle in my belly.

Oh yes. The physical attraction was electric. From the way he spread his fingers out slowly until his entire palm was flat against my skin, I knew he felt it too. I relied on the cool breeze to calm my raucous lady bits. They'd been neglected for a while—and by a while, I meant A WHILE—so any promise of playtime had them doing a happy dance.

"How'd you decide on nursing?" I asked.

Was I curious? Yes.

Was I also trying to see if the word "nurse" was a trigger for insanity? Double yes.

"I couldn't pick a specialty. I wanted to try all the things. Nursing allowed me to do that. And cut down on med school bills," he said. I watched him for any signs of horns or fire breath. So far, so good.

"And you get to save lives every single day."

"I wouldn't go that far. Sometimes it's about convincing a certain recurring patient that he doesn't actually need invasive surgery to get rid of candy he swallowed two months ago."

"Stop it."

"This man is almost one hundred years old, deaf as a doornail, and, besides a bit of hypertension, fit as a fiddle. Unfortunately, we can't convince him of that. His very patient granddaughter brings him at least once a week with some perceived ailment. We've gotten to be fast friends," Trevor said.

I laughed. "I think I'd like to meet him. He sounds like one of our regulars. We have a feisty octogenarian with purple, spiky hair and an attitude to match. Her hang up is the canned goods. She'll spend literal hours inspecting each one for dents, rust, scratches, or scrapes. Bless her."

"Tell me about Costco," he said. "Why there?"

"That's a boring story. I started there part time to help pay for college and moved up the ranks quickly. Once I graduated with a business degree and no real focus, I decided it was easier than starting over somewhere else," I explained. "Tale as old as time."

"Do you like it?" he asked.

"Sure. It's a career. Puts money in the bank. And I get all the bulk shampoo I can handle."

He chuckled. He had a great chuckle. "How can you beat that?"

He slowed his steps until we eventually stopped in a shady spot. I leaned against the railing to face him. His eyes had that smoky look again.

Trapping a lock of my hair between his fingers, he twisted it as the sun glinted on the highlights.

"It must be working. Your hair is beautiful." He leaned in, placing his hands on the rail on either side of me, essentially trapping me. My heartbeat went into overdrive.

"You are beautiful, Marian. I'd like to kiss you now," he said, closing the distance between us.

"Yes, please," I whispered just before our lips met.

My eyes fluttered closed. His hand moved to my face. He tasted as good as he looked.

The kiss was light and lazy at first. He caressed the curves of my lips, licked the seam without demanding entrance, nibbled and sucked. I was merely along for the ride. I wrapped my arms around his waist, feeling his muscles move under his clothes as he angled his head for better access.

Taste, touch, smell, sound—it was like the powers that be designed Trevor to embody all the perfect senses. His other hand moved to my hip as he deepened the kiss, now demanding access to lave the inside of my mouth. Tongues entangled. Mind erased.

Just when I was sure my body was going to burst into flames, Trevor broke the kiss on a groan. He pressed his forehead to mine while we both caught our breath.

Then he reached into his pocket for his cell phone, effectively ending the moment. "I'm sorry. I have to take this."

What—and I cannot stress this enough—the fuck? He's taking a call in the middle of the hottest damn kiss I'd had in years?

I adjusted my dress and tried not to spit on him. Stupid Six and her stupid dating app.

When he looked up from the retched device, his face was full of apologies. "I'm so sorry, Marian. I'm on call. They need me at the hospital. Apparently, there's a bad accident on the interstate."

The wind went right out of my petulant sales. I'd have to be the biggest bitch on the planet to be mad about that. Still, who makes a date when they're on call?

As if reading my thoughts he said, "I was so desperate for a second chance with you, I jumped on the first date you suggested. It wasn't until later I remembered I was on call. They rarely ever call. Just my luck, today is the day."

I shook off my annoyance, which had more to do with being kissed into a horny frenzy without an outlet and less to do with the actual situation, and said, "No worries. Go save the world."

The worry lines around his forehead decreased a little. I puckered up for a good-bye kiss. Then peeked an eye open when none was forthcoming.

He was looking at his phone again. "Thanks, Marian. I'll message you."

Then he squeezed my shoulder. Like a little sister.

Like we hadn't just shared a panty-melting kiss.

Trevor’s chances were starting to flatline.

Chapter Four
Trevor: Date 2

Longest. Shift. Ever.

On autopilot, I taped IVs and poked needles and flushed lines and placated nerves. I think I may have even helped intubate at one point, but I can't be sure.

My mind was full of Marian. My senses were full of Marian.

I'd catch a scent of vanilla and be transported back to that walkway with her hair tickling my cheek as we kissed. I'd take a quick sip of water between patients only to long to be tasting her instead. I'd run my fingers across a cotton sheet only to be reminded of her soft skin.

Man, I was in trouble. Her pretty face and supple mouth were enough to keep me in a state of semi-hardness all evening. Not a great look for a nurse who is trying to put patients and families at ease.

Not that I would admit any of that to Rob. If he heard me talking about longing and tickling and softness, he'd revoke my man card.

But he didn't see her in that dress. I had a small pulmonary embolism when she spun around revealing the smooth expanse of her back. Lightly freckled. No bra strap. My cock noticed too and had been pointing the way to her ever since.

Touching her there hadn't been a decision. It'd been a necessity. An instinct. A compulsion.

I kicked myself all the way to the hospital for not kissing her good-bye. What was I thinking?

I was thinking about the people in the pile-up. The on-call messages made the situation sound worse than it was. I should know better by now; they always sound worse. Maybe I'm a bit jaded after being in the ER for so many years—I've seen it all—or maybe they do it on purpose to get us to hustle. In any case, I definitely had time for a good-bye kiss.

Stupid work. Stupid distracted drivers. Stupid me.

During a lull while we were waiting for test results, I messaged Marian.

Me: Thinking about you. Wishing I was still on that bridge.

She hadn't responded by the time I had to rejoin the team. I tried not to let her delayed response distract me. It didn't work.

Was she mad? She said she was fine with me leaving. Go save the world, she'd said.

Was she busy? Not everyone checked their messages twenty-four-seven.

Was she drafting a flirty reply? Please let it be that one.

I checked again when the Chief of Staff deemed it

stable enough for me to leave. No response. Fuck.

Me: Just got off shift. Up for a nightcap?

Her response was swift and short. Not good.

Marian: Not tonight.

Me: Rain check?

Marian: Why don't you pick the date this time. Preferably when you aren't on call.

Me: Absolutely.

Me: I can still taste you.

Marian: Is that good or bad?

Shit. She was salty about something. How could she not know that our kiss kept me adjusting my pants all night?

Probably because, like a jackass, I squeezed her shoulder like a child instead of killing it with a follow-up kiss.

Me: Intoxicating. I was distracted all shift.

Marian: Hard to tell since you left in a hurry.

Me: Worst decision of the day. That and agreeing to help flush a catheter.

She sent a smiley face emoji. I was back in the race.

Me: FYI. I might have a crush on you.

Marian: Might?

Me: I need more market research. We were rudely interrupted last time. It won't happen again.

Marian: Just so happens that part of my boring job is market research. I'd be happy to give you a few pointers.

I typed in, "I'll be the one giving you the pointer," but thought better of it before pressing SEND. I'd save that for after I actually closed the deal. If the universe decided to stop fucking with me and gave me a fighting chance.

Me: It's a date. Wear the same dress. I couldn't take my eyes off you

After checking my calendar a kajillion times, we settled on a date later in the week. Please, for the love of blue balls, let this one go well.

Marian: I'm sick.

Me: Netflix and soup?

Marian: I'm probably contagious. Reschedule?

Me: Symptoms?

Marian: It's your day off. No need to nurse me.

Me: Symptoms?

Marian: I'll be fine. Just need to rest.

Me: S.Y.M.P.T.O.M.S.

Marian: 😄 Fine. Chills, cough, stuffy nose, stuffy head, stuffy everything.

Me: Temperature?

Marian: I don't have a thermometer.

Me: You're killing me, Smalls.

Marian: Uh-oh. Is no med kit a deal breaker? I

can scrounge up a dusty band aid.

Me: Not with you.

Marian: Sorry. I was looking forward to tonight.

Me: Me too. Rest, liquids, repeat.

Marian: And call you in the morning?

Me: Call me anytime.

Ser-i-ous-ly. Who did a guy have to blow to catch a break around here? Could nothing go right between us? The first Cloud 9 connection with actual potential and it's been nothing but a series of cock-blockable events.

Now, decision time. I had an extra couple thermometers. I also had cool compresses, a supply of fever reducers, a blood pressure cuff, an odometer, and a stethoscope. You know, typical first aid stuff. That Marian apparently did not own. I could easily go to her apartment and take care of her. Show her my sensitive side and amazing bedside manner. Let her know I was in this for more than just sex. Because I was.

Unfortunately, I also had a hefty supply of indecision. There was a fine but firm line between being sweet and being a stalker. Technically, this was our third date. However, since the other two were cut short, this was more like our first and a half date. Too soon to show up unannounced? I mean, I was a professional, so didn't that make it a bit less creepy?

In the end, my need to care for the sick and hurting overcame my fear of sending creepy dickhead vibes. What was the worst that could happen? She wouldn't answer the door? She'd kick me out?

She'd never want to see me again...

On the other hand, she could think it was sweet, and I'd be

skating on roses.

Before I gave myself an ulcer, I took some Vitamin C to ward off the plague, grabbed a can of chicken soup and my med kit, and got in my car to drive the short distance to her apartment. If I didn't puss out on the way, I'd be there in about fifteen minutes.

When we exchanged addresses earlier this week—the actual plan for date three was to pick her up for dinner—I was surprised at how close we lived. Sure, this was a city, but it wasn't a booming metropolis. Presumably, we'd shopped at the same stores, frequented the same bars, walked the same sidewalks. Yet, we'd never run into each other.

I'd totally remember if we'd had. My dick had a photographic memory for hot chicks. And Marian wasn't only a banging body with a great smile. She exuded a vibrancy that matched her hair color. A no-nonsense confidence that was sexy as hell and drew me in. Her deep brown eyes were sharp and assessing. No wonder she'd moved so fast in her career.

No, I definitely would have looked at her twice—or thrice. Or tripped on my feet staring at her—if we'd ever passed on the street.

Somehow, I made it to her door without shitting myself. I knocked, hoping she had enough strength to come and open it.

"Who is it?" her feeble voice called.

I held up the med kit in case she peeked through the peephole. "Nurse Trevor. I bring pills and soup."

Silence from the other side. I had a brief moment of panic that she was blowing me off. Using being sick as an excuse not to see me. Hurriedly shoving some other dude into a closet so she could get rid of me.

I held my breath and counted down from ten. I got to seven

before the lock disengaged.

"You had me at chicken soup," she mumbled, swinging the door open wide enough for me to enter.

I'd love to say that she looked beautiful despite being sick. That the fever caused her skin to glow and pink. But I couldn't. Because I couldn't see her at all.

A blanket covered her from crown to calves. One squinty eye peeked through a small opening by her head shape. On her feet were those thick, fuzzy socks girls like to wear. These had avocados printed on them, I think, but it was hard to tell in the dim light.

She shuffled away from the door to a pile of tissues resembling the shape of a couch. I shut the door behind me and gave myself a moment to both revel in the fact that I'd made it through the door and also let my eyes adjust to the dark.

When they had, I absolutely snooped around on my way to the kitchen to start warming the soup. Besides the new pile of sick detritus on the coffee table and sofa and floor and credenza, her space was clean and uncluttered. A few photographs with Marian smiling in groups and pairs adorned the walls. Her blue and gray color palate was eerily similar to mine. As far as I could tell, she didn't have cats everywhere or multiple crochet patterns or large blow-up penises or bridal magazines strewn about. All things I'd seen before on dates. All in the "delete contact" column.

A series of tiny, high-pitched sneezes from the next room refocused me on my task. In the kitchen, I easily found a pot, started the soup, and then approached the couch with my med kit in tow.

Resisting the urge to put on rubber gloves—not a look that screamed "Swap spit with me later"—I pushed aside a mountain of tissues to sit on the coffee table across from her. I peeled the layers of fabric away from her face.

She tried, unsuccessfully, to bat my hands away, but the sickness made her weak.

"Don't look at me. I'm hideous," she said.

"You're beautiful," I said, pushing her damp hair off her forehead. She was hot to the touch.

I opened a new thermometer and popped it in her mouth.

"Lean into me so I can listen to your lungs." She put her head on my shoulder. Subconsciously, I matched her breaths as I moved the stethoscope around her back, taking much more time than necessary. She felt little in my arms. Little and right.

"This is nice," she whisper-slurred. "You're, like, a really good nurse. A really good kissing, sexy voiced, cutey nursey nurse."

My chest rumbled with a laugh. The fever made her loopy. "I'm glad you approve. I'd like to do that again sometime."

"Nurse me?"

"Kiss you."

"Not now. I have snot on my face."

I kissed her forehead instead. She hummed against my chest.

"Is something burning?" she asked.

"Oh shit. The soup." I leaned her back gently on the couch and scrambled to the kitchen.

By the time I returned to the living room with her bowl of soup, she was asleep. I adjusted the blankets and settled in for a

Netflix marathon while I waited for her to wake up.

Chapter Six

Marian: Date 4

"So, he just sat in your apartment and watched you sleep?" Six asked when I called her a few days later. "You didn't think that was a little creepy?"

"He's a nurse, Six. That's what he does. Takes care of sick people," I reminded her.

"Still. You hardly know the guy."

"You weren't there. He was so sweet and didn't try to take advantage at all."

I remembered letting him in. Remembered leaning on his shoulder while he rubbed my back. I think we talked about kissing. I'm sure we did because that kiss consumed my every waking thought since it happened.

I don't remember falling asleep. But when I awoke, Trevor brought me chicken soup and a cold compress. We held hands, exploring the ridges and lines, the slopes and curves of that appendage, while watching a movie. It was comfortable and easy and nice. Surprisingly, I wasn't overly embarrassed by all my bodily fluids. And he wasn't grossed out.

When it got too late, he kissed my forehead, gave me strict

instructions, and locked the door on the way out.

"And you're seeing him again now that you're not full of mucous?" Six asked.

"Tonight. We're going to dinner."

“Are you wearing fuck-me undies?”

I shifted the phone to my other ear. “Yes, I am. If our kiss the other day was any indication, I’m in for a treat tonight. Barring any national emergencies or wild bird attacks.”

It seemed like anything that could have gone wrong during our first few dates had. I actually contemplated having dessert first—if you know what I mean—if only to make sure it happened. Because let’s be honest, dinner was just noise until I invited him back to my apartment.

I put Six on speaker while I finished putting on my make-up.

“So, you actually like this guy, huh?”

“I think so. It was a rocky start, but first dates are always high stakes. No one is ever truly themselves,” I said.

“I guess so. Do you want me to read your tarot? I can see if there’s any indication that he’s just biding time until wham-bam-thank you, ma’am and ghost.”

“Remind me again why we’re friends?” I asked.

“I keep you grounded and your chakras open.” She sighed. “Seriously, though. Go get ‘em, tiger. I want a full report tomorrow. Let me live vicariously through you for once.”

“You could come with me sometime. There are other singles at the bar, you know,” I said.

“No thanks. I have a not so great history with the bartender.”

“If this doesn’t work out, I can always choose a different bar next time," I offered.

"That's the positive spirit I know and love." She chuckled. "Remember, keep a diary if you have to. I want a play by play." She disconnected.

Right on time, Trevor knocked on the door. He held a bouquet of wildflowers and a dazzling smile.

"These are gorgeous," I said when he handed me the flowers. I hadn't gotten flowers since my high school graduation. From my mother. I hid my overly delighted face in the blooms.

Although we'd had some flirty messages over the last few days, I wasn't entirely positive Trevor still saw me as sex material. At least not this close after our last mucous filled "date." For all I knew, he'd had enough of my bodily fluids, and this was a "thanks but no thanks" break-up date. I was probably squarely in the friend zone. Or even worse, the just another patient zone.

"Not as gorgeous as you," he said, letting his eyes wander down my body. I'd chosen a low-cut turquoise dress to compliment my hair and accentuate my breasts. It was my typical "I wanna get laid" outfit. Baby, don't fail me now.

"Cheesy. But I like it," I teased. "Let me put these in some water."

Trevor followed me into the kitchen. He leaned a hip against the counter to watch as I found a vase and filled it. His eyes were focused and dark. Maybe he did still find me attractive.

"How are you feeling?" he asked. And there went that theory. He was conducting an out of office follow-up visit.

"One hundred percent back to normal. Not even a sniffle." I put the flowers in the water.

When he spoke next, his hypnotic voice was in my ear. "Good

to hear."

He put his hands on either side of me, trapping me against the counter, his chest to my back. My breath hitched. He swept my hair off my neck and brushed his lips over my skin. I shivered involuntarily.

"Your skin feels hot. Sure you don't have a temperature?" he asked, placing another kiss on the curve of my neck. I leaned my head back on his shoulder as he lit little fires across my skin.

Trevor moved a hand to wrap around my waist, pulling our bodies together. I could feel his erection against my back. Channeling my inner slut, I rubbed my ass against it. He groaned and nipped my collarbone.

"I can't stop thinking about our kiss. About what tasting the rest of you would be like," he said.

I think I managed to murmur, "Me too," but the blood rushing through my ears was deafening.

He moved his hand, and I braced myself for where he'd touch me next. My hip? My breast? My aching lady bits?

Instead, he pushed back from the counter away from me. I turned, my face flush with desire.

He looked just as affected.

"Dinner?" he asked, his voice still husky from our connection. His desire was on full display through his khakis. I couldn't stop myself from staring at it. And thinking about his lips on my skin. His breath in my ear. His skin against mine.

"Eating is overrated," I said. Like the demure, sensual being I was, I crossed the kitchen and climbed him like a tree. I wrapped a leg around his waist and slammed my lips against his. No preamble.

No easing into it. No teasing.

I wanted him. Now.

He didn't hesitate. Immediately his strong hands gripped my ass and lifted me, twisting to set me on the counter. Our tongues collided in a frantic attempt to taste and taste and taste. His hand moved up my thigh under my dress as I untucked his shirt to run mine over his abs and chest.

He shivered and moaned my name when I scratched my nails lightly over his heated skin which only served to fuel my desire. I grappled with his fly, my fingers fumbling in their haste.

Trevor pulled the sleeve of my dress off my shoulder to nip and bite along the exposed skin while his skilled fingers brought life back to parts of me that needed nurturing. I rolled my hips to give him better access to those parts. He took the hint and ran a finger under the lace of my underwear. So close to home, yet still so far away.

Finally, he pushed the lace aside to caress me while at the same time dipping his head to my breasts. I held him there, completely at the mercy of his touch. He was going to make me come right here on my kitchen counter. Almost fully clothed. With the lights on.

First time for everything.

When his fingers pushed inside me, I cried out and grabbed his wrist. He stilled for a moment. Looked at me.

Oh, hell no. "Don't stop. Please, for the love of pickles, don't stop," I begged, squirming to feel him move inside me.

He chuckled and kissed me as he pushed me over the edge

without even removing a stitch of clothing.

Her body convulsed as the orgasm—the orgasm I caused—rolled through her. That was the hottest thing that ever happened to me. God, if she was this responsive from only my fingers...

My cock pushed against the fabric of my pants. I can't remember the last time I'd been this hard. I wanted to make her come again. I wanted to come with her. Again and again and again.

She hung limply on my shoulder as she came down, but I wasn't done yet. I lifted her off the counter, squeezing her tight ass. She wrapped her legs around me.

"Bedroom," I said.

"Last door down the hall." Her voice was breathless. She dropped her mouth to my neck as I not at all clumsily moved us in that direction. In my defense, her lips on my skin were highly distracting. As were the little noises she made in her throat.

I set her down on the edge of the bed and stood in front of her to kick off my shoes. This was actually happening. After all our starts and stops, this was finally happening. Please don't let me embarrass myself by being a five-second-Freddy. With my schedule, finding the time and a partner was tough. It'd been a while.

Somewhere along the line, she'd undone my fly, so pants followed shoes into a pile on the floor. I went to add my boxers when her hands pushed mine aside.

"Let me," she said.

"By all means." I took off my shirt while she released my super-charged cock. She took it in her hands, stroking, then her mouth, licking. I grunted from the unexpected pleasure. Her mouth was magic. If I didn't want to be inside her so much, I might have let her finish. I was too damn close.

"Wait, Marian." I pulled her chin up. "I want us to come together."

She slid her arms up my torso. I used the opportunity to pull her dress over her head.

Fuck. Me. Siren red lace barely covered her fun zones. My dick pulsed in appreciation. She smiled coyly and moved up the bed. Her copper hair spread out behind her as she lay back on the pillows and hitched a finger at me.

Uh, don't have to tell me twice. I kissed my way up her body, worshipping her skin. She squirmed and writhed and pulled at my hair. I paused at the apex of her thighs, letting my breath hit her through the lace.

"I want to taste you here," I said. I pressed my lips against her hot folds. "But first, I want to be inside you."

"Yes. Please, Trevor."

Hooking my thumbs in the sides of her panties, I slid them off her legs. She unfastened her bra and threw it on the floor, baring herself to me. Gorgeous.

"Condoms. Top drawer." She pointed to the bedside table. She stroked me as I retrieved one and opened it, then slid it down my length.

"I can't promise this won't be quick," I warned as I positioned myself at her opening. "You make me so hard."

"Quick. Hard. Fast. Don't care. Just please fuck me before I combust."

I do love a woman who knows what she wants. As I slid into her, slowly at first to savor the feeling, she arched under me, gripping my ass to push me in deeper.

"Yes. So good," she moaned.

We moved together, matching our rhythm to our increasing heart rates until I felt her clench around me and let myself go too.

"Marian," I whispered when I was able to find my voice.

"Hmmmm," she hummed, limbs slack around me.

"I want to do that again."

Her chest shook under my cheek with a slight laugh. "Me too. Sorry we missed dinner again."

"I'm not. Although maybe we should go."

She lifted my head up with her hands so I had to look at her. "You want to get dressed and go to dinner?"

"We'll need some nourishment for what I have planned."

Epilogue

Marian: Date 63

I was sick. Again. I blamed the poor ventilation in the store and all the customers touching everything. Retail stores had more germs than a dog's tongue. And they ate poop.

Luckily, I had my own personal nurse to help me through my sniffles. He also made house calls. He was on his way over now with his signature chicken soup, cold compresses, and lectures about why I didn't have these things myself—obviously, so he'd be forced to bring them, and his sexy self, over to take care of me.

Adorned in my fuzzy socks, sweats, and an afghan, I sniffled and coughed my way through an HGTV marathon while I waited for Trevor to get off shift.

When his end of shift came and went and I didn't hear from him, I started to get a bit worried. Not that anything happened to him, but that he wasn't coming. He'd been acting weird lately, evasive. And we'd been spending a lot more time at my apartment than his. Over the last nine-ish months, it'd been a pretty even fifty-fifty split. Now it was my place or out in public.

I did the only thing I could do in place of having a panic

attack. I called Six.

"I think Trevor is hiding a secret harem in his apartment," I said when she answered.

"You sound terrible. Have you been crying?" she asked.

"Not yet," I sniffled. "Just sick."

"What's this about a harem?"

I told her about how Trevor had been evasive. "I haven't heard from him today either. He got off shift over an hour ago."

Ever the supportive friend, Six advised, "Marian, don't turn into a clingy melodramatic worrywart. Trust me, that isn't a path you want to go down."

"You wouldn't be referencing your sordid past with the bartender at McConnells would you?" I asked.

"One and the same. When he ghosted me, I became a ghost of myself. Not worth the tears or the trouble or the amount of sage I had to burn." She laughed sardonically.

"So I should just cut the ties and move on?" I asked. My chest suddenly felt like an elephant was sitting on my chest.

"No. Sorry. Don't listen to my cynical ass. Trevor hasn't gone radio silent, right?"

I sighed. "No. He's just acting weird. I'm just nervous that he's getting sick of me. That our relationship has run its course in his mind. And not inviting me over to his place makes me think he's hiding something."

"Like a secret harem?" she said.

"Okay. That may be a bit dramatic. But what if some ex showed up pregnant and is demanding he marry her? Or he's got a side piece that leaves her toothbrush there?"

"Have you asked him about it?"

I coughed, partly due to the cold and partly because I'd rather die than ask him straight out. "No. I don't want to accuse him of something and start a fight if I am being melodramatic."

She sighed. "Pull up your big girl panties and ask the man. Do it like a joke if you have to." When I just sniffled, she added, "Do you want me to do a reading? I can send you a meditation for the Vishuddha chakra. It'll help you communicate better."

I smiled. Typical Six, fixing things with tarot and crystals. "You're saying words, but I don't know what they mean. I'm going see how today goes. Something's gotta give soon, or I'm going to 'what if' myself into an anxiety induced cocoon."

"Keep me posted. Maybe I can live less cynically through you."

"Maybe you should take your own advice and just ask Brendan what happened," I suggested. "You know where he works."

"Maybe I'm better at giving advice than taking it," she shot back. "My tarot says I'm not quite ready yet. I tend to agree. Plus, I just met this new guy, Timber, and my college best friend, Nora, is coming back into town. I've got a lot on my plate. Reconnecting with Casper is not one of them."

"Casper—'cause he ghosted you." I chuckled. "Good one. And thanks, Six. I'll let you know how today goes." We disconnected.

Was she right? Should I just outright ask him? I didn't want to open a can of worms I couldn't close. Then again, Trevor had never given me reason to doubt his affection before. Probably the fever was making me delirious. Still, I was almost to the point of marching over to his place and putting my mucous-filled nose in his business when he finally texted me.

Trevor: I know you're sick, but can you come to my place tonight. Long shift.

Holy shit. He wanted me to come to his place! I tried to put a lid on the hope threatening to push the elephant off my chest. This didn't mean that he wasn't hiding anything over the last few months. Maybe he finally found a place to hide the dead bodies other than his closet. Still, I was cautiously optimistic. And abundantly curious.

Me: Sure. Everything okay?

Trevor: It will be when you get here.

Me: I'm bringing my fuzzy socks.

Trevor: I would be disappointed if you didn't.

Me: See you in fifteen.

Trevor: I'll start the soup.

My heart did a little flip-flop in my chest. I worried for nothing.

Trevor greeted me at the door with a forehead kiss then wrapped me in his arms.

"You don't feel too feverish. That's good."

"It's still ramping up. I'm hoping a cute nurse will help me stave it off."

He released me but didn't move away from the doorway. Just looked at me with a mix of... what? Hope? Panic? Surprise?

I narrowed my eyes at him. "Can I come in?"

He took a deep breath. "You know I love you, right?"

"You're kind of freakin' me out, Trev. What's going on?"

"I want to show you something." He took my hand and led me

through the living room down the hallway. Besides a few missing pictures on the walls, everything looked the same. No crazy animals or a harem or a long-lost child.

His bedroom, though, had been almost completely rearranged. Half his closet was empty. The dresser, once centered on the wall, was now pushed over asymmetrically to one side. All the stuff usually spread on both nightstands was now confined to one.

"I don't understand. Are you hiding a blood stain? Did you accidentally kill someone and need help hiding the body?" I asked.

He ignored me. "I love you, Marian. I've loved you from the first time you jumped me in the kitchen. I love talking to you. I love not talking to you. I love taking care of you."

"I love you too, Trevor. All of those things."

"Good. Because I think I would love coming home to you too."

"You do. We see each other practically every day."

"Not enough. I want to wake up to you in the morning. Go to sleep together every night. Not have to lug a bag between our apartments. I want to come home—to our home—every night," he clarified.

I swallowed and blinked at him, speechless.

He continued, "Your lease is up next month. Move in with me instead of renewing. I've already made space. We can negotiate the furniture."

"You want me to move in with you?" I asked. An hour ago, I thought he wanted to break up with me. Now, he was moving our relationship forward. In the best way.

I was so relieved, I laughed. His face fell. Flashbacks to our first date, when I had a similarly inappropriate reaction, surfaced. Oh shit.

"I know it's kind of sudden. But I've been thinking about it for a while. I wanted to have everything ready so—"

I interrupted him by throwing my arms around him. "Yes. Of course I'll move in with you. Of course."

He picked me up and twirled me. "Really? When you laughed, I thought..."

"Relieved laugh. I thought you were breaking up with me."

"Breaking up with you? You're the best thing that ever happened to me. Thanks for not giving up on me after my first date freak-out," he said after setting me down again.

"That was very generous of me," I said. "I'm glad I didn't either. And I guess I owe Six a thank you for making me download the Cloud 9 app in the first place."

"Want to know the best part about this whole plan?" he asked.

"You won't have to drive to make a house call when I'm sick again."

"Well, that. And you will finally have a fully stocked med kit."

He erased my scowl with a scorching kiss.

If Cloud 9 made you look for love…

Learn more about Karigan Hale's How to Date Series in the About Author Section.

We hope you've enjoyed each and every romance in ***Heroes with Heat and Heart.***

Thank you again for helping keep those we've lost close to our hearts. While we hope we brightened your day, we also take your faith in us very seriously.

If you want to receive regular updates about how your donation contributed to the 9/11 Memorial, please join our newsletter by visiting https://carinaalyce.com/911-charity-newsletter/

For more information about the 9/11 Memorial & Museum, visit 911memorial.org

Turn the page to learn more about the authors.

About The
Authors
9.11.01

CARINA ALYCE

Carina Alyce is a full-time practicing physician who moonlights as a steamy romance writer and mother of six. Her MetroGen Downtown series is described as Grey's Anatomy + Chicago Fire+steam+actual medicine. She joined the anthology because she worked for years in the ER side-by-side with many firefighters and EMTs.

Tempted's steamy yoga session between the fire chief and his subordinate continues in ***Smolder*** - Book 1 of MetroGen Forbidden Love Duets. https://www.amazon.com/dp/B091MTCS3C/

If the stolen kisses of *Sampled* is your style, find out the sultry complications of doctors dating medical students in ***High Risk*** - Book 2 of MetroGen Forbidden Love Duets.
https://www.amazon.com/dp/B092CJ4XBX

EMKAY CONNOR

EmKay Connor is the author of contemporary romantic fiction infused with quirky humor and engaging characters. Her bright and breezy romances are set in small towns, tropical locations, and glamorous destinations where her heroes and heroines discover passion and fall in love. As a former Navy wife who lived on a military base in Washington, DC, during the 9/1l attacks and aftermath, she believes in honoring those serve and sacrifice for the USA.

Her S.W.A.T. romance *Brave Enough to Love* is first in a new series, Heart of a Hero. Look for more stories about these everyday heroes and heroines as the series continues.
https://www.amazon.com/EmKay-Connor/e/B00GF3WI4M

KARIGAN HALE

Karigan Hale is a wife, mother, high school teacher, and photographer who is highly allergic to poison ivy and early mornings and highly addicted to fountain sodas and true crime. She writes steamy, slow-burn romantic comedies full of sarcastic females and the hot males trying to keep up with them. She chose to participate in this anthology to honor the amazing first responders that not only were heroes during the attacks on September 11th, but also during the recent pandemic.

If you thought Nicole and Marcus were on fire in *Incendiary*, then you should see the heat between Nicole's friend Kennedy and her nemesis Brock McCallister. in ***Cowboy, Take Me Away***.

https://www.amazon.com/gp/product/B08XP43N41

And if you enjoyed *Love on Call*, read ***How to Date Your Ex***, Book 2 in the *How to Date Series,* for more about Six and Brendan.

https://www.amazon.com/gp/product/B085N7YM35

LOLO PAIGE

LoLo Paige is an award-winning author who lives in Alaska and writes full time. Her Blazing Hearts Wildfire Series are action-adventure, romantic suspense stories set in the dangerous and exciting world of wildland firefighting loosely based on her experiences as a wildland firefighter in Montana, California, and Alaska. She joined the anthology because she supports all firefighters who put their lives on the line daily.

Her story *Alaska Dawn* was just the beginning. Read the exciting conclusion in her debut novel: ***Alaska Spark.***

https://www.amazon.com/gp/product/B0871428MS

LC TAYLOR

LC Taylor is a full-time educator that moonlights as a romance author. Starting out as a paranormal romance author, LC found she loved writing about Alpha Male Heroes. Which led her to writing about first responders. As a former police officer and married to one, LC found her niche in writing. Most of her recent books have a police, fire, military, or EMS undertone. And everyone gets their happily-ever-after. The reason LC chose to participate in the anthology because she worked alongside police officers and firemen for several years.

Broken Promises was just the beginning. Find out what happens to Kerrigan and Lorelei in B***roken Vows***, Book 1 of Crossroads Heroes. *https://www.amazon.com/dp/B09B8TCH78*

SAMANTHA THOMAS

Samantha Thomas is an author who loves to write sweet, clean books, filled with lots of fun banter, good-hearted men, and the happiest of ever afters. Participating in this anthology is a privilege that allows me to honor the New York community, as well as my family and friends that work as first responders, in all capacities, every day.

If you have a hankering for a Hallmark type cozy romance after reading An *Irresistible Spark*, check out Book 1 in her Talisman Series, ***Healing Hearts***.

https://www.amazon.com/gp/product/B07TXMZR8X

Please share our project with others!

You can help us honor 9/11 heroes and preserve their memories by sharing a review on Amazon, Goodreads, or BookBub to keep the good word going.

Join our mailing list for updates about contributions to the 9/11 Memorial at *https://carinaalyce.com/911-charity-newsletter/*

For more information about the 9/11 Memorial & Museum, visit 911memorial.org.

HEROES WITH HEAT AND HEART

Lightning Source UK Ltd.
Milton Keynes UK
UKHW010953060223
416537UK00007B/1512

9 781955 832014